ROCKHEAD

ROCKHEAD

A NOVEL

SEAN TOREN

ISBN 13: 978-1-63489-261-2
LCCN: 2019908107

Printed in the United States of America
First Printing 2019

23 22 21 20 19   5 4 3 2 1

Cover design by Luke Bird
Interior design by Patrick Maloney

Wise Ink
807 Broadway Street NE, Suite 46
Minneapolis, MN 55413
wiseink.com

This book is dedicated to the many climbing partners I've had over the years (especially Bart, Pablo, Martin, and Rainer)—and to Georgeanna and Bruno, the best partners in life I could imagine.

But thought is one thing, the deed is another,
and the image of the deed still another:
the wheel of causality does not roll between them.

—Friedrich Nietzsche

On the third planet from the sun,
I've been trying to get the funky job done . . .
G-R-A-V-I-T-Y—Gravity, the big G.

—James Brown

MINNEAPOLIS

ODOMETER (1)98,194

LAT. 44.94° N LONG. 93.44° W

ALT. 873 FEET

JUNE 28

CHAPTER ONE

Yosemite," he said to me in the dark. "You and me and a big, bad wall. Maybe Orion or even the Seven Seas."

It was my climbing partner, Dade, and he'd just woken me from a dream. I could see him in my mind's eye, hulking there with his terrible posture on the other end of the phone. I swear I could smell him too: the smell of some feral animal. Of fear and fearlessness at the same time. I turned my head to make sure Olive was asleep, and then gently cleared my throat.

"Come on, *Uhtlas*, it's the last chance I'm going to have for a while—and the Booty just said it would be okay."

This is how Dade, a junior high science teacher, talks to me on the phone—always mispronouncing my name with a bad Scottish accent—though I've never been able to figure out why, since he's mostly Greek and I'm mostly German. He has twisted names like this for everyone. His wife, Beverly, a tenured physiology professor at the U, he calls the Booty; and their unborn baby he's christened the Crackmeister because he thinks it will climb so hard (and not, he likes to say with a wink, "Of whence it will enter the world"). Usually he would feign the Scottish thing for at least a few sentences, but he cut it out this time.

"Go on, tell him you said it's okay," I heard him stage-whisper to Bev, and then, faintly, I heard her yell, "Yes, Atlas, go! Get him away from me!" She was laughing, and I could imagine her tiny four-month swell of belly jiggling with the Crackmeister.

"What about my job lined up in New York?" I finally whispered, squinting at the still form of Olive again. Her breathing was even and light, but I could tell by the tense angle of her ear that she was actually awake. Listening, not laughing.

"They can wait or find someone else. Come on—we've been talking about getting back to Yosemite since the last time we drove away from it, *over two years ago*, right? It's going to be that many years before I get time off from the Crackmeister, and by then my shoulders will be trashed from diaper duty. Why have we been training three days a week if we're not going to go for it? It's like we're meant to do it and you can't offer one good reason not to go. Plus you can do Son of Sam on the way out there."

He was trying to push my buttons by dropping the name of a new route I was hot to do, but what he cagily didn't mention (in a kind of reverse psychology) was that it might also be the only chance for me to find my "rockhead," a.k.a. "letting the thing be the thing," before I settled into the beige half-walls of the office gig Olive had found for me.

The rockhead is a state of intense focus that Dade claims he's had while climbing, and he says it's the thing that will let me rise to my potential and finally be the climber—and the man—I'm supposed to be. Olive thinks he's just talking about an adrenaline ride or what adventure athletes call "flow." But Dade says it's bigger. Wider. Deeper.

"So what do you think? Three more weeks? You could fly out of San Fran," Dade pushed. And then he said, as if it were ever a good idea, "Let me talk to Olive."

"She's asleep," I said, still whispering, "And anyway, you know I don't have any money."

This finally got the bed shaking as Olive sat up to listen better.

"Ha! That's why I'm calling right now," he said, exultant as if checkmating me, "I just landed a cherry roofing job—the special ed teacher from my school had some roof damage during the storm the other night and called me. No tear off—just a sheathing repair and re-shingling on one side. He's getting a check for eight thousand bucks."

"We'll talk at the house," I said, referring to the painting job we were just finishing. Then I hung up, his *two years* still ringing in my head; it wasn't just how long we'd been away from the Valley, it was also how long I'd been with Olive. And about how long I'd been having the exact same dream every night. The dream Dade's call had torn me from.

In the dream I am flying through space at some incredible speed—close to the speed of light—and though I have no mass or shape at first, I begin to assume shape and then mass, and then I realize that I am falling above the earth through what seems to be warm, buoyant air. As I fall, however, the air cools and thickens into a kind of transparent gel that gradually slows me down. The weirdest part is that I'm desperately trying to reach the ground—and I positively know I will. Nothing is more important than that I can touch it, and as I "make" myself heavier and heavier to get through the "air," I grow so heavy I become something else, something without thought. Something not human. I become a hundred times my normal weight, then a million. But in some freakish ratio, the air-gel continues to cool and thicken around me, always just dense enough to slow—but not stop—my fall.

Each time in the dream I am absolutely sure I will reach the ground, and each time when my body is only a single humming atom away from infinite mass, I realize that I will never reach the ground. Then I wake up.

I turned to look at Olive. I could barely make out her face, just the soft, lovely curves of her body inside one of my old T-shirts. She didn't have her arms crossed over her chest, but that was just a trick—I could feel the weight of her disapproval squatting there along with the dozen packed boxes that filled up the room. In two days she would leave for New York for a job at a German TV station. I was supposed to drive out with her, but the house-painting job I was on with Dade kept getting delayed by Midwestern storms and I still had at least a week to go on that before I followed her in my little Corolla. As soon as I arrived, I would "interview" at the same station for a gig preparing weather reports if the present weatherman couldn't get his work papers straightened out; really, though, the job was mine if I wanted it. A "perfect fit," as Olive said, where I could use not just one but both of my employable skills: speaking the German I learned at my mother's lumpy shins, and applying my knowledge of physical geography and meteorology learned over my seven-year tenure at the University (where I'd taken summers and several autumns off to climb).

I cleared my throat, and then, after a dozen or so heartbeats of her silence, jumped in: "Dade just wants me to go climbing—to help him with a route he wants to fire off before the baby comes. He says it's our last chance for a while. That I need to suck it up and go with him . . . to Yosemite."

"Yosemite?! Again? What about the job? What about your debt?" she asked, crossing her arms in spite of herself.

"He just scored us a roofing job—it'll let me pay off what I owe you. Or most of it, anyway."

She sighed. Then I sighed. Then we both sighed and she got out of bed. I could hear her rustling around in the dark and turned on the light to find her putting her hair up, which is what she does whenever she has to think hard. Or win an argument.

"Why don't you want to move out there?" she asked.

"I'm not saying I don't," I said, as a feeling of rising and spinning began to uncoil in my spine. It was a problem that had been growing worse for about a year and a half, and it had even started to mess with my climbing. I'd get hung up sometimes on easy stuff and actually panicked a few times on harder routes. Dade had given me some breathing exercises to do while climbing, and I tried to do one that night, but then Olive was talking again and I couldn't focus.

"I can tell you don't. I can tell that you're not sure about us. You're such a . . . such a *waffler*. You're waffling now like you always do. It's like you need your decisions made for you, so I'm telling you that this is the right thing. That you should come to New York with me and not give away that job. Jesus, Atlas, at some point you're going to have to *suck it up* and work," she said.

That's when the room grew still and tight, like it had been breathing, but then stopped. Then it all began to swim, and I spiraled upwards so fast my thoughts were flung away from me. Before I lost all my words too, I tossed out a few of them like little anchors: "I didn't say I was going—I'm just telling you what he called about. Jeese."

And then the dizziness began to slow, and then it receded to the periphery.

"I'm just not sure," I should have said right then. "I'm not sure I want to work in a cube. I'm not sure about us." But I didn't— and to defend myself, it wouldn't have worked anyway. *I'm not sure* isn't part of Olive's vocabulary. She's über-organized, slightly embarrassed by talk of emotions, and an incredible multitasker— she's super smart, super capable, super logical. Olive majored in

English but minored in German, and the first time we ever spoke German—at a student beer-drinking group—she corrected my grammar, though she'd only learned the language as an adult while for me it was a *Muttersprache*. I lost the argument to her persuasive, canted eyebrows (and all those soft curves), and even though it turned out later that I was right, it didn't matter; she had managed to set some kind of precedent. She even talked me into saying that I was sure I loved her after we'd been dating two or three months, when I wasn't sure at all.

I stood up and went to her—I always feel better when I'm in motion—and touched her face beneath her cheekbone, then laid a finger like a clasp upon her lips. Olive has the sweetest, most gentle lips I've ever felt, but I didn't want any more words to come out of them just then.

"Do you love me?" she asked, her lips moving under my fingertips.

"Olive Juice," I always said—my nickname for her—but this night, as if the German were somehow safer, I said, "Ich liebe Dich."

She kissed me and said, "It's going to be a big change, but it's going to be great. It's going to be an adventure." Then she kissed me again as if to punctuate the sentence; as if trying to be sure herself.

We went to bed but she never got under the sheet, hugging me tighter and tighter as the night chilled. I don't think she even fell asleep until daybreak, when I got up for work. I think she may have been crying.

She left Minneapolis two days later, scooping me with a tactical move by saying that she needed to take my hamsters Eenie Meany and Miney Mo "to ride shotgun" as protection for the trip (maybe thinking that if I wouldn't come for her, I'd come for them). We packed up her car with everything she needed, as well as the hamsters who were indeed riding shotgun, hanging tough.

We had made very sweet, "in-love" kind of love earlier that morning, surprising both of us, and for some reason making us both cry afterward. But when she left she seemed happy (or maybe just a little manic), cupping my face with her two hands and kissing me for too long on the lips—as if to impress something upon me.

"I can hold them off a couple days, but you have to come the second that roofing job's done. See you out East!" she yelled as she drove away, her arm stuck out the window for the entire block.

I was left standing on our quiet street, holding a hand high and squeaking goodbye to my guys, already missing them but feeling, strangely, happier than I'd been in months.

That morning I loaded what few possessions I had into my old Corolla and carted them over to Dade's garage for storage until I left. Then I set up camp in "the Rig"—Dade's green, 1980 Chevy Sportvan, also known as *Makin' Bacon* because it had that faded bumper sticker on it when he inherited it from his uncle.

We'd been on a dozen trips in *Makin' Bacon* over the years and had slowly turned it into the perfect climbing machine. There's a tiny porcelain sink, a two-burner range, and an old-style icebox that came with the van originally, along with a series of padded wood panels that fold down and clap together to create Dade's bed downstairs. Upstairs is a scavenged vw pop-top that we installed, which opens as a wedge surrounded by a fabric screen and zip-up canvas, making the front of the roof higher than the back. It offers more room but is also more subject to the weather and car headlights and birds pecking at the soft screen. That's where I sleep on our trips.

The Rig has mostly gray carpeting except for the faded purple shag on the dashboard, and it has mostly white cupboards except that you can't really see them for all the climbing photos and topo maps that have been put up over the years. Many of them are of routes that we've done, but some are of those that we hoped to do.

Lying downstairs in Dade's usual bed, I had a vantage of the ceiling where Dade had hung a map of us climbing areas—the summer circuit through Wyoming and the winter circuit through Las Vegas, both dotted and linked together like constellations, their common pole star our Mecca, Yosemite Valley. We've been in the Valley five times, once for two months but never less than two weeks. And every time we've been on El Capitan.

Part of the attraction of El Cap is that few places in the whole wide world offer such high rock with such an easy approach. With over three thousand feet from toe to tip, El Cap is a mountain. But, then, with the climbing stripped down to its most technical side, with no snow-slogging or glacier aprons to deal with, it is also a crag. The vertical granite touches its sandy, horizontal base with the simple ease of a living room wall to a Berber carpet. And the transition to climbing is even more bizarre: one moment you are standing on the ground, where you can walk back to your car in twenty minutes, and the next you have entered a super-vertical wonderland, so huge and so different you're an astronaut leaving the stratosphere for space—or a surfer in Nazaré, Portugal, dropping in on an eighty-foot wave.

It's what Dade was dreaming about, and, it turns out, what I was dreaming about deep down too. A way to find my rockhead. But I didn't have the time or the gumption to fight it out with Olive. At least, that's what I thought that week while we finished the house-painting gig. But things changed when we started on that roof.

We arrived just as the dumpster was being delivered and hauled our heavy, forty-foot ladder into the backyard, walking through piles of sawdust where the downed tree had been cut into pieces before being hauled away.

"Pretty nice house for a teacher," I said after we set the ladder down.

"His wife's some marketing exec," said Dade, plucking a tiny apple out of his pocket and taking a bite. He wrinkled his face up: "Sour."

"It looks like a crabapple—where'd you even get that?" I asked.

"Bev. From the co-op," he said, biting into the apple again so that his teeth, as thick and utilitarian as a tiger's, were suddenly exposed.

His teeth naturally draw attention to his rough, hatchet nose and the notch on top of it; to the pair of awkwardly taped prescription safety glasses he always wears when working or climbing; to his wildly curly, tar-black hair. Dade, who's slightly famous in our circles for having dated over fifty women, certainly isn't what you'd call handsome in the normal sense of the word, and he never takes a good photo, part of it simply from genetics and his mostly terrible posture and part of it from teenage years as a Golden Gloves boxer: that nose comes from a break during his fifth fight, when he was sixteen, and peeking out from behind the left side of his glasses there's a little scar that curls out of his eyebrow and follows his eye socket for almost an inch. It's stupefying to straight men who don't know him, but somehow his confidence and charisma let him flirt with abandon. And no one is exempt: the cashier at the grocery store, the retired gay professor who lives next door, the professor's giggling, eight-year-old granddaughters. Even Olive.

Olive and I were talking about what turned our respective cranks one night and even she admitted that she was attracted to Dade, saying he was like a half-tame wolf. In his cage he has too many sharp angles and looks too rangy, too awkward, too high-strung, but let him out—and let out a rabbit (or a woman or a hard route) for him to chase—and he is bursting with fluid muscle and beautiful to watch. She made me jealous when she said that, and all I could think to do (not very smart, but then this was early in our relationship) was to ask her how she'd describe me.

She'd clearly thought about this already, and her eyebrows, much darker than her light brown hair, rose slightly as she spoke: "You're like some lizard that only likes it in the sun." She didn't fill in the rest, though I saw her analogy: slow to act, a hibernator, something "lower" on the evolutionary bush. The thing she didn't know, but which I would realize later that summer, was that lizards also have something powerful in them; they can give up a part of themselves for escape, then grow that part back again for another try.

Once Dade and I got up on the roof and looked under the huge tarp, we saw that the job was bigger than Dade's colleague told us it was, with not only the sheathing punched through but at least four of the rafters destroyed.

Even with the extra work, we were going to make out like bandits, and by early afternoon we had already pulled off the old sheathing and repaired the rafters and were back up on the steep hip-and-valley roof with the first sheet of plywood. I was straddling the roof, and Dade was below me with one foot on a bare roof jack and the other stemmed into the valley. Our relative positions gave me a quick memory—like mini déjà vu—of being in some granite corner high on a wall.

"This dough should get Olive off your back," Dade said.

I thought he was actually being nice until he turned and I caught the glint of his eyetooth, as if he had just sharpened it. I set a nail in the plywood and then, as Dade started talking again, drove it home with a few good whacks.

"Did you say something? I couldn't hear you."

"What are you going to tell Olive at the end of the summer after we've finished the Seven Seas and you decide you're not moving out East?

"You know something I don't?"

"My grandpa, the one who was a veterinarian, always said that if you're going to shoot a horse, do it sooner rather than later— preferably in a place where you won't have to move it."

"I guess that's better than beating a dead horse."

"So you're going to make Olive end it? When you've finally worn her out? That's not fair, either."

"Why are you riding me about her?" I asked. I snapped my hammer back in its loop and humped myself along the roof crest to the next rafter before I looked down at him.

Dade can somehow change the shape and color of his pupil and then make it even worse by causing that scar that hooks around it to hum at a violent frequency. It's his "don't bullshit me" look—his boxing look—and it shut me up for a second. But then it didn't: "The fact that you need a belay slave for Seven Seas isn't helping any, is it?"

He frowned. "Atlas, the point is that you don't love her enough and she's crazy about you." He lifted his hammer from the head, pointing the handle at me like a gunslinger: "She's been holding back for a year and a half and you know it."

Well, I couldn't say anything to that, either. It was probably true, but I still didn't understand how she could care for me so much. Looking at us from the outside, Olive with her drive and smarts was clearly the better catch. I was the lizard. The waffler.

"I did almost tell her last week," I said, giving in, "the night you called about the trip."

"And what happened?"

"I wasn't sure if it was true or not," I said, and then, trying to sound confident: "I really do love her, and sometimes I think I love her a lot."

For some reason, this softened him: "Look, I'm not saying you've been acting badly, I'm just saying that if you don't stop it now you will be."

I set a nail and whacked it hard a few times as I wondered: Why was it that people like Dade and Bev and Olive could always be so sure about things so big, when I'd never known such surety in my whole life? Were they actually sure, or did they just decide they were and then sort of live their way into it? I didn't know, but I set another nail and started pounding, then pounded in another. The pounding seemed to help.

Later that afternoon, on my last run up the ladder pinch-gripping a half sheet of plywood, I was caught by a rogue gust of wind and almost fell just as I reached the roof. I twisted weirdly to the side to recover but finally had to grab the gutter for balance—and drop the sheet—just as I saw Dade round the corner.

"Rock!" I called instinctively—it's what you say when you're climbing and something gets dislodged—and the plywood, as if encouraged to cause greater damage, flew away from Dade but in towards the house, landing edge-first right on my backpack (destroying my cell phone and my coffee thermos, I'd later find out) before flopping onto the grass in front of him.

"Damn, son, pay attention!" said Dade, staring up at me. "You get hurt now and you're going to ruin our trip." Then, before I could repeat that I wasn't going or even apologize for almost hitting him, he asked, "What's that your mother always says about paying attention—'pop-off' or 'Passover' or something?"

"*Pass auf.*"

"Yeah, *pass auf,*" he said with a strangely good German accent. "Passing auf is key."

CHAPTER TWO

We finished the roof two days later—on the Fourth of July—and had to clean up and load scraps into the dumpster in the dark, fireworks over the Mississippi popping in the distance. I was supposed to call Olive and confirm that I would be leaving the next morning for New York, but I was so tired I just fell into *Makin' Bacon* without brushing my teeth, or even eating, for that matter.

That night I had a dream, and for the first time in two years it wasn't the "thickening" dream. In the dream, I was standing on a flat, black field, in a dull, gray light, as if the earth itself were made of charcoal and its dust also filled the air. I was a boy and stood holding Ursula, a German exchange student who became my first real girlfriend when I was a junior in high school. But then it wasn't just her and I was suddenly much older. I stood in the same place, holding a woman who was really all the women I'd ever dated. It was Ursula, but also Olive, and also my college love Gillian, and also Ruby, a woman I'd almost dated just before Olive. Among these women were others that I felt love for but didn't recognize.

I woke up to find myself in *Makin' Bacon*, not even a sheet on me, chilled in the early morning air. It was only a couple weeks after the summer solstice and, at 5:00 a.m., the northern sky was already growing light, with a few sparrows calling to each other through the blue-gray air.

There was nothing scary or even bad in the dream—in fact, it was strangely soothing—but wide awake, I found myself thinking about one of those women in particular: Ruby Goldberg. She was a housemate and climber I'd lived with in a ratty student house during my last year at the University, the year before I met Olive. Because Olive had a complete lack of understanding for climbing, I always thought of Ruby as the opposite of Olive. The anti-Olive.

The day I met Ruby was during a (then) rare visit to the local climbing gym. Dade and I mostly trained in his extensive basement torture chamber, which he called "The Beast," but sometimes we'd go to the gym's bouldering cave for a little change of pace. I didn't really see her initially, but rather heard her yell from the bouldering cave with a scratchy, ornery voice that I didn't recognize.

"I was already on the wall—you came up under me!" came a second voice that I did recognize: Dade.

I saw her back first when I turned the corner. She looked like a too-tall gymnast—or a too-muscular dancer—and over her mound of wavy, black hair I could make out the upper half of Dade's exasperated face. Ruby turned around and mumbled, "I'd never come under you, you nasty old goat," before dropping her savage brown eyes on me. When she realized that I'd heard her, she gave me an exaggerated wink as she walked past as if to mess with me too, and I could see that the left side of her face was red, as if with a floor burn. She was wearing a climbing tank top, showing off her muscles and breasts, but the thing my brain hung onto from her was the smell of sweat and chalk and the shredded rubber tire that covers the floor of the gym—and some other scent that I couldn't identify at the time.

"Dude," Dade said when I walked up to him, "She got under me and when I popped off I accidentally kicked her in the face. I felt terrible until she turned all wolverine on me."

I looked for her the rest of the evening at the gym so I could explain what had happened or explain gym etiquette or some such nonsense, but she was gone. I thought I'd probably never see her again, but then she showed up two weeks later at my student house for an "interview" to see if she could move into an empty room we'd been trying to fill all semester. She was brought into the fold by a fellow housemate, Fran, one of the hardest climbers (and spiritually nuttiest people) I've ever known. Fran liked to plant herself in the kitchen so that she could talk at you about her climbing "way," which borrowed the animism and pipe-smoking aspects of the Lakota Sioux from her Lakota ex-boyfriend and the more esoteric parts of Hinduism (mostly the reincarnation ideas), with a little Buddhism and Amazonian shamanism thrown in for good measure. She'd mercifully stopped talking to me about them when I started to poke back by calling her religion "the Hokey Hindu Hookah," which she considered racist and Western but at least shut her up.

Ruby looked like a different woman that night. There was no hat and her hair was big and messy and sexy; her face was freckled under smiling eyes, and though she wore loose jeans and an oversized Norwegian ski sweater that should have hidden her body, her hard angles and fit curves were still able to make an impression. Sitting in the living room that night besides Fran were a chain-smoking, undersexed German philosophy student named Wolfie, Clem (Ruby's future boyfriend), and me. Between Fran and us three defenseless, testosterone-crazed males, she was voted into the house with embarrassing speed.

I didn't think she recognized me at first, but as she left that night she stage-winked at me again and handed me—since I was standing closest to her—a sheet of paper with her name and number written on it so large that the words barely fit on the page. That's when I noticed that her right front tooth was twisted slightly—just like Ursula's had been—though Ruby's, in her more beautiful face, had more power. It said, "I just don't give a shit. I am more than my tooth. I am a baby wolverine."

The trouble started on her first night in the house. Clem and I were friends, but we were also competitive in a way that Dade and I aren't. Somehow I always annoyed Clem because I could climb better than him in the gym—in front of the ladies—while he annoyed me because he got good grades though he never seemed to study, as well as the fact that he was tall, had the jawbone and shadow-beard of an REI model, and was used to getting the women he wanted.

The night Ruby moved in, which is when Clem realized that I was more than just a little interested in her, he turned his competitive eye on her. He made sure he was in the kitchen when she was in the kitchen, in the basement climbing gym when she was in the gym, even walking to class or the library whenever she was walking. It made it hard for me to hit on her myself.

Only two weeks later—the weekend after spring finals, when it was warm enough that people were finally wearing just shorts and T-shirts—we threw a house party. Grain Belt beer was involved, as well as dancing. Or dance music, anyway: it was mostly a climbers' party, so everyone stood around in groups of three or four, their hands gripping imaginary holds in the air as they described a recent move or route or fall. I only had one autumn semester left to graduate and was leaving with Dade the next day to spend the summer climbing out west. Up in my attic bedroom, I'd pulled out all the gear I thought I'd need, and then, unable to stand the thought of packing it all, finally descended to find the party in full swing.

I saw Fran out on the living room dance floor, her dread-locked hair tied up like a shock of wheat, wearing a see-through, sleeveless shift over her sports bra to show off all her tattoos and piercings and generally ripped body, stomping her boots like an '80s punker even though the music was funky pop. And then I saw Ruby—right when she saw me—shimmying around Fran and laughing too loudly. I'd never seen her in a skirt or with her hair done up or even in heels, and I think I simply stared at her, slack-jawed, until she stuck her arm out toward me, miming the act of hooking my shirt collar and reeling me in. I smiled and began to walk toward her just as Clem magically appeared and started busting some moves. He can dance better than I—there was no competition there—but he couldn't keep up with Ruby. He was fist-pumping and Ruby pumped back, overemphasizing as if making fun of him. He did a little worm, pulsing a wave through his body, and Ruby got slinky-nasty and pulsed around him, rocking her hips and rolling her shoulders to the doosh-doosh-doosh, and she was laughing, laughing, laughing.

Through the moving screen of Clem's arms and body she kept looking for my eye, and for a moment I thought she was doing it all for me, not him. But when he grabbed her by the waist and started to air-grind with her, she didn't stop him. I couldn't watch. I vanished from the doorway when she wasn't looking and then slunk back up to my room.

But instead of packing I sat down at my desk and picked up the classic photo book *Yosemite* by German climber Reinhardt Karl that I was re-reading. I had been sitting in my desk chair, reading for only a few minutes, as the music pumped up from below, when I realized that Ruby was standing in my doorway, still sweating from the dancing.

Before I could react, Ruby walked in and sat on the bed, saying, "You should have joined us."

I shrugged, then said, "You're a great dancer." I couldn't look into her eyes, so instead picked a place just above her breasts— her collarbones. They were the most beautiful collarbones I'd ever seen. Almost as beautiful as her jawline—and eyebrows. And the slight jag at the top of her nose. Even her knuckles looked pretty good.

She laughed, her eyes flashing at me. "No, I'm just great at making fun of myself when I'm dancing."

"Clem seemed to miss the joke," I said.

"He's pretty literal," She mimicked the funky-man lip bite, extending and retracting her head but making it faux-funk. Anti-funk.

She stared at me for a moment, then said, "Unlike you. You're the opposite."

"The opposite? What's the opposite of literal?" I asked.

Something flitted across her face then, something she wanted to say, but she reined herself in. Instead, she shrugged and looked around the room at all my gear spread out. "It's like a tornado hit. What's all this stuff?"

It was an odd question: I knew I'd mentioned several times I was heading out west and I finally figured out that she was drunk.

"It's all wall gear. I'm heading out to Yosemite with Dade . . . he's the guy who kicked you at the gym." I realized as I said it we still hadn't talked about the night we first met.

"I was having a bad day that day," she said, making a loose, dismissive gesture toward her face. "But then he did kick me pretty hard."

"He felt terrible. We looked around for you to make sure you were okay, but couldn't find you."

Ruby turned a little red then and stood up and shook her hands, as if to discharge some energy: "Actually, I was having a bad month . . . I'd just broken up with my ex that night. That's why I had to get a new place to live."

"Was he a climber?" I asked.

"Ha. A social climber, yeah," she said, picking up a wall hammer from a pile of aid gear and turning it over in her hands. "He's in law school. I barely saw him after he'd started. He had to put me into his schedule to even . . ." She paused and then set the hammer down. "Whatever. I'm pre-med right now, but watching him—and knowing med school's worse—now I'm not so sure."

After a beat, she took a wobbly step toward my desk and lifted the cover of *Yosemite*. Her long, bare leg was only about an inch from my own, and I could feel the heat and sweat rising off it.

"Wow," she said, looking at a two-page spread of huge rock and huge sky. She flipped to another page, then said, "You're getting on this? It looks insane."

Somehow, leaning over the book, Ruby accidentally bumped my leg with hers. She didn't comment on it, and I leaned forward to look at the photo of El Cap too, so that my leg bumped hers back. Suddenly our legs were pressing against each other. Skin on skin.

Then she was pulling me up into an embrace and I was sinking my hands into her thick, black hair, pressing her against the desk. I was filled with that smell I couldn't identify in the gym—the smell of anise and something sweet, like molasses—as if her hair held black licorice among its strands. Suddenly we were kissing and I felt like I was twelve again, the time I got my first real kiss and a light popped behind my eyes and everything went soft. I felt that softness again with Ruby, soft and then softer—as if I were falling into her.

She started to pull my shirt off, and that's when we heard Fran calling for her from the bottom of the attic stairs. Ruby quickly pushed me away and tugged her blouse and skirt back into place. Her lips were swollen and wild, her eyes even wilder, and as I reached for her hand she also reached for mine, but it was our eyes that seemed to catch hold of each other and get all tangled up.

For a second I swear I saw something in them—not just the distorted reflections of me in her dark pupils, but something deeper, behind the reflections. It was as if there were a little piece of me in them—a piece of myself I had lost or never even known about. It overwhelmed me and I tried to look away to recover, but my eyes kept snapping into focus on hers as if trapped in a conduit or tunnel between us.

Fran called again and this time Ruby yelled, "Hey, coming—just trying to talk Atlas into dancing," as she walked backward towards the door. Her eyes were locked to mine until she turned to disappear down the stairs, finally breaking the connection.

Which is why it surprised me the next day when she came out and sat on the stoop with me, hung over and drinking coffee, and barely said a word while I stretched out on the grass and waited for Dade to come pick me up. Ruby was acting as if nothing had happened between us the night before, and each time I tried to look into her eyes she looked away before any kind of conduit could form, or our selves could get tangled up, or I could catch sight of that little piece of me inside her. When Dade arrived she didn't even come over and hug me, but instead stood up to wave from the cracked concrete stoop, joking with a thick, slurred voice (that made her sound mentally handicapped) that she forgave him for kicking her in the head, before she disappeared back into the house.

I sent a few emails to her over the next six weeks, even some pictures from the big wall aid routes Dade and I did, but she didn't write back, and when I returned in late summer (nursing a cracked rib and a broken toe from an awkward fall) I found out that she and Clem had been an item since right after I left. If I had stayed around that summer it would have been me and Ruby, instead of Ruby and Clem. Or maybe not. Was it real, what I'd seen? Or was it a trick of the eye that showed me what I wanted to see? A trick of the heart for what I wanted to feel?

Whatever it was, I couldn't stand being around them. Ruby's bedroom was just below mine and I could hear everything. The last straw came a few weeks into the fall semester when they had sex and then got into a spat. Ruby came up to my room, leaned against my desk—the desk where we'd kissed—and started complaining about Clem.

I told her I was working on my thesis and couldn't talk right then, and I wasn't even able to look up until she'd left the room, when the lack of her presence, which should have felt like a vacuum, instead felt like a dense and heavy thing.

I moved out only a few weeks into the semester, just a few days before I met Olive. I told my parents that I just needed a place where I could concentrate on my thesis, and they were so excited I was finally finishing my degree after seven years that they let me back into the house—but warned me that it was short-term only. I wouldn't be sleeping until noon in the basement trying to figure out what to do with my life.

That's part of what got me to move into Olive's apartment just after Valentine's Day: to get my parents off my back. The other part was so that I could feel like a grown-up. Except it turned out being with Olive didn't make me feel grown-up at all. Just the opposite, in fact. This is what I was thinking about after my dream of the women, and I slipped back into a troubled sleep, my last thoughts about how maybe I just needed to get away from all of them. Or at least from thinking about them.

I woke to the sound of thunder.

CHAPTER THREE

"Climbing, climbing, climbing!" Dade sang as he pounded out the theme to *Hawaii Five-0* on the side of the van. And then, after loudly cracking open the side doors to let in the morning sun and the chirping of the goddam sparrows, he whispered in his bad Scottish accent, "We're on the road today, laddie, so get your arse in gear."

He sat down in the doorway of the Rig, a cup of coffee in his hand, then pushed his safety glasses back up onto his nose.

"That for me?" I asked, sitting up in bed and squinting at the outline of the coffee.

"Only if you're doing Seven Seas."

I took the cup from him, surprising myself as I said, "I'll go to the Needles to do Son of Sam—and to the Tower, if *Makin' Bacon* can make it that far—but you have to give me a couple hours to get ready."

Dade whooped once and started trotting an imaginary horse in circles in front of the van, spanking his own ass as he sang, "Sweet dreams are made of these, who am I to disagree, I've climbed all over the world, now we're TEAM SEVEN SEAS . . ."

I started to repeat that I was only going as far as Devil's Tower, but he reached into the van with his index finger and thumb like an *okay* sign—our old carabiner handshake—and stuck them in front of me. After a tiny hesitation I linked my fingers into his and then we snapped them away. Through his safety glasses

I could see that he was grateful, and something else: that he'd known I was going all along, though I hadn't even admitted it to myself.

Then I prepared myself for the call to Olive. I hadn't had time to replace my cell phone after I'd crushed it with the plywood two days before, so I borrowed Dade's and then snuck out to the van as Dade ate breakfast with Bev. I was breathing slowly in and out, counting my heartbeats as I organized my thoughts. I was just going to tell her that I'd be a couple weeks late.

Amazingly, though my stomach flipped, I managed not to panic as the phone rang. I hadn't rehearsed the actual words but had the feeling of them in my throat, so I could just open my mouth and let my feelings do the work, separate from my brain. If my brain got involved I knew I'd get into trouble with her.

When she finally picked up, however, I could hear her typing briskly in the background.

"Multitasking?"

"I'm sorry, yeah . . . I got my first presentation to the team at nine thirty," she said, still typing.

I held my breath, taking too long as I let the pressure build up in my throat, and she finally stopped typing: "What's up?"

"I'm just going to go with Dade out to the Needles and the Tower to get some climbing in and then I'll be right out," I said in a rush. Things had started to spin a little, but I managed to get the words out first.

There was an unbelievably long pause, then, somehow, another long pause.

"You're all set up for the interview, what am I going to tell them?"

"Tell them I had to go to Germany to see my ailing *Opa*—then when I get back I'll be the best office drone they've ever seen."

Silence. Like deep space. There wasn't even any static on the line.

"Olive?"

Still not a breath. That's when the phone made a clicking sound as it hung up from her end. Yikes. She'd never done that before.

I called back but it went to voicemail, and though I was going to leave a message, when it clicked over to the recording I couldn't find any words. After an eternity of not saying anything, I simply hung up.

I sat in *Makin' Bacon*, staring at the phone in my hand. I should have told her. I should have said that I needed time, that I needed to rethink us. That I wasn't ready for the cube. I should have let her go. But once again I didn't. I didn't know how to say the words, or if they were even true. I didn't know what they were, hours later, when we finally left town, or when we crossed the Missouri River at dinnertime, or even when we drove past the sharp, eroded buttresses of the Badlands of South Dakota as the sun closed in on the horizon in front of us.

Dade didn't have much to say, either—or could tell it would be better to say nothing—and both of us pretty much stayed silent until we started to wind our way up into the Black Hills and past Mt. Rushmore, driving through a landscape that quickly shifted from the dry grasses of the plains to lush, mixed pine forest; from the violently eroded sandstone, siltstone, and mudstone deposits of ancient seas to even older, harder quartzitic granite that stood in great fins and whalebacks of rock, its igneous layers thrust vertical. All of a sudden, after ten hours of already, technically, being on a climbing trip, I woke up as if from a dull, hot dream: my hands grew sweaty, my heart rate speeded up.

This was our world—the world of rock. The world of tectonic plate shifts and exploding volcanoes and enormous floods, where stone has been freed by the minuscule friction of single drops of rain, by the tiny but constant pressure created by snowflakes that have melted and then refrozen millions of times, making a finger crack for me here, a hand crack there. It's the world in its most elemental state of weather, of life, of pure striving.

I looked over at Dade. He was in the passenger seat with his feet propped up on the shag carpeting of the dashboard, the yellowish light from the console not really reaching him except for the lenses of his safety glasses. All of a sudden I was telling him my dream of falling at the speed of light, then slowing and growing so heavy. Of air so thick that it slowed me as I tried to reach, but then didn't quite reach, the ground. And the weirdest part, I told him, was that for the first time in two years, I'd just had a different dream.

Dade barely waited for me to finish, as if he'd been waiting for something—anything—to talk about, clearing his throat in a pedantic way that told me he was going to use his powers of "Dade-uction" (which was mostly just induction and sometimes meant being the devil's advocate).

"Well, you don't need Carl Jung, or even the World's Greatest Junior High Science Teacher, for this one," he said, poking himself in the chest with that last part to indicate himself. "We set out on a climbing trip and the night before you dream of some enormous fall. The Big G, my man. Gravity. Ground fall. Game over. Or maybe it's just this dizziness you keep complaining about, infiltrating your dreams."

He winked when he said this last part—he thought my dizzy spells were about Olive, since they began just after I started seeing her.

But I didn't bite: "You weren't even listening. I *didn't* dream of falling last night—that's what's odd. And more importantly, in the dream I'm super calm—with no dizziness or fear at all. The heavy feeling—when I feel like I'm as heavy as the whole world—that's what's weird. In the dream, I want to be that heavy. And then there is no 'me.'"

"Maybe you *are* afraid, though. Maybe you always have this dream before you go on big walls like Seven Seas, you just haven't remembered it before."

"Okay, maybe we do need more than the World's Lamest Junior High Teacher for this," I said, but before I could finish he had started talking excitedly over me.

"Maybe you did have other dreams, but they were trapped on the other side, as a kind of 'fixed state memory'? You know, like when you learn something on caffeine, then have better recall when you're on caffeine again? Except with dreams you only really remember them when you're asleep."

In spite of my annoyance with him, that got me thinking. It was like one of those monkey traps in Thailand I'd read about. Kids put bait through a small hole in an empty coconut, and these greedy little monkeys would reach in. With their fists too large to come back out of the hole, they created a ball-and-chain that kept them from climbing trees or running away so that the kids could catch them. The monkeys never got to "bring over" the goodies from the inside. Had I really had dreams I couldn't bring over? Did it have something to do with Olive?

Just as I turned to him to say that maybe he was onto something, I saw him wave one hand in the air, as if to dismiss what we'd been talking about. Then that hand flicked up to his throat. I couldn't see what he'd done, but guessed he'd touched his wedding ring, which, on climbing trips, he always hung on a braid of leather around his neck. He called it his "juju." Before Bev and his wedding ring he'd always worn the broken gate of a carabiner that had snapped apart on a nasty aid fall, and I'd seen him touch his gate—and later the ring—to calm himself while climbing, but I never understood it. I never wore anything like that, never counted on anything for luck.

I was about to hit Dade with that, to tweak him a little about not being able to "let the thing be the thing" without his pacifier, when I realized that he had been talking, his voice so quiet that I had missed the first few words: ". . . a dream a couple weeks ago. I'm driving the Rig, all alone, down some superwide highway. It's like nine or ten lanes wide, just the one side, but there isn't any traffic at all. I'm driving way too fast, like the car is accelerating without me, but then I see headlights up ahead. They should be on the other side, but then I realize they're in my lane."

He looked over at me, but when I looked back he turned towards the window, so that he was speaking away from me. "I cut right, cut left, but can't seem to get out of the way . . ."

"And then what happens?"

He waved one hand before him, as if he were shooing a bee away: "I don't know. I always wake up."

"They call it *Geisterfahrer* in German when someone drives in the wrong lane. *Ghost driver*," I said.

Dade didn't react.

"Well, you don't need Carl Jung or even the World's Greatest Underemployed Geographer for this one," I continued, pointing a finger at myself. I was about to connect the dotted lines out loud—baby coming, unavoidable responsibilities—but he was frozen, his fingers locked onto his juju, and I guessed he was making the connections himself.

I drove us the rest of the way to a secret camping spot just a few miles past Mt. Rushmore, hidden off the main road by a large boulder and a hairpin turn.

We drove into our spot slowly, a little surprised that no one else was camped in there, and bounced our way into the woods. The road grew rougher and Dade got out to help guide me in to a flattish spot, pointing with his headlamp at places that seemed best. Once we found a good site, he guesstimated how un-level it was and took a few thick squares of plywood we keep in the back of *Makin' Bacon*, laying out two for each right-side wheel before I lurched the van up onto them.

After almost eleven hours of the engine roaring and wind tearing through the windows, the quiet at our spot felt odd, like we had walked in on someone else's important conversation and made them stop. But there was no one else, only the sound of branches bending against each other and then the hush of us both peeing out into the night, our shadows hidden within the shadows of the trees.

Inside the van, we popped up the top and got ready for bed without speaking, tired but performing our routine by muscle memory. By eleven thirty I was upstairs and settled into my bag, and Dade turned off the light. After a moment I heard him sigh, something he rarely did. Then he sighed again, although this time it was almost a groan. It seemed that he should be happy, but I knew from the length and tone of these sighs (from all my training with Olive) that he was not. I waited.

"Five months and I'll be a dad."

I shrugged, though he couldn't see me. "Pretty exciting . . ."

"I guess," he said, rocking the van as he rolled over. I didn't hear from him again.

THE NEEDLES

ODOMETER (1)98,919

LAT. 44.93° N LONG. 103.44° W

ALT. 5,042 FEET

JULY 6

CHAPTER FOUR

When I woke up the next morning I had the feeling I sometimes had as a child of not knowing exactly where my body was—that there was no border between me and the rest of the world. With my eyes closed, I toyed with the idea, moving my fingers, wiggling my toes to discover where they were. But instead I waited, letting myself balance on that incredible edge between acting and not acting. Between my own borders and no borders at all.

Then suddenly the van was rocking—the door slammed hard and I found my body rushing back into me in a single burst, like a flash flood filling a dry creek bed. I was lying on my right side, with my right hand curled up by my chin and my left hand between my knees.

I opened my eyes. Outside the screen I could see fast-moving clouds flying so low over the rough land that they tore their bellies on the sharp rocks and spires and pine trees. And I could see Dade too, stepping up onto a tree stump with his phone held over his head, trying to find a signal. He was only wearing a T-shirt, and I could tell by the way he was moving that he was cold. I curled up a little tighter in my bag and watched him jump down and walk to another spot, then look at his phone and give up. He walked back around the side of the Rig and disappeared, then opened the door and got back in with a slam.

After a moment I heard him light the propane stove and felt him sit down.

"I hate this thing," he said, talking about his phone, I guessed. "But I want to know the weather."

"It's cloudy. And cold," I said, wriggling over to the edge to look down at him from my upstairs bunk. "Aren't you cold?"

"I read in a *Science Weekly News* that there are guys in Nepal who can actually raise their body temps a few degrees—just sitting, not moving around."

"But you're not Nepalese," I said. "You're barely human. I bet back on your great-great-grandmother's side there was some interspecies fucking. And I'm not talking Neanderthal—probably goat."

Dade bleated and started to rub his arms briskly. With all his muscles bunched up and his crooked nose and buggy eyes, he did look like a satyr who'd had a particularly rough night. And he was being particularly stubborn.

"Why don't you put your jacket on?" I asked.

He grunted and turned on the portable radio, flitting from one staticky station to another while he made our coffee. His refusal to put on a coat wasn't "letting the thing be the thing" or anywhere near the rockhead. It wasn't even close to being mindful or "present," either.

He flicked the dial again, and for a second I recognized the fleeting strains of classic rock, wailing about how "cryin' won't do you no good." Just when I was about to yell, for crying out loud, how he should just stick with a station, he found a weather report with the next twist of the dial. A low-pressure system was about to pass over us, and there was potential for another one in two days.

"We're getting a late start and there's rain coming—we better hustle if you want to warm up before getting on Son of Sam,"

Dade said in a told-you-so kind of voice, as if I should have been out of bed hours ago.

Oh, yeah. Son of Sam. I wanted to get on it—ostensibly why I'd driven eleven hours with Dade—but also, in this moment, didn't. It was a new, super-hard test piece in a large cave, the roof just high and awkward enough that the wrong fall could be deadly. I don't know why it had lit my imagination, but some routes just do that. Like Seven Seas had possessed Dade. But now that we were closer to it I could feel its danger, and I suddenly felt scared. Like I didn't want to get out of bed.

"Let's go, Team Grape-Nuts," said Dade, pouring his cereal into a bowl. "Time to go pull the fucker down."

I groaned, but fifteen minutes later, before I'd even finished eating my own Grape-Nuts, Dade was backing us out of our camping spot. Sunlight popped like a slideshow between the clouds and pine trees, lighting up the purple dash of the van and the steam from our coffees. Son of Sam was in one of the newer climbing areas called Clubland, which included several cliffs with the names of rock and roll clubs like CBGBs and First Avenue, and which we'd only just started to explore.

First Avenue had lots of easy sport routes so we could just get onto rock and warm up without getting into too much trouble, and though we expected it to be crowded so soon after the Fourth of July, when we got to the pullout for it there was only one other car—a beat-up PT Cruiser with North Carolina plates. It had climbing stickers plastered all over the back window and a high school graduation tassel hanging from the rearview mirror.

"Weird . . . not much company," I said.

Dade looked out the windshield at the quickening sky and I followed his gaze. There were at least three layers of cloud—with a dark, blue layer above them—and they were moving in different directions like the wavelets of a choppy bay.

"Maybe they know something we don't," he finally said, pulling out his backpack and a couple ropes. I stuffed the full trad rack into my bag, along with a couple pairs of shoes from my quiver of five, before hopping out of the van.

Dade slammed the door after me with a flourish, only then checking to make sure he'd hung the key and its loop of shoelace around his neck, and then we crossed the road and its broken asphalt, dropping over the side and romping down into the trees to find ourselves in another world, our shoes padding over the sand and rocks and needles of a path that was really just a linkage of bare spots between the pine trees. I saw a pair of jays flash between two of those trees and heard a woodpecker nearby, gently tapping its way up a trunk.

The path eventually widened out to a twenty-foot spread between two lumps of rock and I moved abreast of Dade. He took off his hat and swept it before him with a grin, his spiky hair almost as scraggly as the trees around us. I knew exactly what he meant—that we had landed, that we were home—and we walked side-by-side for about five minutes, neither of us saying anything, until we reached a pair of giant fins that marked the entrance to the First Avenue area. We squeezed through the slot between them and came out on top of a steep rock gulley. From that vantage we could see, stretched out for miles, a great maze of trippy granite battlements and spires, their edges round and soft like dripped sandcastles at the beach. We scrambled down the gulley into a little slot canyon—right at the base of the cliff that held our first climb, Do the Hustle.

"Who led last? Me, right? At Willow River last time? So you're up—and this is a cakewalk," Dade said as he scrambled the lead rope onto a garbage bag he'd spread out on the sand.

We'd trained hard all spring and I was fit, but because bad weather had kept us off rock this season I felt a little rusty, like I sometimes feel the first time I get up to dance at a party. But when I laid my hands on two fat knobs, their shape a little bit like barnacles, I could feel the old beat again.

That's when it started to rain as if the sky had opened up.

"Friggin' weather again!" Dade yelled, taking me off belay, then stuffing the gear and the guidebook into his backpack.

"The cave is about two hundred yards south," he yelled, and then he was off through the rain, channeling a bit of his rough-night satyr as he bounded away. I gathered up the rest of my gear, cradling the mess of rope in my arms, and started chasing him only to trip on a pine root and go down, bashing my knee in the stumble as the rope splayed out before me. I tossed its loops and bights around me again as if wrangling a big octopus, and then I zig-zagged to the cave, leaping over rills that were gushing off the cliffs and forming streams on the already soaked ground.

The main entrance to the cave was about forty feet high and maybe just as wide, and was ringed all the way around with a two-foot overhang. Rainwater from the upper sections of the massif rushed over the cave opening in a wide waterfall, parting and blending as it fell. Shimmering behind the curtain, way up at the top, I could see the anchor bolts for Son of Sam.

"We're going to have to get wetter to get dry," Dade yelled, leaping through the veil of water ahead of us as if into another dimension. I followed him with a burst and found myself in a stiller, drier place, the sloped cave floor dry and sandy and littered with boulders.

Sitting on one of these boulders were two other climbers with beer cans at their feet and a glass pipe which one of them, who was so gangly and whose hair was so red he looked like a strike-anywhere match, had just finished lighting up. They were both maybe eighteen, young enough they could have been in one of Dade's science classes a few years before, and they looked a little nervous, as if they might have to share with strangers—or that we might take their goodies away.

"We're just going around letting people know that it's raining," joked Dade before shaking himself off like a dog. We were both soaked.

"Yeah, man—thanks for the tip," laughed the shorter one as he took the pipe.

Looking at his stocky frame I wondered if he'd been a wrestler, just like I'd been a million years ago when I was in high school. I was still holding the mess of rope in my arms, looking for a place to set it down without getting it all sandy, and Dade saved me by digging a garbage bag out of his pack and laying it out on mica-flecked ground. I dumped the rope onto the bag and started to work my way into the tangle. It was wet and had patches of sand stuck to some loops, which I carefully brushed off as I got to them.

"Did you all get any routes in before it hit?" the stocky one asked.

"Squat. We were about to get on Do the Hustle around the corner," Dade answered, his hot breath steaming from him like the smoke these boys were blowing. "How about you?"

"We've been working Johnny Rotten back in the Mudd Club. My man almost got the redpoint today," he said, and his friend lifted a beer can to himself, shrugging it off like it was nothing. A redpoint is when you try a route one or more times and finally do it without falling.

Dade just said "huh" and then started to take everything out of his pack, including his lunch and a thermos. He sat down on his pile of gear and unscrewed the thermos, pouring himself some coffee.

"You all been on it yet?"

"Nope," lied Dade. I had been there the day Dade did it on-sight, the year before.

"Man, you should check it out—outrageous undercling move with a left knee scunge, then a dyno to a tiny pebble about as big around as Red's pupil." He pointed at Red's eyes and then laughed with a short bark: "Haw."

Dade started to laugh—at these guys, I knew—but the stocky one must have thought he was laughing with them, because he stood up and said, "Hey, I'm Luther—and this here's Red."

Dade leaned uphill toward Luther and shook his hand, then waved at Red, pointing to himself with the other hand.

"I'm Dade and he's Atlas."

"Atlas, no shit? Like a road map?" Red asked.

I held up a handful of rope as a wave and nodded.

"No, it's like the guy who holds up the world," said Luther.

This confused Red, who was about to light his pipe but stopped: "I thought it was turtles that hold up the world. Four turtles."

"That's some other story—we read it at a rest stop the other day," Luther says for our benefit, and then, back to Red, "Atlas is Roman."

"Yeah . . . Greek, actually," said Dade.

"Right," nodded Luther, who then picked up a beer and held it up as a salute to Dade. "Want a beer? We got plenty."

"Thanks, but not when we're climbing," Dade said.

"Climbing's done for the day—haven't you all heard the report, Mr. Weatherman?" Red asked, letting out a cloud of smoke and pointing with his pipe to the world beyond the waterfall.

"We got a full rack, and this seems to be staying dry," said Dade, as if just noticing the steep, violent crack of Son of Sam, which split the roof of the cave, then topped out over the cave's mouth into a second overhang, just inside the stringy curtain of water.

Red laughed again and pointed at the crack, saying, "This here's the big league, not some T-ball Do the Hustle warm-up. Plus it's kind of warm. And damp. This is more of an autumn climb."

"Yeah, maybe, but I think Atlas has got it," Dade said, picking up Red's gauntlet before turning to me. "If he can just get the rope straightened out. You need a hand?"

This got me hot and I stepped away from the mess. "Have fun."

"Where you all from?" Luther asked, taking another sip from his beer.

"Minnesota," Dade answered, pulling quickly at the rope, letting some loops rest on his shoulder while others dropped to the bag.

"Babe the Blue Ox and Swedes and all that?"

"Yeah, except neither of us are Swedish. But let me guess," Dade said, lifting a big loop up and stepping through. "You two are from . . . North Carolina, right?"

"Hey! Yeah. How'd you know? It was our accents, huh?" said Luther.

"Yeah, they're pretty strong," Dade admitted, winking at me before finally feeding the rope out in one long, unknotted strand. I didn't know if he was winking about baiting the boys or about getting done so quickly what I couldn't even get started.

"So you get so good climbing," said Red, who maybe saw the wink, "climbing on all that Minnesota rock?"

Luther barked out another "Haw!" at this, and for some reason it got me even hotter. Suddenly I was scrambling up into the back of the cave to get a better look at the crack, which arced away wildly over our heads with a 60° pitch toward the curtain of water, making a zig and a couple of zags along the way.

This was a "trad" or "traditional" climb, as opposed to a pre-bolted "sport" climb, which meant that protection in the form of metal camming devices and wired stoppers had to be placed in the crack and then clipped to the rope. It's an art where you have to translate the organic shape of a crack in the rock into a negative space, and then fill that space with offset angles and logarithmically spiraled curves of aluminum. Dade was a master at it, and I asked him his advice.

He finished flaking the rope and then came up to where I was and looked it over carefully, as if it were a painting job he were about to make a bid on: "Number three cam right here . . . and a handful of one through two cams . . . and a couple longer slings to turn the roof."

Then, trying to copy the boys' accents but sounding more like a bad Elvis, he grabbed his crotch and said, "Plus some really big nuts."

A cold breath was flowing out of the crack and I finally reached up to put my hands in it. Its edges were covered in rude, sharp crystals like the teeth of a small shark, but I discovered that it was slightly incut, which would make it easier to climb—and easier to shut these guys up.

I picked up the loop of sling we'd clipped the gear to and slipped it over my right shoulder, then took my tape gloves out of the top of my pack, feeling a surge of power when I slipped them over my knuckles. After I taped the gloves on tight, I crammed my feet into my too-small climbing shoes while Dade built an anchor around a low boulder in the back of the cave where the route started. Our cavemen cohorts took this all in with interest—I caught them exchanging a look like they were two shade tree mechanics watching a couple of bankers get ready to drop a transmission.

Dade caught the look too, and to make us seem even more bumbly, he made a staticky sound, as if he were Houston and I were Neil Armstrong, before he said, "Team Grape-Nuts, you're on belay."

"Copy that," I said. Then I stood on my toes to reach the start of the crack and did a pull-up, v-sitting my legs up into the crack, so that I was hanging from the roof by my fingers and toes.

"Fuck me—" I said, as I was hit with the great pull of gravity. I reached up high and deep into the fractured crack, where I got a solid jam, and crammed both feet in to free an arm and get in the first pieces of protection—a number two cam and one of those big nuts. It was like climbing on the underside of a jungle gym— if you could make one out of alligator jaws. After making sure the gear was good I reversed the moves, grunting with each one, and dropped back down to the ground.

"How's it feel?" Dade asked.

"Hurly-burly."

I shook out my arms and rolled my neck and shoulders. After a minute I got back on it, snaking my way through six or seven moves until I finally got within striking range of what looked, from below, like the rim of a big, fat bucket.

"Keep moving," Dade said, and right then I did feel a weakness—a willingness to give up that swelled out of my throat. The wrong side of fight or flight.

"Come on, pass auf," he snapped, and then I found myself moving, trusting my left hand long enough to rocket my right and touch what indeed seemed to be a deep hold. I regrouped and snapped for it again, this time hitting it so hard both feet popped off, so that I was hanging off my right arm only, my feet dangling as if I were hanging off a two-story basketball hoop. For a brief moment, I felt like a total animal.

"Yee-haw!" I yelled.

"Yeah, man," said Luther, giving me back a little respect.

"Just get some gear in," scolded Dade quickly.

I matched hands on the bucket and got my left foot deep into the crack, my right leg angled for balance beneath me, but I was positioned so weirdly that if my hands popped out before my foot did, I'd pivot around it and fall head first—especially dangerous since I'd managed to leave my helmet back with the big wall gear in the van.

I knew that I could fit something into the crack above and thought it was probably a number one cam, but the gear hung awkwardly off the sling and I could only find the number two.

I tried to place it only to confirm that it was too big, as I should have known it would be. Hanging parallel to the ceiling from one arm, one foot, I panicked and ripped the whole rack up onto my ribs, knocking the number two out of my mouth. I finally got my hand on the number one and then tried to jam it in as fast as I could, but that feeling of weakness—of "will-less-ness"—was back.

"Come on, you idiot," I heard myself say, and then, abruptly, my body—or its drill sergeant—took over. With a thick spritz of adrenaline, it supercharged me and shifted me into simple, balls-out go-mode. I slammed the cam in and then exhaled hard, realizing that I hadn't even been breathing, and felt myself grow a little lighter as I took in oxygen.

"Slack!" I yelled, already tugging on the rope and using too much muscle, and then the cam was gone and the hold was gone and I was falling.

The world fractured into pieces, the action discontinuous: my knee trapped in the rope; my body upside down; the smell of mildew replacing the breath left above and behind me. As the rope snapped tight I roared in an arc through the air, down towards the big boulder waiting at head height—but Dade had somehow shortened the line so that I only whiffed over it, its cold edge only parting my hair instead of splitting my skull.

I had dipped headfirst but swung up a little before I slammed into the back wall, and so I caught it mostly with my feet but also with part of my butt and tailbone. Then I bounced off the wall and pendulumed to a stop ten feet below the piece that had held my fall. The whole event had taken only a fraction of a second.

"Yeah, man!" yelled Luther, clearly impressed. "Y'all is some crazy motherfuckers!"

I was still hanging from the rope, pushing myself away from the boulder, and then I was on the ground and Dade had taken me off belay and had a hand on my shoulder.

"You okay? You smacked the wall pretty good."

I was grimacing and couldn't think of an answer yet, and then when Dade touched my head to see if I had somehow hit it I jerked away and said, "Yeah, I'm okay. I'm so okay I'm gonna chew my fucking arms off."

He didn't know what to do with this comment but kept his hand on me for support.

"That was outstanding if that's how y'all climb over in Minnesooda," drawled Red, clapping slowly.

"Fuck you," I spat. In that instant, with enough go-mode to heave a boulder, I was more than ready to throw down and knew that if I couldn't take him, Dade's golden gloves could.

"Naw, naw, no disrespect. That was a good fight. You didn't pussy out, you totally went for it. Couldn't do it, but you went for it."

"Damn, Red, lay off of him," Luther said, and then, turning to me, he said, "That was the real deal. You want a beer off of me you got it, anytime."

I shrugged and nodded, as the wave of adrenaline and endorphins that would have carried me over Red started to be replaced by the other real deal: pain. There was a sharpness in my ankles and knees that would turn to a deep ache when I was in bed that night, and also a pain in my ass from how I'd smacked the wall.

"I feel like a giant cramping asshole," I said to Dade, standing up, hands on my knees, feet wide apart.

"Yeah, Ut, sometimes we all feel like that about you," he said dryly as he worked my knot loose.

I laughed in spite of myself, which made things hurt worse, and then I noticed that Dade's eyes had grown serious.

"But you're okay?" he asked.

I nodded yes, and he stood back up and stared hard at the route with that boxer's look, the myopic look, daring it to drop anything else from its skin besides me. Then he began to move deliberately and quietly about the cave, as if he were afraid he might wake someone. Before I'd even gotten my breath back he had pulled on his shoes and tied them tight, transferred gear off my harness and rack and onto his, and pulled the rope back through the pieces I'd placed, leaving their carabiners swinging in free air.

"If we can't climb this now, I don't think we're going to get too far on Seven Seas," he said, his voice so sharp that it sounded mean, though I don't think that's how he meant it. He was still wearing his fat wool hat but no tape gloves, and as he tied into the rope I heard him mumble to himself. Then I saw his hand rise up to his wedding ring so automatically it seemed the ring had drawn his hand to it. When his hand fell away, his whole body was calm and loose. Present. Letting the thing be the thing. The opposite of how he'd been that morning.

"Let's do this thing and get out of here," he said, looking at the roof and not at me.

I was still shaking from the fall, still feeling my head whiff! against the boulder, but I put on my jacket and clipped myself into the anchor just before he started climbing. He struggled with the beginning moves just as much as I had, hanging almost upside down and wrestling with them until he clipped the first cam and nut, then placed another. For a moment, an evil fraction of a second, I was jealous. I hoped he'd fail and see how hard the route really was. But then that feeling was gone. I didn't want him to get hurt—and I also wanted him to shut Red up.

He plugged a cam in at the lip where I had struggled and fallen, and then he just kept going, grunting through his teeth and reaching blindly over the lip to find the holds I hadn't even gotten to. As Dade turned the lip, exiting the cave completely, thirty feet off the cave floor and out of my sight, I noticed that the rain had stopped, though there were still thin streams falling behind him, flowing and splattering sporadically as if the massif were some giant still dripping from the shower. I could tell by the movement of the rope that he was shaking out one arm, then the other, and I saw one foot swing into view, then back out as he figured out some strange move. Dade hooted and groaned down to me after that, admitting that the route was really, really hard.

Luther had hopped down to the entrance of the cave to get a better view and yelled information up to me, like, "He's clipping a bolt," or "He's going to need slack in a second." Between that information and what I could feel through the rope, I knew Dade was being a machine—maybe even in his rockhead—with all those hard, lean angles cutting their way into the world, making me proud to be his partner.

When Dade reached the belay bolts he somehow knocked his hat off, and it fluttered down to the pool below like a shot bird.

"I'll get it," Luther said, scrambling down from his vantage near the entrance to fish the hat out. Then there was a hard jerk, then another, as Dade clipped the anchor bolts.

As I lowered him, the perspective in the cave, along with the pale skein of dripping water behind him, made it seem as if he weren't dropping plumb to the earth but was being tractioned outward—as if the water were creating some weird gravitational force that drew him toward it. He was rotating in a slow spiral as he came down from the lip, and I was sure of the triumphant face I was going to see when he swung around toward me, but when I finally saw him I was surprised to see another look there: a look of anger.

"Team Son of Sam," I said loudly, purposefully not looking at Red, while Luther handed Dade his soggy hat and slapped him on the back. I unclipped and hopped down to him, to help him untie his knot this time, and when I told him again what a great job he'd done he shrugged. His third knuckles and the backs of both hands were bleeding, the bright red limned with pink where blood met chalk, and he'd bashed and cut his lip somehow too. I handed him a handkerchief and tried to get him to look at me, but he avoided my eyes as he tamped the blood from each hand. Then, facing away from me as he looked out through the dripping water, out toward the trees and the earth and the wind, he said, "I think I'm done for the day. You get to clean it."

CHAPTER FIVE

Usually when I think about thinking—when I notice myself thinking—I feel like it happens up in my head, up in the control room with all those eyes and ears and taste buds working together as a team, driving the rest of me like an elephant wallah goading his beast to work. The old homunculus, running the show. But I woke up in *Makin' Bacon* the next morning climbing Son of Sam all over again—not in my head at all.

It was a dream, but I was also sort of awake enough to consciously replay the moves from the route, and my decisions about how to climb and the intention to do it were down in my hands, freed from the burden of language, blind and deaf and scentless. And perfect. I was taking the rock with precision, and each move was like putting a key in a lock, the key snapping into place as if magnetized. Then I was waking up, my mind flowing back up into my head, and there were no more keys in any more locks—only the "whiff" of my head just missing that boulder.

I vaguely remembered half-waking in the night and fending off dripping water, my tailbone and ankles—and my neck—all aching, and I rolled my face away from a wet spot to look over the edge of my mattress and see my pillow far away on the floor of the van. As the blood began to fill my head, making even my eyes feel thick, I was reminded of the bunk bed I shared with my brother, Gus, when we lived outside of Laramie, Wyoming, where my parents were finishing their PhDs in geology (my father) and biology (my mother). And I was reminded of one particular day.

My mother had asked me to clean up my dinosaurs and Hot Wheels while I waited for *Ren and Stimpy* reruns to come on. I felt Time right then—Time, which had always been a mostly constant but external force—suddenly become my property and split into two halves as cleanly as a banana from its skin. I knew that I could wait for the TV show upstairs in my head, and downstairs, in my body, I could put the dinosaurs away. I had learned in one moment to double the things I was able to do at one time.

Looking down at my pillow in the Rig, it struck me that in order to divide time I also had to divide my thoughts—my intention—and like a river split into two, each fork could only maintain half the force it had before. But when I was at my best in a wrestling match—and, sometimes, climbing—I got back to that one thing and could *undivide* time so that there was only one river. A Mississippi of me. An Amazon of intention. But I hadn't managed it on Son of Sam. Or the day Olive left town. Or maybe any day with Olive.

I had an extended moment of nothing after that, just my heart thudding through my swollen hands as I listened to the rain on the van roof, and then I slowly brought my eyes into focus to realize that Dade was staring up at me. Embarrassed, I said, "No climbing today."

"I feel like hell anyway," he lisped, his lip swollen on the left side where he'd smashed it turning the roof of Son of Sam.

I nodded and retracted my head, rolling over to spy what must have been the leak in the roof above me, a fat drop of water forming only two feet from my eyes. It was something that I'd need to fix later in the day—maybe after replacing my cell phone—but we'd start the rain day off with some rest and recovery. Team R&R.

Without either of us saying a word, both of us working in slow motion, I broke down the pop-top and Dade folded and clapped his bed away. Then we drove down to Hill City, full of jewelry stores and biker joints and one great deal: Alonzo's All-U-Can-Eat, where for the slim price of a latte and an artisanal scone somewhere else you can eat away the hours and drink as much cheap coffee as you'd like.

The surroundings were a little dingy, with wagon wheels and ratty horse gear hanging on the walls, and there was graffiti written with Sharpies on the vinyl of our booth seat, including "Juanita and Dennis," and, strangely, "Arlene Rubiduoux—grandma whore." But then the seats were also comfy enough to ease the pain of my tailbone.

The all-you-can-eat part of the restaurant was a bit of a torture for us, since we were both trying to stay climbing-lean, but I had a buckwheat pancake to go with my eggs, and Dade got extra bacon to wash down his. Then Dade took the *Rig Veda* out of his day bag and started documenting our climbing from the day before, slurping carefully through the right side of his mouth. This was the fourth of the journals he'd kept while I'd been around, though he called each one the *Rig Veda* since he always kept them in the Rig. He draws lots of pictures in them (he can draw really well), records how much money we've spent, and lists where the Rig is by latitude, longitude, and odometer reading. It's also where he writes down the date and place of the climbs he's done, as well his old "percentage" ranking for the hardest moves on the climb—the chance of falling off or staying on a particular hold.

I've never kept a notebook, since it feels too fusty to me, but Dade argues that journaling magically makes you a better climber (or science teacher or husband, for that matter) because it forces you to replay and think about what you did so that you can learn from it and better visualize yourself the next time you're doing something. Like losing your shit on Son of Sam. Or screwing up a phone call with your girlfriend . . . or ex-girlfriend.

I had a photo of Olive that I'd placed demonstratively in my wallet the night before she left for New York, and I took it out to look at it. It was my favorite photo of her. I'd taken it when we'd just started dating, when we were visiting her friends up at their family's lake cabin. In the photo, Olive is sitting on the edge of a big boulder, at twilight, her bare feet just touching the water so that her toes and nothing else spread rings on its surface. She had been looking straight at the camera, but her eyes had been caught at the end of a blink so in the photo they're closed. The grainy arc of lake behind her follows the curve of her brow and lends a tension to her eyes, making it feel like they could pop open at any moment. That weekend contained that kind of tension too—the feeling of potential—and every moment was relaxed but exciting as we mixed up our hearts and let our feelings for each other out into the open.

I put the photo away and groaned. Was the feeling still there, somehow hidden by the mess of our day-to-day lives? I needed to call Olive—to hear her voice, to hear about how the job was going and whether or not she was speaking much German, to find out how Meany and Mo were doing. All that, and to apologize for my cowardly phone call.

I promised myself that I wouldn't tell her about my fall on Son of Sam (because she always got so freaked out), and I secretly hoped her sweet, honest voice—the one that wooed me in the first place—would tell me that she missed me and that she wanted to be with me. Maybe it would save me from myself.

I looked at my watch. It was ten thirty in the Needles' time, which meant it was twelve thirty on Olive-time, which meant it was possible I could catch her eating lunch at her desk. She always ate lunch at her desk. But I needed a phone.

I held my hand out to Dade: "I'll buy a new one today, but can I borrow yours for a second? I got to call Olive."

He pushed his glasses back, his tongue unable to leave his swollen lip alone.

"Why?"

"Because, you know, like you said—I need to tell her things."

"No, I mean, why get a phone?" he asked. Then he pointed at the *Rig Veda*. "I was just writing about how distracted we're getting. I mean, society in general, but also you in particular. Like how you couldn't stay focused on Son of Sam. Maybe a phone is just one more thing that gets in the way. It's like noise pollution in a city—you don't realize it's messing with you until it's gone. I mean, who do you need to call? What email do you desperately need to check? You're just addicted to your phone." In his bad Scottish accent he then said, "Cut yourself loose, man, get off the teat!"

I didn't love the idea, but before I could form any kind of argument, Dade went off about the evils of multitasking and how there was no reason for us to get on the internet on this trip because we already knew where we were going. Plus there were always pay phones if I really needed one. Or his phone, for that matter.

"If we can still use payphones, then why don't you get rid of yours too?"

I thought I'd boxed him into a corner, but he started to nod with Dade-like intensity.

"All right, I'm with you in spirit," he said, looking at the ceiling.

"But you're not going to do it . . ." I said, nodding.

"No. Bev won't go for a full no-phone thing. Plus it's crazy not to have a phone with us traveling and climbing, right? But I tell you what: I'll commit to black-out times with it—I'll turn it off except for one hour in the evenings. We can both check voicemail or make calls. And I'll go on sabbatical with email. I'll put my vacation message on."

"All right. No phones. Just climbing. Team Luddite," I said, holding a loser "L" up to my forehead.

"Team Luddite," he said, smiling, putting an "L" to his forehead too. Then a look came over his face: "Unless there's an emergency . . . or Bev demands I call more often."

"What? You can't bend the rules already—you just made them."

"Rules for rule-making follow the five-second rule. Like for food."

I shook my head, laughing at him: "You're impossible, but, then, all right, give me your phone. I got to get through to Olive again—it's kind of an emergency—and she doesn't know about Team Luddite."

He squinted briefly, as if trying to see his way past the angle I'd gotten on him, then reached deep into his shorts pocket and handed it over. It was still raining when I got outside, and I stood under the awning and dialed Olive's number—then suddenly felt swoony, the awning and the gray sky spinning away from me. I hung up, almost frantic. What was I doing? Calling her to have a little chat? The last call I'd made, I'd started to break her heart. Where was my undivided Mississippi? My Amazon of intention? My one thing I should be doing? Before I called, I needed to know what I wanted.

To stop. Or take a break, anyway. I needed to call and tell her the stress I was feeling about us and not worry about how it came out or what the repercussions would be. I needed to man the fuck up. This last part I even said to myself in Dade's Scottish accent, and I started to pump myself up, imagining myself dialing and saying the words, like I was about to get on a climb. This was it. I felt heavy and a little rattled, like I'd just had an argument with someone, but I managed to redial the number—this time, through some fluke in the phone system, she answered before it rang.

"Atlas," she said flatly, apparently recognizing Dade's number from the last call.

"I'm calling from the Needles. Where you at?" I asked.

"I'm in Manhattan. At work. You know, because I have a job."

Yeeouch. That's all it took to kill my psych. To buy myself some time, so I could psych myself up again, I asked her about the hamster pirates: "How my boys doing? Settled in?"

She sighed. "Mo got out again, but I'm sure he's somewhere in the apartment—the food I put out keeps disappearing."

"Through the lucky lookout? You know you have to tape that shut," I said. She always forgot that and it drove me nuts. When I finished speaking I heard a man's voice in the background.

"Just a second," she said, covering the phone. After maybe twenty seconds she got back on the line: "Yeah, I know, I mean, I don't know. Um, look, I have to shove off—I'm getting lunch with some of the guys." She spoke as if scolding me.

Before I could answer I heard her sigh, and then, finally sounding like Olive, she said quietly, "We really need to talk."

Then she hung up.

"Some of the *guys*?" I said out loud, actually holding the cell in front of me so I could stare at it. "Shove off?" I wanted to smash it—or at least hang it up with a slam, like you can really only do with an old landline phone. But instead I just pressed the off button as hard as I could and shoved the phone into my pocket, as if to punish it. I stared out at the street. I felt empty. Hollow. And not really ready to talk to Dade about "how it went."

After a long moment, the letters on the sign on the awning across the street, which I'd been dully staring at but which really hadn't entered my consciousness, resolved into words: "Last Chance Antiques." Dade had found an old ring piton in that very store once and later hammered it into a perfect, rounded sky hook for aid climbing. I decided to wander over there and see if I could find one myself. Or at least kill a little time.

The place is more of a thrift shop than an antique store, and there was no one else in there at that early hour besides the old lady working behind the counter, who was busy cleaning a black and gold ceramic lamp in the shape of a rearing stallion.

Right in front of it was a shelf that held souvenir knickknacks, including postcards of fish that were larger than the canoes they'd been landed in, of hunters with grasshoppers as large as deer, of Mt. Rushmore and the forever-unfinished Crazy Horse monument. Beneath the cards, sitting alone on the bottom shelf, there was a spiral-bound *Wyoming!* notebook with the famous, mythical creature of the plains, the half jack-rabbit, half antelope "jackalope," looking glassy-eyed from the cover. It was just the kind of kitschy, dorky thing that Olive always got a kick out of, and I decided to buy it and mail it to her as a peace offering.

On the counter itself there was an old, rotating drugstore watch display, which leaned drunkenly to one side. It was full of broken pocket watches and rusting jackknives and not a single piton. At the bottom of the case, however, hidden under some ladies' watches, was a white badge that caught my eye. I asked the old lady about it, and she took the four steps over to me as if my request and her approach were simply a coincidence, then opened the case to take it out and hand it to me. It had a few black ovals on one side, and on the other was the simple outline of a fish.

Suddenly she smiled and took it back from me. "Why, I haven't seen one of these in ages—a whirligig," she said, awkwardly flipping it back and forth in her knotted, wrinkled hands. "It just needs some string."

She pulled an impossibly long carving knife and a roll of packing twine out of her apron pocket, then cut two lengths of the twine, deftly threading it through holes in the top and bottom edges of the badge so that she could spin it back and forth.

"See?" she said breezily.

When it was spinning fast, the fish looked like it was inside a fishbowl, though at the end of the spin I could clearly make out the fish and the bowl as separate entities. It was like a flipbook but with only two images.

"They always used to have cardboard ones at the fair," she said, still spinning it, "Back when I was a little girl."

I bent over to see it better, since she was holding it low, and then she clapped her hands together, cupping the twine and disc between them as if she were passing me a baby bird that might hop away. I stretched out the twine and spun it a few times, putting the fish into the bowl, then taking it out. Putting it in, taking it out, until she smiled—more from her memory of it than the trick itself, I think. I smiled too, though for a decidedly different reason.

It was my "objective correlative," as Olive, with all her lit-crit jargon, might have said. Atlas flipping one way, then the other. And if he does it fast enough, yells the carny, there appears to be a seamless whole—or maybe just an unseemly asshole.

"Five bucks," said the lady, removing the twine from it as if that were too precious to give me for free, and I bought the whirligig along with the *Wyoming!* jackalope notebook. I felt oddly happy as I handed her the money—as if I'd finally caught the name of a song that had been on the tip of my tongue—and walked lightly out of the store.

Back in Alonzo's, the mood had taken a turn for the worse. A scrawny mother with a baby in a high chair was sitting directly across from our table in the other row of booths, and the baby was crying. Or maybe bleating. The father figure reached their table about when I reached Dade, and as soon as he arrived the mother got up—without saying a word—and went to refill her plate. This did not calm the baby down, and it strained for its mother with tiny, syrup-covered hands—which prompted the father, even taller and scrawnier than the mother, to wipe them.

Dade had the local newspaper, the *Nugget*, held up in front of him; it had been rustling casually between his hands when I arrived, but it suddenly froze completely. This was it. This was the *Geisterfahrer* coming at him at ninety miles an hour. He lowered the newspaper, and though he didn't say anything, he looked me in the eye and then at my hand, which was spinning my new whirligig on the tabletop like a coin, the fish landing in the bowl, then coming out again as it made an annoying, rattling sound. Then he looked over at the screaming baby and its father and began to shake his head.

"You can really wear a hole through a guy," he said through his swollen lip as his hand snapped for my toy. I was too quick for him, and by the time he had leaned back in his seat I had already spun it again, cupping my hands around it so he couldn't snatch it. It seemed to spin faster and faster as it slowed down until it rattled itself to an abrupt stop, its sound somehow in sync with the baby's wail.

Dade stared at the whirligig and sighed. "It's all over when the baby comes."

"Oh, come on."

"Yesterday," he said, sitting very still, looking at me hard. "Yesterday, when I finished that route, I was terrified."

"But you cruised it. And on-sight at that."

"I did NOT cruise it. I barely hung on. What if I'd whipped from way up and hit that boulder like you almost did? What would Bev do alone with our new baby—a baby without a father? I'd rather—"

"Chew your own arms off?" I asked, trying to make fun of what I'd said after Son of Sam.

"Kill myself, is what I was going to say. But it's just as stupid."

He sat still for a moment, then grunted a short, bitter laugh at the absurdity of it all, his wet eyes darting from his coffee cup to me and back again. "You got to watch me," he said, his voice straining. "You got to super pass auf."

"Dude, I'm always there when you're climbing—"

He said nothing more but stopped me with his stare, his eyes strangely large.

"Okay," I said, my hands up in the air.

"Promise?"

"Passing auf—110 percent," I said, making the ring of our carabiner handshake and giving him a boy scout salute with it.

Dade seemed calmer after my effort, but then I realized that it was probably only because the baby had stopped crying. In that moment the parents—and everyone else in the restaurant—seemed to relax a little bit, with talk and laughter filling in the vacuum that was left. That's when I realized the rain had stopped.

"Even if it dries out by tomorrow, I don't know if I'm up for a redpoint on Son of Sam," I said, looking at Dade only to find him still staring at me.

"I saw it in my mind's eye," he said slowly, "you falling right before you fell. That's why I was able to get enough slack in, but even then I thought you were going to hit that fucking boulder."

He held out his two palms like a scale: "That was a fifty percent hold for both of us. I rolled a fifty-one, you rolled a forty-nine."

"But I climbed stupid. I should have stuck," I said.

"Yeah, you really did climb stupid."

Before I could react he said quickly, "I could see from the ground that you wanted it to be over. Past tense."

"You did too."

He nodded. "But not when I was actually on it."

"Well, you're a big fucking stud. What do you want me to say?"

"God damn it, Atlas—you're so strong you should be cruising everything we touch! You didn't even fall on Son of Sam when you seconded it and pulled the gear. Don't you see you could climb harder than me? But whenever something's difficult you let yourself get rattled."

Staring at me, he stuck his right arm out to his side, straining two fingers in a V to get my attention, then snapping them to his eyes like some demented Navy SEAL: "You didn't *see* Son of Sam just like you didn't *see* how to undo the tanglefucked rope. You need to focus. You need to get myopic on that shit."

I was about to argue with him but then, partly because of my moment with the number two cam when I knew I had the wrong gear and tried to use it anyway, and partly because his swollen lip made words like "myopic" sound silly, I admitted that he was right: "Okay, I freaked a little. I was pumping out and didn't read it right. But that's not the same as the rope—"

"It's exactly the same as the rope," he said, exasperated. "I don't understand it because you always pay incredible attention when you belay me. You always seem so careful when you're painting, or when you're driving—whenever the heat is off—but they're all the same thing."

Dade paused for a second to touch his swollen lip, then snatched up the whirligig when I wasn't concentrating. "Like with Olive—"

"I just tried to have it out with her," I said, throwing my hands up in the air, "and we agreed to talk later."

"Good. Because there's a point when *not doing things right* is more than not focusing. It's doing things *wrong*. The Golden Rule kind of wrong—like *cunt*," he lisped.

My jaw dropped and Dade's confused look prompted me to whisper the word back to him in disbelief.

"I said *Kant*! Immanuel Kant's Golden Rule," he over-enunciated, "Ow . . . just let me finish: It's a kind of stealing. Especially since you two could be right for each other, if you could just grow up. You need to get into your—"

"What? My *blockhead*? My Team Seven Seas?"

"No," he said sharply, "More like your 'girlfriend head.' Your Team Olive."

I was stunned. *Right for each other*? I couldn't even go there with him about Olive in that moment and waved him off, but he definitely had my attention. This weirdo *did* have a wonderful wife, and he *had* seen the future and stopped me from splitting my head open the day before. And he *did* just say that I could potentially climb harder than he could. If I was going to pass auf and climb better then I needed to pass auf here too, and listen when he was trying to tell me something important.

"Do you know how to get to your rockhead?" I asked, all the fight gone from my voice.

"I don't know anymore . . . I used to think I did," he said dully, setting his forehead down on the table as if exhausted. "When I was there, there was no Bev to get in the way. Or, she was there but I could always push her aside. Except now I can't. Not with the baby. That's the problem. They're either always there, or they come flashing in right after."

All at once I felt exhausted myself. I laid my own head down on the table to think about the rockhead, but found myself instead listening to the hollow sounds of the restaurant: clinking silverware and simple chatter and the baby back to crying with its little bleats. After a while I could feel my heart beating in my forehead, and then I realized that I could feel it pulsing in my cheeks and lips too—where Olive had cupped my face in her hands to kiss me before she left for New York.

As my heart banged away it seemed to be drawn down into my sore tailbone and even sorer ankles, and before I could stop it I felt the panic—as if in a waking dream—of being back on Son of Sam, peeling from the crack in a violent, arcing swing, my head whiffing past the edge of the boulder, the pain electric through my bones.

CHAPTER SIX

We pulled out of our secret bivy for good the next morning and headed up to Sylvan Lake, the switchbacks coming tight and twisty once we'd passed the 244/89 junction. We squeezed through the tunnel that sends many a large RV back to whence it came, and soon saw more rock than we could do in a lifetime spread out beneath us.

But I could tell by the way Dade was pushing the van, lips zipped tight, that he wasn't thinking about climbing, but rather about a text message Bev had sent early that morning that he wouldn't talk to me about. I didn't feel like talking much myself. I'd tried to call Olive the night before but couldn't get a good enough signal, and the tension about the call I still needed to make, as well as the feeling of my head whiffing past the boulder on Son of Sam, were weighing on me.

The only thing going for us was the weather, which was sunny and cool and perfect for climbing. Of course, the one thing I'd learned after dozens of visits to the Needles is that if you know anything about the weather, it's that you don't know anything—my experience backed up by the standing daily weather report that always posted a 50 percent chance of thunderstorms for the afternoon. Every afternoon.

Dade pulled over at the crest of the hill where it flattens out, right where you either turn left to take the Needles Highway past Sylvan Lake or continue straight to roll down into Custer.

The crest is about the only place, besides down in the towns, where you can always pull a strong enough signal to make a call. Dade hopped out of the van and walked about half a rope length ahead of the van, dialing the cell phone before putting it to his ear and then holding it there with both hands as if that could somehow bring it closer to him. I needed to stretch out the kinks still left in my body from Son of Sam, but this wasn't a good place to do it; instead I stared at a smooth, iridescent puddle of mixed water and gas that shimmered just in front of the van.

I could see the chemical colors of the gas slowly folding in on themselves and could see more too; "beneath" the gas I could make out the dirt shoulder, and "above" it, superimposed on the polychrome swirls, was a reflection of the clouds overhead. As I stared at it I thought about the fact that I had known I needed a number one cam on Son of Sam, but then rushed and tried to make the number two fit—making things harder for myself by not accepting the truth at hand.

Before I knew I was doing it, I found myself digging in my day bag for a pen and Olive's jackalope notebook, almost as if those hands from my dream the day before, not my brain, made the decision for me. I just wanted to borrow a single page from her. In the back of the notebook I wrote down the question, "Seeing?"

But then it wasn't so much a problem with seeing for me (since I had *seen* what I needed to do) as with being lazy. But then it wasn't just laziness, either. It was more like a weakness. A weakness that had been growing worse over the last year.

I wrote down a few more words.

Seeing?→ *lazy*→ *weakness*→

Then I finally wrote down where this was really heading:

→ *Olive.*

I wrote it again and whispered her name out loud a few times until the sounds became slippery, transforming themselves from 'Olive' to 'all of' to 'I love.' I love all of Olive. Olive juice. Olive-ederchi. I looked back out at that swirling mess of a puddle.

Maybe I should just write out the words I needed to say to her, I thought, since I couldn't seem to have the conversation on-sight. If I could practice the words here to get them right—work them like the moves from a hard route—then maybe when I had to say them I could do it as if from muscle memory. A red-point phone call. A red-point relationship.

"Olive," I wrote again. "Olive. Olive. Olive. Olive."

I wanted to write the words, "I can't be with you," but it seemed so harsh there, all alone on the page. Too abrupt a start. Instead, I wrote, "I've been wanting to talk to you for a long time, to talk about us."

What could I say? That I should have stopped "us" before New York? That you knew when we met that I was a climber and that I wasn't going to stop? That you should be mad at me, but then, since you've expected this all along, maybe this will be satisfying, your prediction finally come true?

My eyes became damp and foggy—the beginnings of a cry— and I felt other words that could be written rise up from within me, words from some deep drawer in a deep room deep in my mind, hidden in a tiny wooden box, wrapped in a worn handkerchief. Words that said, *I'm not ready yet. I'm not ready for you.*

Was it true? Had Dade infected me with his talk about how Olive was right for me, but that it wasn't the right time? The words on the page were still out of focus, and after looking up to blink a few times I saw that Dade was loping toward me, eating up ground like some carnivore on the hunt, only three minutes after he'd gone to make the call. I quickly wiped my eyes again and shoved the notebook into my day bag, wondering what shit had just hit his particular fan, as he jumped into the driver's side seat and slammed the door way too hard.

I didn't ask what was up until he looked at me.

"Nothing, except for a pregnant wife and her raging hormones, who now thinks that there's too much to do around the house and that I shouldn't be gone so long. But I maybe talked her into it. We're supposed to talk again tomorrow."

"Can you still go to Yosemite?"

"What do you care? You're not going anyway, right?"

I held my hands up in submission, his anger at me seeming out of proportion with his response. Until I remembered the scream-ing baby at Alonzo's. The *Geisterfahrer*.

"Maybe she'll back off. You guys made a deal."

"My stupid fate," he said, his hand rising to his swollen lip and then dropping. "This whole baby thing . . . one thing leading to the next and the next and the next until I'm dead."

I stared at him. He often went to the worst-case scenario and had to be argued back from the brink. Or at least have his skitter-ing brain distracted.

"That's not fate. It's just old-school determinism," I said, trying to engage him. "Fate is like how Oedipus was supposed to kill his father and mount his mother and in spite of a million attempts to avoid it, he did just that. Or, wait, do you think Bev is your mother?"

Dade held up his powerful, gnarly hand and started flicking out digits, beginning with his middle finger: "One, Bev's scent somehow addles my brain and lures me to her—after all those other women. Two, we decided to have a kid, but I thought it would take a while, right? I've been wearing tight-ass underwear my whole life, over-heating my boys, but no, she's fucking preggers the month after we pull the goalie. Four—"

"You're only on three," I said, to show I was paying attention.

"Four," he repeated, stressing his middle finger again, "Her happy love hormones are raging, so all in a dewy glow she says I can go to Yosemite . . . then, her other hormones—the uptight tiger-mother ones—start raging and she says I can't. It's like her self is gone . . . she's just driven by chemicals, and I'm driven by chemicals too."

Dade's non-climbing posture, usually bad, had taken on a particularly malevolent form, his back hunched and his shoulders rounded so far forward he could have steered the van with them. He sat like this for a while, staring with glazed eyes at the iridescent puddle in front of us like I'd done earlier, and then, his eyes suddenly focusing, he said, "Okay, you're right. Not fate. Determinism. It's all just . . . triggers. We're just triggered to do stuff. We're stuck in a line of dominos, unable to avoid the one behind us or banging into the one ahead."

When he finished speaking he froze. I think he was holding his breath because after a half minute he let out a really big sigh, then took in an equally big breath, his shoulders opening up a little with the inhale. He seemed to hold his breath again, then breathed out and in. His shoulders spread a little more and then he kept doing it, as if he were inflating himself. After a minute of this, his shoulders wide, his head balanced perfectly on the top of his head, he started the van and clunked it into gear.

"Whatever, Bev. What-fucking-ever," he whispered, calmly. Then he flicked a look at me and said, "Let's go pull some shit down," before driving us right through the puddle he'd been staring at to turn left and head down the Needles Highway and into the park. Although I couldn't see the puddle in the side mirror, I imagined that it was roiling, the iridescence trying to flatten out and gather itself again.

Twenty minutes later I was standing at the top of a little pedestal, at the start of a route on an enormous blob of rock not far from Sylvan Lake. Small quartz crystals, far more typical of Needles climbing than overhung Son of Sam, pressed out from this wave of granite like coral bloom undersea, arching up and away from me for eighty feet. The climb was called Mudskipper, a relatively easy but X-rated (that is, death fall) test piece Dade talked me into, arguing that I needed to get back on the horse that bucked me.

"You couldn't fall off this if you tried," Dade said as he scrambled the rope for me, and it was almost true. It was easily within my soloing ability. I'd headpointed, without a rope, stuff much harder than this, and here I even had a single, lonely bolt just below the crux to protect it.

There was only one problem: I couldn't seem to get started. When I reached up to take the first crystals I could hear the roar of gravity—and the *thuk* sound my head would have made if it had hit that boulder on Son of Sam. I tried to regroup and looked up at the clouds overhead, then watched a wren dart from branch to branch in a nearby tree, her wings flicking more for show, it seemed, than to fly.

"Come on, Uhtlas, I know that fall was freaky, but you have to move through it. You have to break the spell," he said. Then, making a motion as if he were flicking a spider off the back of his hand he said, "Remember when I took that fifty-footer at The Chief—when I grazed the ground with my feet? You made me get right back on it. You made me snap out of it. Well, you need to snap out of it. Come on: take a big, deep breath, then start climbing."

I took a breath and held it, like he'd done in the van, then took the other. Then took a few more. Nothing happened.

"You got it, just stay loose," he said, "And pass auf."

Hands high, stepping up . . . and again I imagined, unable to stop it, me popping off Mudskipper, catching the pedestal to twist backwards and crack my cranium with a dull, horrible *thuk*.

There it was again: I couldn't get my thoughts "right" any more than I could reach for the right gear on Son of Sam. Where was the "me" that had reached for that cam—or took the notebook out of my day bag and started writing to Olive? Where inside me was the part that acts? And why couldn't I control it?

As I chewed on this, a gust of wind tangled in the trees around me, and it made the tree with the wren in it burst with a little rain left over from the night before. I saw the wren fall away in flight, and then had the upside-down sensation that it was the tree, not the wren, that was in motion, dropping ballast to somehow rise off the ground.

It left me hyperaware of the weight of the rope at my waist, of the swing of the quickdraws on my harness, of the sharp edges of the crystals in my hands. For one flat, humming moment, each thing *lined up* just right with the others, like cherries in a slot machine. Except there was an extra column—me—and I wasn't lined up. I didn't fit into the world the way I should have. I chalked up again, set my hands back on the two knobs, and tried to bridge between my thoughts and (I don't know how else to say it) my "self," until it suddenly felt like I'd crossed my thoughts like I sometimes cross my eyes.

And there it was—with another burst of wind there was a burst in me: for a moment I seemed to be both a filter-feeder and a pollinator at the same time, absorbing the world and spreading myself into it simultaneously.

My feet were lean and light, my hands taking the crystal knobs with surety, and the sun was bright, the rock warm, the wind lifting me a little as if I were simply a bubble rising to the surface. I knew deep down that whether Olive and I ended up together didn't matter; we would live good lives either way. I rode that surety all the way through the crux before the feeling of being lined up began to dim. Even though I tried to focus on it, to "listen" for it like a sound that was fading, it was finally gone and I was simply climbing again—good and calm but "normal"—all the way to the rounded top, where I was able to stand up and yell "Off belay!" down to Dade.

I tugged on the line and yelled through the wind again, finally getting enough slack to sit down and set up the belay, and for a moment I was awash in scent, encased in that mixed smell of lichen and rope fibers and chalk and even the rock itself, which smells a little bit like all those things. I looked up again at the clouds, so confident in their journey, and it seemed like I could hear them, their sound like a giant yawn or chant that was stretched out and slowed down and very far away. And beneath me: I slapped the hard mineral I was sitting on and pressed it into my palm. I was made up of minerals—and chemicals—too; my body was constantly drawing in air, splitting it, taking what it needed, and sending the rest back out into the world. I was only one breath away from the wind that carried that wren, only molecules away from the rock I sat on.

But just because I was made of this physical stuff, it didn't mean that it was all just determined, did it? What Dade dubbed the "triggers"? It was true that every time I had to have a difficult conversation with Olive the stress had started to cause a Pavlovian response and got me all woozy. But was that stress brought on by the fact that, even though we were maybe intellectually and emotionally right for each other, we had the wrong pheromones or genes or even gut flora? That is, was it ultimately determined by the triggers? Or was it simply because "I" couldn't make the decision to settle down? But then, who or what was making the decision? I had no idea why I did anything: Grape-Nuts or oatmeal? Follow Olive east or follow Dade west? Do the route or lose my shit? No idea. Maybe I really was just riding a giant domino to the ground, ready to smash into the next one (and the next one and the next one) all the way to the last domino—my gravestone.

And yet . . . if my actions were just a series of dominos, then what was that vaporous "focus" I'd just found, when I lined up those cherries to finally climb like I was supposed to? It felt different from any other decision I've ever made; like I'd somehow tapped my true, capital *W* will. Or were those just other, hidden triggers? Triggers so deep they fooled me into thinking I had any sort of will at all?

I didn't know. All I knew was that I was excited to have glimpsed something important—something that seemed to let me move through my fear—and when Dade jerked the rope three times to let me know he was starting to climb, I let out a big "Whoo-hoo," flicking the extra line behind me like a ranch hand, like a sailor, like anyone else in the world who is intimate with rope. It was ridiculous, I knew, that I had such a hard time getting started, and even more ridiculous that I was proud of myself that I *did* finally start. But there I was: stoked about the day and psyched to be climbing with Dade.

"Nice job," he said to me when he topped out, only ten minutes later, fighting the wind to take my hand with a deep grip. The climbing and the beautiful day had lifted him out of his funk too—or at least were helping him to ignore it.

I shrugged, as if it were nothing, and then gathered up the rope and walked over the other side of the cliff, over the humps and around a small pool of water to set up the rappel, which fell free off the overhung backside to a giant boulder. I rappelled first into deep shadow, finally sheltered from the wind, and spun very slowly downward for half a rope length, my feet never touching the wall. As I spun, my view shifted from the wall of rock to the upslope side of a hill that abutted it, and then to Sylvan Lake, lying cobalt blue in the sun. Harsh winds skated across the lake in fits and starts, sometimes coming from straight above in downbursts to create star-shaped patterns that feathered the water in all directions. When I looked up above me, I could see the rope vanishing to a point where the rock met the sky, the rope my true zenith above and also my nadir below, pinning me along a line of gravity.

By the time Dade had fired off an overhung clip-up and I had followed it, it was eleven thirty and the sky had clouded up. It was classic, capricious Needles weather, but we both thought that we could still maybe sneak a little more climbing in before the rain hit. There was a route on the other side of the Needle's Eye that Dade had long lusted after, the Melvillian Queequeg's Revenge, and right near that was a famous, though not very difficult route I'd always wanted: a free-standing spire called Monkey Rope. The name (the guidebook told us) also comes from *Moby-Dick*, and refers to a short rope that is tied to a man on-ship as incentive to better belay a mate who is butchering a whale at sea level. If the man below is lost to the ocean, so too will be the man on board.

We found chaos at the Needle's Eye area, where the asphalt road, right before the entrance of the one-lane tunnel, spreads wide like a gopher in a bull snake's belly. A climber was just threading the eye of the needle, and the parking lot was full of video camera–wielding tourists all focused on the sideshow before them, getting in the way of traffic, each other, and our quick exit out of the area. Too bad they didn't turn around to see the main attraction.

Queued up with a couple of other cars and a Bounder RV, waiting for traffic to come through the other side of the one-lane tunnel, we witnessed quite a sight: a Winnebago ridden through the tunnel by a pair of feral, Amazon commandos. They had crouched down to make it through the tunnel but then stood up, shirtless and braless and waving big sticks. They established clear control by whacking the 'bago on the head a couple times before leaping onto the slope alongside the tunnel opening and scrambling back over the top of the granite shoulder they'd just gone under, leaving the older man driving the RV to stop and get out, thinking he'd been rear-ended.

Dade yelled, "Winnebuckaroo! Whoo-hoo!" and honked the horn, cheering on the old tradition of tormenting RVs that we'd also participated in once years before, when I'd first started climbing.

I was about to yell "Whoo-hoo," too when I was struck dumb. One of the women, romping up into the rocks like a female satyr, had blonde, dreadlocked hair tied straight up like a shock of wheat. The other had oceans of wavy, black hair and sinewy legs that glistened in a column of sunlight. I almost saw her face, but then she turned and scrambled over the top of the rocks that rose over the tunnel, so that my last sight of her was her bare back, disappearing as if over the edge of the world.

"It's Fran and Ruby," I yelled more to myself than Dade. I jumped out of the Rig, intending to go surprise Ruby, when I realized that startling the two of them without their tops on would be a bad idea and climbed back in.

"Let's go catch them on the other side," I said.

Dade pounded the steering wheel with a "Yar!" and guided us through the long, narrow tunnel that had been dynamited out of the granite. As we came out the other side, back into the light of mixed sun and cloud, I recognized Clem's big, yellow International Harvester truck, complete with extended cab and double-high topper, parked next to a new vw bug.

"Definitely them," I said, nodding, directing Dade to the far side of their truck at a pull-out that looked out over trees and rocks and scrub that reached all the way to Wyoming. I popped open the side doors of *Makin' Bacon*, which faced the driver's side of the truck, and sat down just as I caught sight of them. Now wearing their tops, they made their way down between pine trees on a slope so steep they had to drop from tree to tree, finally jumping the last yard down onto the shoulder of the road as a load of needles and dirt cascaded down after them.

They hadn't noticed us yet and ran, laughing, across the road, bumping fists as they reached the truck, only realizing in that moment that the guy sitting in the doorway of the van was me.

The last time I had seen Ruby was when I'd moved out of the house, my heart a tiny bit broken, but I wasn't worrying about that. In this moment, grinning like an idiot, I felt my old excitement for her fully formed, ready to find that lost part of me in her eyes again. Ready to kiss and feels stars pop behind my eyes. Ready to make something happen with her. I was ready for all of this, even though, in the back of my mind, I knew Clem was still mixed up with her somehow. Just as Olive was mixed up with me.

"Well, speak of the devil," Ruby yelled, grinning and throwing her hot arms around me for a hug as I stood up, "Atlas Taugenichts."

Ruby's lips were dry and a little cracked, her face simple from sleeping in the back of a truck, her voice a little hoarse from hollering. All that and her goddam quirky tooth. She was so beautiful I felt out of breath.

"You saw us, huh?" Fran asked Dade.

"Yes—like *Lord of the Flies*. Well done," he said, trying to talk clearly over his still-swollen lip.

Ruby crossed her arms over her sports bra then: "We didn't know you were over there—I never would have . . . you know—"

"—used the sticks?" I joked, but she was serious now, embarrassed.

"No . . . bare-chested and all," she said, flashing a look at Dade.

"They didn't look like any bears I've ever seen," said Dade.

Ruby seemed displeased by this, but Fran barked out a laugh. Although she'd seemed enormous atop the Winnebago, standing before us Fran was back to her tiny, tattoo-flashing self. She had wrapped a narrow sarong over her climbing shorts, and was wearing a short, sleeveless T-shirt with the words "organic = orgasmic" printed above and below her breasts. The shirt showed off her muscles and a small silver ring in her navel, which was styled to look like a carabiner. Fran reached out a hand (looking, I swear, for a ring on Dade's finger) and stepped between me and Ruby to shake with him.

"Dave, right? I recognize you from the gym. I'm Francis—but you should call me Fran," she said to him, her hair jiggling as she pumped his hand once, smiling with her pixie face. Fran had always been such a nut I don't think I'd looked really hard at her, but right then she struck me as quite beautiful. She struck Dade too.

"It's Dade," he said, hanging onto her hand, and then, in an Elvis voice: "Rhymes with 'suede.'"

"And 'well-made,'" she said, making fun of him with her own bad Elvis voice—and not letting go of his hand right away, either.

"So where's Clem?" I asked, making a show of looking around the parking lot. "That's his truck, right?"

"*Old Yeller*, yeah. I kind of got custody of it for the summer," she said, waving at it. "We finally hit the skids this spring, right around when I found out I was accepted at USC medical school."

"I'm sorry, that must have been rough," I said.

"Yeah, being a doctor will really suck." She smiled for a long beat, then said, "He's an idiot. But then, you knew that."

"I never thought he was an idiot, just an—" I started to say, but before I could finish she was talking over me: "What about you? Still with . . . what's her name—Onion? Okra?"

"You mean Olive? Yeah, well . . . she moved out to New York," I said, looking away and making a complicated wave of my hand. It was too much to go into in that moment—especially with Dade standing there as my chaperone.

"That doesn't sound like much fun, either," she said, giving me a sympathetic look.

"It's not—it wasn't," I said, feeling guilty—both for dissembling about Olive and for sneaking looks at Ruby's waist and legs and breasts. "It's a long story."

"Maybe you'll get to tell it to me—which way are you guys heading now? We're heading to Colorado. I think."

"Dade's heading west too—to the Valley, eventually—but we're off to the Tower next. He's got his eyes on something."

"And you don't?" she said, her eyes laughing at me.

I turned to Dade, embarrassed for getting caught checking her out, only to find him leaning in close to Fran's hips. He was tracing, without touching, the long, thorny rose-stem tattoo that ran all the way up her spine into her hair and all the way down it into her shorts, which she had just pushed down a little more in order to show him the full artwork. At the base of her spine there was an oval scar, about two inches across, encircling the bottom of the rose stem.

"Go ahead, touch it—it's crazy," she said, craning her neck around as if she could see it too. "A friend did it for free. Hurt like hell."

I knew that it was a bad idea. I knew that Dade shouldn't get his hands on her, but he had already laid his right index and middle tips on either side of the circle, brushing them along the scar before taking them away. She had raised her eyebrows at him, as if to say, *Pretty good, huh?* but then they sank, startled, when he touched her. He had busted out his old charisma—his old flirt. His old goat.

Fran pulled up her waistband quickly, clearly shaken by his touch, but Dade acted like he wasn't tracking any of it.

"I've got one of those too," he said, lifting up the side of his baggy shorts to show off a long, jagged scar on the outside of his muscular leg, "I got this one for free too, or through insurance, anyway."

Fran, having found her composure again, didn't miss a beat and reached out to touch it, boldly running her thumb hard along its length, all the way to his hip joint.

"Wow. You get it falling?"

He nodded: "Caught an old bolt hanger in the Valley. Eighteen stitches."

I had a sudden vision of Dade and his fifty women all lined up, with Fran here butting to the front of the line, and decided to play a little chaperone myself.

"All right, enough war stories," I said, turning Dade around and pushing him back into the Rig as if putting him back in his cage. Then I pointed up at the fast-moving clouds and said, "Time to get climbing. We were heading to Monkey Rope before the weather hits. You probably saw it if you drove through the ten pins already—it's the one that looks like a big, flat shark fin."

"We haven't been able to find a single route here—or a camping spot at Sylvan, for that matter. The guidebooks for this place suck," said Fran.

"We'll take you to it—it's on our way," I said as I got into the passenger seat.

"Lead on," said Ruby, getting into the driver's seat of the truck and honking twice. She looked at me hard, fixing her eyes on mine until Dade backed up. I lost her eyes and then caught them again for a moment in the frame of her side-view mirror; then Dade pulled away.

"Too yummy! That woman is too much," I said, sticking my hand outside the window to curve and dip and ride the fast air like a wing.

"*Two* too yummy . . ." he said, looking a bit Neanderthal with his lip thick and pouched forward.

"What are you talking about? You got no right to lead Fran on. Plus she's a total kook."

He sent me a look of shocked delight, like a kid misbehaving who thought he was cute, then said with his Scottish accent, "My dear Uhtlas, what on earth are *you* talking about?"

I looked at his hands on the steering wheel, the ones he'd touched Fran with, then back at his face: "You have a pregnant wife named Bev."

The smile on his face vanished.

"Hey, I'm just counting coup—you're the one about to draw blood," he snapped, suddenly sober.

"I'm doing it tonight," I said about my call to Olive, "even if I have to leave a message."

Dade shook his head in disbelief, but I really meant it. The decision had finally hardened in me, and running into Ruby had been the catalyst. If I could have gotten cell coverage I would have called Olive right then, my fingers itching to pop out the numbers, my mouth and throat ready to bring it all out. I felt no nervousness, no dizziness, at the thought of it.

We drove the few minutes to the trailhead for Pitchpole and parked across the road from it. Doors opened and doors slammed. I heard Fran hassling Ruby about something on the other side of their truck, then heard both of them cackle, though they shut up when Ruby spied me through the side windows of the topper. Above them, to the west, the sky was darkening, with thicker masses not so far away. It wasn't enough to stop me, though; I wanted another shot at forcing myself to focus—at "dropping ballast" like I had on Mudskipper—even if it meant separating from Ruby right then. Dade and I led them down the faint trail about a hundred and fifty yards into the forest to the foot of the climb. It was a free-standing pole of rock about fifty feet high, which loomed weirdly off-kilter.

"Looks like a zig that should have zagged," said Fran, dropping her pack behind us.

"Looks ready to fall down," said Ruby, clearly nervous. It was going to be her lead. Dade gave Ruby details about the route as she put on her shoes, then warned her not to spend too much time placing gear after the crux, since she could blast to the top at that point. Then he started clucking his tongue about the weather.

"We're gonna get hit . . ." he said quietly to me, staring off to the west.

"We'll be all right," I said with more confidence than I felt.

"What's going to hit? Is it going to storm?" Ruby asked. As if to scare her more, a cool wind picked up and blew over us.

"Not if you hurry," said Dade, starting back toward the Rig.

"Don't listen to Chicken Little," I said, trying to un-spook her. "It still might blow over."

Ruby looked nervous, all racked up and ready to go, and I knew that, unless she was climbing a lot better than she used to, this would be hard for her—and hard with trad gear usually means scary. I wanted to hug her or kiss her or somehow touch her, but I didn't want to throw her off, either, and so I held out my thumb and index finger in a ring. I pincered them together a couple times, indicating that she should make the *Okay* sign too, then "clipped" mine into hers and pulled away with a snap. She smiled briefly, but then the smile was overtaken by a small and serious frown.

"We're off to Monkey Rope," I said, "You can see it from the road a half-mile down. Come meet us when you're done here, and we'll show you where the free camping is. And don't worry— you'll cruise it."

She nodded, flashing me a quick look before turning back to the rock.

"You're on belay," I heard Fran say, and as I rounded the corner of the path I caught a last glimpse of Ruby with her hands on the climb, her right foot just leaving the ground.

CHAPTER SEVEN

By the time we reached the parking spot for Monkey Rope, only minutes later, the wind was coming in hard bursts, and behind the bursts there was a constant blow, sharp and menacing. It made the Monkey Rope spire, which we could see poking out of the trees, seem scary, the triple horns on its top more like the encrusted tines of a great frog gig.

"What do we need on this thing?" Dade asked from the back of the van, rifling through the gear sling.

"Small cams and nuts, extra slings—and I've heard small tricams for the crux."

He grimaced. He'd always hated tricams because he had one rip out on him in a fall once, plus they can be a bitch to pull.

"I hate tricams," he said, clipping two of the smaller sizes onto the lead sling. We had tried to do this famous route years before, but there were climbers lined up to do it then, and Dade isn't too good at waiting when there are dozens of other routes around and he's got climbing on the brain.

I ran ahead of Dade to get to the base. Monkey Rope was only forty feet high, like many of the spires in the Needles, but set against the darkening sky it seemed larger, its holds smaller and sharper. And its color, without the sun to lighten its mood, seemed to be just a darker version of one of the clouds above. I scrambled the rope quickly, then tied in. I waited a minute like that, then another, and still no Dade.

"Let's GO!" I yelled toward the Rig, only to have Dade emerge from the trees right then.

"What took you so long?" I was about to ask, but before I could get the sentence out I saw that he'd brought my windbreaker for me. I could only thank him and pull it on, the hood catching gusts like a little sail.

"I don't know if you're even going to have time," he said, curving his arm as if to point behind Monkey Rope. "I could see a really big thunderhead coming this way."

"Who knows when we'll get to climb again, at this rate," I said, trying to push his buttons.

He shrugged, putting me on belay. "Your call."

Suddenly I wanted it badly. "Climbing," I said, pulling into the first move. The rock surprised me, radiating its summer warmth to my hands even though it looked like it should have been cold.

I worked my way up the first ten feet, not even hesitating at the start, and placed a small nut. Then I climbed another five and futzed around for a while, trying to get something into a pinky-sized cavity behind a flake. The slot was too narrow for a TCU, and I finally pulled the smallest tricam I had off my rack.

I heard Dade groan from below, but he was in luck—this didn't fit, either. I looked up at the crux just above me—and the gray sky roiling beyond that—then back down at Dade, who was shaking his head with some urgency.

I needed something to protect the crux there and realized that the tricam "hole" was really a slot that I could probably sling with something skinny—like the six-millimeter prusik cord that always hung on the back of my harness. I managed to thread the cord through the hourglass-shaped slot with one hand, then back-looped and clipped it. It seemed to work, though when I smiled down at Dade he only made an impatient motion with his free hand.

I knew the crux was easy enough that I could do it without being anywhere near my rockhead, but I wanted each move to feel perfect and important again, like they'd been on the start of Mudskipper that morning. I wanted to feel different from five minutes before when I rushed, hectic, up to the route; different from how I had been when I talked with Ruby. But standing on a knob, my other toe hooked beneath a flake edge, the incoming weather made everything feel desperate, as if it were a layer between me and the climbing I wanted to do. And Olive was another layer, and the worry about the gear another layer, and even an old classic rock song, which had been cycling around my head for days, created yet another layer between us.

I tried hard to focus on the trees dropping ballast, to let myself drop ballast too, but nothing happened.

"Go," I whispered to myself, "go, go, GO. Float." But it didn't come. What came was the sick, dreary sound of wind ripping through the rappel slings up above, and then a shock of adrenaline deep in my stomach as the wind caught me and tried to twist me from the rock.

"Uhtlas, get moving! What are you waiting for?" Dade hollered.

"Figuring out a move," I lied, my voice sucked away by the wind. I waited one more moment, hoping for that feeling that had come at Sylvan Lake, and then finally pulled impatiently at the rock, hard and with no finesse. I was fighting the wind as much as gravity and making decisions about climbing purely from my adrenal glands.

I stepped, pulled high, and got through the crux, and then placed a last stopper before clipping it. I would have been pretty safe if I'd fallen at that point, far enough off the ground that I wouldn't hit it, but my adrenaline didn't believe that and raced me up the last ten feet to the knuckled top. I wound one hand into the slings and flung my torso between two of the three rumps, then tossed a leg over for good measure so that I finally straddled the top, hanging on like a bronc buster about to rip out of the chute.

Up there, I could finally see what the outcrop had been hiding and was startled by a beast of a thunderhead dumping rain into the valley. As if to let me know who was boss, I got hit right then with such a fierce gust of wind it that actually lifted my body a bit. *Jesus.* My stomach flipped inside out, shaking out the old adrenaline to make room for some new, as I clung to crystals to keep me from falling *up* into the sky. After ten seconds, the gust died down and I pawed through the mass of old colored slings up there, unable to find a rappel ring and finally clipping a single carabiner into a few of the healthier-looking slings.

"Okay, now. Lower me. Now!"

On the way down, Dade stopped me at my top two pieces so I could retrieve them. But then I wasn't able to pull that prussic sling, which was woefully stuck in the hourglass slot.

"Forget it!" Dade yelled. As he said this came a flash of lightning and, maybe three seconds later, its boiling thunder; the strike was less than a mile away. I should have just bailed off the route right then, but I didn't want to leave the sling I'd placed—I'd had that prussic for years. Plus, maybe I wanted to punish myself just a little for not being able to focus and climb right.

"Just leave it!" Dade yelled, but I couldn't, not yet. I worked at it with my nut tool, twisting it, tickling it, and finally got it unstuck so I could unthread it from its lair.

"Down!" I yelled, holding the prussic up like a trophy, but Dade was already lowering me—just as an enormous, black cloud to my left threw down a big, bad bolt of lightning.

"One"—BOOM!

"Two"—BOOM!

"Three, fuck me," I said bitterly, my voice cracking with the beginnings of panic.

Ba-BOOOOOOM!! BOOM! KRR-Krrssshh! came more thunder, simultaneous with its strike, the sound bashing its way up and down the valley—all the way to Ruby, I thought. *Why did I talk her into doing Pitchpole?* I wondered, and then I didn't have time to think of anything else as Dade dropped me to the earth, the descent so fast that I landed in a squat, my butt only inches off the ground.

He had a freaky giggle going, and I started to giggle too as I untied from the rope, both of us shaken by the danger of the storm and the stupidity of trying to beat it. I pulled the rope as fast as I could—afraid that lightning would chase it like a harpoon line to hunt me down—and watched its white tip race up the rock and finally pop through the lower-out biner to fall on top of the pile at my feet. I felt safer for a brief moment, but as I started to unbuckle my harness, I realized that all the hairs on my body had pricked up. When I looked over at Dade, he was holding his arms out stiffly at his sides, trying not to touch the metal gear hanging off his harness. He was staring at the gear rack I'd just taken off, which was glowing with the luminescent green of a firefly, and in our total silence the air started to buzz like a swarm of mosquitoes.

We both stood frozen, our combined and magnified vision of the St. Elmo's fire dividing us from the rest of the world in that moment. There was a growing tension in the space around us, the earth a massive clock-spring about to move its spire-sized second hand, drawing out time and space until a great blitz of lightning finally struck simultaneously with its thunder one spire over. Eyes full of afterimage, ears still ringing from the booming thunder, we ran, hobbled by our harnesses as we tore them off, sprinting the last hundred yards to the van and its insulated chassis, me fumbling with my key until both of us piled in on top of each other through the passenger door.

"Jingus, Murder, and Jehosephat!" yelled Dade, slamming the door behind us.

Lightning struck several times nearby—the concussions rocking the van like someone bouncing up and down on the bumper—and then it finally hit Monkey Rope too. There was an explosion of water on the roof and windshield, as if the lightning had somehow primed a pump in the sky, and the rain came down so heavy that within seconds the air seemed as dense with water as Sylvan Lake.

"Amazing," I hollered, pressing my hands flat to the windshield to feel the ball-peen hammering of hail.

"Yeah, so amazing that I give up," Dade yelled over the noise, ripping off his raincoat in the cramped space of the driver's seat, "This weather . . . I think the climbing gods are angry or something. We either have to sacrifice a virgin or just leave for the Tower."

"The Tower has the same weather as here, though, it just gets it earlier," I lied, thinking of Ruby.

"That's not true—it's lower altitude. And anyway, it doesn't matter because this place has worn me out."

He was serious, and I wasn't sure how to argue with him, finally settling on—and yelling out—the truth: "Okay, I'm cracking too, my man, but Ruby is here and I want to see her some. At least, I hope she's still here," I said, pointing to the storm as if it might have swallowed her up.

"Well, I'm CRACKED on this place—past tense—and I'd rather hang at the Tower in bad weather than here. Or better yet, just get to Yosemite."

I pulled my wet windbreaker over my head, struggling as the van rocked in the wind, my hands trapped in the elastic wristlets, and when I finally got it off I was frustrated enough to ball it up and throw it on the floor. Neither of us said anything for a minute, but I could tell that Dade was struggling with something else. And then I knew what it was: back home was his pregnant wife—and the *Geisterfahrer*—and right here was Fran, a person who could distract him, if just for a moment, and who also couldn't really endanger his marriage. Still, he could get himself into a bit of trouble with her, and he needed to escape her to save him from himself, while I wanted to stay there with Ruby.

As I tried to come up with something that would save me, I looked out at the road, which had turned into a river, and with huge relief saw *Old Yeller* appear all at once before us, the visibility so bad that I didn't see its lights until I saw the truck itself. Ruby pulled up facing us, parking about a car length from our nose.

Through the two windshields and the rain and hail I could barely see them, but I could tell that they were laughing and singing something together. And I could see that whatever had just happened made both of them stronger and more vital. And beautiful.

Dade must have thought so too, because, instead of driving us away, west to Devil's Tower, away from this trouble, he said, "I guess for your sake we can hang out a little longer—but you'll owe me one: I get first try on the Gibraltar pitch on Seven Seas."

There was no joke in his voice this time, and I knew I had to give him something—at the very least admit that I was going to Yosemite with him—and so I sat with that idea for a long moment as the rain slowed, then turned to him and nodded. Yes to Yosemite. Yes to Seven Seas. Yes to Gibraltar.

He didn't say anything more but grinned and backhanded me on the chest, then signed to Ruby and Fran with his big, scabby hands, indicating that they should come over to the roomier comfort of *Makin' Bacon*. It was still raining pretty hard, though the hail had stopped, and somehow, before I could even say that it was a bad idea for him and Fran to hang out together, in the frenzy of boys and girls and post–lightning strike adrenaline, I ended up running to *Old Yeller* in the downpour, just as Fran and Ruby got out to join us in the Rig. As if it had been choreographed by the Keystone Cops, Ruby and I dove back into the truck, and Fran jumped into *Makin' Bacon* with Dade.

"Augh, I'm soaked!" Ruby laughed, shaking water out of her hair, filling the truck cab with the scent of licorice and rain and her fear-laced sweat from leading Pitchpole.

From the driver's side, she turned and leaned through the rear window, which opened into the covered truck bed, to grab a towel.

"How was Pitchpole?" I asked, leaning back against the passenger door, making as much room for her as I could. I was ready to tell her about where I was at with Olive, but was still looking for a way into it.

"Fired it off," she said as she worked the towel through her thick, black hair, her voice full of fake bravado, "All you hardmen better watch out."

Then she frowned and said, "Except for the part where I was stuck at the crux for maybe ten minutes, crying for Mommy, downclimbing to my highest piece, then going back up three times. Fran finally started yelling at me to go, to tear it up, and somehow her badgering worked." She was beaming, but also shaking her head. "That climb isn't even a warm-up for Fran— she's mutant strong. Just like when we were kids in gymnastics. She's only climbing with me now because she's injured . . . resting up her middle finger."

"So that's how you two know each other."

"Yeah. And then when she started climbing, she got me into it."

"How's her list going?" I asked. I knew she had a hit list of all the hardest routes in the US and was slowly ticking them off.

"Not much climbing this year. She was getting certified as an EMT, plus she just got through an icky breakup with her boyfriend. I got to hear about it *ad nauseam* on the way out here. But she's got a new list going: 'The Errors of Man.'"

I raised my eyebrows.

"I've got a little list of my own going now, after Clem. And Aaron."

I shrugged, not knowing who that was.

"Aaron was my boyfriend before Clem. The one who broke up with me?"

"The law student."

"No, before him, though he broke up with me too. I'm talking about the nut job—the guy who had kids? I never told you about that? Whole nutha' story . . . but, Clem, he's my main man on the List. I can't believe we were about to get married—or that I was going to get my tooth 'fixed' for him. God, I'm such an idiot. You used to live with him too—why can't he just say what he wants? Why can't he tell me what he's thinking in that uptight head of his?"

I didn't know. My brain was still trying to process that part about almost getting married—and ruining her tooth—but before I could say that she was poking me in the ribs with her towel: "Not that you're any better! I thought you were just dense—until I realized you just weren't into me."

"Not what? What do you mean, 'dense'?"

"My god, Atlas . . . there were so many moments. My phone number—do you remember that? I wrote it as large as I could on a piece of paper?"

"Yeah, but you could have handed that to any of us! I thought—"

"But I handed it to you!" she said, exasperated, "And then at the party, I tried to get you dancing, but you wouldn't come out. I had to come upstairs after you. We even kissed! I mean, we *really* kissed. And the next morning you just ignored me, got in a van, and drove away. Wham, bam, thank you ma'am."

I was in shock—joyous shock. Or maybe a mild paralysis, since I couldn't seem to work my jaw. But it was true: she'd seen some part of herself in me too.

"You . . . you never said anything," I stammered.

"I 'said' it all by coming up and kissing you." Her voice was contained, and I realized she was actually mad and also embarrassed. She'd been holding this in for a while. More than two years.

"Then I guess I am dense, but it sure wasn't because I didn't want you—I mean, like you," I said. I wanted to say more, like how she was the one for me and how I'd screwed up and how I knew that partially because I knew Olive wasn't the one for me— plus, by the way, I was breaking up with Olive. But I didn't know how to fit that all into a sentence.

"Whatever—I'm not fishing for compliments. I shouldn't have said anything," she sighed.

"No, you're right to say something. We could have been . . ." I paused, not sure what the word was. It was all happening so fast. I was the anti-flirt. The anti-Dade. I was the idiot.

"Soaking wet?" she finally asked, snapping her wet jog bra.

"Something like that—for sure," I said, shrugging. My words were bad, but I caught her eye for a moment and I know she saw it—saw the intensity of my feelings for her. Then she smiled and looked away, and I had the vague sensation that she'd prevented herself from winking. Suddenly I wondered if I'd just been played somehow: set up and knocked down.

"Hang on a sec, I need to get out of these clothes—don't peek," she said. She turned and slipped her arms through the rear window, getting ready to climb over the bench seat and into the back of the truck, and I couldn't help but see a tattoo (inches from my face) on her lower back. Peeking out from the top of her shorts were the thick black lines of a Chinese character.

"What's the tattoo of?" I blurted out.

For some reason, this startled her. She jerked back into the cab, looking at her stomach, it seemed, and then, relieved, pushed the top of her shorts down an inch: "These are the characters for gecko, which literally means 'wall tiger' in Chinese."

The calligraphy was especially bold, the lines powerful and thick and masculine, as if they belonged on the chest of some Japanese yakuza.

"You know that saying? 'Each thing in its right place and for every thing the right word'?" she asked. "I figure this is the right word."

"Um, no, but the tattoo looks great," I said. The intimacy in the cab was too much, her body too much, and I practically flattened myself to the door as I spoke.

She let her shorts back up and then clambered through the window into the truck bed, telling me again not to peek. I stared at the floor and thought about how Olive had always wanted a tattoo and how I'd always talked her out of it. For straight acting, egghead Olive, a tattoo seemed too put-on, too wannabe. But on Ruby, seeing the way each character possessed its territory, how they owned the skin stretched tight across her sacrum, all I could think of was that I wanted to touch them with my fingers, to feel the border of the black lines on her taut, smooth skin. To pull her to me and cup the words with my belly.

Ruby changed into loose jeans and a T-shirt and started speaking as she shimmied, feet first, back into the cab: "I got the tattoo just before the trip. I wanted to try to make myself lead harder stuff."

I was about to open my big mouth and ask how that could help, but as she turned and dropped onto the seat she cut me off: "It's stupid, I know, but I need a reminder to help keep me focused."

But then it didn't sound stupid at all.

"My mother hates it, so I guess it's a good thing she doesn't know about the one on the other side," she said, tapping the button of her jeans. "Below the belt."

I'm pretty sure I blushed right then, because Ruby lit up with another enormous smile and said, "I'd show you that one, but then I'd have to kill you."

"That's all right, I'm not ready to die yet," I mumbled, my hands held out before me as if to stop her from disrobing—and from wrapping me any tighter around her little finger.

We had been in the truck long enough that the windows had completely fogged up, and in the humid lull between us, I realized that it had stopped raining. I wiped the windshield in front of me to get a look at the Rig, and could see Dade sitting in the driver's seat, one arm over his head and the other stuck out his open window, describing a climbing move to Fran. Probably his conquest of Son of Sam. I opened my window to a blast of fresh, cool air and saw that the sky was clearing.

"We should probably find out what they want to do," I said.

"Brrr," Ruby said, as the cool, post-storm air rushed in. She reached down for her shoulder bag, which was sitting on the floor of the cab between us, and took out a long-sleeved shirt, flipping it over her head, then arching her back as she pulled it on. The fabric strained against her rib cage and her perfect breasts, and then I couldn't stand it anymore.

"You are something else," I said, surprising myself—though I think it wasn't a surprise to her.

"What?" she said, laughing as she zipped her bag back up.

"Nothing, I mean . . . Clem is a fool."

"Yeah, he is. For lots of reasons."

"I mean for not staying with you."

"Well, you didn't stay, either!" Ruby shot back. She tried to make it a joke, but there was something sharp about it too. Before I could counter, she continued, "And what makes you think he had a choice, anyway?"

"I mean, for not . . . for not trying to . . . never mind. I can't say it right."

"I broke up with Clem—if that's what you're wondering," she said, all joking gone from her voice.

"But you lasted a long time with him. Two years is a long time," I said.

"Yeah. Especially since two years with Clem-the-dog would be like fourteen with anyone else," she said, stepping down from the truck, "But, whatever. I figure everything happens for a reason."

Olive hated that default phrase, and even went so far as to say that the world could be broken down into those who think everything happens for a reason and those who don't. I guess I was one of those who don't, but I was curious about what Ruby thought.

"Or things happen and we learn from them," I said gently.

Ruby narrowed her eyes with a flash—not far from Dade's boxing look, as if ready to argue—then just as quickly softened them and fluttered her eyelashes at me in a faux-coy way, flirting by making fun of flirting. "Well, then I guess what happened was that I learned who was wrong for me . . . so I'd know it when I found the one who was right."

Twang. Arrow to the heart. I think I blushed again and Ruby covered for me by asking, "Was Okra wrong for you? I know Clem will be wrong for me for the rest of my days."

"Her name's Olive," I corrected again, finally realizing that Ruby was getting Olive's name wrong on purpose for some reason. Just as I was about to say, "And speaking of her," in order to finally explain my soon-to-be free-and-clear dating status, Dade honked long and soulfully on the Rig's horn, then stuck his head out the window and yelled, "The rock's all wet, and it's got to be five o'clock somewhere in the world."

Ruby looked at her watch, confused, and said, "It's five o'clock here."

"See!" he yelled before tooting his horn again.

I got out of Ruby's truck and ran down the path to Monkey Rope to retrieve all our soggy gear, surprised to find the ground still covered with pea-sized hailstones, which were so hard they didn't break apart when I stepped on them but instead shot out of the way or dug into the wet earth. When I got back to the Rig, Ruby was standing at the open side doors.

"So what should we do?" I asked.

"Make supper. Drink a beer," said Dade after looking at Fran and Ruby. Then, really fast, he said, "Atthesupersecretbivy."

"The supersuperbivy?" said Fran, trying to say it just as fast. "The one you were at last night?"

"Nooo, that was the steaalllth bivy," Dade whispered slowly, smoothing the air out with his hands. "Thisisthesupersecretone, on the way out of the park. It's also free . . . if we don't get caught."

"Not like we got a lot of options," said Ruby, getting out of my way so I could dump the wet gear on the Rig floor.

"Right. Let's check it out. This . . . supersecretbivy," said Fran.

"Guess it was meant to be," said Ruby pointedly.

I held my hands up in surrender and said, "Okay, okay, maybe some things are. You can follow us."

Then I hopped into the Rig and they got into their truck, and Dade turned us around and headed in a direction opposite from Sylvan Lake and the ten pins—and away from better cell phone coverage and my call to Olive. That was my chance, I'd realize later. The chance when I could have ridden the dominos down another path. But I couldn't see it right then. All I could see was *Old Yeller* right behind us in the rearview mirror, with Ruby and Fran singing and laughing along with the car stereo again, each of them with a hand outside the window, catching wind.

CHAPTER EIGHT

Warning. Bison are wild animals. Do not enter enclosure. No trespassing," said the sign, complete with a silhouette of a buffalo knocking a child into the air.

That's where we turned in on the faintest of dirt tracks, which cut up a hillside between a few large boulders and then disappeared over a little rise. In the hectic bump and grind of the side mirror, I saw *Old Yeller* turn in behind us and follow us for a tenth of a mile to a rugged, steel gate.

I hopped out and opened the gate with a high-pitched, rusty screech, only then thinking to look around to make sure there weren't any of the wooly ones nearby. Dade drove in and waited, and Ruby pulled through and idled her truck alongside him.

"Uh…isn't this kind of dangerous?" she asked while I shut the gate. It screeched again but at a lower pitch.

"Nah," Dade said, keeping a straight face, "I've never seen rangers back here."

"I mean because of the buffalos."

"Oh, right . . ." he said, winking at Fran, "I think they hang out at the other end of the field."

Fran grinned, then pounded the dash two times before pointing her index fingers straight ahead like six-shooters. Dade pressed forward, *Makin' Bacon* jerking and rocking like a prairie schooner, and I stepped onto *Old Yeller*'s sideboard and hung on as Ruby followed him. He only went another hundred yards or so, so that he was hidden behind a stand of pine trees. I hopped off and scouted the ground until I found a flattish spot so he could park while Ruby and Fran did the same, dropping anchor about forty feet away.

I helped Dade pop open the top, as we always do when we've parked for the night, only to discover that almost everything up above—the canvas siding, my bedding, even the thin foam mattress—had been thoroughly soaked by the storm. I'd completely forgotten about the repair job I'd needed to do, and now I would pay for it.

"Man, this is going to take forever to dry out," I said, dropping down to the first floor.

"You might want to put up a tent for tonight," said Dade.

He started heating water for spaghetti, and I hung up all the wet climbing gear—including Ruby's and Fran's—between two trees, then went around to the backside of the Rig to dig out my old, freestanding tent. It was wedged against the haul bag, and when I popped it out, I discovered it had been hiding the end of my own portaledge, which I'd need to sleep on if I did Seven Seas with Dade. He had never doubted for a minute that I was going with him and had stowed it secretly. I tugged hard on the portaledge a few times to pop it loose and placed it on top of the Rig to get it out of the way. Then I freed the tent and a couple pads and walked about a hundred feet from the Rig to set things up.

I'd had this tent since I was sixteen, and even though I hadn't used it in a while, I knew it well enough to set it up blind. What I'd forgotten, though, was the dry, musty smell trapped in its nylon walls, and that the last time I'd used it I had been with Olive— the only time we'd camped. She had been difficult to camp with, her need for cleanliness a little too intense, but she was excited about the trees and the little brown bats that jetted between them.

She was excited to make love in this tent in the outdoors too. That was the trip when I really started to fall for her.

Once I had the tent set up, I lay down on the floor, my wet feet sticking out the door but the rest of me encased in its scent, and felt myself transposed for a moment. My heart was beating with its old love for Olive, and my head was full of indecision—and the fear that by leaving her I'd be making a mistake. But as I lay there, I began to lose the musty scent to the smells of the pines and Dade's spaghetti and could hear parts of sentences between Ruby and Fran and Dade—all of them somehow combining to pull me into the present. I felt myself slowly ebb away from Olive and flow toward Ruby.

Dade finally called me to dinner. When I got up to walk to the Rig, I found the sun clearly in view, though low in the sky, and the angled summer light added a soft glow to everything— even the shadow from the portaledge I'd placed on the roof of *Makin' Bacon*, which stretched across the open doors of the van and then bent onto the earth like a stick refracted by water. Ruby, approaching from her truck and looking at me, was caught in this gentle light too, her brook-water skin sunset-struck and blending into orange and rose.

This vision froze me in place, and I saw myself as if from thirty feet above. Ruby's face and my face were luminous, our bodies cast long shadows, and I felt so dizzy I began to swoon. Ruby continued to walk toward the Rig, though she was watching me with a funny look on her face; then I was back on the ground and walking up to her as if nothing had happened, ready again to fall into her eyes like I had that night at the party, over two years ago.

We ate upon a variety of seats, Ruby and Fran in their lawn chairs, Dade on a little camp stool, and I in the doorway of the Rig with my plate perched on my knees. We even made it through dinner, some chocolate, and a couple of bottles of wine that Fran brought out (Dade and Fran flirting mildly through it all) before Dade had to go and ruin everything.

Fran's sarong had slipped down a little, and as she stood up to pour herself some more wine a tattoo could clearly be seen rising out of the fabric. I couldn't make it out but made a mental note to ask Ruby about it—maybe as a way to get to see Ruby's own below-the-belt tattoo.

But Dade dove right in.

"You have another tattoo," he declared, pointing at the spot just next to her hip crest with his mug of wine.

Fran was genuinely surprised to find the tattoo visible and hiked her sarong up a bit. I think she was embarrassed but was so used to acting like a tough guy all the time that she couldn't just blow off his question, so she took a sip of wine and patted the side of her belly, saying "Roy. My ex."

"Do you regret getting that, now that you two have split?" asked Dade, simply trying to make idle conversation, it seemed.

She let out a short, bitter laugh. "I'd like to cover it up if I could find a good design — or a guy named 'Royal.' But no . . . I mean, I think I was meant to get it. So it can be a reminder for me."

"For what?"

"*Not* to fall in love with the wrong guys. And that I should stop being in love with them." As she said this last bit, she looked pointedly at Ruby.

Dade laughed out loud at this: "As if we have any control over that."

"I do," Fran said, not laughing at all. "I decide who I fall in love with now, and when I fall in love."

Dade was shaking his head. "I don't believe you can control that."

"That just means it's not in your experience."

"Dying's not in my experience, but I'm pretty sure I can't control that, either."

Fran looked confused. "I don't know what that means," she said.

"It just means it's a given that you can assume some things without going through them," said Dade with his slightly pedantic, dade-uctive tone. "Just like it's known *a priori* that people in love can't help how they act. They can't control how they feel."

"Well, I can," said Fran, throwing one hand in the air, easy as pie.

"So when El Roy the King decided he wasn't in love anymore, you just turned it off?"

"I think I was meant to be with him precisely so I could learn that lesson. It's part of my path," Fran said, taking another sip of her wine. In the twilight, her pixie face seemed to be hardening.

"I don't buy it," said Dade. "I mean, things hurt in a breakup precisely because we can't just turn things off."

Fran stood up: "Things hurt because most people aren't strong enough to stop old habits of being with that person—obviously where you're still stuck."

"Oh, come on. Part of being in love is that we *don't* have a choice about it—"

"Because that's how you define love. I define love as where there's a choice about things. That's what I know *a posteriori*," she said, sticking our her sarong-clad ass and smacking it.

Then she turned to Ruby, "What about you? Don't you think you have a choice about Clem?"

Before Ruby could answer, though, Dade was talking: "Wait—why did you get a tattoo of Roy's name? You loved him so much that you wanted him as a part of you and then you found out that he was wrong and now you're—"

"Who the fuck is this guy?" Fran said, jerking her thumb at him while looking at me and Ruby. I realized when she said this that she was more than a little drunk—and that Dade was too.

"Maybe love comes in different forms . . . maybe you've only had weaker forms of it. Forms less evolved," she said to Dade.

"Dade," I said as he got up off his stool, "ix-nay on the dade-uc-ion-shay." I wanted to stop this, but then I also wanted to know what Fran was saying about Clem. And why she used the present tense.

"I'm just saying . . . I've been thinking about getting a tattoo of Bev and the baby, and I'll stay committed to them and admit that I loved Bev so much that I didn't have a choice. And if she leaves me then I'll be out of my fucking mind."

By this point Fran stood up too and said: "If you think you can't make choices about love, and you'd be out of your mind without your wife, then how come you're not with her right now? And what were you doing flirting with me earlier?"

Dade froze when she said this, as if he'd been slapped. Fran froze too, so surprised by the effectiveness of her barb that she seemed to need all her energy just to frown her eyebrows.

"He's even more messed up than I am," she said. Then she turned around and walked quickly to *Old Yeller*.

All that was left, with the sun well set but still casting twilight, was Dade standing next to the Rig, shrugging his shoulders.

"I didn't mean to push it that hard," he said quietly to Ruby and me.

Ruby just raised her eyebrows and looked into her cup, and I shook my head at Dade, stunned from what, in terms of the energy expended and what little time had elapsed, was the social equivalent of a volcanic eruption.

"I think I'll just go to bed," he said, stepping up into the Rig so that I couldn't really see him anymore.

"Hookaay," said Ruby, slapping her thighs once before standing up, "I'd better go see how Fran is doing—that was enough to make her start smoking again. Hell, it's enough to make *me* start smoking."

She started to walk away, but then she stopped and turned to me. "But we should probably take down the gear you hung up, in case the rangers come and we have to bail, huh?"

I nodded.

"I'll be back in a few minutes."

I waited a second for her to be out of earshot and then went to *Makin' Bacon.*

"What the fuck?!" I whispered to Dade, who was sitting on the small bench seat.

He shrugged. "She was pissing me off, denying love like that."

"She's fresh off a divorce! Her heart's busted up. If you really believe we don't have a choice, then you should have known she didn't either and let it go."

"Okay, I know. I pushed too hard. I should go apologize," he said, though he made no move to get up.

"And what's this about a tattoo? I thought you hated tattoos."

"I've never hated them, I just never saw the reason for them. But I'm in a new stage in my life and I kind of get it now. It'll just be Bev's name," he said, pointing at his left pectoral. "Or maybe something more meaningful about her. A beaver."

"A beaver?! With Bev's name on it? My god." I wasn't whispering anymore.

"That's what Beverly means: 'beaver meadow.'"

"Yeah, your students are going to love that. Plus it'll keep stray women away from you—oh, I forgot, your charming personality will do that."

"Actually, I have a wedding ring to do that, thank you. But I guess it wouldn't hurt. Fran probably got her tattoo to scare men away, right? A kind of chastity belt? It seemed to work pretty well for that tonight, it's just that maybe she doesn't want it working anymore."

I didn't know what to say to that, so I just reached in and grabbed my headlamp and day bag, saying "Sweet dreams," as I jumped out of the van.

I put on my sweatshirt, sat back down in a lawn chair to wait for Ruby, and watched the night sky open up. Except for the telltale twinkling of the stars that signaled moisture in the sky, I would have sworn there was a vacuum between my eyes and their light. While I stared at them, I ran through the dialogue I was going to have with Olive the next day. I wouldn't have to tell her about Ruby, I reasoned, since it wasn't about her (and nothing had happened yet), but about me and Olive—that we were wrong for each other. She'd be mad and try to reason things out, but I had the upper hand since it had all crystallized in me. In my mind, after playing through a few different scenarios for the breakup, I'd made myself out to be a kind of good guy for saving Olive from any more wasted time. We would each hang up our phones saying we were sad that it had gone that way, but that it was all for the best.

I'd wrapped this all up so nicely in my head that by the time Ruby had returned, slipping into the lawn chair with a sigh, I sort of felt like I'd already cleaned the slate for her.

"How's Fran?" I asked.

"Whew, pretty hot. Dade has definitely added a few more bullet points to 'The errors of man.'"

"He was out of line."

She shrugged. "Yeah, well, she's always talking her crap and touching her chakra. Maybe Dade *was meant* to rub her chakra in it. I mean, if she had a choice and could simply stop her habits, then she wouldn't be so worked up about it now, would she?"

"I know—which is why he should've laid off."

I could see Ruby's outline with my eyes adjusted to the dark, and watched her slump into the chair, blowing a flat raspberry as if trying to get rid of some bad juju. She sat there looking up at the sky, and after a minute she seemed to lighten a bit and turned to stare at me—or rather, my silhouette.

"We should take down the gear, huh?" she asked, standing up.

"I'll do it," I said, getting out of my chair. I started walking toward the tree we'd hung the rope on, and then found Ruby right alongside me, taking my hand to stop me. I couldn't make out her face in the darker shadows of the trees, but I could smell her chalk and sweat from climbing, and on her lips was the taste of wine and chocolate and all that lovely licorice.

I tossed Olive high like a jacks ball then to snatch up this sweet prize, overwhelmed by Ruby's touch, by the pressure of her body against mine in that humid air, and by an overwhelming sense of rightness—of belonging.

Pulled off balance with my eyes closed, I slipped and almost fell to the damp ground, but Ruby caught me, her hands rough on my arms as she pulled me up, then gentle on my back as we slid back into a kiss. As I gave in to that softness for a second time, I was sure that I knew absolutely nothing about anything anymore, least of all Olive. I knew nothing except for the kiss and Ruby's scent and her body pressing up against mine.

In the tent we lay down on my pads, and even though I knew that nothing could happen yet, my body kept saying "yes" and "yes" again as we struggled out of our clothes. But then I froze. I'm not sure if it was the scent of mold that reminded me of Olive—or if I was worrying about Fran's cryptic comment about Clem—but suddenly I couldn't breathe and had to sit up. Before I knew what I was doing, I said, "We should talk about some stuff."

Ruby nodded vigorously, pulling my sleeping bag half around her, so that we both sat cross-legged in front of each other in the darkness. I didn't know what to say, though, and after a weird pause Ruby finally said, "You mean we should talk about the things we might have."

Now I was really surprised. "Um, yeah . . . I think I might have one in my bag, but—"

"No, I mean . . . what about things we can give each other?" she asked nervously. "STDs?"

For a second I could only think of climbing gear, like TCUs, and though she couldn't have seen my face she must have sensed that I was still confused.

"Sexually transmitted diseases!" she said too loudly, embarrassed. "Damn, Atlas, haven't you ever talked to anyone about this stuff? Okay, do you have syphilis or crabs or rabies or mad cow disease?"

"Me? No, no, none of them."

"Are you sure? It doesn't seem like you know what they are."

"Okay, obviously mad cow. No, I just thought . . . I mean, I got tested with Olive—when I was with Olive. I haven't been with anyone else since then."

"All right," she said, quietly again. She hugged herself, and then pulled on my T-shirt, complaining of it getting chilly, though if anything our heat and the minimal ventilation made it hotter in there.

Then I got it: "So . . . what about you?"

"Herpes 2," she said clearly, a hint of defiance in her voice.

Without thinking, suddenly jealous, I asked, "Who'd you get it from? Clem?"

"No, someone else—the boyfriend before him. But I mean, it's totally under control. I've had it a couple years and I almost never have outbreaks, and when I do, I have this medication that will suppress it."

"So I won't get it from you?" I asked. My brother Gus had had herpes 2 for years, and I knew it didn't trouble him that much.

"Not if you use a condom."

"And . . . what about if I use my mouth?"

She laughed so briefly it was more like a pant. "You could get it, I guess, but look—I'm not having an outbreak right now. If I'm not having an outbreak, you can't get it . . . except for like three days before an outbreak."

I chewed on this for a moment. "But you don't know if you're having the outbreak three days before, right, since you haven't had the outbreak yet?"

"Rrright . . . but—"

"—so I could get it?"

She pushed me back and straddled me, placing one hand on my chest. In the darkness I could just make out that she was pinching her other thumb and forefinger tight together, like she were squeezing a tick. "The chances are this slim," she said, then leaned back as if to say, *So what'll it be?*

I had my hands on her hips, the edges of her T-shirt lapping at my fingers, her smooth expanse of skin and her puckered belly button waiting for me. I worked a little dade-uction on myself: I knew I should keep the moral high ground for Olive, but then admitted that if I didn't move forward with Ruby, right in that moment, she might think I didn't want to be with her and was using fear of getting her disease as some kind of excuse—but I did want to be with her.

Shit, I was already in trouble with Olive, and Ruby was the

person I wanted to be with. But if she was someone I wanted to be with, then I should tell her about it all. While I thought this out, however, my body had already made a positive decision, and was pressing back against her as hard as she was pressing against me.

The first time with a new partner has always been awkward for me, mostly because I can never seem to read them, and they can never read me. This was certainly the case between me and Ursula, my first real love, and also with several lovers after her—and especially with Olive, with whom it took a bit of work to get things right. But something happened this time with Ruby that had never happened to me before.

Ruby started to kiss me again, grinding me, getting us ready, but as I held her I had another wave of feeling for Olive. It was probably just that I hadn't made love to anyone else for years and was used to Olive's broader hips between my hands, her sweeter scent, her thinner arms. But Ruby had put the condom on me and was getting ready to put me inside of her, and so, out of desperation, I tried to "drop ballast" like I'd done earlier in the day on Mudskipper, to let go of thoughts of Olive and get myopic on Ruby. I turned myself into the filter-feeder/pollinator and then felt things shift ever so slightly. Just as Ruby put me inside her, I found that I was wide open, all energy—the cherries all lined up. My focus was only on her and me and the planet beneath us.

As if breathing through my skin, aware of everything around me, I swear I could feel where her veins were, where her lungs and heart hovered over me. I felt, too, that some deeper part of her self, her *Rubyness*, was wrapped inside and all around me—and then came the feeling, like waking from a dream, that I'd been right there, in this very moment, my entire life.

I was overwhelmed by my feelings for her, their intensity never matched by anything with Olive, and those feelings grew in size and weight until—like in the "thick" falling dream—I had so many of them that I was only feelings, so overwhelmed by the sense that I was only sense.

Ruby had stuffed the T-shirt into her mouth to muffle her cries, but I heard her yell "Umph Gdd," through it anyway, and then an "Oh, God," when the T-shirt finally slipped out, the words so loud they hurt my ears. The sound cracked me open even further, until, as she moved into and around me, as I moved into and around her, I felt a piercing ache that began at the back of my jaw. I started to cry as Ruby kept pushing off my chest with one hand and pressed the T-shirt back into her mouth with the other.

There was that bubble again, the wordless thing/place/time inside of me that had started to rise to my surface when I was on Mudskipper, only this time it was wrapped up in Ruby too. And then Ruby yelled "Come!" through her teeth. "Come!"

And I did.

CHAPTER NINE

"Hee-yah!" I heard from the depths of some uncomfortable dream. "Hee-yah!" as I woke up in my own body, surrounded by the wild, funky smell of old cheese and dust.

"What stinks?" Ruby asked, sitting up to stare pointedly at my feet, "It's terrible."

Her body had been tucked up into mine, her wall-tiger tight up against my belly.

Before I could answer Ruby, though, we heard Dade's voice loud and clear:

"Get out of here, get out of here!" he yelled, just before we heard a strange, low moan as someone stepped near the tent. Not someone—something.

"Buffalos," Ruby and I whispered together.

I opened the screen and then the rainfly of the tent as quietly as possible and we both leaned out to look: between us and *Makin' Bacon* there were over two dozen bison, their giant heads full of watery eyes and flaring nostrils, their hindquarters so small it seemed their back halves were taken from some other, more delicate, species—though one still capable of giving off such a funky scent that it could maintain its own presence in the field alongside them.

"Never seen 'em back here, huh?" whispered Ruby, a little bit scared but mostly excited.

Dade opened up the side door of *Makin' Bacon* then, yelling

"Hee-yah!" again and clapping his hands a few times. Several of the calves jerked away from him, but the others were unimpressed, and one large male, its head as big around as a car tire, took a few steps toward him until it was fifteen feet from the van.

After they contemplated each other for a moment, Dade disappeared and then reappeared in the doorway with a long carrot, at which point he started to make squeaky noises as if he were calling a cat.

"Here you go, big boy," said Dade, holding the carrot out as far as he could.

The buffalo stretched its neck out for a sniff while all the other buffalo watched, and then, working its massive head for a little momentum, walked casually up to the Rig to take the carrot, chewing it up right there.

"We shouldn't be feeding them," said Ruby, somewhat amazed. Then she leaned forward for a better look.

Somehow this shadowy movement of Ruby's was scary to them where all Dade's yelling and clapping hadn't made a dent; the buffalo spooked as one, charging briefly until they'd put about fifty yards between us and them, stopping in their cloud of dust as if suddenly forgetting why they'd run in the first place.

Dade looked over at us as he got out of the Rig, stage whispering, "Did you see that?" before walking around to the other side of the Rig to pee.

"I got to see a man about a horse too . . ." said Ruby as she crawled out of the tent, surprising me by already being fully clothed. She walked cautiously towards a stand of pine, clapping her hands a few times and yelling, "No stray buffalos in here?" before disappearing into it.

Behind her, the sun was just cresting a low point between a pair of hills, casting great blocks of air into shadow and light, their monumental planes made visible by the dust the buffalos had kicked up. I sat back in the tent, a little stunned from the quick wake-up.

Then all at once, the weight of making love to Ruby—and of cheating on Olive—hit me. I had wanted to do the right thing so badly, and once again, by not doing right, I'd done wrong. And I wondered again about what Fran had asked Ruby: "*Don't you still think you have a choice with Clem?*" But I couldn't ask Ruby about Clem until I'd told her about Olive—and I couldn't tell Ruby now until I'd broken things off. But if I broke things off quickly enough, maybe I wouldn't even have to tell Ruby, came the weaselly thought, though that wasn't good or right, either. I needed time to get my head straight so that I didn't do or say anything else that might get me in more trouble. I needed to crawl back into my bag for twenty-four hours.

"I'm making pancakes," Dade yelled cheerily from the Rig then, as if trying to atone for his cock-up the night before, "and coffee—who wants some?"

"I do," I heard Ruby say as she walked past me toward the Rig. Then, using her best Wyoming drawl, she said, "Time to get up, big guy," without even looking back at me.

I pulled on a shirt and shorts and walked over to *Makin' Bacon* with my sleeping pad so I could stretch out a little before climbing. It was already growing hot—the first day of the trip to really feel like July. When I reached her, Ruby made a little gesture with her chin, over her shoulder, indicating that I should look behind me; then she threw her leg up on the back of her lawn chair as if to stretch out her hamstring, though she was really just sneaking a look under her shoulder.

Dade was walking away from *Makin' Bacon* with a cup of coffee held up as an offering. Fran watched him approach, leaning against Ruby's truck with her arms crossed. When Dade got close he held up his other hand as if to say, "*Who knows anything,*" his head penitent with apology by the time he reached her and started to speak. We couldn't hear what they were saying, but after a moment Dade gestured toward the tent, and Fran barked out a grudging laugh and finally took his offered cup of coffee. He came back to the Rig seeming much relieved and turned on the stove while Fran made her way over to us.

Ruby groaned as she lifted her other leg onto the chair back, shaking her head.

"Achey from Pitchpole?" I asked.

"Yeah, I'm a little sore . . . it was pretty hard for me."

Fran was in earshot by then and snorted a laugh, a gleeful look on her face as she said, "Yeah, we heard all about it last night."

Ruby dropped her leg to the ground and looked confused for a moment, then narrowed her eyes to slits to give Fran a murderous look.

"Hey, there's nothing to be embarrassed about," said Fran.

"Nothing wrong with two consenting adults, uh, consenting," Dade said from the stove in the Rig. I couldn't see his face, but I could hear the smirk in his voice.

This infuriated Ruby, even though we were all basically friends. She snatched up her coffee and walked quickly back to her truck, saying something about getting her plate.

"Hey, I like to get laid too, whenever I lead a route that's hard for me. It's a good release," said Fran as a parting shot.

I don't know why I hadn't caught it up until that moment, but there was clearly some stress building between them. I hustled after Ruby and caught up with her just as she reached the hidden back of her truck. She had tears on her face.

"Hey, hey, what's going on?"

"She's just so . . . ugh!" she grumbled, and then, mimicking Fran's higher-pitched voice: "*Sure, I'll climb with you until my finger's healed up*—as if it's a mercy fuck."

I pulled Ruby close and hugged her. We stood still like that for a while.

"I guess we were a little loud, though," I finally said, leaning back to smile at her.

"Yeah, when I dropped the T-shirt." She laughed, though she cried a little bit too. "But Fran's always done this. Ever since high school. She has this way she talks about sex—and everything else—like she's some super cool seventies hippie . . . like everyone else is a child and she's the grown up. She did it when I got stuck at the crux of Pitchpole. She tries to ruin things."

I was about to say that nothing could ruin what we'd done the night before, but Ruby jumped in again, this time mimicking Fran's brassy voice: "'I like to get laid too, whenever I lead a route that's hard for me.'"

I shrugged, suddenly not sure what to say to calm her, when Ruby dove in again.

"It could also be that she's gone off her meds . . . she's always snappier when she's not taking them."

"Meds? For what?"

"Depression. Anxiety. And if she's off her meds, drinking seems to make things worse—but don't say anything, I'm not supposed to tell."

"I won't."

Ruby moved away from me and scooched up onto the open gate of her truck. Then she sighed.

"It's great that we can figure out everyone *else's* problems for them."

"You think we have a problem?" I was surprised but tried to sound light.

"That's what I'm trying to figure out."

I shook my head. "Well, it's not from my side—not from me. I mean, last night . . . that was amazing."

Ruby blushed and pulled me into a hug, her legs wrapping lightly around my legs.

"You too. I mean, for me too," she said over my shoulder, "I just sensed something this morning . . . I don't know. It made me wonder what was going on with you."

"There's nothing going on with me, besides thinking about you," I lied.

I felt her nod her head, though she didn't say anything; then she pulled back so she could look at me.

"Me neither. Anyway, I got my plate—and the pancakes are probably ready, huh?" she asked, smiling. She pushed me away so she could slip off the gate and then led me around the truck and back towards the others. While we walked, I noticed that the buffalo had drifted, along with their dusty cloud, another fifty yards away while those great blocks of shadow and light had been washed away by the more intense, though somehow duller, light of mid-morning.

Dade handed me a plate of pancakes when I reached him, and I said, "Time to get climbing," as an attempt to normalize relations. Fran and Ruby were so busy ignoring each other that they didn't seem to hear me, but Dade, always psyched to climb, started to nod his head in time with his chewing as if mesmerized by the action.

I suggested we all climb together and do some hard classics in the Outlets, and though no one said a word, I assumed we were all in agreement, since everyone packed up and loaded themselves into, respectively, *Old Yeller* and *Makin' Bacon*, and drove back to-ward Sylvan Lake.

Dade was strangely silent in the Rig, as if still mesmerized, and didn't say anything the whole ride. I didn't want to rile him and get him going about Olive and Ruby, but after we parked in the lot, he immediately jumped out of the Rig and started walk-ing away. I finally had to ask him if he was doing all right.

"It's just that I got to call Bev," he said, over his shoulder, point-ing ahead of himself up the hill, where he'd gotten cell phone coverage the day before, "and Yosemite is on the chopping block."

If he was calling Bev, then it was time for me to call Olive too, but I couldn't risk Ruby overhearing everything and knew I'd have to make some excuse in the afternoon to get alone. I had no idea what I was going to tell Olive now—even thinking about it made me feel crazy. I'd have to tell her everything, I realized, and then I started to spin and accelerate upward, my heart beating quickly. I closed my eyes and focused on my breathing to calm things down, and then the spinning did slow as the rising stopped. When I opened my eyes again, I found that Ruby was standing next to the side door of the Rig, watching me with a quizzical look on her face.

"You okay?" she asked.

I waved it off. "Too much coffee, I think. I'm fine."

"Fran doesn't want to climb with Dade—and I don't want to climb with her," she said, sitting down in the side door.

"I don't blame her—or you," I said.

"I still don't get it, I thought they got square this morning."

By stretching my neck high to look through the windshield, I could see Dade approaching the top of the hill. I pointed to my left ring finger and said, "It's all fun and games until someone gets their heart poked out."

Ruby eyed me seriously for a moment, as if she'd follow up on that idea, but after a pause she stood up and, saying she had to get her gear ready, went back to her truck. I coiled the still-damp rope and then organized our great mess of gear, which I'd gathered from the line and simply thrown into the Rig. By the time I finished racking it all Dade had returned, looking determined as he got into the driver's side seat. He was testing his lip with a finger where the swelling had retreated, leaving only a thin, pink vertical crack.

"What's wrong? Is Bev okay?" I asked.

"Bev calmed down. I got her back on the old schedule—at least until the next hormonal wave hits," he said, not looking at me. "But I got to get out of here. I'm done with the Needles—with all this weather and all this fucking around. We need to get on some longer, harder routes and start getting in shape. We need a Valley Day to get things jumpstarted."

A Valley Day was when we climbed as much real estate in one day as we would on a big, Yosemite free climb—anywhere from ten to thirty pitches and balls to the wall. I looked out demonstratively at the clear blue sky, holding my hand out as if to say, *"We could try for a Valley Day here,"* but he just slammed his door as confirmation of his decision.

I was about to argue with him, even though I knew it was probably useless, when I realized that deep down inside I was relieved that we'd be leaving. It was all moving so fast with Ruby—I needed to sort things out. And if we left it would be easier to call Olive.

"You'd better go let them know we're heading to the Tower," Dade said as he started the engine. "You can blame it on me."

I looked over at *Old Yeller* just as Ruby slammed the gate, her backpack already on, while Fran walked over to the trash cans with a milk carton. I jumped out to meet Ruby so I wouldn't have to have the conversation in front of Dade or Fran.

"You guys ready?" Ruby asked, cinching down the straps on her pack. Then she saw my face. "What's wrong?"

"Dade wants to head to the Tower. Right now. He wants to get on some longer routes so we can get some momentum going." I held my hands up to let her know it was all beyond my control. "I'm amazed he made it this long."

"Fran thinks he can't take a strong woman like her around him," she said. Over Ruby's shoulder, I saw Fran toss the milk carton into the trashcan and start walking towards us.

"Yeah, maybe. It could be some other things too."

"It's a common trait. I see it all the time," Ruby said, almost squinting at me.

I was embarrassed, unsure if she was talking about me too, but then she stepped forward to give me a hug. My arms were awkward on her climbing pack until I reached up and held her head from behind. I was surprised by how hot her black hair had grown in the sun.

"You're not crazy, are you?" she asked, dead serious, still holding me tight.

"What do you mean?"

"I mean, you're not going to wig out on me, right? You're not all fucked up and stuff, are you?"

I laughed and pulled myself away so I could look at her. Her face was flat and something had shifted in her eyes, as if their color had lightened the tiniest bit. The question seemed fair.

"Totally sane," I said.

She pulled me back to her. "That's good. I am too."

Before I could think it through, I was saying, "You should come to the Tower—talk Fran into coming."

"I'll try, but we're supposed to be in San Francisco in like six days. That's when she has to be at the tradeshow for her sponsors."

"Kissy-kissy," said Fran then as she reached us, hefting her own pack off the ground, "Didn't get enough of that last night, huh?"

Ruby let go of me abruptly and said, "The boys are taking off for the Tower."

This seemed to startle Fran, though she recovered with the motions of adjusting her pack.

"Dade wants to get on longer routes there so we can get ready for the Valley—you should come with," I said.

"You should," said Dade from the driver's seat. "I'm just totally fried on the weather here."

I saw Dade's eyes as he looked at Fran. They held frustration and also an apology, I thought, but if she caught these things she didn't acknowledge them.

"Right . . . well, let's get rolling, Ruby, I want to get on some of this 'classic' rock before it gets too hot," she said, starting out toward the path that circles Sylvan Lake and waving dismissively to Dade and me over her shoulder.

Ruby turned to me and we kissed on the lips again. Then she quickly wrote her phone number (as large as possible) on a receipt and handed it to me, winking, before she turned and hustled after Fran.

"Long, beautiful routes. Prairie dogs. Giant jackalopes," I yelled after her. "All at the Tower."

Ruby turned around, but kept walking backward and held up what I thought was a peace sign before mouthing the words "*Two days.*"

I watched her until she reached the path by the lake. Then I turned to Dade.

"You owe *me*, now."

"I owe you big-time," he said grandly, trying to make light of it all. "If you keep being nice, maybe I'll let you do the Jaws pitch on Seven Seas."

I climbed into the van, acting testier than I actually felt, and said, "If we're going to go then let's go. It's already ten o'clock."

"To the Tower," he said, trying to sound jaunty, "to train for YO! Sem-I-tee!"

"Uh-huh," I said dryly. "It'll be easier to train without Fran around."

He backed out of our slot and then looked over at me as he yarded on the steering wheel. I was ready for an argument, or at least some response like how it'd be easier for me to call Olive without Ruby around too, but he just rapped the doghouse twice with his thick knuckles—somewhat conspiratorially, like together *we'd* gotten away with something—and then ground the gears into first before pulling away. I had a powerful sense in that second, a feeling of being in on something—as if I had once robbed a bank with him and he had pulled on the steering wheel just like that, in air exactly this warm, in another life.

And then, as we cleared the hill at the top of the parking lot, I remembered again what I'd forgotten when Ruby and I made love: I never had Ruby show me her "other" tattoo, the one on her front side. For the first time I tried to imagine what it might be. More characters? Clem's name? And what was that line? Each thing in its right place and for every thing the right word? What was the right word for us? For what we'd done last night? Where was the right place for us to be?

CHAPTER TEN

We made it about two miles down the road before the day really went to hell. The temperature gauge spiked into the red, as if to taunt us, then dropped back down. Then it spiked again. Dade pulled over alongside a field and jumped from the Rig, pointing at the heavens with two defiant, quivering middle fingers.

Then he crawled under the front to have a look. This was his territory (car repair), so I stayed where I was, with my feet on the dash, and waited for his judgment. Through the doghouse I heard him sing a classic rock song with his bad Scottish accent, only with new lyrics—something like, "Mean old climbin' gods, won't let me go climbing, no . . . mean old gods, they threw Uhtlas a bone . . . now it's the last straw and I'm ready to go-oo home," until he finally hollered that the fan belt was okay, and the hoses too.

"Must be the pump," I yelled, sure he was about to yell the same.

"Or the thermostat," he said, crawling out from beneath the Rig. "And according to the *Rig Veda* I replaced it only twenty thousand miles ago." He went around to the back of the van to get the toolbox, but I just sat still and looked out over the field next to us.

I noticed a few pale, brown cow pies nearby, and then a few brown longhorn cows too, at the other edge of the pasture. Above us, in the sky Dade had just cursed, there were several fat, fair-weather clouds taking up as little space in their domain as the cows did down in theirs. They gave me one of those sensory over-laps, their bright white-on-blue smelling like a combination of chlorine and wind-dried cotton.

One of the clouds, shaped like an axe head or maybe a thick hourglass, floated its multi-acre shadow across the grass and the cows and the cow pies no faster than I could walk, and its pace was a powerful sedative on me. I let out a long, slow breath.

Dade jumped back in and slammed the door: "We'll have to wait for it to cool a bit. Then I'll take out the thermostat, though I'm pretty sure it's the pump."

He leaned forward as if to better see the road, which dropped off into the trees ahead of us, and said, "We might make it all the way to Custer if we can coast the downhills."

I sighed but didn't say anything.

"What?" he demanded. "You want to say that if we'd only stayed with them we'd be climbing by now."

"No . . . all I need to say is the truth to Olive. And now I got plenty of time to figure out what that's going to be."

He nodded. "With Ruby and everything?"

"If it comes to that?"

"How's it the truth if it doesn't come to that?"

"If I just stick to me and Olive and how we're not right for each other. That's the core truth."

"Well, you'd better prepare yourself for it; Ruby is going to come up."

"I really messed up."

"Yeah, you did," he said too quickly—not even trying to console me or agree it was a difficult thing.

This annoyed me. I waited a moment, then said: "You were no peach with Fran, either, speaking of messing things up."

"Maybe she just bugged me, in spite of how hot she is, and I couldn't help but bug back," he said, annoyed. Then he started to nod: "But the result is that I managed to keep my future self from having to make the kind of phone call you're making to Olive."

I scoffed at him. "Oh, I see. You acted out of your own, zen-like self-awareness."

"Sure, subconsciously, anyway. It was just the triggers, but they were my triggers and I'll take credit for them. And maybe your subconscious triggers had you sleep with Ruby so you'd finally have to break up with Olive. Even your own self couldn't stand how indecisive you were being."

Just as I started to counter, he held up his crooked left index finger to silence me, then started to wag it at me: "Yeah. You wait and wait and DON'T make a decision about one thing so many times in a row that you finally do something else to impact it. It's as if your subconscious finally has to take charge. Yeah. You're a *waiter*. You always wait for things come to you, whether it's school or climbing or women."

"Enough with the psychoanalysis, Christ," I said, holding up a hand and turning away from him to look out the window, where there were no more cloud shadows but only sun and cows.

I stared at a longhorn for a while. It stood very still, simply chewing, its horns swaying lightly with the action, and somehow this helped me admit that Dade was on to something. Olive had called me a "waffler" and now Dade said I was a "waiter," and maybe they were both right. I created bad habits for myself pretty easily, and the waiting was a habit—the result of being a waffler. And waffling was a habit too. And suddenly it struck me that maybe I'd created a habit about love too, with Ursula, that German exchange student.

Even though we were only juniors in high school, we were very much in love. Or in love enough, anyway, to give me a real understanding of it, so that when I first told Olive I loved her, I knew that deep down it wasn't exactly the truth, and not exactly lying, either. It was more like a hope, a hope that over time I'd come to truly love her.

Ursula and I were racing the clock, though. She only had a year in the US, and then would have to go back for her last year of *Gymnasium* in Germany. This time limit built a tragedy into our love—a tragedy that was somehow "adult," I realized, looking back on it—and we threw ourselves into it with a kind of rapture, in awe of our new feelings and each other.

Maybe the way I fell in love with Ursula had determined my rules—or my habits—for being in love. That is, I'd had the template of tragic love for my first love, and I needed those conditions to really feel that I was in love again. And since things with Olive hadn't been tragic at all, I was never able to feel like I was in love with her like I had been in love with Ursula.

It was like I'd learned to play basketball on sloped alley concrete, with special rules for two-man teams and the too-short hoop, and then couldn't change my habits enough to make the shift to an organized team playing zone defense indoors. Shit. I had some unlearning to do, and then some relearning to do with Ruby, because I knew, deep down, that I really could love Ruby right.

"I just got to figure out the rules with Ruby," I said out loud, turning my gaze from the field back to Dade.

He looked at me, puzzled for a second, and then nodded, as if this simply confirmed what he'd said earlier: "You'll have to stop waiting, then—go after it."

"Uh-huh. But if it's all just triggers, then how can I *go after* anything? To go after it I have to have free will. In your causal cage world, I'd really just be fulfilling my nature."

This almost gave him pause, but then his mouth started moving: "Well, maybe we do have free will in little decisions—like how Uhtlas should fucking pass auf and not procrastinate. But that doesn't mean we're not on a big, determined ball that keeps spinning no matter what we do."

"That's bullshit—it doesn't follow. It can't be all determined and then, on special Dade occasions, not be."

"Who says it has to follow? If you're never going to travel anywhere, does it really matter if you believe the theory that the earth is round or the theory that it's flat? Either way you get up every morning and eat your Wheaties, crap after coffee, and yoke the oxen. At night, when the *sun goes down*, it doesn't matter if you believe that the earth rotates on its own axis or that the sun goes around the earth."

"It matters because one's the truth, and the other's *myopic* and ignorant," I said.

"So you're not a flat-earther? Do you know for a fact that the earth is a sphere?"

"Will you quit?! I'm serious. Can I change bad habits and be with Ruby or not? Did you do Son of Sam because you willed it, or because it was your nature to shut up Red and Lex Luther?"

He shrugged, and I mimicked it back to him like an eight-year-old, bobbing my head and almost sticking out my tongue. The field was still stuck to the planet like a postage stamp, the clouds intrepid in their journey above, all of us rotating with the earth and revolving around the sun. I wanted Ruby, and I wanted to do the right thing with Olive. I hadn't done the right thing with Olive up until then, and that would have to change. I would have to start exercising my couch-potato will like I exercised my body. I was about to admit as much to Dade when he looked at me with a little goat in his eye.

"Things aren't meant to happen *for* a reason, like Fran thinks—like there's some grand plan. Things happen *because* of a reason, because it's causal. It's still all determined—I'm just built by nature to forget this fact and try to twist things in the world, like when I tell you to pass auf. And maybe that's something that's determined too. Like, you're causally determined to become a better human, but only if there are triggers from the outside world to make it happen. I'm the triggerman. It's all connected, but so complicated we can't see it all."

He seemed supremely satisfied with this twisted solution and how it fit the facts.

"If someone beat you in the fifty-yard dash, you'd figure out they'd taken the wrong number of steps," I said.

He grinned. "As my grandpappy used to say, if you ever catch a wolverine by the tail, you better keep swinging and never let go. Or throw it really far away."

"Yeah, the phrase is '*tiger* by the tail', for your information, and it's not just your grandpappy who says it . . . and anyway, at some point your arm's going to tire out."

He flexed his impressive right bicep, popping out a vein like an exclamation point, and raised both eyebrows. Then, without another word, he got out of the Rig and started to work on removing the thermostat in case it was broken, so that the cooling system would be wide open.

We drove about a mile before we hit a hill long and straight enough that Dade could kill the engine to coast. Floating down the road, hearing the pull of the tires and the bounce of the frame instead of the engine, made me feel like we were kids in a grocery cart careening down an alley. We had to stop and cool off a couple more times—it was the pump—and finally hit Custer around two o'clock, not far from the edge of the state, rolling to a stop at a full-service Sinclair station, the Rig panting steam under the shadow of the big, green dinosaur sign. It had grown beastly hot.

A wiry, zero-body-fat kid, probably just out of high school, sat on the stoop watching us. He wore a Colorado Avalanche baseball hat and a green, pin-striped Sinclair work shirt a size too big for him, and though he was looking in our direction, clearly taking in the steam roiling out of the front grill, he somehow managed not to look at me or Dade at all. He spit leisurely into a Mountain Dew can as though he never needed to move from the stoop, but as soon as I hopped out of the Rig he rose from his squat and walked slowly inside, the shape of a tobacco tin worn into his back pocket.

As he went in, a serious-looking dog, tail-docked and cross-eyed, came out of the garage. The dog was part pit bull, part heeler maybe, and was so muscular it looked like it could wag a telephone pole if you could somehow attach one to its stubby tail. I whistled at it to say hi, but it simply froze as if I'd broken some law, and as I neared the glass door it sauntered stiff-legged back into the relative cool of the garage.

Although the kid had entered the office silently, I tinkled the cowbell attached to the door when I walked inside and was instantly enveloped in the cool, sharp scent of mint air freshener and burnt coffee and rubber. "Everett" (the name on the kid's shirt) seemed to float above the counter until I realized that he was sitting on a tall bar stool.

"I think we might have a bad water pump," I said, careful not to spook him.

"What you got there?" he said, leaning to look out the window after checking out the muscles in my arms.

"Chevy Sportvan—nineteen-eighty."

He squirted another shot of tobacco juice into his Mountain

Dew can and then hunt-and-pecked his way through the auto parts website on his computer. Once the kid found the serial number, he slipped off his stool and walked into the garage, moving like he was forty years old. There was an old Toyota pickup on the near lift with its transmission dropped and balanced precariously on a metal cart beneath it, and along the back wall of the garage was a very high and deep metal shelving unit with more parts than I'd ever seen in so small a space. Everett kicked the rolling ladder ahead of him and right over the dog, which lay on a piece of old carpet beneath the shelving, and started climbing up to the highest shelf when he reached what I took to be the water pump section. I hesitated before passing in front of the dog's line of fire, but Everett looked down at me, almost spitting juice but controlling himself, and said, "Don't worry about Foursey, he only bites if you run or something."

He rooted around on the shelf, and then came coolly down the ladder.

"Don't got it."

"Yeah . . . I didn't think you would. Is there an auto parts store in town?"

"This is it," he said, walking ahead of me to the front office, "Used to be a Napa in town, but they went belly up." This made him grin.

"So where do you get parts, then?"

"The boss just drove to Rapid to get a clutch plate. Sometimes we have to go to Casper."

"Shit."

"Life's a bitch," he said, strangely cheered. I nodded with him a couple beats, trying to figure out how to get him on our good side, and then Dade came in.

"No go," I said, "And the boss already left to get parts in Rapid."

"When did he leave?" Dade asked the kid.

"My dad? About a half-hour ago," he said, checking out Dade's ripped arms too. "He'll be back in a couple hours or so."

Just then the phone rang and the kid answered: "Custer Sinclair . . . nope, Old Everett's out for a couple hours . . . yeah, I'll tell him."

We all stood staring at each other for a second after he hung up, and then, to fill the silence, Dade said, "I figured you were Everett," pointing at his shirt.

"It's my dad's shirt."

"So who are you?"

"Oh, I'm Everett too."

"Everett 'two'? Like Everett Junior?" said Dade, holding up his middle and index fingers.

"No, the Third. But they all call me 'Young Everett.'" He lifted his left shirtsleeve to show off the tattoo of a monster truck inked onto his bicep, complete with *Everett* on the door and wheels bursting with power. Beneath the truck, in ornate calligraphy, it had the Roman numeral *III*.

"Nice tat," said Dade. "Where'd you get it?"

"This one, right here in town. But there's a really good guy in Rapid," he said, lifting up his right sleeve to show off another tattoo: *South Dakota State, 138 lbs.* "Personally, I'd go to him."

"Yeah, I've been thinking of getting one myself—just my wife's name."

"Or maybe a beaver," I said, looking at Dade and sticking out my front teeth.

Everett the Third couldn't possibly have understood my joke, but he seemed to warm to us then, and, after looking up at the big Sinclair clock over the door, said, "Well, maybe I could catch my dad before he leaves Rapid."

"That'd be great—and we'll need a gasket too," said Dade, catching my eye as Everett dialed the number with the end of a pencil.

Everett held up a finger to silence us as the call rang through, though we weren't talking, and after a series of *heys* and *huhs* let us know that his father was still at the Napa store. They found the pump and gaskets at another store across Rapid, and he'd pick them up for free if he was doing the job; he'd pick them up for twenty bucks if we were.

"Deal," said Dade, taking a couple Cokes out of the refrigerator.

I walked outside to the Rig while Dade paid for the Cokes, and opened up the small hood of the van to help things cool off before we got to work. Then I sat down in the side door. Inside the station I saw Foursey (a nickname for "Everett the Fourth," I guessed) sniff at Dade's sock, then back up and let himself be patted casually before Dade came out to join me.

While we melted into the heat, drinking our Cokes, two girls rode up on beat-up mountain bikes, both of them maybe sixteen years old, one with skinny hips and big breasts, the other skinny all around but with rock-star lips. The dog came out ducking and wagging his stumpy tail, making himself sweet as could be, until the girls called to him, "Hey Foursey, c'mere, boy," when he bounded over to snuffle and expose his belly to them. The girl with skinny hips bent over to give Foursey a scratch; he stretched mightily on the concrete until Everett came out of the office, when the dog snapped to his feet as if embarrassed to be caught enjoying himself.

Everett had both sleeves rolled high to give his tattoos some air, and started to push a broom around the pumps to flex his muscles. The girls talked and leaned their shoulders against the glass of the office, alternating between puckering and biting their lips, scratching the dog, and yelling things like, "Caitlin was talking shit about you!" or, "When you get off?" and then whispering to each other with giggles.

About fifteen minutes later, after the girls rode away and Foursey stumped back into the garage, we borrowed a pan from Everett the Third and got to work draining the coolant and pulling off the hoses. Or Dade did, anyway; I mostly fed him tools and put parts in an orderly row on an old, spread-out newspaper.

It was a pleasure to watch Dade work on the Rig. Once he calms down he's attentive and detailed, just like when he climbs, and he worked carefully on the problem, checking out everything in the system again, hoses and radiator included, before soaking the pump housing bolts with WD-40 so they could loosen up. He waited about twenty minutes and then pulled the pump and carefully handed it to me from beneath the Rig, as if it were the barely-alive body of some mechanical sprite, his greasy hands dripping with dirty, greenish radiator fluid. I could tell that the earlier trouble with Fran, and even breaking down on the side of the road, were nothing to him. It was a good day for living; a good day to repair something and do it right.

"Now we wait," I said, setting the pump on the newspaper, while Dade finished shaving off the old, dried gasket with a bare razor blade.

"And hope Everett the Second brings the right parts," he said, sliding and rocking himself out from under the Rig. I brushed sand off his back for him, and we walked over to the surprisingly clean, cool bathroom to wash up. I had grease up to my elbow from handing tools to Dade, and had to scrub at it hard. Then, while Dade washed his hands at the sink, I peed at the urinal. And farted.

"Sounds like you oughta' be sitting down," said Dade, mimicking the kid's drawl perfectly.

I laughed stupidly at this, almost missing the urinal. "He'll have one of those girls pregnant within a year."

"Both—there's nothing else to do in this town," said Dade, pumping more soap out of an old, nozzle-style dispenser. He looked at the powdered soap in his hand, then over at me, and froze.

"I just had the weirdest déjà vu. Like I've been right here before, talking to you about that kid . . . the smell of this soap," he said, holding his hands to his nose. "I was just reading about déjà vu in *Science News Weekly*."

I thought about whatever it was that I'd felt when we'd left Sylvan Lake that morning, when it felt like we'd been conspirators. But that wasn't really déjà vu—it struck deeper somehow.

"What did the article say?" I asked, zipping up.

"They think now that it's a moment when the body actually incorporates a memory into the brain—as if we're feeling the brain event. Like when your muscles twitch after you've been training for power."

"It's always felt to me like I was just being reminded of something similar—a similar place or scent."

Dade started talking again, but I didn't hear him; I was on the edge of a thought, just about to grasp it. It had something to do with Olive and Ruby and me and even Dade. It was like a name I could almost remember—a brain beetle scrambling, its legs almost bridging a synapse—and then it was gone. I wouldn't see it again until our last day on the Seven Seas, and when I saw it the second time it would change everything.

"Well?" Dade asked.

"I'm sorry, I missed what you said . . ."

Dade looked at me queerly. "For the third time, do you ever have déjà vu?"

"Yeah, sure . . ." I said, shrugging. "Sometimes."

Dade shook his head as he pulled open the bathroom door, the interaction clearly strange to him, and said he was going to take a nap while we waited for the parts.

That's when I felt the faintest tendril of dizziness—as if an alarm had gone off, a Pavlovian phone ring—and I knew I had to call Olive.

I didn't want to have the conversation in front of Dade (or Everett, for that matter) and headed down a side street with Dade's cell phone heavy in my pocket. I finally stopped about a block away, right at the spot where the sidewalk dropped from one level to another, the distance bridged by a single concrete step. I took the phone out of my pocket and apparently had enough momentum from the last two days that I found myself dialing the numbers without getting dizzy. Then it was ringing, and then Olive was picking up the phone.

"Olive, it's me," I said, though it sure didn't feel like me. It felt like there was someone else inside me, doing the talking for me.

"Where are you?" she asked dully—more of a statement than a question.

"We're in the Needles, on the way to the Tower. How you doing?"

"Okay. I guess. I'm glad it's Saturday. I'm producing this great show on expat German artists, and it's been pretty hectic." She sounded cagey. Then she sighed: "So how's the climbing going?"

"It's good . . . well, actually, it's been pretty sucky. We got caught in a nasty storm yesterday, and now the Rig's broke down . . ." I said, looking around to make sure no one could listen in on me.

There was a long silence then, maybe fifteen seconds, when both of us froze.

"Atlas, what's going on? You sound really weird."

"I have to tell you something," I said, and then I started to spin and couldn't line my words up right, and then she was crying.

"God damn it," she said, almost choking. "Now you tell me? What happened, did you meet someone else?"

"Olive . . . it's just that I don't think I can move out there. Dade wants me to go on to Yosemite, and I—"

"There is, isn't there? I know, because you're too weak to make a decision on your own. You need someone twisting your arm or giving you candy."

"It's not like that . . . and now that I'm out climbing, I know I can't take New York." I was swooning, spinning, and rising, but still I was talking; I was doing it. I was calling the thing by its right name.

"But you knew that when I left, didn't you? You were just too weak to say it. I'm such an idiot . . ."

Another silence, this time for a minute. It wasn't about Ruby, I told myself, my thoughts growing clearer as the spinning stopped, but then I hadn't called Olive until after Ruby, either. Maybe I did need someone else to make my decisions. Maybe I was that weak.

"Okay," I finally said, switching to German. "Es gibt jemand anders, aber sie hat nichts damit zu tun . . ." *There's someone else— but she has nothing to do with this . . .*

"Stop."

I heard Olive put the phone down and run away from it, the wooden thuds of her footsteps growing ever fainter, though they never quite seemed to stop. I waited on the phone for one minute, two minutes, before finally sitting down on the stair. I had threaded the whirligig on a shoelace earlier, sitting in the Rig on the side of the road, and I pulled it out from my shirt and began to spin it, putting the fish in the bowl, letting the fish get out, my mind a complete blank except for the waiting.

She returned to the phone so silently she must have taken off her shoes to sneak up on it, and she cleared her throat to let me know she was there.

"Olive, baby, I'm so sorry—"

"I just threw up," she said, announcing it like little kids do when they wake up their parents, but then she steeled her voice: "I can't believe you're such a rat. Even though I always knew you were. You and Mo both—you both turned out to be rats."

But before I could find out more about Mo she launched in again: "So tell me about her, is she a climber? Of course she is. If I had been a climber this wouldn't have been a problem. I could have climbed with you during the day and fucked you at night and you'd have been in heaven. That's your dream, isn't it?"

"Olive, no." I didn't know how to tell her that I'd always hoped I would get there with her. That she was so amazing, but I just didn't find my way.

"The rules didn't fit with you," I finally blurted out. "I didn't know I had to learn others. It's like I learned to play one-on-one basketball on the street, then had to work a passing offense with you."

"YOU were on the offensive with ME? Atlas, you were always the one who couldn't commit."

"No, not offensive . . . look, that's a bad analogy . . . here: I had bad habits from way back with Ursula, okay. And then with you—you're like perfect, but we weren't tragic, and I needed it to be tragic to *be* with you. But since I really *could* be with you our love *couldn't* ever be tragic, so I never really felt we were enough in love."

I was clear about the logic, but knew the words were muddy.

"Tragic? Since you *could* be with me then you *couldn't* be with me? The bitch must have hit you hard on your little head to get you this messed up."

"Look, she's not a bitch, okay? It's Ruby—you know her—Clem's girlfriend. I mean, his ex-girlfriend."

"Ruby Goldberg?! Your old housemate? What's she doing with you? God, what am I doing with you? How do you manage to pull good, strong women into your crazed little world? You know what? I was mad, but now I'm relieved. I knew this was coming and I knew you were too weak to do anything about it and for some reason that made me too weak to do anything about it too."

She muttered something I couldn't hear, and then said: "And I've had this producer at work *falling* at my feet, begging me to go out, but I keep saying, 'Really, Klaus, I've got this great boyfriend. He's on his way out here to get a real job.' Right. I know what I'm doing tonight."

She cried through another wordless minute, and then, because he was my boy and I had to know, I sighed and asked again about Mo.

"He was missing for a while, right? And I was putting out food for him and he was eating it?"

"Right . . ." I said, standing up.

"Only it wasn't him!" she said, choking on a little sob, "Two days ago I saw it was a fucking rat that was getting into the apartment. I'm afraid the rat maybe ate him . . ."

"No way. He's like the Dirty Harry of hamsters. He's probably got his own crew already, getting strong on cats, shaking down those miniature Dobermans . . ."

This made her laugh in spite of herself, but I felt utterly defeated. I didn't know what else to say but, finally, the bones of it.

"I kept thinking it would hit, Olive. You're so amazing that I

knew that I'd fall madly in love with you. I KNEW I would, so I
kept waiting . . . but then it didn't happen. Or it didn't happen like
that. I do love you, though. I just don't love you enough, and so
I'm finally going to make a decision for once and stop it."

"Then why did it have to become about someone else?" she
asked, almost whispering.

I started to answer, or, at least, words started to come out of
my mouth, but I realized that she had hung up and I was still
standing on the edge of a step, on the edge of the world, with the
phone in my hand. Was this what Ruby meant when she asked if
I was crazy? Did she really mean: was I the kind that could break
her heart? Yes, I thought—but then she was too, and really, who
fucking isn't?

I HUNG UP, pressing the button as gently as I could, and just stood
there for . . . I'm not sure how long. After a while I found myself walking, and somewhere along the way went into a hardware
store to buy caulk to repair that crack in the Rig's roof—as if the
mundane act could ground me. Then I walked back to the Sinclair,
arriving just as Everett the Second, driving the vehicle of choice
around there, an abused Ford 250, pulled into the parking lot. The
back of the truck was dangerously full of parts big and small, but
Foursey managed to leap up and scramble over the gate, winding
himself between an engine and a transmission to pop up on the
cab roof as the truck came to a stop. He leapt to the ground with
one bounce off the hood when Everett the Second got out.

I waved at father Everett, who was smacking the now-happy
dog hard on the head to show his love, and thanked him for going
out of his way to pick up the parts for us. By physical appear-
ance he was clearly kin to Everett the Third, though a little bigger around the waist and arms. But that's where the resemblance

stopped. Old Everett must have been forty-five but moved in a frenzy, as if he were eight years old. It struck me that maybe things were flip-flopped out here: you start as a slow-moving runt, then get up off all fours and just keep accelerating until you've sprinted into the terminal velocity of death. On the way are gum-popping girls and dogs that won't lick your hand and a world of guilt for screwing up all down the line.

I paid for the pump and the gasket and chatted with him about how lucky we were to catch him before he'd left Rapid, and then, still numb, I walked back to the Rig and woke up Dade. He looked at me, knowing me well enough to see that something was wrong—and well enough to know not to ask—then yawned and crawled back under the Rig to put the pump in place while I sat alongside and handed him his tools.

Hours later, after we'd crossed into the red sand and crumbling buttes of Wyoming, we pulled off the interstate to make sure that the pump gasket wasn't leaking, then rumbled over a set of cattle grates to pull back on.

The sky had grown bigger—three, maybe five times the sky of the Needles and all its spires and trees—and to the west-northwest the sun was trapped between the earth and low clouds, its rays of light like the spokes of an immense wagon wheel that rolled over the land ahead of us.

"So how'd it go?" Dade asked suddenly, as if the bump of the cattle grate had finally jarred the question loose.

I shrugged.

"Did you break things off?"

I nodded so slowly he couldn't have seen it, and then said, "I just hope I still have the wall-tiger by the tail."

Without looking, I guessed he'd pursed his lips to correct me, the word *wolverine* caught between them, but he stopped himself and didn't say another thing until there was only the wind coming in through the edge of the window, the rough, strong growl of the engine, and the sky turning from reds to mauves to purples.

About twenty miles later, when the purple finally turned to the heaviest of blues, I caught my first glimpse of the Tower. Its dark shape was like a hole in the sky—a deep, matte indigo that sucked the last light out of the evening, as if it were trying to be the one thing in the world that was the opposite of glowing.

DEVIL'S TOWER

ODOMETER (1)99,032

LAT. 44.59° N LONG. 104.72° W

ALT. CAMPGROUND 3,858 FEET

ALT. TOP OF TOWER 5,117 FEET

JULY 9

CHAPTER ELEVEN

There's no explaining obsession. In the dark of the Tower campground, and the deeper dark of the Rig, we fell asleep talking over the game plan for our "Valley Day," picking four multi-pitch routes—eleven pitches total—that would get us in a Big Wall frame of mind. But Dade woke up with a completely different plan, and there was no shaking him. He felt strong, he said, and he wanted to get on the Devil's Workshop, champing at the bit to free its third pitch, Spanish Prisoner, aka, the hardest trad pitch in Wyoming.

Triggers, I thought as we signed in at the Ranger's station; some tiny trigger flipped a tiny switch in Dade's tiny, emotion-controlling amygdala. Maybe it was a dream. Or maybe the special Devil's Tower scent of sage and cottonwood and something acrid in the dust—prairie dog or roadkill raccoon—had combined with the sour funk we'd generated in the Rig after days of unwashed clothes and cooking and a leaky roof. Or maybe it was just that the many visits over the years had accumulated a certain weight that pushed him over the edge.

I wasn't feeling it as much. I woke up with the idea of the lots-of-easy-climbing in my head, plus the whole Olive-Ruby thing had me feeling a little low. I hadn't changed gears yet.

"Maybe we should warm up a little, get our feet wet on something else first," I said as Dade caught up to me on the Tower path.

But Dade was already singing, to the tune of John Denver's

"Blue Ridge Mountains": "Devil's Tower, Wild Wyoming, gonna pu-ull this motherfucker down-down-down . . ." his toes all but scratching at the pavement as he cupped the back of my head in his big hand and started nodding it for me, singing, "Are you ready to pass auf, my Uh-uht-las?"

He kept nodding it for me until I realized that, yeah, maybe I could make myself ready. Maybe I could fill my brain with something—anything—and not leave room in it for thoughts about how I'd hurt Olive or whether Ruby would show up. And there was no better way to do that than get on something insane. How else was I going to find my rockhead?

"Born ready," I said on an upswing, my feelings and my words suddenly in step.

"Good," he said, letting go of me, "because I'm gonna pull this bad boy *down*."

We headed to the northwest face, clockwise around the path, and although I'd seen it dozens of times, I was struck by the Tower's perfect size that morning. It is the biggest thing on the plains, but small enough that you can see it all at once. It is enormous—a monster—and yet you can walk around it in twenty minutes. And like man-made objects—an oil tanker at sea, or a giant sculpture in a building—it is just the right size to let you see how big it really is, while at the same time remaining dwarfed by what surrounds it.

I knew that we looked like a couple of pill bugs crossing a pile of gravel to any climbers up on the wall, but down on the slope we were surrounded by boulders as big as washing machines—a few as big as *Makin' Bacon*. Cool, musty air rose from their shadows, along with chipmunks which, spoiled by tourists, were bold enough to follow us a ways, their tiny bodies covering ground even faster than we could. Or faster than I could, anyway; I'd ripped my shin open here before and picked my route carefully, while Dade found his inner mountain goat and leapt nimbly from rock to rock, building momentum and flowing over the rough edges and steeplechase gaps.

I reached the base about half a minute behind Dade. It was already blustery there, with winds coming from either side and also from behind, as if they were confused about why they hadn't yet worn down this old volcano plug and were unsure what to do next.

Unlike Dade, who knew exactly what to do next. He had somehow tempered his hot psyche during the approach into a cool concentration so that there was no more singing, or any other sounds for that matter, coming from him. He must have been looking for his rockhead; I saw him touch his wedding ring–juju more than once as he looked over the rack, making a last-minute decision to ditch a few extra TCUs to cut down on weight.

On a route this hard, we couldn't risk the rope getting hung up at all. I realized I hadn't carefully looked it over in a long time, so I fed every inch of it through my hands, feeling the mantle for any fraying, as I flaked it into a delicate pool at my feet.

Dade romped up the first easy pitch and set up the belay; I organized the thin backpack, with our 8.8-millimeter rappel rope and water, and followed him up into the wind, pulling the three nuts he'd placed along the way.

The pitch two finger crack, a Tower test piece, was mostly vertical and much harder, and I looked the route over carefully before I left the belay chains. I knew from the guidebook that the endurance crux ended just below a dwarf pine tree that grew straight out of the rock, seventy feet into the route, and that things got easier after that. I pulled the whirligig out of my shirt to touch it, hoping the act might help me get myopic like it seemed to help Dade, then turned to the crack.

THE INSIDE OF it was cooler than the air, and I tried to think about that feeling of expansion that had come on Mudskipper—and while making love with Ruby—and then I slipped my feet into it as if I were mounting the stirrups of some familiar beast. There was no initial hitch this time as there had been on Mudskipper, even though the climbing was much harder. This time it was like there was a "me" that was always climbing, and I was able to simply step over and into that me. Twenty-five smooth feet later, I came to a fat three-fourths-inch ledge—big enough to shake out my forearms—and looked down to see Dade staring up at me, exuding calm and strength by the way he held the rope. Far beneath him, down past the talus on the asphalt path, I could see a family bunched together, passing binoculars back and forth, and dozens of miles away I could see another outcropping of rock, maybe another volcano core.

Then I looked at my next placement. If I had fallen from here, with no gear in, I would have gone past Dade's belay with the twenty-five feet of rope that was out, so that I would have fallen that amount times two (swinging around my fixed point of the belay), which would be fifty feet plus any rope stretch and slack that Dade left in the system. That is, I would have gone sixty feet and hit the lightly curving wall beneath Dade. That is, I would have been seriously fucked.

But I tried not to think about that by focusing on my protection, letting my actions, including my yell of "Slack" to Dade, be enough to focus me. As I clipped the pinky-width nut, suddenly safe, I felt a shift. For just a moment the rock and the cam and the air and my body all felt of the same stuff. Cherries lining up.

THEN FOR A little while there was nothing else. I was all myopic and all climbing and I was fearfully strong, yarding on the rock as if I were hoisting a sail.

I climbed like this for maybe twenty feet, on moves that were pretty hard, then placed a good nut the size of my index knuckle and went another twenty. I was in my rockhead, I was sure; I was cruising in control but not on cruise control.

"Pass auf!" Dade yelled. I was over twenty feet out from my last piece—two hundred feet above the base—hanging on only by my thin fingers and toe tips in a crack that was just too hard not to be putting gear in. Like a novice fisherman I had been so proud, so excited to get a bite, that I forgot to set the hook, and now I scared the moment away as quickly as it had come. I misjudged a swelling in the crack, couldn't get the nut in, then fumbled with the next size trying to make it fit, when I noticed that the dwarf pine tree that had been so far away was now only ten feet above me.

I took off for it, cranking my fingertips as deep as I could get them, my forearms and calves burning, and managed to reach the tree and grab hold of it, forcing myself through its stubby branches. The tree, its trunk as big around as my neck, was uncomfortable and it tore my shirt as I scrambled through it, but it was super solid—an oasis on a vertical desert.

"What was that all about?" Dade hollered.

"The climbing was just so good I thought I was okay," I lied, wrapping the trunk with a sling.

He looked down and away and said nothing more. After a short rest, I finished the last fifty feet of the pitch, following a mixed corner of vertical and horizontal cracks which ended in a series of pedestals that rose up like a great, three-tiered wedding cake, topped by a two-foot ledge.

By the time Dade finished the pitch it was almost ten thirty, and the long shadow that spread from the Tower during our approach had tucked up tight to the base of the route. Dade clipped into our anchor chains and then surprised me with a hearty slap on the back.

"I should have gotten some gear in," I said, to head him off at the pass.

"Yeah, you should have. I don't know how you can freeze on some nothing route like Mudskipper, and then cruise something that would give most people serious pause—including me."

I nodded. I wanted to talk to him about the rockhead—about whether what I'd just experienced was a piece of it—but then Dade needed to get his own head together and I didn't want to throw him off. He stretched out his forearms, untied and retied his shoes—kissing each one on the very tip—then looked over the pitch. The walls on either side started out close together and formed a kind of chute at first, but then widened out after about forty feet. All that was left from there to the top was seventy feet of razor-thin seam, which finally passed though an eight-foot bulge. That was the technical crux, where the crack didn't change in shape but overhung slightly. The real crux, however, was placing gear just below the bulge. In his conversation with a ranger that morning Dade got the beta on gear: a point-five TCU or an Alien just below the bulge, then a small but solid nut about ten feet after it. The ranger had to rest on the TCU below the bulge, then pumped out trying to place the nut and took a thirty-foot whip. We'd read in one of the magazines, however, that the Slovenians who put up the route had simply blasted right through the crux on their redpoint, not even slowing down to place gear afterwards.

Dade changed the order of his rack a few times as he looked over the route, getting the tiny RPs and nuts and TCUs in just the order he thought he'd need—and then he did something odd, something I'd only seen him do with dogs. He grasped my head with both hands, pressed the crook of his nose to my forehead, and held us for a moment, his safety glasses pinned between us. Then, with the briefest of eye contact, he clicked his cheek with a horsy giddy-up and turned to face the rock, so that I was looking at him from the side, his shoulders square and wide.

"Watch me close," he said.

"I will."

"I'll probably have to hang beneath the crux, depending—today's probably just recon."

"I know."

"Not too tight up till then. Keep the rope—"

"I got you."

He worked the sidewalls as long as he could, spread-eagled as if he were climbing inside an elevator shaft; then he stuck to just the right side in a layback, pausing for a long, casual rest—and a couple good friend placements—about fifty feet out. That rest (I'd find out later) was just a thin edge, about the width of the back of a good kitchen knife, but Dade had balanced there with an ease that those people down on the trail, who were still watching with binoculars, probably didn't have standing on flat ground.

With his hair whipping around his head, he checked over his gear and then set out on the completely vertical line, only able to stuff his first digits in by torqueing them hard.

He did this left fingers, right fingers, foot, foot; left fingers, right fingers, foot, foot, moving fast until he reached a place in the seam you couldn't see from below, where it opened up and he could get his whole hand in. He punched his left into this, then bone-hanged, his body turned sideways to the rock as he slammed in a good nut and clipped the rope—all of this as if in a single movement. This was the last good rest until past the

bulge—another fifty feet away—and his veins already seemed as
thick as the rope in my hands. He shook out his left arm, hard,
then made a few more moves to get his left foot into the slot
where his hand had been.

"Aaah-oooow!" he howled, setting off again aggressively. He
was climbing fast, even for him—only getting in fingertips, only
able to smear his feet—and barreled right through a section
where he might have gotten another piece, finally pausing on an
edge where he could set his toes. It was too hard, I realized. He'd
taken on too much and was so far out that if he fell he'd go fifty
feet and come to a stop just above me—and that was only if the
last nut held.

"You're getting pretty run-out!" I yelled, over-gripping the rope.

He managed to get in a tiny RP, then went another ten feet
where it seemed he'd found an edge for his right foot, maybe
eight feet below the bulge.

"This is some serious shit! I need to hang a second!"

"Can you down climb to the RP?" My stomach was so knotted
up I could barely yell loudly enough.

He couldn't, though. I could feel how hard it was through the
rope. It was thin and crimpy and on the other side of the spectrum from big and burly Son of Sam—as hard as the crux pitch
of Seven Seas would be. Then he was moving again, almost at the
bulge and twenty feet above that RP—its cable so thin it would
surely break if he fell that far on it. I could hear his gear tinkling,
the wind ripping around us, and my own heart, beating not so
much faster as with more depth, as if I were a great drum.

"Fucking pumped!" he yelled at the rock, not calm anymore. He
got an arm free long enough to swing his rack around and then
pulled off a cam. His left ring and middle fingers were locked into
the seam straight above me, feet smeared and seeming stable, and

just as he started to pop the cam in he slipped sideways, barn-dooring out over me in a millionth of a second. In my mind's eye I saw him falling then, perhaps like he'd seen me on Son of Sam, and I locked the rope down hard and waited for the bomb blast. But it didn't come. He was hanging from his two left fingers, frozen over a seventy-foot fall, the cam tearing through the air toward my face. I thought myself small, my teeth tight, as I hunkered in and watched Dade, faster then I could comprehend, stab his right fingers back into the seam and freeze his cartwheel off the wall, his two hands and one foot sucking at the Tower's hard skin while his other leg flagged the rock for balance.

The cam just missed me, landing on our pack with a waspy buzz, and when I looked up again I saw the puffing white of Dade's hand as it snapped out of his chalk bag. Dade let out an unearthly cry then—almost a roar—from deep down in his belly. He was fighting as hard I've ever seen anyone, his elbows winged out to the side, his whole body trying to suck itself to the rock. With each move it seemed he would fall, and I braced over and over for it, but then his hand or foot would snap back into the rock—punching the clock in the Devil's Workshop—screwing another lid onto another jar of gravity.

If I'd thought of it, I would have been crying, but I didn't have room for anything else besides my heart beating *Don't fall, don't fall, don't fall* and the sadness that swelled out of my bones. Even if Bev and the Crackmeister could live without him, I didn't know if I could. I powered my love for him up the rope, pulsing and pushing him upward, trying to bubble him off from gravity by wishing he were light as a feather, strong as an ape. Though I could barely stand to watch him, I had to, because he was amazing and if I didn't focus my spell of *Don't fall* up the rock then he really might fall. I squeezed this thought dry until he reached

the top 110 feet above me, his feet skittering and almost popping
one last time just before his hands caught the sloping ledge and
mantled him out of sight. I choked once, lost to the wind, and
then Dade's head came into view.

"Fuck meeeeeeee!" he screamed out over Wyoming. "I am a bad
man! I am a fucking monster of the earth!"

"You are, my man, you are—and you did it!" I tried to yell but I
couldn't say it right because my heart had filled my throat, beating

thankyouthankyouthankyou

thankyou thankyou thankyou

thank you   thank you   thank you

until it had dropped back into my chest, splashing down in a
sea of adrenaline.

"YOSEMITE, HERE WE come!" I said, breathless, when I arrived at
the sloping, bench-sized alcove. I clipped myself into the belay while Dade tied me off, and then reached out to shake his
bleeding hand. It was so heavy with what he'd done it felt as if I
were grabbing the rock one more time. He didn't reply, though.
His eyes were glassy, the calm after the storm, and I could smell
the bitter scent of panic that must have washed over him when
he barndoored.

"We need to re-name this whole route Dade's Workshop," I
said, sitting down next to him, our feet dangling off the unusual,
wavy granite ledge, which seemed to hold the crenellations of a
seafloor in its skin. I was psyched, partly because I'd climbed it
(on top rope, hanging twice but piecing the crux together) and
partly because he was such an animal, but I only got a thin, forced
smile out of him.

"You still want to take it to the top?" he asked flatly.

"Dude, you flashed it! Practically solo! Who else will have

flashed the hardest route at the Tower and taken it to the top? It's
. . . it's historic or something."

I slapped him on the chest just to touch him again. This gave
him an odd face, as if he had a smile laid over a frown, so that he
looked intensely proud and also terrified.

He held out both hands so I could see his fingers, which
jumped and shook like he was playing boogey-woogey piano, his
forearms still hard with their pump. "I'm bonking."

My own arms were unbelievably pumped too, and it was an
effort just to get the water bottle open and pass it to him. Then I
pulled a couple Fruit Roll-Ups and a small bag of gorp out of the
pack. Both my first index knuckles were raw, with ghost-white
flappers of skin curled away from the flesh, and I had to lick the
drops of blood away before I put my hand into the gorp bag. I
handed him the bag but he took a roll-up instead, peeling a ty-
rannosaurus off the backing before biting its head off. I wanted
to talk about the killer crux section where the rock felt like it had
been cut with a great scalpel the exact width of my fingertips,
forcing wild tensioning and insane footwork—but he cut me off
just as I was about to speak.

"I'm never doing this again," he whispered to himself, and then,
loudly, to me: "I'm a fucking idiot. If Bev could have seen me just
now, she would have died from fright—or divorced me. I've convinced her that I never get into trouble. That I'm always safe. That
I'll always be there for our kids . . . and I almost took the way-
whip again—just like on Son of Sam. I'm oh for two right now."

I started to protest, but he slapped the ledge we were on and
said, "I almost popped on this last, easy mantle move."

"You've always said that if you didn't fall, you weren't pushing
hard enough."

"On sporty clip-ups, not death falls! Christ, what are you think-ing? I couldn't get any gear in."

"It's just that I can't believe you did it! That I could even follow it . . ."

"After that barndoor, believe you me, you would have had enough juice to follow it," he said, taking a swig from the water bottle and handing it to me. "And you'd be just as mad at yourself."

I went to take a sip and froze when I saw a thin snake of blood from his cracked lips swelling in the water, diffusing until it mag-ically disappeared. Then, too parched to care, I took a swallow and stared out into sky.

Could I have done it? I *had* known exactly what to do—even the weird crossover undercling—my hands going left, right, right-right-left, while my feet did an intense, slow-motion rumba be-neath me. And it wasn't just from having seen Dade do it, either, because I was too consumed "helping" him up the rope and had no real idea what moves he'd made. I'd had a top-rope, it's true, but I was also carrying the weight of the pack with our rappel rope in it, which made it even harder. Plus, on the sharp end I'd have had a little more incentive.

Of course, I might have just panicked, gotten dizzy with ver-tigo, fumbled the gear, and fainted myself right off the rock to splatter on one of those washing machine–sized boulders. Now I'd never know.

The wind, made up of fingers of different temperatures, pulled at the rope and then my shirt, finally deciding on a wrapper from one of the Fruit Roll-Ups, which it snatched and pulled straight out from the Tower.

As I watched it flutter downward, I felt something whip past my head. I jerked back, thinking it was a rock, just in time to see the blurry trail of a second something rocket past.

Swallows.

We both leaned out to watch them go, crying to each other as they ripped mad patterns through the air, arcing out of sight but returning immediately to shoot straight up to the top of the Tower—an ascent that would take us another half hour. Way up in the sky, they seemed to disappear into each other, but then they grew larger until they spun past us, joined like a pair of wind-tossed oak seeds, chirring wildly for the several seconds of their mate. Just as they reached the ledge at the top of pitch two, they burst apart and shot back up past us again, still screaming with their anger or lust or whatever they scream about.

"Noisy little bugger-ers," I joked as another swallow whistled past, gliding sideways over vertical rock as if they were flying horizontally over the earth.

Dade mumbled something I didn't catch. Then, for no reason, the world fragmented into a shard of wind, a sliver of raisin scent, a hollow of pain on the shoelace where I caught my knuckle. A pang for Olive. These sensory snapshots were interspliced with lightning images of my feet hanging below me, blood at my knuckles, a drop of white chalk on rock. Each snapshot was disparate, each one a hard fact from a world that had been torn apart, and then I felt the shards begin to weave themselves together until they had sped back up into the normal flow to leave me sitting in the broad, blue sky.

"My glasses are killing me," Dade said then, pinching the bridge of his nose. "If you want to top this out, we'd better get moving."

I re-racked the gear and set off. The short final pitch was easy, but chossy, and I slowly worked my way up a series of blocky steps, placing long runners at each piece of gear. Near the top of the pitch, the swallows long gone, things got really ugly, with lots of loose, bread loaf–sized rocks all over the place, caught in their moment (geologically speaking) when they were no longer quite part of the Tower, but also not yet one of its eroded remnants at the base. I moved carefully there, but a hold broke away in my hand anyway and fell, bouncing once off a ledge to become a deadly missile.

"Rock!" I yelled down to Dade—like I had days before from the house roof, when I almost hit him with that sheet of plywood.

There was total silence, and then I heard Dade yell "Rock!" too, to warn anyone who might have been beneath him. In the last ten feet I had to trundle some smaller rocks too—knocking them off in a controlled way instead of just letting them fall—and yelled "Trundling!" and "Rock!" and "Sorry!" each time.

Dade started to yell "Fuck" and "Be careful" to me, though there was nothing I could do, since even the movement of the rope was sweeping bits off.

"It's terrible up here," I yelled when I got to the last set of anchor chains, set into the topmost, vertical edge of the Tower, about ten feet from the top. The rock and even the chains were covered in pigeon and vulture guano, and though I just wanted to top out I knew it would create too much drag on the rope to pull it over the last, blocky section of the route, so I set up my belay there. It took Dade a while to get started, and after loosening my shoes with one hand, I stared out toward the north. I'd heard that on a good day you can see all the way into Montana from that side, but there are quite a few hills in between, and it could be just a myth.

"Can you really see Montana from here?" I asked Dade when he reached me, but he ignored the question and simply grunted out a "Yuck."

"I know—just keep going," I said. He had to climb over me and place a hand on my shoulder as he moved past. I belayed him until he was out of sight on the summit, and then broke down the belay and followed him.

Up on the rough, rocky prairie top, the altitude at which small planes fly, the wind came gusting from the west, filled with the sweet smells of sage and scrub brush and gravel. I'd been up there plenty of times—even saw a small rattlesnake swollen with prey once, lazing in the sun—but this day all I saw was the rope strung out ahead of me. I followed it over a hillock and past some small boulders to find Dade splayed out on his back on a big, flat spot, untied from the rope with his shoes off.

I sat down next to him, unclipped the water bottle from his harness, and took a sip, then brushed some gravel out of the way and lay back with my hands over my head. But as soon as I lay back, Dade stood up and said, "Let's sign the register and get out of here."

As he walked away, I groaned, picked up the other end of the rope, and started to coil it, my exhausted arms spread out cruciform as I made each loop, counting them off to myself. As I neared the end of the coil—24, 25, 26—I saw my first vulture of the day float up above the Tower near where the route had topped out, its wingspan almost as wide as mine, rising over and then behind me to briefly screen the sun. It eyed me over its long beak and then turned away to fight a confluence of winds at the edge of the Tower. Its primary feathers, translucent at their tips, bent and shifted like cattails down in the Belle Fourche over a thousand feet below us; then it angled its wings slightly and wheeled out of sight.

When I caught up to Dade, he was sitting cross-legged next to the summit cairn with the register pulled out of its heavy steel canister.

"Did you see the turkey vulture?" I asked, squatting down beside him.

He had just finished writing in the notebook and handed it to me, standing up and shaking his head *no* at the same time. I turned the book around to read what he'd written: "Devil's Workshop, Spanish Prisoner—FREE. The Monster from Minnesota and Atlas holding up the world."

I crossed out "Devil's," wrote in "Dade's," and added "Dade Eleutherios, On-sight Spanish Prisoner." Then I wrote down the coordinates for the Tower that I'd read in the rangers' station that morning, as if to pin us down for once on this spinning earth:

44° 35' N/104° 42' W

5,117 ASL

As I started to shut the book I noticed the last entry from the day before, from "Collin from Fort Collins." He'd topped out on McCarthy West Face and wrote, "The thought is one thing, the deed another, the image of the deed yet another still; the wheel of causality does not roll between them. F.N." I'd seen the same quote written on the bathroom wall that morning and had wondered about it.

"What the hell is that supposed to mean?" I asked Dade, but he was already out of earshot, walking to the rappel station. Over to the west there were a dozen more vultures riding early thermals, and I yelled to Dade, pointing at them and wishing I could just spread some wings and float back down to the campground. I said as much to him at the rap anchors, just as he tossed one coiled rope out into space, but when he held his hand out for the second rope it was as if he were looking right through me.

CHAPTER TWELVE

We were back in the campground by three o'clock, both of us so worn out that we crawled into the Rig and lay down. I wanted to sleep, but was somehow too wound up, and stared out at the cottonwood leaves flipping back and forth in the light breeze. The campground is a simple place, broad and open in a way the Needles' camping spots aren't. Huge cottonwoods—the ones that are still standing—stretch out of the prairie grass and into the sky as if luxuriating with the sheer size of it. Beyond them winds the Belle Fourche river, whose workman-like flow comes to a crawl as it curves around the Tower—as if pausing to take in the sights—and then continues eastward with greater urgency to swing wide around the Black Hills and finally join the Cheyenne River in South Dakota.

I'd been to the Tower nine times. One of my visits had been during high school, while I was with Ursula, when I'd first started climbing; six visits when I was at the U, while dating a couple other women; two while I was with poor Olive. And then this time, when I was with Ruby. Well, when I was sort of with Ruby—and sort of alone. It's like I'd been doing laps over Wyoming, I thought, but with each lap I'd barely changed at all, while my women changed like the seasons. Then I felt the inverse of that: what if I was frozen in space, always locked in the exact same co-ordinates in some objective universe? I was the needle of a record while the world spun flat beneath me, playing out my life as I slowly spiraled toward the end.

Somehow these thoughts didn't help me fall asleep, and I finally gave up and tried to do something Dade says he always does—mentally re-climb the route we'd just done to try and learn from it. I replayed the crux moves from Spanish Prisoner and also, because it had felt so good, my run-out to reach the tree on the pitch below it. On the second time through it, though, I became fixated on the ledge at the top, the one with the rippled seafloor pattern I'd never seen in granite before. It felt like a limestone erratic, but then it was definitely granite. I found myself wondering, from inside the canvas walls of the poptop, if its sheared cast were down below in the talus field—and if I'd scrambled over it on the approach without realizing it. What was its fall like? After ten million years of slow weathering, of water freezing and wedging it apart, there were two or three seconds of simple free fall—a nothing in time—witnessed by the wind and maybe an ancient antelope or some soaring bird, then ten million more dull years again before I crawled over it. I thought about this block falling and then fell into sleep myself, though I didn't remember it all.

When I woke up, it was very slowly, and I had the numbing sense that my tongue and skin and eyes had been hammered flat, my whole body aching from the exertion on the wall. But I was incredibly calm, with no stress from thinking about Olive or Ruby, and that made me wonder what I'd dreamed—or if my calm came from not dreaming at all.

With my eyes still closed, I could sense that the canvas sides of the poptop were seething in and out with the hot winds, as if the Rig were slowly breathing in the afternoon air of the campground.

But it wasn't the canvas top that was seething—the air was too still for that. I realized that I was seeing, through my eyelids, something dilating, then contracting, from light to dark. As if the sky itself were pulsing. I opened my eyes and lost track of it, but when I closed them again, the pulsing returned, with about one cycle for every six heartbeats, and I realized it was all happening on the inside of my eyelids. Or even my optic nerve. After a while, as I came fully into waking, the pulsing seemed to skip beats, then fade, and then stop completely. Weird.

I lowered my head into the opening, looking for Dade, and saw him sitting outside at the picnic table, writing in the *Rig Veda*. From my perspective he was hanging off the bottom of the planet like a stalactite, the trees and picnic table sucked up tight. Just like me.

I slipped "downstairs," my body so sluggish that I almost crumpled, and then half-stepped, half-fell out of the Rig. It was cooler outside and even cooler at the picnic table in the shade. I sat down across from Dade and yawned, the world upright again.

Dade flipped the pages of his book once, then started working on it again. I realized he was drawing and craned my neck to see what it was, but he's left-handed and his wrist blocked my view. My hands were so thick from the climbing that I couldn't have held a pencil if I'd wanted to.

"What are you—"

"The crux of Spanish Prisoner," he said, annoyed for some reason, holding up the *Rig Veda* and then flipping the pages, as if to cut to the chase about all the questions I was going to ask.

Dade had boxed off the bottom right corner of every free page in the book and started drawing an animation of the climb, beginning with his barn door and the dropping of the cam, culminating in his body moving through the crux, his hands going left-right, right-right-left, while his feet did that slow-motion rumba beneath him, just like I remembered my own hands and feet doing.

"That's pretty great," I said. "Can I look at it?" I held out my hand so I could flip it myself, but he closed the book.

"It's not finished," he said. "And anyway, I need to go down to the store to get some ice."

"Dade, wait—can we talk? You're acting all bitchy, but you did an amazing thing today. That was your hardest on-sight ever."

"And probably my last," he said, peering at me through his dirty glasses. He looked like he'd aged ten years since his manic singing of John Denver that morning.

"Not if you flash the crux pitch on Seven Seas," I said, trying to encourage him.

He got up from the table and then gestured dismissively at his chest. "You ever hear that mice and elephants have the same average number of heartbeats before they die? That there's a limit? Just over a billion?"

I nodded. I knew it because he had told me at least twice before.

"Same with engines," he said, pointing at *Makin' Bacon*. "And generators. My gas generator is rated at two thousand hours, at full capacity. You go over full capacity, drive the engine at six thousand RPM all the time, and you wear it out faster . . . you know what I'm saying?"

"But you also told me that humans are the only mammal that the heartbeat equation doesn't hold true for—that we should die at thirty-three or something but we live way longer."

He nodded, taking in a big breath as if preparing to dade-uct against me, but then he just blew the breath out, climbing into the van before asking me if I was coming with him to the store.

I dropped the poptop and we drove out through the camp-ground, the late afternoon air full of tents and camping gear but strangely devoid of people, the hum of the engine somehow making that feeling of flatness that I'd woken up with even more intense. Then we curved our way down the asphalt to the general store just outside the entrance kiosk. They have lots of tourist junk for sale there, with chefs' aprons that say things like "Cut the Bull" and "Give the Cook a Goose" and shot glasses with images of both the Tower and a Harley Davidson logo on them, but they also sell ice cream and milkshakes and beer. I bought a quart of chocolate milk and a bag of ice while Dade called Bev from the shade of the store's front porch, then walked back to the Rig and, after dumping out some of the melt water from our cooler, poured the ice in. I sunk my hands into the freezing water (the questionable half-and-half and tub of cream cheese floating in there with them). Just to take my mind off the pain, I tried to replay the moves from Spanish Prisoner again, in case I got the chance to redpoint it myself, but I discovered that Dade was standing behind me before I could really get going.

"Bev can't talk right now. I'm heading into the store," he said flatly.

"Wait," I said, drying my hands off on my pants. "Let me borrow your phone."

Neither of us said anything about Team Luddite or how we weren't supposed to be using it now, and he just handed it over. I took the receipt with Ruby's phone number out of my wallet and stared at the enormous numbers for a while, then turned on the cell and started to dial—only to find myself calling Olive. All of a sudden the afternoon wasn't flat or dull anymore: it was tall as the Tower, as sharp as the vicious edges of Spanish Prisoner. It rang once, abruptly, and then, with equal abruptness, Olive picked up.

"Atlas?"

"I'm sorry, Olive. I dialed automatically." I was weirdly relieved to be talking to her. I was also incredibly calm—no feeling of dizziness anywhere—as if there had been some holdover from the calm pulsing I'd woken up with.

"I don't even know why I answered . . . it's worthless. You've ruined me," she said.

"Ruined you? What do you mean?"

"I don't know . . . why did this happen? Why can't we talk it out?"

I thought about what Dade had said—"Right for each other but not right now"—but I still wasn't sure how much timing had to do with it. Instead I said, "It isn't right for me—and it really isn't right for you."

She let out a strange laugh, almost like a moan, and then said, "I don't think that's true."

"There's . . . I don't know how to say it, but it's like there's a little edge that's missing. Some . . . *thing*. We don't have it."

"We have it," she said defiantly. "You're just denying it, and I don't understand why."

"I'm not, really," I said, shaking my head. Or was I? Suddenly it was so complicated.

"I wish we could do this face to face," she said. Then she sighed. "Remember that time coming back from the North Shore? We almost hit a deer that night. You swerved and missed it somehow and we ended up in the sumac . . . the smell of it. You put your finger on my lips—and that was IT, wasn't it? That was IT and we were right for each other! God damn it!" She started crying.

I started crying too. I was sitting in the doorway of the Rig in Wyoming, but I could smell the sumac. That *was* it. We *were* right.

"Yes," I said.

"Then what's happened?"

I didn't know.

"You said you loved me. Did you?"

"Yes."

"And now you don't?"

"I don't know," I thought. It was so different with Ruby. She lit my imagination a little like Son of Sam had. I wanted her— but I didn't know exactly why. With Olive, right in that moment, though, I knew that there was something else, something deeper and different. But I couldn't say it. I couldn't say anything; it would give too much false hope to her. And maybe to me. Suddenly I regretted everything, all the dominos back to that first one when Dade had called about Yosemite, including the one that was running into Ruby. Everything except that I'd started having different dreams again. And what happened on Mudskipper.

"I never had any dreams when I was with you—except for the one," I said. "Why was that?"

"Because you felt trapped," she said without hesitating, as if she'd analyzed it long ago. "Unable to decide."

"Maybe. Maybe it was something else . . . I've started to dream again."

There was a long pause, then: "Do you think it was about you falling out of love with me?" she asked, her tears clearing a little.

"I don't know . . . I don't think so," I said. "But I think it's something important. And what I'm doing now is important."

"Are you with her now?"

"No. I haven't seen her since before I told you."

"Are you going to see her again?"

"I don't know," I said honestly. "It depends on where they climb—and how Dade is."

I told her about Dade's almost-fall, relieved at first not to be talking about me and Olive, but telling someone else about it made me realize how close it had really been. Suddenly I was appalled with myself for making him top out after the third pitch.

She sighed. "And every time I think that it might be you."

I didn't know if she was talking about me getting hurt climbing, or about me being her partner.

"All I ever wanted was for you to be happy with me," she said after another long pause.

"Olive, that's not true. You were hell bent on your school, on getting the perfect job and the perfect career."

"So?! That didn't have to exclude you."

"*But it did!*" I almost said, but that would have started up a whole other argument, so I kept my mouth shut. Instead I blew out a big breath of air.

"Just let me know before you go up on a big wall. And when you get down," she said. I'd always done that in the past. Big wall climbs always scared her.

"Olive, it'll just make it worse—"

"Just . . . I need to know you're okay for a while."

"All right," I said. Then she was off the phone and I realized that I hadn't even found out how Eeney Meaney was doing, or if Miney Mo ever showed up. But then, maybe I didn't deserve to know those things anymore, either.

What I realized, though, picking up my milk and walking back to the Rig, was that I had stayed completely calm through the whole conversation. No dizziness at all. Was it because now I was free of Olive, or was it something simpler? Something I'd taken away with me from Mudskipper, from making love with Ruby—or even that pulsing I'd just woken up with, the leftover of some unremembered dream?

Maybe it was a little bit of each of these things. Each time I put my hand in the monkey trap, even though I couldn't steal the prize, I made the hole a little bit bigger—and a little bit of its scent rubbed off on my hand.

CHAPTER THIRTEEN

The next morning I woke up just after dawn, my body so sore I couldn't find a side that was comfortable. Again I could see something pulsing behind my eyelids, and I focused on it while the day lightened up. *I should write something down about this pulsing,* I thought, along with all the other stuff that had happened in the last few days, including that quote from the register: "The thought is one thing, the deed another . . ." The one that I'd also read in the bathroom. But when I picked up a pen to write, I found my fingers about as light and flexible as lead pipe. I started stretching them out and then heard a strange sound at the side of the Rig, like the snort of a baby buffalo. Then I heard it again.

I craned myself around as well as I could to look out the screen—I could see the tiny Chevy Metro from Carolina with a bright blue tent set up behind it.

Then I heard a weird, faux-deep voice say, "Knock, knock."

I shot up: "Ruby?"

"Hey neighbor, you have any sugar for me?" she asked, still with a false bass. Then she laughed.

I pressed my face hard against the screen, trying to look down at the side of the Rig, but I could only make out her black hair until she stepped back. She was swaying a cup of coffee back and forth, as if to lure me out.

"You came," I whispered. For one brief moment I was disappointed to see her, as if I weren't ready for her yet, and I was as surprised by that reaction as I'd been the afternoon before when I'd dialed Olive's number.

"We got in around midnight and I didn't want to wake you," she said. "But this morning I couldn't wait any longer. Sorry."

"I was awake anyway, trying to write in my . . . my climbing log," I said. I held the notebook up to show it to her through the screen.

"Well, come on down here and get some coffee," she said, waving her cup again.

I watched her walk over to the picnic table, thinking about how my women problem had flip-flopped, though the problem was still the same: how to tell one person about the other, about something bad I had done or had to do. I wasn't dizzy or swooning, but then I didn't feel good, either, and I counted out five breaths to get myself in sync before I climbed down from my bed. Maybe the breathing helped: when she took me in her arms, my nose buried in her thick hair, my feeling of not being ready left me as quickly as it had come.

"I'm so glad you made it," I said, squeezing her tighter, and then, trying to sound casual, "What's with the Carolina boys?"

I was pretty surprised she'd brought them along, but then I'd never told her about our run-in with them at Son of Sam.

"We kind of caravanned it with them from the Needles," she said quietly, leaning her head towards their tent. "Fran assumed it would be all right that they camped here, since nothing else was open. They're a riot."

"Yeah, a laugh a minute—we met them in the Rushmore area. So how long can you stay?"

"A couple days, then we have to head straight to San Francisco for the convention. Fran can't climb at all right now. She tweaked her shoulder training yesterday and might be out for a week. So I'm a *loba sola* . . . wanna climb today?"

I groaned and held up my fat fingers as proof that I needed a rest day. I told her about Dade's triumph on Spanish Prisoner, that I'd done the moves too and wanted to go back and redpoint it. I must have unconsciously touched the whirligig hanging around my neck as I talked, because she reached up and pulled it out from my shirt to finger it.

"I got it in Hill City," I said, lifting it over my head and spinning it for her. The fish was in the bowl at first, and then came out of it as the whirligig slowed down.

"I had a coin like that once, with a hole in either end," she said, clapping her hands on it to stop it. She caught it with the bowl side up.

"Here—let's flip for whether you climb with me today or not," she said. "Heads—that'd be the bowl—and you head out with me. And if it's tails—"

"I get some tail?"

She laughed and slapped my arm, and then nodded sharply, fake-spitting into her hand to shake on it with me.

I spun it, holding the string horizontal in front of me, and she clapped her hands on it to show which side it "landed" on: tails. Without missing a beat she said, "Best of three, right?"

She made me spin it again and slapped it to a stop, then lifted her right hand to see what luck had brought her.

"TWO *COILS* OF rope," said Ruby as we reached the base of her route, Even Cowgirls Get the Blues. "Three *slabs* of rock."

"What are you talking about?"

"I just realized that climbing has all these measure words— more than regular English."

"A *rack* of gear," I offered.

"That's a good one, but I think that's a collective noun. Measure words are for counting individual things . . . like 'two *books* of matches.' Collective nouns are for groups of things—the famous one is a 'murder of crows.'"

We had just crossed the area below the Meadows under the south face of the Tower, a zone sometimes called the Bowling Alley because so many rocks get knocked off from the loose, grassy slope above to carom down the granite lanes. Partly because of what had happened on the last pitch of Devil's Workshop the day before, and partly because I was with Ruby and wanted to keep *her* safe, we were both wearing our helmets.

"So we have a 'hassle of helmets,'" I said, flaking the rope for her, trying to get into the spirit of things. "A 'load of Luddites.'"

"Right, and I'm living in a 'ship of fools' right now—no, a 'fracas of Frans.'"

"A 'fracas of Frans'?"

"She's been driving me nuts with all her karmas and chakras. And dogmas."

I wanted to hear some more about that—some flat-out gossip—but Ruby's easy mood evaporated as soon as she tied into her rope. It was like a light bulb had gone out in her.

"Come on—this is a perfect crack for you to get used to the Tower," I said, trying to get her psyched. "Solid, small hands and good gear all the way."

She sighed, then looked over the gear on her rack for the third time. There were fear and angry determination in her face, which had the effect of winching her eyebrows together.

"Climbing," she finally sighed, as if resigned to a walk to the gallows.

She placed a small cam, worked herself about ten feet up to a little ledge where she shook her arms out, and then started to fumble around, fitting in another cam when a big nut would have been bomber.

"Whew," she said after finally clipping it, looking down at me from fifteen feet above, "I'm getting pumped already."

"Only 135 feet to go," I said, smiling, but she didn't like the joke and looked away.

There were other climbers off to our left, hollering about something, and as I looked over the leader took a short, five-foot fall. He was okay, but he cursed the rock and the route and himself violently as he hauled himself up to his top piece.

"Nothing to see here, folks," I joked again, trying to keep Ruby on task, but she was clearly rattled—although she kept saying, "Okay–go," to herself, she didn't move at all.

"This is what happened yesterday, when Fran got so mad at me and had to go off bouldering and hurt herself," she finally said, looking down at me. "I froze."

"Maybe you should come down for a minute and shake out."

"Yeah, okay. Lower me," she said, relieved.

"Why don't you downclimb—it won't be an on-sight if you lower," I said, afraid she'd lose all her gumption if she hung on the rope.

"A 'Goldberg of wimps,'" she said when she finally stepped down next to me.

"Just three days ago I froze on a route that was easy for me. You're doing good, just take a rest."

She leaned out to see the climber who'd just fallen, hanging on his high piece; then she jerked slack from the rope so she could sit down.

"What do you think? Will you be pissed if I bag this?"

I held up my hands again, the joints taped up to protect my wounds from Spanish Prisoner, as my answer.

She blew out a big breath, smacking her thigh in frustration: "This is so wimpy–I never keep my psyche going on trad routes . . ."

I was about to say something pat about getting psyched, about sucking it up, but then, looking at her sweet face, I had a vision of us making love back in the buffalo field. When we were making love, it was all I was "doing" in the world, all I *wanted* to be doing, and those things had merged into one glorious . . . something. Suddenly it dawned on me that maybe I had been in my rockhead while making love to her and hadn't even recognized it. My thoughts and my voice rushed into each other.

"Get myopic," I said, holding my fingers in Dade's V. "Re-focus. You don't really want to be here right now . . . you want the route over with because you're afraid, or because you want to tell Fran you did it and that you're not being 'wimpy,' or because . . . because whatever. But you need to get myopic on it."

She looked at me like I was speaking Hungarian.

"You just have to focus on it as hard as you can. You have to want to be there, like when . . ."

I wanted to say, "Like when we made love." Like when all our softs and hards and wets and meltings came together and there was nothing else in the world but us locked in for the ride. *Climbing is like that,* I thought—*well, just like that except with climbing it's also like there's someone screaming at you over the barrel of a shotgun to "stay calm" and "don't panic."*

It's about letting the thing be the thing, I finally thought. And then I said it.

"What? The thing's-the-thing?" She was frowning.

I reached into the air before me, as if I could pull an example from it, but it was impossible to show or say and I ended up strangling an imaginary chicken. No wonder Dade never wanted to talk about this stuff.

"I sort of know what you're getting at," she said, all serious, craning her neck up to look the route over once more. "But I need some external impetus, like . . . if I fall on this I'll have to sherpa for you in the valley. That's my bet."

"I don't want to bet you—this is too dangerous for that. I just want you to not get hurt."

"No, I need the bet. Just to get me to the ledge. Once I'm there, I'll be too high up to want to come down. It'll focus me. And if I don't fall, let's see . . . you'll have to change the oil on *Old Yeller*. The pan nut head is stripped."

"Okay. I hope you fall."

She stuck her tongue out at me, then climbed like a stud up to her high piece—way better than I usually do when I have to regroup—and continued that psyche for the next hundred feet, when she abruptly headed off-route.

"Keep to the crack," I yelled as she clipped the belay anchor for Dude Ranch—the route that ran next to us. The anchor was maybe six feet right, only ten feet above her last piece. It would make for some heinous rope drag.

Ruby looked down at me, unsure; then, instead of unclipping from the anchor, she extended the sling and sideshuffled back to the crack, creating a big zigzag in the rope. About ten feet higher, she started to get into trouble.

She yelled "Slack!" thinking that I wasn't feeding her rope, but I held up a shallow loop to show that she had plenty. She had to reach down between her legs and pull up enough slack for every move she made, wrenching it up to her teeth each time, her arm muscles flexed to fight the incredible friction she'd generated by clipping that bolt.

"Slack!" she yelled again, and suddenly I got a flutter in my stomach. Without time to think, I did the opposite of what she asked, locking down the rope just as she pulled herself right out of the crack.

Before I even had a chance to worry about it, Ruby had fallen twenty feet, landing so hard it jerked me up and smacked my helmet against the rock. When I finally looked up I had the weird sensation that I'd seen her fall and land at the same time. But she was hanging on the rope, and I had caught her.

"You okay?!" I yelled up at her.

She looked at her right forearm, then held it out to me, and even from a hundred feet away I could see the blood. I snapped into go-mode, already figuring out how to lower her off and how to tear my shirt to bind what might be a compound fracture in her forearm. I knew completely that I wanted her in my life and didn't want to lose her to this . . . this shit. Within seconds I was bargaining with the climbing gods: "I'll give up everything if she's okay, I'll never climb again," I promised, and then her weight was off the rope and she was back on the rock.

"I'm going to climb back up, okay?"

"What?!"

"I just scraped my arm. I'll finish the route."

"You sure?" I asked, but Ruby had started climbing back up and there was no answer. I hadn't lost her: the muscles in her bicep, her sharp spirit, her attempts to make fun of me. Decades of love.

When she reached the height of that off-route bolt she tensioned over to unclip the sling, and then she finished the last thirty feet of the pitch. On top, finally clipped into a hanging belay, she let out a "Whoo-hoo!" that rivaled the one Dade made at the top of Spanish Prisoner. The climber off to our left, who we'd seen fall earlier, was still down working the crux of his route, but he let out a "Whoop!" for Ruby too. Twenty minutes later, when I finally reached her at the belay, Ruby was beaming.

"Nice job!" I said after I'd clipped in, shaking her hand with two good pumps, and although she brushed this off, rolling her eyes at the scrape on her arm, she was also grinning with pride, her sweet, crooked tooth making her look even sweeter.

"I should have downclimbed at my next piece to unclip the bolt. I made an easy route hard."

"And then did the hard route."

"With a fall . . ."

"You were burly and stayed on track. Better than I would have done after a fall like that." And something that Olive could never even understand, I reminded myself.

This time Ruby just shrugged, looking at her arm, which had started bleeding again.

"I'm a mess, huh?"

"You look beautiful," I said. "Good enough to sherpa for me."

All of a sudden I was intensely proud of her, my feelings for her expanding. Hanging there alongside her, the sides of our hips pressed into each other, I slid my hand behind her helmet, grasping her hair so that she couldn't look anywhere else but into my eyes. Then, with my mouth as light a moth wing, I kissed her lips.

She pulled my hand away roughly, no longer beaming, and then took off the gear sling and handed it to me, clearly pissed off. I'd ruined her moment somehow and, because I didn't know how to repair it, not even sure what to apologize for, I started to re-rack the nuts and cams, both of us silent until she saw that I was ready to go.

"You're on," she said.

I unclipped from the anchors and started to climb, but in the slightly overhung corner I was forced to clamber over her, straddling her for a few awkward moments as I got off the belay.

"Sorry," I said after I almost sat on her helmet. Then I did sit on it, lightly: "I think I have to re-rack my nuts."

She wouldn't even laugh and pushed me off her.

Five feet up I looked back down at her. "I'm sorry for whatever I did."

"It's not . . . let's just talk about it later."

"I'm just so proud of you for thugging it out."

Her helmet moved, so I guessed she'd nodded, but she didn't say anything and I started up the off-hands crack. It was hot and a strong wind had picked up, which seemed to break apart the cloud cover that had dogged us all morning. I had been thinking of telling her about Olive after the climb, about how there had been "overlap," but now I needed to pull myself out of the frying pan—to catch a breath—before I dropped myself into the fire.

I climbed slowly but easily after my warm-up on Ruby's pitch. Just as I reached the top of the route I heard a distant yell; then, on another gust of wind, the names of animals and people being called out for a rodeo, which must have been starting up at the small arena just outside the monument. I could hear the names perfectly in the wind, though the rodeo must have been more than a mile away as the buzzard flies. I seemed to smell manure on the wind too, along with alfalfa; then the wind changed direction and I could only smell rock and chalk and sweat and the musty scent of dead pill bugs from deep inside the seam I was working. And then, after all those smells, I seemed to smell Olive—her hair—though I didn't know why, since these smells were nothing like its sweet, fatty scent.

It made me wonder about something Dade had read to me from a science magazine as we made one of our several "cooldown" stops on the way to Custer. Researchers found that if they gave three words in certain pairs to American test subjects, they could get certain associations out of them. Their example was with the words "Sansabelt," "Florida," and "plastic." "Sansabelt" and "Florida" made the subjects think of elderly people, while "Florida" and "plastic" made them think of the beach, and "Sansabelt" and "plastic" made them think of "tacky."

What was it that made me think of Olive? Certainly not dead pill bugs and sweat. Maybe just achy pain and sadness. Or maybe the musty smell just reminded me of my tent, which reminded me of Olive. Or maybe, like that old classic rock song that seemed to be in my head all the time, she was just circling round and round at another layer of thoughts, ready to pop up when there was nothing else in my mind—like at the store the day before when my mind went blank and I was dialing her number. Or maybe it was more complicated than that. Or less complicated. That is, more or less complicated.

I was left hanging at the belay, the wind playing with my hair and my shirt. Ruby was yelling something up to me, something about being ready, and so I pulled a bight into the belay plate and got ready for her to come up into the sky.

CHAPTER FOURTEEN

It felt like the set for a surfer movie back at the campground. Red was manning the grill, cooking up bratwurst and banging his head in time with the vintage Jane's Addiction blaring out of the Chevy Metro, standing in the ankle-deep water of a blow-up kiddy pool, while Fran stood on the edge of the picnic table with her sarong tied high between her legs, directing Dade and Luther in some strange activity that involved positioning head-sized rocks in a kind of compass rose. We parked in front of the Rig and got out. Or rather, I got out; Ruby popped out of the truck like a super ball and bounced over to the picnic table to tell Fran all about her success—and to get away from me, it seemed.

We'd barely spoken since I'd kissed her, and as we drove down to the campground I came up with my own explanation of what had happened: Ruby was proud of her triumph, and by kissing her I had somehow taken this triumph away from her, as if I were trying to make it "our" triumph—something I hadn't felt at all. I decided to just let things calm down before I talked to her about it, and went over to Dade to find out how he'd maintained the truce between him and Fran and what the boys from North Carolina were doing there.

"We got a regular Beach Blanket Brady Bunch going on here," I said, watching as he rolled a rock into the eight-foot circle.

"We're making a 'Wheel of Causality' for Fran, since she can't move the rocks around too well."

"Wheel of Causality? Like the quote from the register?"

"Well . . . that's just what I'm calling it. She called it the 'Peace Circle.'"

"Five minutes to eat!" Red yelled over the Jane's Addiction then, stepping out of the kiddy pool to grab some buns.

I froze, saying nothing for a while as Perry Farrell trembled over the thick air:

I was made with a heart of stone, to be broken with one hard blow, I've seen the ocean break on the shore, come together with no harm done.

It ain't easy livin', I want to be, as deep as the ocean, mother ocean, yeah.

I made sure no one could hear me, looking first at Ruby, who was replaying her fall for Fran, then at Luther, who was over in a neighboring campsite looking for another rock, and asked Dade, "What's with the cats and dogs living together?"

Dade stopped rolling the rock around and stood up to look at me. "I had a long talk with Fran today about how we'd gotten off on the wrong foot—my wrong foot in my big fat mouth."

"And the *All-y'alls?*"

"Red apologized this morning, after you'd left."

"They found out you flashed Spanish Prisoner, huh?"

"Yeah . . . that's why they're cooking dinner—to fete me."

"To *fete* you? They just know your *Minnesooodan* ass is going to be in the climbing mags."

He stood up, shaking his head: "Maybe they needed a way to apologize for being eighteen, and this was the only way they knew how. I was worse than them at that age, strutting around with my Golden Gloves wins—something you've never had to learn to deal with."

Before I could respond to that last dig, Dade said quickly,

"Anyway, Bev keeps telling me I should try to do things for the right reason."

"You were about ready to beat him down in the cave five days ago—just for making fun of me."

"Well, I wasn't trying then—and I am now," he said, grunting as he rolled the rock into its final resting place.

"And what's this all for—this 'Wheel of Causality'?" I asked, my hand dismissing the rocks.

"Fran wants to thank the Tower for letting us climb here," he said, sitting down on the rock he'd just gotten in place. "I'm pretty happy I didn't fall off it yesterday, so I figured I'd like to thank it too." He gave me his "look" then, the faintest glimmer of the boxer in it.

My heart jumped. We were lucky Dade was alive, so why was I being such a brat? I was about to blurt out an apology for making him go all the way to the top of the Tower after his Spanish Prisoner pitch, but when I tried to catch his eye again he wouldn't look at me, wandering off to find another large rock for the wheel.

I caught Ruby watching me then, and when I did manage to make eye contact with her she seemed to challenge me about something before turning away to talk to Fran, her eyes lagging behind the movement of her head.

A couple hours later, with the sun on its way down and our bellies full of brats and beer, Fran urged us with her slightly pedantic tone to take a place at the Peace Wheel. She was careful to take the north-northwestern point—so that the Tower was directly behind her—but left the rest of us to arrange ourselves however we wanted. It was a little kooky for me, this pseudo-spiritual world, and it didn't help that we were staggered around the circle as if about to start a funky, pagan version of musical chairs.

"Thanks for joining me," she said, wearing her sarong and a

strange woven wrap that looked almost like burlap. She pulled a large leather bundle out from her wrap and placed it on the ground. "Here's the deal with this ceremony—it comes from one of my exes, Roy Carlson Talking Crow, who was Lakota."

As Fran untied the leather bundle, Ruby gave me a look, her eyebrows raised, to tell me that she was even more annoyed with Fran in that moment than with me. Fran opened the leather swatch to expose a rust-red stone pipe with a black-and-white stem and long feathers tied to it.

"He won a grant to study with Roger Erickson Lame Deer, a famous Lakota pipe carver, and he carved me this pipe, though this ceremony is really my own version," Fran said.

Chanting quietly to herself, she took tobacco out of a pocket from the inside of her wrap, also held in a piece of leather, and took a few fat pinches of this with her right hand and placed them in the bowl. Next she struck a match—a bright, tiny blaze in the drifting twilight—and drew deeply as she lit the bowl, her cheekbones bright.

"By smoking this holy pipe you will walk as a living prayer. With your feet on the sacred earth and the pipe stem reaching into the sacred sky, you will become the bridge between earth and sky and all other things of the world: the plants and the animals, the rocks and the soils, the humans and their families . . ."

She handed the pipe to Red, making sure he held the bowl with his left hand; Red took it from her very carefully and even refrained from making any obvious jokes about pot. Luther and Ruby watched Red, but Dade was watching me—he spooked me a little when I saw that the fingers that rested on his knee were cast in his "myopic" V signal.

While Red smoked, Fran said, "In this state of awareness, it is important to make any other thanks that you'd like—which you can keep to yourself or share with the rest of us. I for one would like to give thanks for my 'moment' . . . for having found my path, when I realized what it is I'm supposed to do with my life."

Red looked overwhelmed—as if it were too much to ask the brain operating his long, wiry body for speech after all those brats and beer—and said, "I'll just keep it to myself."

But then, as he passed the pipe on to Dade, he spoke up anyway. "I'm thankful we didn't get hurt on Hard Day's Night yesterday. I saw my life flash before my eyes, then—swear to God. And I'm thankful for running into all y'all, for letting us camp here." He was dead sincere.

I felt for Red in that moment. Maybe Dade was right—maybe he *was* just young. Maybe he just needed to get the stuffing knocked out of him a few times and he'd come around.

"That's some scary business at the crux," I said, trying to be on his side, but Fran sent me a critical look and reminded me that this was a moment of thanks, and that we should save our side conversations for the "open discussion" later.

I blew my breath out slowly, with my eyebrows raised so Ruby could see, while Dade relit the bowl and "walked as a living prayer."

But when he was finished, he just sat there.

"Please pass the pipe along when you're finished," Fran said.

Dade smiled at her briefly, a smile most terrible, and then, reaching up to touch his wedding ring, said, "I realized yesterday that there is a luck clock somewhere with my name on it, counting down or running out, and that getting to my rockhead can't free me from it . . . but I'm thankful for not falling yesterday, thankful that Atlas was belaying me . . . thankful for my wife and our coming baby. A year ago I didn't know what I wanted, what my 'path' in life was, but now, it's like I know exactly who I am and how I should live out my life. Right now, more than any other point in my life, things branch in multiple directions—even what the rockhead means for me. But then it's like that quote too . . . 'the image of the deed'. . . I don't know what it will be until I'm in it, I just know that I'm on the cusp of it."

He stood up then, handed the pipe and matches to Ruby, and walked away from the circle and into the cottonwoods.

Fran looked concerned as Dade walked away, but then said, "Well, you're not really supposed to leave during the ceremony, but I guess it's all right. This process can be upsetting for some people."

I almost got up to follow him, but Ruby smoked quickly, then paused and gave thanks for learning about "letting the thing be the thing" from me. She looked at me with an apologetic smile as she handed me the pipe, and then it was my turn.

The sky was purpling into dusk, but there was just enough light to make some of the Tower's features recognizable. I lit the pipe and smoked.

"I'm thankful . . . " I started to say, and then I was overcome with emotion. I *was* thankful for the plants and minerals and for the possibility of being a bridge between earth and sky—and a bridge between my thoughts and my actions. And I was thankful that Dade was alive, even though I suspected that he might be backing out of the trip. I was thankful for my years with Olive too, but felt like I had freed up something deep inside of me when I broke up with her. I was thankful for the possibility of Ruby— and also overwhelmed by the need to tell her how deeply I felt for her and about the overlap we had with Olive.

I wanted to say all of this, but everyone was waiting on me and suddenly I began to feel heavy—heavy like in the dream where I'm falling and almost reach the earth but then can't. Only the falling feeling wasn't there, just the heaviness. I was on the verge of passing out, as if from low blood pressure, but I managed to stave it off by taking a deep breath and exhaling with my head between my knees.

"Atlas? Are you okay?" Ruby asked then, her words something I could grab onto.

"I'm not much of a smoker," I stammered, sitting back up, still heavy. I had the sudden sense that I was upside down again, like when I woke up in the Rig and was hanging off the "ceiling" of the earth like a stalactite, so heavy my bonds might break and let me slip out into space. It was so disorienting that I wasn't able to look at anyone for fear of losing myself in their eyes, but I finally got enough in control of myself that I was able to say, "I'm just thankful—for everything."

Then I handed the pipe to Luther.

In the deep dark a little while later, walking toward the dead cottonwood trees with Ruby, I stopped to look up at the millions of stars. They were so rich and deep that they made it hard to even find the lesser constellations, though I could pick out Antares and Scorpius on the southern horizon. I had recovered from my "heaviness" and was almost back to normal, though I was strangely aware of our body heat and the heat radiating from the rocks and the ground, lifting off into the sky I'd almost "fallen" into earlier.

"It's cooling down," I said, almost reaching over to her.

"We need to talk," said Ruby, taking my hand to pull me toward a fallen cottonwood, its trunk bare and horizontal, about the height of a picnic table.

"I'm in a pack of trouble, huh? Or is it a *heap* of trouble?" I said when we reached the downed tree. *A heap of trouble from my pack of lies.*

She half sat, half leaned on the white wood and forced a smile.

"I'm not sure exactly what I did on the route, but I'm sorry for whatever it was," I said.

"How can you be sorry if you don't know what it was?" she asked. She sounded like she was trying to be patient.

"Because I care about you."

She laughed, but there was a bitter edge to it.

"Okay, I know I stepped on your moment—but it was just because I was so proud of you."

"It's more like you *sat* on my moment . . . but that wasn't it at all. You took something that was just about climbing and made it sexual, just like Clem always does. He can never separate our boyfriend-girlfriend thing from our climbing thing. Everything we do—I mean, did—like climbing or studying, had to be sexual too."

"So, what—you had sex all the time?"

"He wanted to . . . I didn't."

"And you didn't with me the other night?"

"God, Atlas, I'm not talking about that. I loved that, I wanted to be with you . . . it's just that climbing today, I didn't want that at all. I wanted to climb."

"I wasn't trying to get anything started."

"Then why did you kiss me? You wouldn't have kissed Dade, would you?"

I shrugged. I had kissed her because I could and because I was proud of her and because we'd just made love the other night and we hadn't kissed since. I flashed on Dade pressing our foreheads together—on my feelings for him that transcended our relationship as climbing partners and even friends. It was more complicated than she was making it out to be, but I didn't know how to explain it. I had a sudden flash that Olive would get this distinction—would allow for how complicated it was. But I wasn't dealing with Olive.

"I guess I wouldn't have kissed Dade, exactly. But I don't stop being Dade's friend—more than his friend—when we're climbing, so how can I stop being your . . . your whatever?"

She crossed her arms over her chest. "You'll have to. I want our climbing and our 'whatever' to stay separate."

"I'm not Clem, you know."

"Thank God for that . . ."

"Look, I won't ever, ever kiss you again unless you say so, okay?"

"That's not what I'm talking about."

"It seems like it is, sort of. You want our friendship to be a certain way, and I'm okay with that, and I'm okay with that because . . ."

"What?"

"Don't get mad at me, I mean, I don't know where we're going or if you even want to be with me, but our time together . . . you're so . . . I don't even know how to say it."

She stood up, her hip pushing off the cottonwood. "So *what?*"

I wanted to say it all. *So bright. So real. So yummy and gorgeous*—words that Olive had trained me to find melodramatic and saccharine. I finally threw my hands up in the air. "I don't know, so *great.*"

She grimaced: "I'm great? Like 'three out of four' stars great?"

"No, no," I said. *Beautiful, intense, amazing,* but all of them sounded stupid, none of them did justice to how I felt about her.

"It's just great being with you, and I wish we could have stayed together in the Needles—that Dade hadn't made me come here without you."

"Right—nice try," she mumbled. Then, as if trying to recover, she used her version of a Wyoming drawl again to say, "Big strong guy like you . . ." and socked me lightly in the arm.

"Listen, I'll prove it to you: We'll have a sleepover. I'll set up my tent again and I won't try to climb on you or kiss you or anything else. We'll just sleep curled up, like hibernating buffalos. Trust me."

She laughed and said, "Buffalos don't hibernate."

"Then like yaks. Really, bring your PJs and a flashlight and your scary stories. Come on."

She leaned back into me then, just breathing. After a while she turned to face me.

"Okay," she said, putting her hand on my arm and squeezing hard, "I trust you. You go get your tent set up. I'll get my sleep stuff."

She started back toward *Old Yeller*, crunching across cottonwood leaves and bark, and then, in a serious voice, she said, "You lied . . ."

I think my heart skipped a beat: "What?"

"Yaks don't hibernate, either," she said as she started to walk away, her voice suddenly light.

Then my heart sank. I had lied—and was still lying—because I still hadn't told her about Olive. I groaned and got up from the tree and started back to the campsite. The overlap was so tiny, so miniscule, I reasoned, that maybe it didn't matter in the grand scheme of things. It could come out years later, in our apartment in San Francisco when Ruby was a doctor. Olive would somehow come up, as exes always do. I would tell Ruby, over chocolate croissants from some fabulous bakery near our home, that I had known I had wanted to be with her, desperately, and just wasn't able to tell her about Olive way back then, when we'd first started. Anyway, *she* was the one to jump my bones, I'd kid with her, and since she'd been my partner for years the whole thing would barely hit the radar. Another neat package, I kidded myself—aware that that's what I'd done the other night, right before I slept with Ruby.

As I got close to the campsite and *Makin' Bacon*, I heard one of the North Carolina boys say, "Buzzard?"

I hung back. They were sitting around a fire in the charcoal grate, though it was really only embers. Red was sitting on a case of beer, and I saw the glint of a liquor bottle as it went from Luther to Dade, who must have recovered from his epiphany at the peace wheel.

"What the hell does 'buzzard' mean?" asked Red, accidentally kicking the pile of beer bottles at his feet.

"Paass aauuf," Dade repeated, over-enunciating and clearly drunk himself. He took a slug and handed the bottle back to Luther.

"'Pause out'? Like 'chill out'? Man, I can't understand your Minnesoodan accent."

"Pass auf! Pass auf! It's a German accent! It's a German word! It means to pay attention, to not get distracted. Like you should pass auf and learn how to say pass auf."

Luther chuckled at this, raising the bottle, to say "Buz-zard!"

"Buzzard!" yelled Red immediately. Then he yelled it again—really loud—for good measure.

"You guys are going to get us kicked out of here," I said, finally stepping into their circle.

"Uhtlus, my uptight boy—tell these *All-y'alls* about the 'pass auf,' they won't believe me. Come on, use it in a sentence."

"Um . . . how about 'I hope you passed auf and left at least two beers in *Makin' Bacon.*'"

"Haw," Red laughed, "that name is nasty. *Makin' Bacon.*"

"Why are you even talking about this to them?" I asked, turning to Dade.

"It's just like the living prayer thing: to walk like a living prayer.

That's what I mean when I say pass auf." He smiled at this as if it were funny.

"I haven't seen you this drunk in years," I said, vaguely disappointed in him. He never drank more than a beer at a time when he was in training. Then I corrected myself: he was almost this drunk at the supersecretbivy, when he offended Fran.

"Buzzard!" yelled Red and Luther in unison.

"Okay, say 'Buzzard' then. Same fucking difference," said Dade, saluting them with his beer: "Here's to Team Buzzard."

Red and Luther yelled "Buz-zard!" again, in response to Dade's salute, as if they had just turned saying "Buz-zard" into a drinking game. Dade raised the bottle to them and took another hit himself.

"You're all nuts. I'm going to sleep in the tent tonight."

"With the Rubes?"

I laughed, starting to walk away, "'The 'Rubes'? You should keep it down out here, I just saw the campground host's light go on."

"Wait, wait, Uhhtluuhs. Hey, come here," Dade whispered. "You keep an eye on the Ruby—she's good at vanishing acts, Fran says. She needs to be the center of it all, you know? That's why Clem keeps getting her back."

"We're sleeping together in the tent tonight."

He smacked me on the ass. "That's good, that's really good. You keep—keep thinking about her."

"I am."

"'Cause she might be a keeper," he laughed. "Finders-keepers, baby."

"Uh, right," I said, walking away.

"That's what I've been talking to you about."

I started to say that, with me, anyway, he hadn't been talking about anything lately, but then Red leaned forward with his beer and cried "Buzzard!"

"Buzzard!" cried Luther and Dade in unison, leaning in to clink bottles with him, just as the elderly campground host hobbled out of his RV, the screen door clattering shut behind him as he came down the stairs one leg at a time.

CHAPTER FIFTEEN

Ruby and I started out just spooning, fully clothed, without even a sheet in the warm Wyoming air. The moon was far from rising, and even with the millions of stars out there, there weren't enough to give us any light in the tent. Ruby was breathing deeply, as if she had already fallen asleep; I just listened and smelled her into me, glad she was in my arms. She had washed up before the ceremony and, though the scent of adrenaline and fear was gone, there was still a hint of anise and cardamom mingled with the Betadine from the bandage on her right arm. And there was something else too, something that was only her. Something *right*.

But she wasn't asleep. She caught me sniffing her and then rolled over to face me.

"That's Fran's problem with Dade; she likes the smell of him," Ruby said, her voice soft, as if our problems from earlier in the day had been forgotten.

"They had a long talk today while we were climbing," she continued. "They talked about his wife and the baby and how he's so into it. And they talked about Fran's ex too . . . and how Dade's pretty much done with this trip."

My stomach flipped. I had guessed that earlier, but it was weird to hear it from Ruby—who got it from Fran. Suddenly I was mad at Dade. And disappointed. Now that I wasn't with Olive and could go to the Valley, I'd have to find another partner who'd want to do Seven Seas—and even if I did find someone, it wouldn't be the same. It wouldn't be Team Luddite or even Team Buzzard. I might as well do some other route with someone I cared about.

"You want to do a big wall with me? Some trad route like the Nose or something to get our teeth wet? You have to sherpa for me anyway . . ."

"Me? I could barely even do Cowgirls today—and I've never aid climbed. I'm not even in your league. Plus I think you mean get our teeth *sharp*—feet get wet."

"Right, whatever . . . anyway, I think you're sandbagging me."

"Atlas, come on . . . you just said you did all the moves of Spanish Prisoner, right? Could you link them next time?"

I shrugged. "Maybe."

"Well, it's only been done by four or five people, including Dade—and not because no one's trying it."

"You're sweet," I said, entirely uncomfortable. I kissed her, then rolled onto my side, pulling her arm along with me to end the discussion. She must have been keeping herself awake by talking, because once we stopped she fell asleep in seconds like some exhausted kid.

I held the cool enamel of the whirligig between my lips for what must have been hours—late enough to see the quarter moon finally stretch across the tent door, so bright it seemed to cut the screen. I had been thinking about the day with Ruby, and the day before with Dade. But when I tried to think about Olive and how I owed her more of an explanation than I'd given her, I couldn't hang on to my thoughts. The next thing I knew, I was in the middle of a dream, oddly aware that I was dreaming.

I was back in the world of the flat, black field, and Olive was there, a gray silhouette. She was enormous, a giantess, and was making love to someone else; then I was holding her and I was a titan too. We kissed, although we were also talking to each other by passing between our lips words as hard and discrete as teeth. I felt a terrible pang of sadness and also of joy when I realized she was on top of me, making love to me, and as I began to rise and spin upward with the beginnings of my dizziness, I reached out and said her name.

"OH, AT-LAST," RUBY whispered, stilling her hips for a moment to lean over me, "You're so sweet."

I had been colossal, sinking into the dust of the flat, black field, passing discrete words to Olive through my kiss, and suddenly Olive was gone and my dizziness was gone and Ruby was there as I swam from one world to the next.

Then I was wide awake: *Olive Juice*. Had I said "Olive Juice" out loud? Did she think she heard me say *I love you*?

"So much for the hibernating yaks, huh?" she whispered in my ear, beginning to churn again. "Not that I'm complaining."

Sunrise wasn't far away, and between the purpling east and the quarter moon above the tent there was just enough light to make out her face.

"I thought we'd just be *hibernating* too," I said, holding her hips still for a moment.

"Well, you started it—sweet-talked me right out of a dead sleep."

My mind was racing. Maybe I was just trapped in Dade's Causal Cage. Maybe Ruby and I were just driven by pheromones to make love out of sleep, or to kiss on the wall, or to follow each other across the country, our bodies conjuring lust from beyond our selves.

And why was I was dreaming of making love with Olive, now that I'd finally ended things with her? But as I thought the question, I also realized the answer: because now we were tragic. It was just like it had been with Ursula; Olive and I had become tragic now that we had broken up, and so now she was more attractive to me. And if I was triggered this easily by past loves, Ruby could be too. She had totally overreacted to my kiss up on Cowgirl, but maybe she used to have to overreact with Clem just to get his attention. So her reactions to me could be old habits from Clem or other lovers or even her family. What was it Dade had said at the grill? *She needs to be the center of it all. That's why Clem keeps getting her back.*

Before I could think anything else, though, Ruby started to rock on top of me to finish in waking what had started out of sleep, and I couldn't do anything else but let the thing be the thing.

We were amazing and *sweet* and *yummy* and *luscious* and *gorgeous. Beautiful, intense, smart, sexy, wet, hard.* This time I did say those words, and she slowed down enough to kiss me and say them back, and when she sat up there was finally enough light for me to make out the tattoo that had been under my nose the whole time.

I had to hold her hips still to get a look at the insane cartoon sprawled out broadly between her pubis and navel: it was an impossible construct of eggbeaters and matchsticks and tiny engines and a nine iron to create what looked like a masturbatory machine, though I wasn't sure, since the business end of the machine was hidden in the rough.

"Wow," I said, my thumbs stretching the skin at her hip bones, "It looks like that Mousetrap game from when I was a kid."

"This is a way better game, though, isn't it?"

I wanted to ask her one more thing, but then she was kissing away all my words, grinding away all my thoughts until there was only Ruby Goldberg and her Rube Goldberg tattoo. That and a little bit of Atlas, pinned to the earth in the great state of Wyoming, both of us letting the thing be the thing.

CHAPTER SIXTEEN

I t's a sandbag," Dade said at noon the next day, hulking over a cup of coffee at the picnic table, hung over. "And it's dangerous if you're not used to the gear. Don't even waste your time on it."

He was speaking to Red and Luther, who, in spite of their own, milder hangovers, were preparing to board the Queen Mary—a 160-foot-long, off-width enduro-crack. They had their rack out before them, slim pickings at best, and still needed at least one big cam to protect it.

"We're trying to do one of every kind of crack here—it'll be some scary shit without a big boy. You said yourself that we had to get our chops in," said Luther.

"One big cam isn't enough, and Scary Mary is not the route to do it on anyway," said Dade, shaking his head as he poked through their rack. The way he said it—the tone of it—I suddenly saw him as a father, teaching his kid how to drive.

"That's why you'll lend us yours," said Red, grinning.

Dade laughed at this—he never lent gear to anybody—but after they badgered him for another minute, he got up, as if he did it every day, and dug out two of his big cams. For some reason he felt like he had to justify it to me, but I didn't care. The night had done me good, in spite of my lack of sleep, and Ruby and I were both raring to go ourselves. Dade was taking another rest day, and Ruby and I decided on a route right next to Queen Mary: the seventy-foot first pitch of Cruise Line. I'd been on it years before and knew its small hands and solid pro would be a good fit for Ruby.

We all piled into *Makin' Bacon*, blaring "Ocean Size" on the way up to the parking lot, then hiked up to the base on the west side of the Tower. Off-width cracks demand strange tactics and equally strange positions, and Red was forced into stacking a hand and a fist to fill the gap, working in his knee and heel-to-toe from the very first move. Ten minutes later, after Ruby re-taped the bandage on her arm and stepped up to begin Cruise Line, Red was still only twenty feet off the ground, although he had managed to get a big cam placed above his head and was pushing it along with him as he ratcheted himself up what, for his skinny frame, could have passed for a chimney at times.

"Fuck me!" Red yelled, one thin hip halfway in the slot. "And fuck the Queen Mary!"

"Maybe I'll just let him clean the route on rap," said Luther as a nervous joke, clearly worried by the outright brutishness of the pitch.

Ruby, on the easy hands of Cruise Line, climbed confidently up to the hanging belay, seventy feet off the ground, which hung forty feet below the belay stance for Queen Mary. Red was about thirty feet above Ruby's belay, five feet to the left, when I reached her there. He looked ready to vomit, overwhelmed by the fat crack, which had trapped him into a kind of knee brace below, with an elbow wedged in above, so that it looked like he were trying force open a door—with the Tower trying to push him out from the other side. He needed to get into a different contortion, but the moves he'd have to do to get there must have been too difficult for him in his exhausted state. He swore again and then, with a mighty effort, managed to shove himself up another two inches.

"Hang in there, Red, it's almost over," I yelled to him.

He'd left his last large cam at the level of his feet—if it were at his chest he could have simply hung on it and rested. Instead, shaking with exertion, he pawed through his rack with his free arm as if he could will another cam to appear—a little like I'd done on Son of Sam.

"Keep moving! You can get something in where the crack narrows down," I yelled.

He fumbled around for another moment, then swore viciously and shoved his body up another inch, his fear infectious enough to get Ruby nervous.

"Maybe you could get just above him and drop a line. The routes almost come together up there," she said to me.

For an instant all I could think about was that Red had made fun of me for trying to be in the "Big Leagues" on Son of Sam, where I'd whipped and almost split my skull. He'd made his bed with the queen—"not even in the same league" as Son of Sam—and now he could lie in it. But I was hanging next to Ruby, and he really was in trouble.

"I don't know if I can do it fast enough."

"It's worth trying."

I looked down at Dade, who was looking up at me, clearly thinking what Ruby was thinking; then he shrugged. Above us, Red had started to curse again, saying "Fuck me" over and over, staring down at the curved base of the route, no longer moving upward but simply trying to stay in the crack. Then, quietly, I heard him say, "Don't fall," to himself; then he said it again, just before his heel popped and he almost came out of the crack.

"Okay, I'll do it," I said. I clipped the rappel rope to the back of my harness and pulled up off the belay. I touched my whirligig to help me focus, but then I didn't need to; the pitch was easy enough that I could romp up it in go-mode. I didn't need to

unsplit time or filter feed. All I had to do was stay focused on Red
and get to the belay as quickly as I could, and in that relatively
easy hand crack I simply placed one limb after the other until I
was about ten feet above Ruby and a little to her left, only twenty
beneath Red and about ninety feet off the ground.

"I'm almost to you," I yelled.

I was cool and clear in that moment, in control, as if I were
up on a roof banging nails. Red must have sensed it, because he
yelled "Thank you" down to me. I looked up to see him terrified,
but calming down, his foot resting on the cam beneath him, and I
realized—I don't know how else to say it—that I was both in my
world and in Red's world simultaneously, as if my act of climbing
and my act of helping Red were wells that tapped the same ancient aquifer.

I looked down at Luther and Dade and Fran sitting at the base,
then at my feet smeared in the crack. I looked for the briefest of
moments out over the land behind me, where I could see those
pill bug–sized people walking on the path around the Tower;
then I zeroed in, as if with a zoom lens, above me on Red's foot
rocking on that cam.

Then I was exploding. Falling.

I was falling and Red had grown too large and an intense
pain burst from my arm, Red next to me for a millisecond and
then falling away farther—so quickly it almost seemed that I was
shooting upwards.

It was all out of order at first, as if Red's fall to the base happened before he hit my arm—even before he stepped on that cam.
Then in the next second I saw tiny white spots and darkness and
there was no order for anything at all. I think I passed out for
a few seconds, but came to in time to see Red hanging upside-
down seventy feet below, while Luther, after letting all the rope

out, still had to climb up ten feet just to lower Red to the base and into Fran's arms.

In a flood of logic, of causal connections after the fact, I figured that Red must have knocked out that cam with his foot, and with his next-highest piece thirty feet below that, he had to fall through almost seventy feet of air before the rope came completely taut. Some part of him—an ankle or knee—must have gotten caught and flipped him backwards so that he cracked his head down where the wall curves out.

It all happened so fast at first and then slowed down. While I hung eighty feet above them with a great pain in my arm, I remember Dade looking up at me, to make sure I was okay. Then I saw him take off across the boulder field toward the ranger station. Ruby was yelling at me and began to lower me to the base.

During my descent, I watched my arm expand so quickly it seemed to be a time-lapse film of some mushroom growing or a cloud expanding—certainly not my own body. By the time I reached the ground, Dade and a couple of rangers were working their way across the difficult boulder field with a basket stretcher, while Fran stabilized Red's neck and back.

As I tried to untie from the rope, I saw more white spots and squiggles that finally curled around the edges of my vision; then I supposedly blacked out again. That's what Fran said, anyway, but I don't remember that. I remember telling the rangers I was okay, and them carrying Red off in the stretcher as Fran, in her EMT mode, did a careful head-to-toe on me. I also remember Ruby leading me past a shallow cup of blood that pooled on the rock Red had rested on.

When I saw the blood, I think I said out loud, "Guess that's why they call him Red." If Ruby heard or reacted, I don't know, but I found this terribly funny. I realized I was crying for him because he didn't deserve it, and maybe it was my fault for not reaching him in time—or our collective fault for not talking him out of it. That's when my time truly split in two, one half of me sick with worry for Red, the other full of razor focus for the boulders and not slipping, my body reading the distances and jumps and steps just like it had read the moves of Cruise Line up above.

By the time I reached the van I felt simultaneously light and heavy: so light that I might float away if I didn't grab the door handle, but also so heavy I might fall away into sky—the two things being the same somehow.

This sense seemed to recede when I got into the Rig, but then everything started to look translucent and also thick, as if light weren't bouncing off my friends but instead were being bent through them somehow, shimmering like heat waves above hot pavement, and I didn't know how to tell them they weren't really solid anymore.

Although everything was a little hazy, I remember that Ruby got in, slammed the door, and said it was a good thing that they'd gotten me down so quickly, and that I then said: "I'm just not used to it yet."

"Used to what?" she asked, alarmed. "The pain?"

"To this . . . this feeling of things being the same density, only with different gravities. Of being on the inside of things."

"That's it. We're going to the hospital," said Dade, starting up the Rig while Ruby helped lay me down in back. We stopped at the store for ice on the way out, to pack my arm, and they kept asking me how I felt.

"Trolling," I wanted to say. Frozen at distinct, unchanging coordinates in the universe, with the land and sky of Wyoming moving past and around me; a fishing lure cast from a bridge in a fast moving river. But I knew that sounded crazy, so all I said was, "Kind of dizzy."

Lying on Dade's bed, my arm propped up by the ice bag, I stared up at the El Capitan topo map on the ceiling, its red and black lines glowing, then looked out the windows at the sky and clouds and telephone poles, wondering if all three states of solid and liquid and gas were really just shadows of some more elemental state that I'd never been able to notice before—an elemental state that, at that moment, I seemed to be made up of entirely.

When we pulled into the Crook County hospital in Sundance, forty-five minutes later, I woke up to the shock of ice water riding down my side, and I sat up awkwardly to discover that my arm had grown even bigger. When Ruby bent over me to take a look at it, she even screwed her eyes up as if something foul might squirt out of it.

It took half an hour to straighten out the paperwork, since I didn't have my insurance card with me, and another half hour of waiting on the plastic chairs in the salmon-colored reception area, Ruby on one side, Dade on the other. That's when we found out that Red had been air-vacced all the way to Cheyenne, since there wasn't room in Casper, but they wouldn't tell us anything about his condition.

I was too out of it to wonder where Fran was at that point, but I found out later that she and Luther had gone to the wrong hospital, in Spearfish. And while Dade and Ruby kept going up to the desk to find out when I could see a doctor, I just sat very, very still, staring at a hexagonal pattern in the rug. There was something hidden in it, like a "magic eye" picture, that I knew I'd be able to see if only I could focus at the right distance. Just as I was about to crack its code, the desk nurse called us, and I was led along the blue and then yellow floor lines to an examination room.

Dade and Ruby tried to follow me in there, but they only let one visitor come along, and I found myself sitting on the edge of a table with Dade standing awkwardly nearby while a nurse took my temperature and blood pressure and asked me questions I didn't understand. After the nurse left, I shrugged at Dade and he shrugged back, just like before I set off after Red, and then the potato-like form of Dr. Holznagel came in. He reached out his thick lump of a hand to shake mine, then realized, with a flutter of eyelashes, that it was my right arm that was injured.

"That's a good-sized bump," he said jovially—a tone meant to squash my fears. Dade told him what he thought happened, and the doctor sucked his teeth. Then, when Dade asked him about Red, referring to him as the "other accident from the Tower," the good doctor, who had been probing my arm gently, said nothing but squeezed it so hard it made me swim in nausea, as if that were part of the examination.

"It's probably just a big bruise, but I'm going to take some images anyway. I've had guys kicked by horses come in here and look like they had grapefruits in their pants."

"What about the other stuff?" Dade asked before turning to me. "Tell him about the dizziness—about passing out."

Dr. Holznagel suddenly looked concerned. I took a deep breath and told him about the squiggles at the edge of my vision, about how I'd fallen asleep for a moment. But I knew he'd overreact if I told him that his body and the air around him were of the same substance that simply held different gravities, which were blending into each other at the border of his skin, and so I left that part out.

He palpated my head for a moment, then ran his fingers along my spine, his hands so careful and expert that I actually started to trust him. He kept asking me, "Does it hurt here? How about here?" but it only hurt where he'd squeezed my arm.

Holznagel sent me to X-ray for the images; half an hour later, back in the examination room, he brought them up on a computer screen and ran a delicate finger over the ghostly bones—more gently than he'd done with my actual arm. Then, again speaking to Dade as if I were too addled to follow, he concluded that it was indeed just a bad contusion.

"It'll be swollen for a few days. Sore for a week or two. Don't let him use it much until it heals. Keep it in the sling."

"And the dizziness?" Dade asked again.

"Well, there's not much fat on him, and his blood pressure"—he looked at the chart—"105 over 60—that's pretty low too. You should get some food into him. And then there's the pain. It must hurt quite a bit, and sometimes we aren't as tough as we'd like to be."

He told me to take 800 milligrams of Ibuprofen three times a day and use lots of ice until the swelling subsided, and then, finally noticing the split in Dade's lip, shook his head and walked off to his next patient.

Luther and Fran had finally arrived while I was being examined and were sitting with Ruby in the reception area. I was having a hard time tracking anything they were talking about at first, though I understood that Red had suffered internal injuries and had also broken his left tibia and fibula, his left femur, and his pelvis, and had fractured his skull. He was still unconscious, but they were doing all they could.

I was having that "trolling" feeling until I heard this, and then, somehow, I split into two again. There was the Atlas tripping in a world of freak density, and then there was Atlas functioning with everyone, hearing what they were saying, watching them all closely, smelling the terror that rose in tiny clouds from Luther's bloody shirt.

That's when I finally realized how upset Dade was. He seemed pale, and when I caught his eye I could tell he was on the verge of tears. Maybe it was about Red—or maybe about his own near-miss two days before. Or both. Whatever it was, after Luther left for Cheyenne to catch up with Red, Dade tried to snap himself out of it by overcompensating, somehow bootstrapping his mood up enough to convince us we all needed to go out for "beer and fats" for dinner, taking us on a whim to the Jackalope Bar on the outskirts of town.

The outside is, naturally, a giant jackalope, made out of concrete and fiberglass like a truckstop T. rex, about forty-five feet high with spotlights all around. Inside it's dark and a little dank and filled with a half-moon bar ringed with a dozen stools, as well as maybe eight or nine tables spread out beneath the largest collection (it claims on the menu) of jackalopes in the world. There were jackalope lamps and jackalope boot-pulls, jackalope heads and jackalope T-shirts. And among all the jackalopes there were stuffed coyotes and antelope and snapping turtles and hawks and rattlesnakes and one dusty bear and one ratty buffalo and a pair of glass eyes to go with each and every one of them—which all seemed to be staring at us. Not unlike the half-dozen locals who looked up from their drinks to watch us walk to our table.

"The clientele are looking as scruffy as the taxidermy," Fran whispered as she took her seat.

"And two of them are just as pickled," said Dade, leaning his head back toward the bar, where the two guys closest to us had a dozen Coors a piece lined up before them. One of them was wearing a black, sleeveless T-shirt with "Mustache rides, 5 cents" written on it, and he was still watching us.

Ruby smiled as if she might laugh, and Dade tried to laugh with her, but the mood about Red was just too heavy and it all fell flat. They ordered burgers and big baskets of fries and a pitcher of beer, and Dade ordered a bowl of chili for me so I could eat with one hand. I barely remember anything else until I'd finished eating, when the food finally hit my bloodstream. The one thing I do remember was a full-sized coyote perched on a big shelf across from the bar. It had its mouth wide open, about to snap up a jackrabbit that was wheeling in front of it. There was something in that frozen moment that I'd seen before in a dream that I could almost, but not quite, capture. Just like I couldn't capture the "magic eye" in the carpet at the hospital.

When we'd finished eating, Ruby and Fran started talking, in hushed tones, about how weird it was to see the fall—how Red seemed to drop from the crack all at once, as if it were a vise that had simply opened up, and how the way he spun coming out put him right in line to hit me. I remember wanting to disagree and explain about the tendrils of gravity and how Red had just hit one that was too thick, but I couldn't find any of the words I needed and instead just stared at the bandage on Ruby's arm, which was magnified and distorted as if I were looking through an old bottle.

After a while, Ruby said something about how if he had just hung on, I would've gotten a rope over to him, but Fran shook her head, her tone as pedantic as it had been during the peace ceremony: "Maybe it was meant to happen—as a lesson for the rest of us. Anyways, in his next life, maybe he'll have the chance to live through this moment again—and hopefully he'll do the right thing that time."

"In his 'next life'? If he dies, that's it! There are no do-overs," Ruby said loudly, before looking at the ceiling and making a vague hand movement as if to apologize to Red for talking about him.

Fran began to respond, but I lost track of what she said when I made eye contact with Dade, who was clearly horrified by the whole conversation.

"We should have talked him out of doing the route," he said quietly, almost standing up from the table, though then he changed his mind: "It's my fault. I should never have lent him those cams."

I tried to respond, but my own mouth felt too rubbery to speak, and then Dade said to me, too low for Fran or Ruby to hear, "It could've been me on Spanish Prisoner. Or you on Son of Sam. It can happen to anyone."

I nodded.

"I shouldn't have given them the gear."

I nodded again, still trying to round up some words, but then the meowing and hissing started from the bar: "Mustache" was making noises toward us, though they seemed to be focused mostly on Fran.

"C'mon, kitty cat," he yelled, elbowing his even larger friend next to him, "Smack that pussy!"

Ruby and Fran stopped talking completely, and then Fran yelled, with her biggest, brashest voice, "Why don't you mind your sweet fucking business?"

Mustache said, "The fucking business? Yeah, that's what I'm talking about! But we could start with a little dance first—I ain't that easy." Then he laughed and said something to his friend before sliding off his barstool. He walked over to the jukebox and put on some pop country star, who after a moment twanged, *"Every time I get a handle on my world, the handle breaks off."* As he walked back to his barstool, Mustache blew us all a kiss.

Fran flipped him off, punchy from her argument with Ruby, and I suddenly felt sick. Wrestling skills don't work so well with guys fifty pounds heavier than you, and with my arm the way it was—in a sling, no less—I was worthless anyway.

Dade, however, seemed positively energized by the interaction, and I saw a wide, bright look on his face that I usually only see when he's about to win a game of Scrabble. That look, once it focused on the bar, quickly stepped down into something more than his "look," and I realized with a stomach flip that I'd never really seen it out of its cage.

Our friend noticed this look too and slid off his barstool. Then, attempting a Clint Eastwood impersonation, but laughing while he did it, he said, "What you looking at, punk?"

Dade didn't say anything but, weirdly, flashed his myopic V symbol over his right eye, snapping it away in a kind of salute. The man and everyone else in the bar froze, and then the bartender said something low to Mustache.

Dade's hands seemed to pulse, though they didn't move, and I was sure that he'd changed his density somehow—like a cuttlefish changes its color. He had been a thin and rubbery line of gravity when we were talking, but now he took on a tensile core that tightened up the air around us.

He didn't move at all until Mustache started to walk over, and then he stood up slowly, holding his hands out before him as if to calm a startled deer that had come into the bar. While he did this he also assumed an odd stance, stepping forward with his left but leaning back. The ceiling seemed to lower, the walls closed in, and then while the guy threw his first slow punch, moving as if in water, Dade became a wolverine, slashing through aether to deliver two stinging jabs to the face, following them with a deep left to the stomach and finally a flat-anvil punch to the side of the head, the last so thick and brutal that it dropped the guy all the way to the floorboards.

The whole thing happened as quickly as Red's fall, and then I heard Dade apologizing to the bartender, saying he was just defending himself as he threw bills on the counter. Then he was motioning at us to follow him as he hit the door.

When I got up from my chair I had to step right over the guy, and, like in the dream with Olive, I suddenly felt gigantic—as if a thousand times my normal size. But there was something different: it was like I was at the bottom of the sea but also *made* of sea, moving as if between tendrils of gravity.

I walked all the way out the door and through the dusk and almost to the van, where I could see Dade sitting in the front seat, looking ready to cry and as beat up as Mustache was. I could feel eyes on me—as if the patrons or even the stuffed animals had all followed me out there—but when I turned to look back I saw only the great jackalope in its spotlights, looming above me, even more colossal than my own colossal body.

CHAPTER SEVENTEEN

That night I barely slept because of the ache in my arm, and had dozens of what must have been dreams, though most of them were of such simple, banal moments I wasn't sure if I'd dreamt them or lived through them. In one such moment I was getting out of the Rig and going out to sleep in the tent. In another, Ruby lay down with me for a while with one hand resting on my forehead, the other on my stomach. One thing that felt like it was real, and not just a dream, happened when I got out of the tent to pee, when I seemed to spy Fran slipping out the side door of *Makin' Bacon*. But that one didn't make any sense at all, and I figured I'd really just dreamt that one too.

By the time the sun had risen a few palm-widths above the horizon, I finally woke up for good, alone in the tent with my enormous, throbbing arm. My mouth tasted like death, my tongue thick and heavy, and every other part of my body had a low-level ache as if it had been infected by my giant lump, which during the night had turned an awful sort of blue-green black.

I unzipped the tent and crawled out, pushing myself up with my good arm, and looked around. Ruby and Fran were sitting on the tailgate of *Old Yeller*, facing away from me, and there was no movement at all from the Rig. The air was so still not even the papery cottonwood leaves were moving, and it was clear that it would be an unbearably hot day.

As I walked over to the Rig, however, and especially when I

grabbed the handle to open the door, I realized that the ground and the air and my body were still "close" to each other; the density feeling wasn't gone, I was just getting used to it.

Dade was in the Rig, lying on his stomach, writing or drawing, and when he heard me he closed up his journal and rolled over to look at me. He whistled when he saw my arm, and as he sat up I saw a condom wrapper fall from his sheet to the floor.

It *wasn't* just a dream. Fran had been in the Rig. All at once I could smell her.

"Ruby told me you told Fran you didn't want to climb anymore," I said before I even knew I would say it.

"What did I tell her?" He had started to pull a T-shirt on but froze with it over his head.

"That you're done climbing."

He pulled the shirt on completely but still wouldn't look at me, and I noticed that he was trying to sit with especially good posture.

"I don't remember saying that," he said.

"Well, are you?"

He shrugged, but before he could really answer Ruby walked up. I smiled at her, but her face was grim: "Fran got ahold of the hospital in Cheyenne. Red's in intensive care and still in a coma. They said the brain swelling is pretty bad. He might not make it."

Dade looked over at Fran, who seemed to be hanging back at *Old Yeller*, and then he stepped out of the van and walked through the cottonwood grove toward the river. Ruby started crying quietly and took my hand, pulling me down to sit on the edge of the doorway. After a while she said, "This is not what I signed up for . . . Red getting hurt—you getting hurt. I don't even feel like climbing anymore."

She squeezed my hand and looked at me. So beautiful. I

started to melt looking into her teary eyes and kissed her on the forehead.

"And I *really* don't feel like dealing with San Francisco yet," she said, leaning away from me to look up at the Tower.

"So don't."

"I promised Fran I'd go—plus I'm her ride and she needs to get out of here this morning."

"I forgot you were leaving today."

"You should come out and visit. Does Dade have time to drive into San Fran?"

"I don't know what he's doing," I said. A hot breeze lifted her hair as I stared at her. "What if I come out with you? Ride with?"

"In *Old Yeller*?" she asked, looking away. "It'd be a little tight."

"I could ride in the back."

"With no seatbelt? Sounds too dangerous."

I looked up at the Tower: "Yeah, you're right, that sounds pretty hairy. Probably safer on a big wall."

Ruby smiled, but the smile faded.

"It's just . . . I think Fran won't be up for it. This was supposed to be a women's trip," she said, but she didn't sound very sure.

I realized in a rush that once again she was waiting for me to speak up, to say what I felt—like I hadn't after we'd kissed at our house dance party. She was waiting for me to act.

"I think I'm falling for you," I said quickly, priming the pump but also feeling other words line up inside.

A wild look crossed her face, like a shiver, and she looked about to say something, but I didn't want to lose my momentum or have her beat me to anything important. Suddenly I was telling her about Olive—explaining that I hadn't technically been broken up when we'd slept together in the buffalo field, but that I'd told Olive immediately after that and ended it for good.

Ruby stood up before I could finish: "Why couldn't you say all this in the Needles?"

"I tried . . . and I was absolutely going to tell her the next day, but it was bad timing."

"Tell *her*? No—when were you *absolutely* going to tell *me*?"

"No, right—of course—I meant you too. Look, Olive has nothing to do with us—with how I feel about you."

"So you just dropped her when you ran into me? And you let there be overlap?"

"There wasn't any overlap in my heart—"

"Out of the frying pan and into the freakin' fire," she said, shaking her head as if at her own stupidity. Then she was walking back to her truck.

"I need to think about some stuff," she said, not looking back.

"Just let me talk to Dade before you do anything," I said, striking out across the cottonwood grove. The huge sky was nothing but blue, the air molten. I looked back to see Ruby talking to Fran, her hands flying up in exasperation.

"Fuck me," I said to myself. "Fuck, fuck, fuck."

I found Dade sitting in the river with his arms around his knees, and though I'd been thinking about how to turn him and get him to continue on to Yosemite, when I saw him there I just felt defeated. Without saying a word—and without taking off my sandals—I stepped into the cool, dark river and found a rock to sit on, twisting my body a bit so I could soak my arm, the water coldest where it lapped at my skin. In our silence I could hear the river ripple past while sunken tree stumps and single blades of prairie grass and our own dumb bodies ruffled the water into brown, cat-eyed curves.

Neither of us moved for a long time, until I pulled a rock

from the mud at my feet and tossed it out ahead of me. The rings it made in the water stretched into ovals and quickly disappeared.

"You ever hear about anyone who's actually had their life flash before their eyes?" Dade asked, not looking at me.

"I've heard the expression, of course."

"But never talked to anyone who it actually happened to?"

"I don't think so. Why?"

"Red mentioned it during the Wheel of Causality and, well, I think something like that happened to me on Spanish Prisoner. Or whatever happens to people when they say that."

"But you didn't even fall—I should have been the one seeing my life flash before my eyes back on Son of Sam," I said.

He shrugged. "All I know is, there was a moment after that barndoor where, right then, that's all I could ever be, you know? I don't know how else to describe it. It was like I needed an answer and I didn't have it. I was trying to find a solution . . . then it was over, but once I'd clipped the chains everything came at me at once. Bev, the baby, this one time I got lost as a kid and couldn't get home . . . the smell of my—" He made two upturned fists and raised them dripping out of the water, looking perplexed. "The smell of my laces. From my boxing gloves. When I trained I'd pull on them with my teeth and wipe sweat off my face and stuff. They'd get super funky. I don't know if that's what people mean—I didn't see my *whole* life, but I saw so many pieces of it. It kind of put me on edge."

"Yeah, I noticed." I didn't know what else to say, but turned to look at him, obviously disappointed.

"You won't be able to climb for a week, anyway," said Dade, still looking at the water.

"I'm going to follow Ruby to California, if you're not going. I'll catch a bus somewhere."

"Let's go visit Red in Cheyenne, first."

I was about to say that it wasn't worth visiting Red because he was in a coma, but when I looked over at Dade he was just staring at the dark water, his shoulders rounded forward as if the bones had gone out of them, and I didn't have the heart.

There was nothing else to say except what I had to say to Ruby: that I wouldn't be jumping ship but would be coming out, somehow, to California—and that I was sorry.

But when I clambered up on top of the river bank I could see right away that *Old Yeller* was gone. I stopped there and sighed, then kicked at the grass with my wet sandal, setting forth a spray of grasshoppers that shot in all directions.

CHEYENNE

ODOMETER (1)99,397

LAT. 41.31° N LONG. 105.58° W

ALT. 7,208 FEET

JULY 14

CHAPTER EIGHTEEN

Dade spent the rest of that day sitting in the van, oozing grumpy vibes that said "stay away" and working intensely on a drawing he wouldn't show me. I mostly laid on my pad in the shade and iced my arm, a study in heat and sloth. We slept fitfully through the night, and when the air finally cooled around four in the morning, we roused ourselves and rolled out of the campground before the sun was above the horizon, trying to lay down some miles before the heat ramped up again.

By eight o'clock, though, bombing down Interstate 25, it felt like we were in a convection oven, with feverish winds raging through the open windows and rattling the big map loose, forcing me to climb in back and tape it in place with one arm. The colors around us were elemental, breaking down into large patches of tawny earth and sage-gray scrub, the heat waves on the highway capturing the bottom edge of the sky in silvery blue pools that disappeared every time our wheels got close to them.

Although the radio was off, I could have sworn at times that the wind was carrying some ghostly sounds from the small towns we passed by, sure that if we were going slower I might be able to make out some wailing song about lost chances. Some song about me losing Ruby. About Red's mother losing her son. About Dade losing his gumption to climb.

In Orin, after jogging west on 18, we caught Interstate 25 south and slowly crept up on an old, green flatbed truck that was hauling the wrecked body of a vw bus on its back. We were only moving about a mile an hour faster than it was, and the driver took a long look at us as we passed, her gaze landing on the ice pack on my arm, my eyes, and Dade's face. She nodded her head about a quarter of an inch, as if to say hello, and then looked in the rearview mirror.

As we passed, I stared at the truck's hubcaps. They seemed to be standing still at first, but then began to rotate, ever so slowly, forward. I caught Dade staring at the wheels too, and then he sneaked a look at me. He cleared his throat nervously, and I thought he was finally going to talk to me about bailing on the trip, but instead he launched off on a science lecture.

"They're like your whirligig," he said, pointing at the hubcaps, "Like how movies work. It's a glitch in the eye's ability to take things in, where your eye sort of takes a snapshot, then wipes that image away to get ready for the next one. Then the brain tries to blend them together to make sense of it. Different eyes work differently . . . like, flies' eyes can take in three hundred images a second."

I reached up to take my whirligig off my neck, but I needed both arms and the sharp pain in my right stopped me.

"I taught this in my human anatomy component last year and had this student who argued that flies must be experiencing more than us and thus must pack more life into each second," Dade continued. "As if the length of life and intensity of perception were an inverse relationship."

I thought about those sensory snapshots I'd had after Spanish Prisoner, when sights and sounds and smells came to me intense but fragmented—as if my brain weren't able to blend them together. And then there was that moment making love with Ruby, when everything in the world did seem blend into a single, extended moment. There was a connection to be made here, but the thought of Ruby sent a pang through me—that, and the fact that Dade had started speaking again, made me lose my train of thought.

"What do you think?" he asked.

"I think I don't want to be a fly," is all I said, adjusting my bag of ice. "Or you, right now."

A moment later Dade flexed his right hand, slightly swollen from punching Mustache the night before. He sighed, then said, "Okay . . . something happened with Fran last night."

I nodded.

"It's not what you think."

"If it's not that you two had sex, then you're right," I said. I immediately felt bad, but I was mad at him for deciding to bail on the trip—and mad at myself for screwing up with Ruby.

"It just started out decompressing from the night. From Red . . . the guy in the bar. We had a few more beers in the Rig."

"You guys were fighting just days ago . . ."

"Fighting to stay off each other . . . anyway, she started crying and said she needed a hug—and honestly, I did too. Then after a while, it just happened."

"What are you going to tell Bev? She has to know the truth—if I've learned anything it's that."

He looked at me, his face fallen: "When I tell her, I will tell her the truth . . . that I'm a rotten, dirty shit and don't deserve her. That I almost killed a guy and then banged some hottie because I was bummed out."

"Dade, come on—she's not that hot," I said, trying to joke him out of his funk, but he was too far gone.

"Old habits, laddie, old *fucking* habits," he said, his fake-jaunty tone etched with acid.

"So that's why Fran wanted to bail so badly, why they didn't even say goodbye," I said.

He didn't nod, but rocked in his seat.

I felt a second of relief, as if Fran's haste to get away were an explanation for why Ruby didn't wait for me. But then, that couldn't really explain why Ruby didn't even leave a note.

"Well, Ruby's all pissed at me too, if it's any consolation. I told her about Olive, and that there had been some overlap."

He eyed me for a moment, about to say something, then thought better about rubbing my nose in it. In the end he just said, "Well, I blew it. I blew my marriage."

"I bet Bev won't even bat an eye."

"And you'd lose that bet. She knew about all the women before her and said, 'You're done with them if you get with me.' And I was, I really was. I don't know what happened."

"Red's accident—that was enough to make anyone need a hug."

"But not start pawing their clothes off . . . but it wasn't like I started it. *She* started kissing me. *She* started pulling *my* shirt off. Crazy women . . . I used to get sucked in by them—until Bev. Why now?" he asked grimly.

I shook my head again. I wanted to talk about Red, about how we should never have let him get on that route, but before I could start, Dade followed his thoughts out loud.

"I guess that old saw, 'Out of sight, out of mind,' is true."

He seemed to chew on his own words, staring out over the broad, deep land before us, and then asked, "Why do we say 'out of sight, out of mind,' and also 'distance makes the heart grow fonder'? They're opposite."

With another pang, I thought about Ruby. And then Olive. With Olive, 'out of sight' finally did put her 'out of mind.' But the more distant Ruby grew, as she drove west and we drove south, the fonder my heart grew—and the larger my pain about screwing up how I'd told her about Olive.

"Maybe 'distance' is about being separated right now," I said, "and 'out of sight' is about someone in the past, so they grow less important with time." Like Ursula. Like Olive.

"No, I get it," he said, cutting me off. "'Distance makes the heart grow fonder' is about old flames, like that crazy hottie I dated—Lana. Now that the bad times have faded away, I only remember how much fun she was. And 'out of sight' is about right now. Bev was out of sight and so she was—I was—out of my mind."

He reached up to touch his juju again, rubbing the ring for a while, and then knocked himself on his head. "At least I used a condom," he mumbled. "Emergency workers can't have STDs, can they? They have to get tested, right?"

I shrugged. "Ruby's got something—herpes. But said I couldn't get it right now."

Dade looked at me seriously for a moment, as if he would say something about that, but then far ahead a movement caught our collective eye.

Up on our left, where a ranch road crossed the railroad tracks that paralleled the highway, an antelope bounded wildly through the scrub brush and then froze with its front hooves poised daintily near the rails, as if sensing a coming train. I turned to see the van's wave of wind reach it and knock it lightly—this seemed to send it bounding up a low hill of taupe and tan, one of its leaps helping it clear the horizon so that it was framed for a brief second by nothing but sky.

"It's just too much," Dade mumbled.

I nodded, not sure if he was talking about Bev and Fran and

doing right in the world—or about the impossibly huge sky. It was enormous like it only gets in great valleys, where the land can stretch out and offer itself as a mirror. Far away, sharp-edged clouds cast gigantic columns of rain and shadow down like fishing nets thrown by titans—as if from my colossal dream.

I turned around to look behind us and was suddenly struck by the thought that we can never take it all in: whenever I was looking for something difficult—like the rockhead—some important part of it seemed to be ever-opposite my eyes, as if projected from the back of my skull. And the farther I turned around to see it, the farther it moved behind me.

"I'm always talking about getting myopic—about 'buzzard,'" Dade said then. "How did I not pay attention with Bev?"

"I don't know," I said, though what I thought was, *Like me not telling Ruby in time, right? It's not so easy, is it?*

"I mean, I can pay attention when I'm climbing—I can find my rockhead some of the time—but then other times it's like the rockhead is changing . . . what I'm supposed to do is changing. Like in the bar. If I was in the rockhead, I would have ducked that punch and walked away from mustache guy. And I would have stopped Red . . . and I would have sent Fran away."

"But you did the right thing with Red, sharing our site with him, giving him the benefit of the doubt," I said. "And, hell, WE did Queen Mary ourselves, back when it was too hard for us, and we survived."

Dade acknowledged this with a sort of sideways nod, but then continued: "When I'm climbing, I almost never let anything block anything from *me*. That's what I mean when I say 'get myopic.' But the rest of the time . . . I'm not a 'bridge,' you know? I don't walk like a living prayer. I'm not telling the truth about things."

"Well, you can tell me the truth . . . whatever it is."

He reached up to touch his juju and then looked at me: "You want to know one of my stupid tricks, since you've been asking? I just tie my shoes really well. I put everything into my shoes. And I put everything into the rope when I flake it. Everything into my knot when I tie it. Then it's easier to put everything into a move when things get hard. It's like I'm warmed up, but in my head."

"But that just sounds like my breathing exercises," I said, and then, with a bad German accent: "Zen und 'ze art of knot tying."

He sighed painfully. "See, that's why I never talk about it."

I wasn't joking, though, not really. "And that gets you to your rockhead?"

"It gets me to the place where I can start to get to it. But I don't really have a trick like that for this other stuff. For Bev, you know?"

I did know—all of this—didn't I? It was like being a filter-feeder and a pollinator at the same time. It was like making love to Ruby when I didn't let anything come between me and her, or me and my actions. It was like unsplitting time.

Was that all he was talking about? Is that all the rockhead was for him? I stared at him as if the meaning lay on the surface of his skin, if only I could read it. But I couldn't read it, I could only guess at it. I would never know what it was like for him in the heat of the moment—barndooring off Spanish Prisoner, cranking through the crux of Son of Sam. Changing the Crackmeister's diaper a year from now.

I wondered if maybe I were ahead of him in terms of "letting the thing be the thing," only I was physically a much worse climber. Maybe I was climbing, in terms of my physical ability, at 99.9 percent, while Dade was climbing at only 90 percent of his potential. Maybe a 60 percent hold for him was a 51 percent for me and I actually stuck better most of the time. We'd never know. There's no bathroom scale for will, no rain gauge for focus.

I thought about this for a long time but didn't know how to say it to him in the right way. After a while, we pulled off the interstate to get gas and more ice for my arm, the awning of the station providing a brief respite from the enormous sky. I thought Dade would try calling Bev again, but he said she had an appointment with the ob-gyn that morning and he didn't want to call in the middle of it. *I bet,* I thought; not with the bad news he was going to share. I was feeling a little more relaxed after our talk, like we'd normalized relations, but when we pulled back onto the frontage road there was a mass of fur and guts up ahead, just on the sunny edge of a cloud-thrown shadow, that tensed me up again. As we passed into the shadow, I saw that it was actually two jackrabbits that must have been hit at the same time. Then, only fifty feet farther along, was the body of a coyote, its torso spiraled into a corkscrew as if someone had tried to wring it out of its own skin.

"Yikes," I said.

We both had our windows rolled down, and I leaned out to get a better look, so that I had to pull my head back in to hear Dade when he started speaking.

"What?" I asked.

"About Ruby . . ." he said quickly, shooting a look over at me. "Uhtlas, this is just about telling the truth . . . okay, so you know what's what. But she's sort of still with Clem. Or they're on the skids, but they're always on the skids. That's what Fran told me the other night. She's going to see Clem in San Francisco, at the convention. I mean, Ruby is."

I knew it before he said it—all the little hints. Why hadn't I put it all together?

"But supposedly Ruby really wants to be done with him. Anyway, I just thought you should know before you made any more decisions," he said.

I don't know why, but I was all reason in that moment—cool and collected.

"Thanks . . . I appreciate it," I said.

He looked at me, as if he didn't believe it, and then slowed to turn off the frontage road and onto the ramp for I-25. I felt super calm but somehow hollow. Just as Dade started to say something else, an animal leapt from the embankment and popped a double kick into the air as it arced below the hood of the Rig.

I felt the impact in my bones as much as I heard it, and then Dade braked hard so that there was only the sound of tires popping on the gravel shoulder as we came to a stop.

"What the hell was that?" Dade asked. "Not a coyote?"

I could have sworn I saw horns on the animal. "A little pronghorn?"

I turned to look out the side window and could see something tawny moving on the gravel. We both got out and walked back to it.

"It's a jackrabbit—a big one," Dade said as we reached it, "Poor little guy."

Its hind legs, the ones that had pumped with futility against the thin air, seemed paralyzed, and there was a red and purple tear in its belly that glistened through its fur. It eyed us wildly, pawing the gravel with its front legs. We both looked at the rabbit, not at each other.

"I should put him out of his misery," I said, stepping next to it.

"Oh man—just leave him."

"So he can just bake here in the sun until some coyote comes by to eat him alive? Forget that."

I lifted the heel of my sandal over its neck, apologizing out loud to it, and though the rabbit tried to bite me once it then relaxed, as if resigned to it.

I wanted to do this in a single motion, to keep it from suffering, and tried to focus everything on this one simple act. I filled myself with breath and as I let it out, deep inside, I saw and also felt that pulsing, and then, deeper still, that bubble began to rise up—the bubble that doesn't contain a question, but only the feeling of one. Time didn't just unsplit but rather fell away from me and I felt enormous, my breathing like weather, my heartbeat lodged in the foot I was about to use on the rabbit, thundering like someone beating the hull of a vast, empty ship.

Concentrating only on this one brutal moment, I laid my left heel on the rabbit's neck and then snapped down with my full weight, the rabbit's wide, moist eyes blasting like a furnace. For a brief, unbearable second—like a waking dream—I could see what the rabbit saw: beyond the scattered blue light of day, raw and deep into space where there are planets and asterisms of another season. I could feel, too, the animation that had carried it through its fast and simple life—the very thing so constant that it was the world itself—expand in a rush to leave what had been a vital, electric body simply a sack of dying cells, their mitochondria powering down, their cell walls no longer keeping the outside out or the inside in.

I turned around, feeling incredible pressure on the heel of my foot, and looked at Dade. He seemed unfamiliar, his skin and clothes matte but bright—just like my sandals and hands and everything else around us. It was as if the air had been cleansed to make it easier to see through. I felt the pulsing even stronger then, and swelled with the feeling that I had already done exactly this thing in exactly this spot. Then the pulsing made everything too white, with brightness popping at the edges of my vision, and I was falling through layers of air—layers of time—each one resisting and breaking and resisting and breaking until, for a few moments, there was no Dade and no rabbit and finally no me, either.

I WOKE UP facing the red gleam in its fur, my throbbing arm pressed hard into the gravel. I remember the smells of dry grass and burnt rubber. I remember the pads of the rabbit's feet and a fly crawling in its fur.

And I remember seeing something else this time as I passed out. This time as my vision squiggled at its edges, I would have sworn I was somehow seeing atoms themselves, as if photons were hitting the inside of my eyes. And like the rabbit had been—like I had begun to sense on top of Mudskipper—I *knew* that I was an animated world unto myself, but also made up of inanimate chemicals—chains of carbon that for no particular reason were on this side of the lifeline, and which would eventually be on the other side. The animate fish in the inanimate bowl.

Dade was listening for my breath, checking my pulse, poking and talking at me, but I pushed him away and got to my knees, then to my feet.

"Uhtlas, answer me. Are you okay?"

"Yeah, I'm good. The air isn't so thick anymore," I said, realizing that the feeling of density I'd had for a whole day—that liquids and gases and solids were all merged together—had diminished a little bit.

"The air is what?"

I squatted down next to the rabbit and ran my fingers through its fur. So warm and soft—it was no longer resigned like it had been when I broke its neck. Being resigned is the potential for something—whatever that something is—and this was the rabbit's something. Suddenly I was resigned too—to confront Ruby. In person. All or nothing.

I carefully, piously pushed the rabbit off the gravel and into the tall, dry grass along the shoulder. The grass resisted, then parted, some stalks bending before snapping back with blood and single hairs stuck to them.

In the Rig I pretty much passed out, exhausted from two nights of bad sleep as well as the pain of falling on my arm, but not before I'd tied the bag of ice around my arm with a towel and pounded more Tylenol. I didn't wake up until after noon— hours later—outside "Cloud Nine," a relatively hip tattoo parlor in downtown Cheyenne, which was wedged between a cell phone store and a café.

I felt like hell, the density feeling still present, but as I crawled out of the Rig I realized that the swelling in my arm had gone down almost completely. I wasn't sure if it had shrunk during my sleep or in the moments after I had landed on it, but either way it had deflated and left my intensely wrinkled skin with a sick, dark hue.

I guessed Dade was in the tattoo parlor and went into the waiting room, which looked a bit like a trendy Italian restaurant merged with a barbershop. It had antiqued walls and lush leather couches and chairs, as well as artsy three-ring binders with rusted sheet metal covers riveted to them, resting on a tropical hardwood coffee table.

I could see Dade in a second room through an open doorway, sitting in an old-fashioned dentist's chair with the tattoo artist hunched over him. The artist seemed to be completely free of tattoos, body piercings, and even hair. He had no eyebrows, no eyelashes, and wore a mesh shirt to show off his place at the other end of the body art spectrum. And though he looked slightly nefarious, when he told me where the bathroom was a kind of corn-fed golly-gee shined through.

When I got out of the bathroom, Dade yelled that he was almost done; in the meantime, I looked through the binders on the table. They were full of sample photos of very white women with Maori designs on their arms and what seemed to be Tibetan and Buddhist symbols etched onto their skinny hip crests. A far cry, it would turn out, from what Dade had gotten.

"They're waiting for Red's parents to arrive before we can visit him," Dade said as we walked out.

"And I finally got ahold of Bev. She had an ultrasound today and the tech screwed up and referred to the Crackmeister as a girl. So now we know—we're having a daughter."

"I take it you didn't tell her about Fran," I said. I was a little shocked by his improved mood, but I basically still felt cool and calm, like I did when he told me about Ruby. Like when I'd killed the rabbit. I wanted the truth out about everything.

"I can't tell her on the phone," he said. He opened up the Rig and sat down in the doorway, holding his right hand over his tattoo bandage. I could see climbing guidebooks spread out on the table behind him.

"It's not so easy, it is?" I asked, noticing that my left hand was resting on my own injury, so that for a moment we each created ragged, mirror images of the other.

"It's not like it matters, anyway. It's not like I'll ever do that with Fran again. She was just a warning for me to stay on the path, you know?"

"So are we leaving today?" I asked, pointing at the guidebooks on the dash. I wanted to bail that second. To catch a bus or even a plane to San Francisco if he wasn't going.

"Well, that's what I wanted to talk to you about. I'm still

thinking of heading out there—but no more short stuff," he said, pointing to the guidebooks. "If we're going to do it, we need to be firing off long, solid routes. All action, you know?"

"Yeah, right. What about your luck clock? Your billion heart-bearts? And what about visiting Red?"

"We're still not allowed into intensive care, but we can call and check in tomorrow. As for my luck clock," he said, looking at the gauze on his arm, "I think I've reset it."

I was about to say how stupid that was, but his eyes shut me up. Somehow, I don't know how else to say it, Dade looked doomed but committed—and brightly resigned to it. If I were a betting man, I could have dade-ucted the roots of it: he didn't want to go home yet because he couldn't bear telling Bev about Fran, and he probably didn't want to climb in Yosemite because he feared he would be killed on the wall by the gods of climbing as "punishment" for sleeping with Fran. But then he wanted to be punished too; and if he could survive his trial by fire, then maybe he would have paid his penance and be cleansed for Bev. And of course—a contradiction—he really did want to get on Seven Seas too, because deep down he was a climber to the bone. And because he was Dade, I'm sure he was able to tie this all up into a neat causal package. If I were a better friend, maybe I would have forced him back to Bev. But I wanted him for myself right then. I wanted him on Seven Seas.

"You are a fucking piece of work," I finally said. And then I pointed at his arm. "So show me—what did you end up with anyway? Let me guess: a giant beaver? Or just a big, cramping asshole?"

"It's what I was drawing all day yesterday . . . and I'm not supposed to take the wrap off," Dade said, pressing his hand more tightly over it.

"They always say that. Come on—show us your tits—I promise I won't laugh."

Dade shrugged a passionate shrug, as if he were letting go of everything in the world, then peeled back the top edge of the plastic wrap and pulled it away. Revealed, under speckles of blood, was a tattoo of a cartoonish *Makin' Bacon*, its corners rounded a little, its wheels showing speed. Its license plate said "BZZRD" and on the side of it was a beaver with a baby in that '70s-style van art. Inside, just large enough to see, there was Dade at the wheel (with glasses). And someone riding shotgun. Me.

I barked out a laugh, in spite of myself. "It's Everett's monster truck."

Dade looked at me then with the opposite of his boxing look, a look he'd never given me so directly before. It was a look of apology, of thanks for understanding. Of love.

"Straight to the Valley?" I asked.

"It's pretty hot there right now," he said, reaching for the Cirque of the Towers guidebook on the front seat and handing it to me. I flipped through the pages and eyed a few of the routes, like Mt. Hooker and War Bonnet, and knew the weather at that altitude would be cool and blue. Almost perfect, actually. But they were too far from Ruby in San Francisco.

"Look, it might be hot out in the Valley, but it's not going to get cooler there for a month, and the best way to train for Yosemite is on Yosemite rock. Those huge walls could be in our hands in a couple days—and we can climb in Tuolumne if it really is too hot. After a detour to San Fran. And I'm talking about the city here, not the hottie."

He paused, as if letting this last part sink in, then stuck out his hand with index finger and thumb in a ring: "For all the marbles . . ." he said.

I clipped my own to his and then we snapped them apart.

"Yeah, we're Team 'Lost Our Marbles,'" I said, grinning.

But I remember thinking, *It's not marbles at all; it's still just dominos.* And I imagined a great chain of fallen white tiles—some the size of the Tower, others only as large as a 1.5 cam, another exactly the size of Olive—that stretched back to the driveway at Dade's house. And I imagined more of them too, stacked off into our future, standing proud. I hoped that one of them was Ruby-sized, and that another one—maybe the last one—would be the exact size and shape of El Capitan; the one that I might ride down myself into the great Pacific sea.

THE GREAT BASIN

ODOMETER (1)99,912

LAT. 40.73° N LONG. 114.00° W

ALT. 4,232 FEET

JULY 14

CHAPTER NINETEEN

I woke up to a smell like Black Cat firecrackers, blinded by white light. I felt like I'd slept for a lifetime, as if in some fairytale. "Where are we?" I croaked, sitting up in the back of the Rig. My arm felt surprisingly good, but my left leg was asleep and I had to bang it to try to wake it up.

"It's alive!" said Dade, attempting a Dr. Frankenstein voice. I couldn't see him for the light, but I knew his voice was coming from the driver's seat.

I had a vague memory of the world passing by the Rig window as if in a time-lapse film. The clouds appeared and then vanished. The sun jerked from behind to ahead of us. High desert heat flared and faded and then flared again. In between these moments there were others where there was no movement at all—a gas station, a stoplight—and then there was only movement and humming and a hot wind all around me.

"When did it get so hot?" I asked, finally standing up in an awkward crouch to stamp my leg, which still hadn't caught up to the rest of my wakened body. My shirt and skin were damp where I'd lain on my side, but the rest of me was as dry as sheetrock dust—especially the inside of my mouth.

"About two gas stops and a pee-jar break ago," Dade said. He sounded more relaxed than he'd been in a week.

We were driving almost right into the sun with the flat land and even flatter sky shimmering outside our windows, and as my eyes adjusted to the light, it seemed that the difference between land and sky lay not in their material form but simply in the shape and color of their brightness.

"I'm going to pull over at the next town so you can drive," said Dade, just after a sign for the exit to the Bonneville Salt Flats shot past.

There were heat waves out the side window, and I imagined that there might be rocket cars out on the cracked land, their wheels and the white earth shimmering into the same motile substance—and maybe even a jet above, its sound booming in frustration when it couldn't keep up. I felt a little like that myself. I had dreamt a lot during the drive—mostly about Ruby and a little about my fall with Red—but the contents had been left behind me like a piece of bubble gum we'd rolled over, a little bit stretched out and lost with each revolution.

Dade pulled off in Wendover, spitting distance from the Nevada border, and went into the gas station to buy us each a quart of chocolate milk while I hobbled quickly to the outdoor bathroom, stamping the last sleep from my leg like some whacked-out clogger. My pee was so dark it startled me at first, and I drank from my cupped hand at the bathroom sink for a long time before I finally came up for air. The creature wiping water off his face—his eyes green under the fluorescent lights instead of brown—looked familiar, but it sure didn't look like me. More like something from my dreams.

When I pulled the Rig back onto the Eisenhower highway, the sun was less than a palm-width above the horizon and I had to flip down the sun visor, then hold out my hand too, to see well enough to drive. In the rearview mirror, our shadow stretched out so far behind us I couldn't find the end of it. I took a long pull of my chocolate milk, all of a sudden hungry, and finished it off with a few more slow chugs before tossing the carton in back.

By then the sun was so close to the horizon I could only squint and look through my fingers. It was changing shape as if resisting the moment its edge would pop below the land, starting as an oval but then flattening out into a line, then a dot, and then—right after it disappeared—a thin, green line again, spread out across the horizon, only to disappear for a second, final time.

For a moment I thought about the dream I'd woken up from when Dade first called me about this trip: the dream of falling and thickening and never reaching the ground. It used to be the only thing I ever dreamed about, but I hadn't had it in weeks.

Something had changed in me.

"I feel good about my chances," I said, looking over at Dade to find him obscured by a dozen or so bright, pale-green ghost spots the sun had burned into my eyes.

"Me too. I think we're going to pull this bad boy down."

"Well, yeah, for Seven Seas too. But I mean with Ruby. In spite of Clem."

He grunted contrarily, then held his milk carton over his open mouth to gently shake the last few drops out of it. When he was finished, he said, "You may have to fight harder than she's worth, you know. And then there's Olive too. Smarty-pants Olive."

I looked sideways at him. "You don't think Ruby is smart?"

"She's smart . . . she's just . . . well, Olive's sort of an intellectual," he said, carefully flattening the milk carton and then folding it into a square. "She cares about the bigger questions. She's passionate about important things in life . . . like the rockhead. She has ideas about it. And she's loyal. She commits."

"Yeah, her ideas are that *you* are deceiving yourself—that the rockhead is just 'flow.'"

"Well, then at least there's a conversation to be had. Ruby's a little more, uh, quirky."

"Quirky?" I said, frowning at him, "What's that supposed to mean?"

"Okay, then how about . . . capricious. Fickle. Volatile. I was trying to be nice."

"All I know is that when Ruby and I first kissed, it was like a switch got flipped in me—just like you said happened with you and Bev. You said that you and Bev were 'meant to be.'"

"I know I've said that stuff, and it's true. But somehow I also love Bev because I want to—like Fran said. She wasn't totally crazy the night we argued at the supersecretbivy."

"But if Bev died, or left you, you'd be in agony. Her leaving would be a trigger to cause a bunch of things to happen in you, right?"

He nodded but then also wobbled his head, setting his immaculately folded milk carton on the doghouse between us. The carton immediately unfolded itself in a determined way, like the time-lapse video of a flower blooming, though it couldn't make it all the way back to its original shape and stopped twitching in mid-bloom, barely half unfolded.

"Here's what it's like. When I first started with Bev, I think I sort of controlled how fast I fell in love with her . . . I let things out or held things back at different times. It's like at the state fair: you have the freedom to buy your little ticket, to get in line for the tilt-a-whirl, or to get some cotton candy first. But when you decide to get on and they pull the gate down over you, then you're in it until it's over. And it ain't over until the fat carny *flings*"—he paused to repeat his dumb joke—"until the fat carny *flings* the gate open again."

I did know this, a little, from how things had started with

Ruby, and was about to admit this to him when he suddenly shifted his tack, unable not to dade-uct.

"But of course maybe we're just triggered into thinking we have free will when we let things out or hold them back," he said, picking up the milk carton again to re-fold it. "You meet some woman like Ruby who's hard to hold or whose crooked tooth makes you wild—or whatever your fucked up thing is—and it brings up old feelings of love or lust that you're used to, and so you DO fall for her."

Like Ursula and my need for things to feel tragic.

As I thought about that, Dade unbuckled his seatbelt and turned to climb in back, setting the milk carton back on the doghouse where it began to unfold again, though with even less gumption than it had the first time around.

"Wait, are you going to sleep?" I asked, unable to keep the disappointment out of my voice.

"Yeah, I've been fighting it for hours," he said, leaning on my shoulder as he squeezed between the seats. "The odometer's going to hit two hundred thousand—wake me when you got a mile left. I want to see it roll over. And set your watch back for the Pacific time zone—you're going to need that extra hour to get us across the state."

I felt like I was on the cusp of something—at least the cusp of understanding what the question was—and needed Dade to keep sitting there, if only as a sounding board, but then he was gone and I was all alone.

I'd been so involved in our conversation that I hadn't noticed that the sky had grown dark, my headlights catching only a thin cone of the highway and its edges, where scrub brush shuddered as if with some excess, internal energy. I was passed by a few sleek luxury SUVs with California plates, and though I barely got a look at them, I thought about that old flatbed we'd seen in Wyoming hauling the vw bus, with its hubcaps rotating, ever so slowly, forward.

If my eyes had been quick enough—three hundred times a second like one of Dade's flies—I could have seen each rotation of the hubcap and turned what seemed a continuous pattern into its discrete parts. But I'm not that quick. I have to take in the world and myself—and Ruby and Olive and Dade—as mini-continuums.

When I was knocked from the Tower by Red, my arm smashed, the world inside out, I could barely make sense of what was happening—at least the order of it all—and for a while I lost that continuum. My "me." My sense of self. It was only after the fall was over that my causal mind could attempt to cobble my shattered memory of it into a cohesive whole. But even that wasn't enough. I needed Dade's memory of the event—and Ruby's—to recreate it for me. It's as if, if they hadn't remembered it for me, my moment wouldn't have existed.

Driving across Nevada, I was aware of the "me" made up of my slippery memories and also the "me" driving—and all of sudden it felt like there was no connective tissue between the two. If I had to rely on others, like Dade or Ruby, for confirmation of my memories—which themselves were build on my dizzy, fallible senses—how could I ever be sure about my memories about anything? How could I be sure they were connected to this "me" driving?

And of course, Dade's own memory had no support, either, and could only be supported by the memories of the people who knew him (including me) so that all of our memories—our selves, really—were spreading and intersecting like choppy ripples, safe only in the Venn diagram spaces of their overlap.

Suddenly the location of my self seemed to come down to a

slick shell game where I was supposed to figure out which shell the ball was under, when I knew that the trick to such games is to make sure that the mark never knows where the ball is—sometimes by making sure there's never a ball there at all.

I put my left arm out the window as if it could ground me, my sore right arm not too sore to handle the steering wheel alone. The air felt thick and warm, then thick and cool, then thick and warm again from heat that was radiating from the asphalt, the cooler patches places where the chilling desert air had pushed the warmer away.

Something glowed along the edges of the hills to either side of us, as well as on a few cirrus clouds and fresh contrails to the north, though the moon was far from rising. I was terribly aware of the sky not as a backdrop for these things, but as some three-dimensional stuff that contained them—like a soft, wax mold. If I could crack the mold open I might blow away the clouds and stars to show their shape in relief; maybe even peel it back from the earth to capture the land's impression like a plaster cast.

I wanted to see the stars and better imagine them held in the casting of space, and found myself reaching forward then—only acting, not thinking at all—to turn off the lights. The road all but disappeared, but I could feel my seat and the van around me like they were part of my own body and for a long moment I seemed to have proprioception for the Rig's hard corners and rubber tires. I had proprioception too, I could swear, for the land itself, right where the pavement came up to meet the wheels. Like I'd had for Ruby's body when we made love.

I wondered why I wasn't more upset about her right then—why I seemed so calm. But I was calm. Ready for whatever the dominoes held in store. In this moment, in the almost dark, I felt that white pulsing again, though it seemed as if it were out there, swelling from the center of the sky like some constellation-sized jellyfish, instead of from behind my eyes. I counted my heartbeats—six for each pulsing—and after a long while my heart slowed even more so that I only had five beats per pulsing; as if the pulsing were the true measure, like a private atomic clock that set the standard for my other rhythms.

For a while then, I don't know how long, there was no Atlas, no "me" that I could point to. No me that could have spoken. I was only driving—beautifully, perfectly—through the starlit land.

SAN FRANCISCO

ODOMETER (2)00,534

LAT. 37.76°N 122.47°W

ALT. 231 FEET

JULY 15

CHAPTER TWENTY

We found them without even having to go into the convention center, right as we pulled onto the top floor of the parking ramp. The expanding, universe-sized selflessness I'd felt the night before had been replaced by my very normal, agitated self. A self that wanted, desperately, to talk face-to-face with Ruby.

I hopped out while Dade drove down the lane to take a parking spot. He'd been mightily annoyed that I forgot to wake him to witness the odometer roll over from all nines to all zeros, but coffee and an indulgent bear claw to watch the sun rise at a gas station in Emigrant Gap had gotten him back on track.

"So, the nice-man cometh," said Fran, stopping in the middle of the aisle. She was decked out in fancy new climbing clothes, her hair bundled up like a shock of wheat for her signature look.

I was so excited to see Ruby—to tell her how sorry I was—that I wasn't tracking Fran very well: "What are you talking about? Where's Ruby?"

"She's back talking with Clem in *Old Yeller*," she said, pointing to the next aisle over. "They're just working their stuff out." Her voice was soft, as if she were trying to be kind to me.

I had known in the back of my head that Clem would be there, but I had somehow managed not to think about it. Stupid. I sidestepped between cars to get to the next aisle and started to jog toward *Old Yeller*, my stomach tightening with each step. I saw

Dade out of the corner of my eye, heading toward Fran, but I didn't pay them any more attention.

When I found Ruby's truck, the curtains were shut and it was shaking slightly. I had the horrible image of Ruby on top of Clem, like she'd been on top of me only days before. I banged "Shave and a Haircut" on the side and yelled, "Ruby!"

There was a bump inside, and then the back hatch swung open to reveal Ruby staring at me, surprised, though not as surprised as Clem, who was sitting behind her. Ruby had cut her hair super short, almost a buzz cut, and had a cold sore on her upper lip. Her face was a little swollen from crying, though she wasn't crying right then. And her eyes. I could barely look into them, but when I did, I did not see a little piece of myself reflected back at me; I saw a look of worry—and pity—that told me I had made a mistake.

"Atlas!? What are you doing here?" She was already climbing over the rear gate, coming out into the sunlight.

"We're not done talking," said Clem, though this didn't stop her.

"I came to see you. I came to try to explain what had happened," I said. Without all the hair her head seemed smaller—and her eyes bigger.

"I can't believe you came anyway. When did you get here?"

"Dade decided to go for Seven Seas—we're going to free the Gibraltar pitch—and so we're out here," I said, shooting a look at Clem. I had thrown the words down as a kind of gauntlet, expecting him to snort or somehow scoff that we'd try so hard a route, but he just looked angry.

Then I turned to Ruby: "And what do you mean, 'anyway'?"

She looked back at Clem, and then at me: "I thought you'd understand I needed this time to get straightened out." She started to walk ahead of me to lead us out of earshot of Clem.

I wanted to tell her that I was confused, but that familiar off-kilter wobble had started, my body spinning around my head.

She searched me with her eyes, and then a sad, disappointed look came over her: "You never got it? The letter I left in your notebook?"

Something solid inside of me tore loose, and my body was suddenly light and rising—as if I were once again a fish being reeled up from a high pier. I took a deep breath, trying to stop the spinning, and put my hands on my knees.

"I tried to explain some things about . . . about how I feel about you, and where Clem fits into all of this."

"I'm sorry about how I handled Olive," I said, finally letting my breath out, "but I thought Clem was—"

"Wait. When I walked away at the Tower I acted like it was about Olive, but it wasn't. It was because I hadn't really told you everything about Clem."

"But you said I should come visit," I said, standing up carefully on the wobbly ground.

"Because I wanted you to right then. Now it's . . . complicated."

"It's only been three days!"

Clem climbed out of the truck and started to walk toward us, but Ruby shook her head sharply at him and he went back to lean against the rear gate.

"Do you still love him?" I snapped, flicking the back of my hand at Clem.

"I do love him, sort of," she said, almost whispering, "But I could love you more . . . it's different."

"I thought you were wrong for each other, and we were right."

"We are," she said. She had lifted a hand up as if to touch me, but with Clem still standing there, she changed this motion into one of putting a hand over a scab on her forearm. It was the scrape she'd gotten the day we climbed together.

"I really wish you'd given me some time to figure this out," she said.

Clem crossed his arms, staring at me as if I'd, well, as if I'd just fucked his girlfriend. Then he held up his ring finger and thumb together and mouthed the word "Asshole."

That's when I realized that I had it all backward: I was the one to get between him and Ruby, not the other way around. Still, the high school wrestler in me wanted to grab his skinny ass and slam him on the pavement—maybe even break a couple of his sport-climbin' fingers—and as I thought this, hardening with a burst of adrenaline, the dizzy spinning almost stopped.

"Fine, I'll go, then. You two will have all the time in the world."

"Atlas, come on. You're the one who said, 'Let the thing be the thing,' so I'm trying to now."

It sounded so stupid coming out of her mouth, just another one of Fran's new-age platitudes.

"Right, and you guys are 'a thing,' so I'll let it be. How's that?"

"Atlas, please, that's not what I want . . ."

I had hoped that with Ruby I'd learn new rules, but suddenly—truly, deeply—I understood that with love there aren't any rules at all.

"Every time it's some new made-up game . . . every time it's the wild, wild West," I said, desperate to look away from her and so looking up into the sky. I felt wildly agitated. Ready to burst. But instead of trying to breathe easy to let that energy out into the universe, I did just the opposite, forcing the black thoughts inward with great pressure by holding and compressing them smaller and smaller and tighter and tighter. Suddenly my thoughts were sharp and clear and infinitely hard.

That moment making love with Ruby when I'd "dropped ballast": was that because she was the one, or because I'd dropped ballast on Mudskipper that very morning and was primed for it to happen? The same thing could have happened with Olive if only I could have been open to it. But Olive was gone. I had been a fool to think Ruby and I were meant to be—that I had found a lost piece of myself within her. And now that I thought about it, I realized that I hadn't lost myself in her eyes or even seen the piece of myself since we'd reconnected in the Needles. The only odd thing that I'd "seen" like that was the pulsing. The pulsing that seemed to come both from behind my eyes and from outside my self.

I was still holding my breath, and the pain in my air-deprived lungs and head finally cut through my thoughts to make me inhale desperately until I was breathing normally again—when I realized that the dizziness had simply vanished. It had vanished and I was gigantic and striding away from Ruby and her words with thirty-mile steps, compressing my feelings for her—and Olive too—into a knot so tight and hard and deep that I knew it could never bother me.

I barely remember buying supplies or leaving San Francisco or even Dade telling me what he'd learned from Fran—that Red had died the night before—but I knew that inside of me my cells were rearranging themselves like alpine flowers turning toward the sun, like iron filings snapping to a magnet.

I knew too, from deep down in those cells, that Dade was right about the triggers: I was triggered to think of "old people" when I heard the words "sansabelt" and "Florida," and I had been triggered to think that Ruby was The One only to find out that Ruby wasn't triggered to fully fall for me—just like I hadn't been triggered to fully fall for Olive.

I also knew that Dade was right about being able to "reset" yourself, like he'd done with his tattoo, because I'd just been triggered into such a reset myself—seared and tempered in a single instant. It was "the moment" Fran talked about during her ceremony at Devil's Tower—the moment when I knew once and for all what I was supposed to do with my life. There would be no more worry about Olive or Ruby. I would follow the pulsing—my own atomic clock—and it would set the rules for rock, the rules for the rockhead, and the rules for climbing Seven Seas.

YOSEMITE

ODOMETER: (2)00,739

LAT. 37.75° N LONG. 119.55° W

ALT. EL CAP MEADOWS 4,370 FEET

ALT. TOP OF EL CAP 7,569 FEET

JULY 16

CHAPTER TWENTY-ONE

"Whoo-hooo!" I howled the next morning as we drove across the bottom of Yosemite Valley. El Cap was finally in sight, its three thousand vertical feet—over three Empire State Buildings stacked on top of each other—lording over the valley while the Cathedrals across the meadow balanced out its great weight. In spite of my bad sleep the night before from parking at a wayside rest outside the park (and no sleep the night before that), I was raring to go, but Dade was in a crummy mood, partially from the bad sleep and partially because of the news about Red.

We parked on the Cathedral side and jogged (at least I did) across the broad field of El Cap meadows to take it all in, our shirts off in the building heat. The sky was blazing blue, the fine-grained granite golden in the morning light.

I scanned the wall for other climbers just to imagine myself up there too. In spite of the almost-perfect weather, I could only count eight parties (when there should have been dozens), including two parties on the Nose and another high above them on Seven Seas with white shirts and a yellow haul bag. The small forest between the base and us obscured our view of the first few hundred feet of the route, but from the Bay of Pigs, a blurry patch of dark in the otherwise gold rock, I could follow the entire route.

I pointed at the white shirts and the yellow haul bag halfway up the wall and grinned like a moron at Dade. For the first time since he'd found out about Red's death, he grudgingly smiled back. How could he help it? It was all so gorgeous—and within our grasp.

We walked farther across the meadow, until we were twenty feet from a muscly young lad with binoculars, and watched someone on the Nose route, one of the most famous Big Wall routes in the world, beginning the wild pendulum traverse to the stoveleg cracks. The climber was six or seven hundred feet up, just a tiny ant of a thing, inscribing a narrow arc along the rock to the left, then to the right, then to the left again.

"He's really going for it," I started to say, but then the kid gasped and looked back at us, exclaiming that someone had just fallen.

"Up and to the right. A few pitches below that giant roof," the kid said.

"On Seven Seas?" I asked. "Can I borrow your binoculars?"

The kid hesitated, but then handed them to me. I could see that one of the climbers was hanging about fifty feet below the belay, holding his knee, and rocking his helmet on the granite. Above him, flattened to the wall next to the yellow haul bag, his partner was clearly yelling down to him.

"They're about two pitches below the roof," I said to Dade. "That's the Roaring Forties pitch, right?"

"Yeah—A4+ hooking till the cows come home. He must have zipped big-time," said Dade, trying to sound calm.

"Probably a ninety-foot fall," I said, my stomach screwing up. That could be Dade. Or me. There are other triggers in the world. Like little A4 flakes whose time has finally come. Little flakes exploding off the wall while your mouth opens wide for the terror.

"So that's Seven Seas, huh?" said the kid, seeing Dade's tattoo and giving him an appreciative look. "The rangers say that after Davy Jones's Locker fell out you could hear the boot creaking."

"It fell out?" asked Dade, looking back up at the route.

"It's not a cowboy *boot*; it's pronounced like *boat*—Das Boooht. And rock doesn't creak," I said testily, handing the kid his binoculars back

"This one *definitely* does," he said, taking aim at El Cap again. "I'm just glad the Nose is out of the fall line."

I knew the kid was probably going up on the Nose and itching to talk about it, but I suddenly wasn't in the mood and avoided saying anything. It didn't matter.

"We're going up on it tomorrow," the kid said, trying to sound nonchalant. "We've got three days of good weather before it's supposed to turn."

As I started to mumble "Good luck," Dade cut in: "I think that guy is jugging back up."

I could see him too, slowly working his way back up his own line, and I was instantly relieved. So was the kid, who let out a long "whew."

"He must be okay," I said to Dade.

When Dade looked at me, he wasn't smiling at all anymore: "Come on. I owe Bev a call, and we still need to see if we can get a site in Sunnyside."

WE COULDN'T. SUNNYSIDE (the famous "Camp Four" of yore) is the only campground in the Valley where you don't have to make reservations a year in advance and where we could literally have "walked in"—except, at 10:00 a.m., we were already so late there wasn't even a ranger manning the kiosk, just a sign attached to the outside of the window that said, *The early bird catches the worm*, alongside a very large smiley face.

The sign had been vandalized, however, with a black Sharpie and horrendous handwriting, to read, *The early bird can suck my dick,* with the addition of a badly drawn penis and balls stuffed in the mouth of the smiley face, which was wearing a ranger hat. *The Mad Marker* was written on the forehead of the smiley face, as if it were carved into it, with a black drop of blood oozing from it.

We walked around to the back of the kiosk, unsure what to do next, and read the postings people had hung on the bulletin board.

"Wanted, lost arrows, long dongs, rurps, hammer—or ride to San Francisco. Mickey, site 8."

"Lost: #2 Camalot. Forgot at base of Cookie. Please return to site 22, Richard, reward."

"Wanted: Partner to climb Central Pillar of Frenzy—must have own gear." Except someone had changed "gear" to "beer."

While I looked over all the ads, Dade took down a two day-old *Sacramento Bee* newspaper from the board and began to read it. While we stood there, a scruffy, ponytail guy wearing a T-shirt that said *Actual Size* on it slipped between us with his own ad and tried to find a thumbtack to post it with.

The guy nodded a hello to me just as Dade started to read out loud: "'In the second major rescue attempt of the season, rangers and the search and rescue team initiated a full-scale effort to rescue two climbers on the popular "Nose" route of El Capitan, in Yosemite Valley. The experienced climbers apparently got into trouble after one fell into a crevasse . . . climber later died from head injuries.'" He folded the paper loudly when he was done, then tacked it back up on the board.

"They always say they're 'experienced,'" I said to Dade. "They never say 'inexperienced climbers'—plus there's no crevasse on the Nose."

"He whipped into the Texas Flake from above," said the ponytail guy, casually, as if he already knew us. He whistled in a descending tone—like a bomb falling—and then made a wet, splatting sound.

"But the pitch above is a bolt ladder," said Dade. "And it heads left of the flake."

The guy nodded, then shrugged, still looking for a tack.

I'd led the Texas Flake pitch, which actually looks like the state of Texas, on my first trip to the Valley when Dade and I did the Nose. The flake is separated from the wall by a few feet, narrower at the bottom, wider at the top to create a chimney. It's only twenty-five feet of climbing tops, but falling into it from above you'd be a human pachinko ball, rattling down the sides until you got wedged in at the bottom.

"Poor bastard," I said. "What do they think happened?"

"Search and rescue guys say the belayer must have screwed up—but they can't figure it out, and he's not talking."

"Hey, what's the deal with Das Boot, on Seven Seas? Have you heard anything about it?" asked Dade.

"Heard lots," said the guy with a grim laugh. "We did Dog Daze two weeks ago—close enough to hear it. It was groaning."

"Groaning? We heard it was creaking."

"It was groaning like an old hound dog when I was up there . . . it was creepy as shit, dude, and that thing's the size of my apartment building back in Oakland. I want to be far away when it gets launched," he said, finally removing the "#2 Camalot" ad and crumpling it into his pocket, using the tack to place his "Portaledge for Rent" ad before he walked away. It was signed

Pistol Pete, site 23 and written with a black Sharpie. I noticed that
the handwriting was suspiciously similar to the Mad Marker's.

"Let's see if there's anyone here we know who we can crash
with," I said, turning to head down the campground path, realizing that Pistol Pete had vanished into thin air.

The dusty campground was barren. Most of the climbers
(whose tents occupied the sites we needed) had abandoned it for
the granite walls that ring the valley. That made it quiet too, except for the Stellar Jays, which hollered at the rough n' tumble
rock squirrels like a gang of thugs warning off another gang.

A sign had been posted on the path that read: *No unregistered
camping: Violators will be prosecuted,* only someone with much better handwriting than the Magic Marker had changed it to *No
uncastrated humping: Vibrators will be prostituted.* "They must be
getting serious," I joked, but Dade didn't respond. He focused his
attentions on a plastic soda bottle, kicking it ahead of us while
we walked, though the plastic itself sounded almost bored by its
torment.

We wandered past a group of French climbers who were
working the famous Midnight Lightning boulder problem, and
then past a couple of ripped kids kicking a footbag. They were
being watched by two Japanese climbers who sat on either side
of a rock, arms crossed and legs crossed and smoking hand-rolled
cigarettes. Dull rays of light fanned out through the trees to give
the campground a flat, sleepy feeling—opposite the feeling found
high up on the granite walls—and the air was thick enough to
slow us to a halt in front of a picnic table where a large, cheap
kitchen knife had been stabbed vertically into one of its many
cracks. A tiny pool of sun landed on the table, about a foot away
from the knife, with dust motes swirling in the column of light
above it.

"We'll probably have to stealth bivy at the base," I said to Dade, still thinking about where we'd have to sleep. We'd done that a few times before when we couldn't get a site. The rangers pretty much leave cars alone that are parked at the base of El Cap, assuming that the owners are up on the wall, but it's hard to sleep with cars driving by in ones and twos all night.

Dade didn't answer me but just stared at the table. I had a flash then, imagining that for Dade, the knife and the sunbeam were symbolic of something: maybe his life now (the dangerous knife = Red's death and his own possible death) versus what it would be like back home (the beatific sunbeam). But then, he turned to me and said, "I'm trying to remember—didn't we camp at this very site once before? The time we did Astroman? I think I recognize that tree there."

I had a sudden scent memory of the two-gallon bucket of peanut butter that someone had left behind in the bear box. There were elephants and seals printed on the smooth plastic, with the words written in a jaunty circus font.

"Yeah. It was here—we ate out of that peanut butter tub for two weeks," I said, warmed by the memory. I was flexing my right arm and realized that, though there was still a pale bruise, it was healed. As good as new.

"And there was still enough in it to leave behind for the next crew," Dade said, turning to me, not exactly happy, but also not ornery. Then, as if still trying to talk himself into it, he said, "You keep looking, I'm going to make my call to Bev."

WE WERE SUPPOSED to go cragging the next day, just to do some nice long routes and get used to the rock again, and while Dade made his phone call I lay in the Rig reading the Yosemite guidebook and spinning my whirligig—putting the fish in, then taking it out of the bowl—as I picked out good multi-pitch routes for us to sharpen our teeth on. I felt even more invincible (if you can add to invincible like you can add to infinity) and imagined myself on the Valley walls, my body brimming over with the rockhead, sending everything I touched. But that day of cragging never came—or not as we'd planned it, anyway.

"Bev's giving me one week," said Dade when he got back to the van.

I looked up from my guidebook to consider him. He still had his shirt off and had a hand on the roof so that it showed off his etched lats and triceps, his pecs lean and serrated where they tried to gap his sternum. He was so ripped even his tattoo was looking burly—all of him built for sending Seven Seas.

"She read about that guy who just died on the Nose. It turns out he was from Wisconsin and climbed at the St. Paul gym sometimes. Jacobi or something. Ever hear of him?"

The name was familiar, but I answered no.

"She had another dream too. In it I was on a snowy mountain, but also underwater, drowning. I was drowning on the mountain, and she knew where I was but couldn't get to me. You were in it too," he said, extending an index finger to poke me, "but you wouldn't help me. All you did was watch."

I held up my palm to deflect him: "Dade, come on—'you and me and a big bad wall,' right? We're meant to send this." I made a ring of my thumb and index finger, trying to get him to do our carabiner handshake, but he looked away.

"I have a pregnant wife to worry about. A wife who's more important to me than doing the Seven Seas," he said, as if he might convince himself it were true.

That was when I realized I was being triggered to push Dade's buttons (and that he needed me to push them), and since there was nothing we could do about it, I pushed all his buttons, all at once, counting them off on my fingers: "Come on, when are going to be this fit again? Do you want to look back at fifty and know that you could've had this route in hand but gave it up? And as soon as you get home you'll have to tell Bev about Fran. And when you finally get her to forgive you you'll have makeup sex and create another kid, and then you'll be forty. Then your shoulders really may be toast. Plus you're leaving me in the lurch—I'll have to go do it with someone else. If I can even find someone as good as you . . ."

The last point was his final straw, I knew, because he couldn't bear it if I managed to tick off Seven Seas and he didn't.

"Then we'd better be off it within seven days from now, because that's when we have to drive back to Minnesota," he said, pushing away from the van.

"Fine. The weather's good for at least four days. Let's get on it tomorrow. Team Seven Seas," I said. I knew that he was mostly hooked; that he wanted to capture this jewel for his crown. But I also knew that I had to call his bluff; like the necessary head bobble in the complex courtship of two Weaver birds, I had to make all the right moves to lure him onto Seven Seas. More than any other time on the trip I felt the dominos crashing into each other, one by one. I was standing on top of the biggest one yet, a domino so enormous I couldn't see the next one in the line-up—or which way it would fall.

"Are you fully committed? For a storm? For no return after the Roof? For Das Boot to come wheeling off in the middle of the night?" he asked, whipping one arm behind him as if it were the granite block itself.

"Yes," I said, and then, waiting a beat to make my last move in the ritual: "Are you?"

He vanished from the side door, and a moment later the Rig shook as he opened up the back. By the time I got out he was already pulling things violently from it: two portaledges; the big haul bag; ensolite sleeping pads; wall hammers and holsters; his big, green tarp to lay it all out on; and, since you have to pack all your waste off the wall with you, our sealable, six-inch pvc pipe "caboose," which would hang off our haul bag and bring up the rear, so to speak.

"If we're going to do this fucking thing, then let's do it," he said, turning the haul bag upside down to shake its gear out onto the tarp. "All I know is we have a hell of a lot to do if we're going to get on it tomorrow."

Rare and specialized wall gear spilled out in a rush like the contents of a deep-sea fishing net. Bird beaks and sky hooks and Leeper Z's and baby angles and bright, beat-up ascenders and aiders and daisy chains and dozens of slings, tangled up in a big nasty pile before Dade dropped to his knees to spread it all out.

I spied that old ring piton–sky hook Dade had gotten years before in the Needles and snatched it from the mess as if it were a treasured pet pit viper, trying to escape. I held it up by its neck: "This bad boy looks hungry."

"Oh, yeah. We're going to need that. Plus all the tapes," he said, "And maybe a forty-foot stick clip for Jaws—you get to do that pitch, since you're so gung ho. And I get Gibraltar."

"We'll throw paper, scissors, rock—as always. Or flip for it," I said, spinning my whirligig back and forth.

He squinted his eyes at me, then nodded. "We'll need thirteen two-liter bottles in this heat. Or make that fourteen—I'm not running out of water again. And soup cans for three days, apples, lemonade mix, canned coffee, Powerbars . . ."

"And Jolly Ranchers," I said, "And kitty litter for the caboose—I'll get it all at the store while you rack up."

"I saw a guy putting out water bottles by the dumpsters this morning—maybe a dozen."

"Good—a *fleet* of water bottles. Or maybe a *raft*," I said, thinking of the collective nouns from Ruby, and then, for a piercing moment, of Ruby's sweet face. Of Ruby and me. Of her letter. Of Ruby with Clem.

Dade looked at me, confused; I'd never talked to him about the measure word stuff, and in my spasm about Ruby I couldn't gather myself enough to explain.

"Never mind—I'm on it," I said, picking up the empty haul bag. "I'll get the bottles first."

I was excited to do the prep work—to be in line for the tilt-a-whirl. I wanted Seven Seas like never before. Or better said, I believed I didn't *want* it any more than a carrier pigeon *wants* to fly home or a cat *wants* to mate. I wanted it because it was wanted for me. Because I was a matrix of switches and triggers that were being flipped outside of my control. I was driven to go and get that thing, but the end result, for Dade and the rest of the world, was the same.

I *decided* to call Olive in the same way.

It was like I had been hypnotized way back when I was at Devil's Tower: Olive had made me promise to call her before I went up on a wall, and now that Dade had said the magic word there was nothing else to do but dial the number. I didn't want to explain to Dade why I needed his phone and so instead I went to the lodge to use a pay phone. I had no idea what I'd say, though I was sure I didn't want to go into it all again and get myself torqued up before the hard climbing. I also didn't want to get her hopes up or make her sad, though my call would surely, at the very least, do the latter. That meant, I told myself, that I shouldn't make the call. And yet I did.

I looked in my day bag for my wallet and also found that jackalope notebook I'd bought for Olive, complete with my notes about her on the back page. I also discovered what must have been the letter Ruby mentioned, peeking out from the middle. I ignored the letter and folded the notebook over to the last page, setting it on the ledge in front of the payphone as if it might somehow help me focus:

> *Seeing?→ lazy→ weakness→ Olive.*
> *Olive. Olive. Olive. Olive. Olive.*

But it was as if the words had no meaning anymore. I dialed Olive's number.

The phone rang and rang, but she didn't pick up. Maybe Olive guessed from the California area code that it was me. Or maybe she was making love to that producer who had been hitting on her. Or in a late meeting. Probably in a meeting, I thought, leaving too long a pause on her voicemail before I found myself speaking.

"Olive, I just wanted you to know that I'm in the Valley and I'm okay . . . I'm just calling like you asked me to. We're going up on a wall tomorrow—on Seven Seas. Dade and I. That's the one we always wanted to do. The big, famous one with the aid pitches that go free. Anyway, things didn't work out with Ruby and she's back with her old boyfriend, Clem. I don't know if you've met him . . . I . . ."

Wait—how could I say that? Why did I say that about Ruby? I wanted to eat my words, suck the whole message back through the line and swallow it.

"I mean, I'm not saying that to get things started again, just to . . ."

What? Just to make things worse for her?

"Just to let you know it's not all roses for me."

Wait, that's not what I mean, either.

"Oh, fuck it. I'm sorry I made this call. I'm not sure what I even meant to say. But then, that's about right, because I'm just a ball of triggers, right? Just a mess of bad decisions and misreads and fucked-up shit. But that's not true, either, because I'm climbing solid now, I can get to my rockhead. I'm going to pull this monster down."

I paused again, and then, just as I was, out of ancient habit, about to say "Olive Juice," I managed to hang up, not even saying goodbye.

I was frantic with what I'd just done, surprised by how much her voice had rattled me. I couldn't figure out why it bothered me, since I didn't want to be with her anyway. But then, maybe I did. What did I know about what I wanted? I did care about Olive, that was true, but did I want to be with her? Was I only reacting to my loss of Ruby? Was I rebounding back to the person I'd bounded away from? Maybe "I" was the Jax ball I'd tossed high when I'd kissed Ruby that night in the buffalo field, while Olive had always been rooted firmly to the ground. As I thought these thoughts, my head hidden in the metal shell of the wall phone as if I were still talking, the phone rang violently. Olive? She couldn't have listened to the message yet and must have simply hit the call back button on her cell.

I found myself listening to the rings. Two. Three. Four. Five. I wasn't going to pick it up, and then the phone was in my hand: "Hello?" I said, my voice cracking weirdly.

"Hello, is . . . who just called me? Is Atlas there? Atlas?"

I started to answer, but then I was crying and the words came out in a shuddering moan. I couldn't even say "yes" without the words melting together.

"Atlas? Baby, are you okay?"

I tried again to say something, to pull myself together, but I was crying uncontrollably.

"Hey, it's okay. Is Dade there? Let me talk to Dade," she said.

I tried to say "No," but it started to come out strange again and then I gently pressed the receiver down. I was sobbing silently, with my eyes closed to make things dark, still hiding in the metal sides of the wall phone so none of the good families in the lodge could see me crying.

I hadn't realized how badly I needed someone to tell me how much they cared about me before I went up on Seven Seas. And then, like pure darkness lit by the tiniest of lights—the pale blink of a firefly—I was able see myself as if from a distance, hanging slightly above and behind my own body: it wasn't just "someone" I needed to hear, but Olive. Olive Juice. I love all of Olive's Olives.

Then the tiniest of lights was gone. The phone rang again and its harsh sound snapped me out of my paralysis, and I was hardening, walking out of the lodge, wiping my eyes as I crossed the parking lot to Dade and *Makin' Bacon* and all our hungry gear.

CHAPTER TWENTY-TWO

We were up before dawn, our tattered haul bag packed, our gear ready to go. Dade took the rotor out of the distributor so no one could easily steal the Rig, and then, in the dusky light, we saddled up. Together we hefted the ninety-pound haul bag—forty-eight pounds of it water—up into the side doorway of *Makin' Bacon*, and I helped Dade thread his arms through the straps.

"This thing is on its last legs," I said as Dade stood up with the weight, slapping him like a mule.

"I wish it *had* some legs," he said with a pant, staggering forward with his first, tentative steps. I took a quick picture of him, with the camera flash on, in front of *Makin' Bacon*. Then I put on the immense chest harness with its double set of Camalots, triple-nuts, RPs, HBs, sky hooks, lost arrows, sawed-off angles, and chains of free biners, finally pulling on the climbing pack that held our storm gear and everything else we needed easy access to, including four liters of water and the caboose. Then I slung the two 60-meter, 10.5-millimeter ropes and the 9-millimeter haul line over my neck, and finally threw a portaledge over each shoulder to strike out into the woods after Dade, my ankles and lumbar discs groaning with the awkward, seventy-pound load.

We walked for about twenty minutes and took a rest, then walked another twenty minutes to the base, picking our way through the red manzanita. Schlepping the load sucked, and getting up at 5:00 a.m. was rotten, but as we walked through the forest we heard only the sounds of our breathing and footsteps and a soft wind in the pines, while the swelling dawn light trickled down through the trees to slowly give form and mass to each discrete object around us.

"It's always like this, and I always forget," I said as we reached the base of the wall, the rock looming so high above us it was difficult to grasp its height. There was a faint, nostalgic scent there of granite and manzanita that I hadn't smelled in a while, along with something else—something sour-sweet that I couldn't quite identify—that all added up to a unique perfume: L'eau de Big Wall. Dade was just ahead of me and had already cut right to skirt the base toward Seven Seas, and then he froze: there was a party already on the wall, not even to the first belay.

"Not again," said Dade breathlessly. "We should have started earlier."

We'd had a party just ahead or just behind us on half the walls we'd been on, and it had been a hassle every time.

"Maybe they're doing Dog Daze," I said as I passed him, since they shared the same start, but he just shook his head.

I mumbled a good morning to the guy belaying, whom I recognized from the climbing mags, though he was much smaller in person. I also noticed that their haul bag was brand new, as were their portaledges.

"You doing Dog Daze?" the guy asked me.

I was shucking my backpack; once I dumped it, I shook my head. "Seven Seas."

He rolled his eyes, then yelled up to his partner, "It sees ten ascents a summer, and now that we're on it it's packed."

His partner—another rope gun I recognized from the sport climbing circuit—was about ninety feet off the deck, not too far from the belay slings, working his way across a field of crimpy flakes. He was climbing with barely any gear, with a single rope and a haul line clipped to the back of his harness. He might as well have been bathing with African crocodiles in just a Speedo and Ray Bans.

"Don't worry," the rope gun said, looking down to see Dade lying on the haul bag like a turtle on its back, "we'll be way ahead of them by afternoon."

I took off the wall harness, the rest of the gear, and my wet T-shirt and walked up to the rock, feeling so buoyant with each step, once the weight was off me, that it seemed gravity had been turned down a notch—or that I was filled with helium. I flattened myself against the rock, my toe tips butted against the wall, my arms spread-eagled as if to hold myself to the earth, and looked up to see granite and then more granite and then the sharp blue sky.

All that rushing the night before, and all our momentum, had been for nothing; now we'd have to wait hours, and maybe wait hours on the rock too in the following days, if they weren't as fast as they hoped they would be.

The first time we'd done a wall, it had taken us days to get ready, triple-thinking every decision, carefully duct-taping all the water bottles, poring over weather reports and gear lists. We had no momentum that time, and it didn't even feel like we'd stay on the route until we'd gotten to our first camp, 1,200 feet off the ground. But that afternoon, looking out over the valley through the humming, crystalline air, I felt like I had discovered a language I hadn't known existed—and like I could speak it. That night, exhausted and half hanging, half lying on an eighteen-inch ledge, I was too amazed by how far and how hard we'd climbed to sleep much; I kept waking up, staring at the stars as they wheeled across the half-sky, moving in bursts between my fragments of sleep.

A yell from above ripped me from my thoughts. Although the middle section of Seven Seas was hidden from us, the pitches beneath the Roof of Good Hope were already in the sun. I could see the yellow haul bag along with the two climbers in white T-shirts—the one's we'd seen fall the day before from El Cap meadow—who were waving their arms wildly at us.

I thought I heard the word *Stein*——"rock" in German—and then the haul bag and one of the climbers started falling. Then only the haul bag was falling. It fell and fell, so bottom-heavy it never rotated but simply wobbled like a shuttlecock. Before any of us could say anything, it hit the ground with a loud crunch, a hundred feet to our right.

"They lost their bag," I said, amazed.

"No . . . I think they're bailing," said Dade as the higher of the two climbers began to lower out. "They must have fucked up big-time."

"Dude," yelled the belayer to the rope gun, "Petr and Jorg are bailing."

Dade looked at me and raised his eyebrows.

"Petr and Jorg? The Schaeffer brothers?" I asked the belayer. The Austrian twins were famous for their hideous alpine routes. They had come to raid Gibraltar.

He nodded to me, and then yelled up to his partner again: "If they're bailing, I'm not going the fuck up there."

"I bet Das Boot really is coming down," I said, trying to make my voice sound worried, then turning to wink at Dade.

"Well, I'm not going up on it until it does," said the belayer.

"Me neither," said Dade quickly, and then, to me, "Come on, let's go check out the haul bag."

When we were out of earshot, Dade made the ka-ching sound of a slot machine: "If they bail now we're golden—with the whole wall to ourselves."

"You're not worried?" I asked.

"These guys are Über-studs, right," he said, jerking his thumb over his shoulder at the belayer. "But they're stressing and looking for an excuse. I mean, come on, the Schaeffer Brothers can't be bailing because of Das Boot, can they? Because they could always traverse left and finish the last couple pitches on Dog Daze. I bet one of them is hurt or they lost gear or water or something."

We stared at each other, trying hard not to grin. I hadn't looked that hard into Dade's eyes since we left Laramie. He was solid, not unhappy, definitely hungry—and I knew that he too had handed over his ticket for the tilt-a-whirl, any thoughts about what had happened to Red locked up tight in the ornate ink of his tattoo.

"I just hope they don't change their minds when they see we're getting on it," I said.

"Let's pretend we're thinking of doing another route and that we need to rest before we take off," Dade said, almost whispering. Then, after a beat, he said, "Team Sandbag Sucker Punch," holding out his hand for our carabiner handshake.

"Yeah. Something equally sick, like Wyoming Sheep Ranch," I said, snapping my fingers apart from his.

We walked back to our packs and lounged while the rope gun rappelled the first pitch. He was mad at the belayer, though he'd made the call to bail too, and it was clear from their sniping that they may not have survived each other, anyway—not an uncommon fate among novice big-wall teams. They ignored us as they angrily packed up their gear, but as they got ready to go, they finally began talking to us.

That's when Dade started getting our gear ready, champing at the bit like only he can do—and starting to get confident.

When they realized what we were doing, things got weird.

"You're still going up?" the rope gun asked.

Dade pushed his safety glasses on his nose and gave them a shit-eating grin as his answer.

"Where are you guys from?" asked the rope gun.

"Minnesoodah. We're going to try to free Gibraltar," Dade said.

"Das Boot has been up there for millions of years," I said. "I doubt it would have come down while you were underneath it."

There was a look on the rope gun's face like we'd pitched quarters and won his milk money off him, but there was little he could do about it at that point—they'd already lost their momentum for the day.

"Yeah, good luck," the rope gun said, recovering enough to scoff at us.

Dade nodded a serious thank-you and said that he was saving up all the luck he could get. And then we got busy.

I opened the Schaefer Brothers' haul bag and pulled out an intact water bottle—they'd be dumping all their water before they hiked out anyway. I drank as much water as I could, then pissed on the ground one last time, realizing that the smell I couldn't identify when we first walked up was simply the scent of a distant bus station urinal—also known as the Nose Route, not far to our left.

Then I started to put on the rest of the ridiculous amount of gear we'd need: on my waist harness I had slings and aiders and jumars and pulleys and my aiding shoes and a water bottle, as well as the haul bag rope and the zip line. On my chest harness I had more than double sets of cams and nuts and tons of biners. It all weighed about twenty-five pounds—an insane amount for free climbing—and would grow heavier as I moved upward and took on the weight of the ropes hanging below me. The only thing I didn't have out for this pitch was the pure aid gear—the hammer and pitons and copperheads and sky hooks and knee pads. Dade would jug after me with those in the daypack.

I tied into the lead rope and made sure Dade watched me while I did it. I'd be tied into this very end for days and Dade would be tied in at the other end, fifty-eight meters of monkey rope between us the whole time. No matter how much rope got used up at a belay, there'd always be this long, strong core between us. I had the quick thought again that I'd had before, that I might as well be stepping off into space, the rope a tether to my capsule. Then I was laying hands on the rock, setting my feet on the very first edge of the very first move in the very first second of what, in my memory years later if I ever became an old man, would be a single, extended moment—the moment of succeeding on Seven Seas. With my hands set on two thin flakes, one foot on the rock, one still on the sandy ground, I turned to Dade and said, "Climbing."

CHAPTER TWENTY-THREE

Five pitches later, 490 feet off the deck, I was deep into the hideous Bay of Pigs pitch—rated A4+, the hardest aid pitch on that first day of climbing. I was standing high in my aiders and working a seam so thin and crooked a dime wouldn't fit in it, my trunk muscles tight to keep me in balance against the fifi hook as I held my breath and pasted a copperhead with hammer and chisel. We had already been in the sun for hours and it was hot, with the wind blowing steady from below to act as a convection oven—gusting so strong at times that it jerked my aiders above my shoulders to snap at my helmet.

My gear was so sketchy and thin that if any of the aid pieces failed, they would all fail, unzipping to send me past the belay. With thirty feet of rope out, including rope stretch, that would be over a seventy-foot fall—and I wasn't even to the hard part yet, a blank stretch of rock I'd have to traverse with a sky hook and a fifteen-foot pendulum.

With that last thought, I froze—not because I was scared, but because I wasn't. In the past, I'd compared aid climbing to super strenuous roofing—with a gun pointed at my head. But during this pitch I'd known, with the quickest of looks at a placement, exactly how to move and exactly what gear I'd need, pulling it blind off my chest harness. Each location in the rock was like the mold of the piece I'd find to place inside it, each pasted copperhead or delicate RP almost the same density as the rock I'd connect it to.

This climbing was the same—except for some reason I didn't believe the gun was loaded. But that was four moves before the seam died out—four moves before I reached the skyhook pendulum. Normally in a pendulum traverse you create a solid anchor and lower out to swing along the wall—running back and forth like a skateboarder building up momentum on a ramp—to get the next crack system. But this was too dicey for any aggressive movements, and I'd have to claw my way sideways like a bat to get over to the next vertical crack. I'd heard the first party actually taped their sky hook onto the rock with a big *X* of duct tape to keep it in place, but I didn't think I'd need to go that far. Instead, I simply snicked my sharpest hook on the slightly rounded, quarter-inch flake and had Dade lower me down fifteen feet, so that that I was dangling beneath the hook, about ten feet right of Dade, twenty feet above him. The last piece before the hook was a fat RP the size of my eyetooth, and there were seven copperheads before that. It was a delicate chain that should have had my stomach in knots, but I was calm, confident that I'd make the next seam even when I started pulling myself across the rock, climbing sideways under so much tension it was as hard as climbing directly against gravity.

I was about to yell about how hard it was, but the words never made it to my mouth. Like the tip of a bullwhip being cracked, I was accelerating at an absurd rate toward the ground, the gear disintegrating with high-pitched pings that I felt more than heard, the rock rushing past in such a terrible blur that time didn't have a chance to slow down.

AND THEN, JUST as abruptly, the rope came taut and slammed

me into the wall eighty feet below where the skyhook had been, knocking the wind out of me. I couldn't draw air for a few seconds, and when I could, the blown skyhook and RP and copperheads sizzled down the rope as if on a zipline, racing toward my harness to snap at me.

"Uhtlas!" Dade was screaming, "Uhtlas, are you okay?!"

It happened so fast, and when it was over it was as if I'd been trapped underwater, too stunned to scream or even cry. Then I broke the surface with a long, deep breath, and the moments of the fall came tearing back into me. I remembered the rock as mostly a blur except for a star-shaped flake as I dropped past, my gear jangling as something hit me in the chin. My right elbow was bleeding and my knee pad was somehow torn, and I felt something like a charley horse but in the bones of my hips, which left my legs slightly numb. I didn't have a thought for the first second or two, and then I only had one thought, which was *Scary shit*. Scary, scary scary. Shit, shit, shit. Then I had another thought (maybe when the adrenaline really hit): this fall was really no different than the fall Red had taken; I had fallen eighty feet and was fucking okay. In fact, I was more than okay—I was invincible. I was a hardwired badass, and my whole being throbbed with the surety that I would succeed on Seven Seas. I held up my thumb and fingers in an okay sign to Dade and yelled, "I guess I should have passed the fuck auf!" I laughed, and, stunned, he laughed back.

From a few hundred feet above us, I heard someone calling and realized that it was the Austrian brothers, hooting when they saw me wave to Dade. And someone else too, though I couldn't locate them. The Austrians were rappelling Desert Rat, which crossed Seven Seas about midway, and which had bolted rappel stations all the way to the ground.

I jugged back up to Dade, mad on adrenaline. He checked my bloody elbow—just a nasty scrape—and offered, for only the third or fourth time in our climbing partnership, to take the pitch off my hands. But I wanted it badly and set off again.

It took almost an hour to get back up to my high point, the rock bearing little whitish flares where the gear had torn out. And this time, when I hung the skyhook, I did put an *X* of duct tape on it to help persuade it to stay in place, though I might as well have placed the *X* on my own chest for the amount of good it probably did. I pulled downward as much as sideways when I tensioned rightward this second time, and then I was at the seam, where I jammed my thin nut tool into the crack like a log pike to create a handle. Twenty feet above it, I built a nest of gear for the belay and watched the taped skyhook pop off and tinkle sideways down toward Dade. Then I weighted my new favorite place in the world and the slack went out of the line.

At the top of the Bay of Pigs pitch, I set up the pulleys and jumars to Z-haul the bag again. This had been the worst part of the first and third pitches earlier that day, when I had to throw my body off the rock, pushing with my hands and feet like I were on some demented Nautilus machine to inch the 120 pounds of haul bag and portaledges and our caboose up after me. The honeymoon was over then, and I was reminded that this is what big walls are made of: in between the fierce, brittle moments of climbing—aid or free—it's really just ditch-digger's work, coal miner's labor. But at the base of the Rhumb Line pitch, I was safe, hanging on some big honkin' Camalots, and the hauling was almost a joy because no matter how hard I had to work, I at least couldn't peel off from there and fall: I was happy to dig ditches, elated to work the mine. Plus, ahead of us were the two fine pitches of medium-hard finger-crack climbing, where we could free climb again and make better time.

"Whoo-hoo!" I yelled to Dade as he did a version of the pendulum himself, using the zip line to let himself out sideways from the last belay as he simultaneously jugged up the lead line to pull the gear.

I heard another "Whoo-hoo!" come from the Austrians too, just above us and about a hundred feet to the right.

In the spirit of things, and feeling good about getting Bay of Pigs behind me, I yelled to them in German: "Was ist denn passiert? Taucht Das Boot runter?" *What happened? Is Das Boot going to take a dive?*

"Nee," yelled one of them with a crazy accent, my German not fazing them in the least, "Mein Bruder Jorg ist verletzt worden," he said, pointing at his partner.

Peter told me that Jorg, who had already rappelled out of sight, had been hit by the haul bag during a pendulum pitch. It had gotten loose and side-checked him hard enough to crush him into the corner wall above the Tropic of Skin Cancer pitch. His knee was so swollen he couldn't even bend it. They were heading down, but claimed they'd be back as soon as Jorg was fit again.

"*What about Das Boot?*" I hollered, continuing in German.

"*Something falls every few minutes—gravel and dirt, mostly,*" he yelled back, still rappelling.

"*Do you think it's dangerous?*"

He paused to laugh and swept his free arm in a broad circle, encompassing his brother and El Capitan and maybe the whole wide world outside Yosemite too, shrugging as if to say, "What isn't dangerous?" Then he disappeared after his brother.

It was odd passing them like that, close but also at a distance, like two ships at sea, and when they rappelled out of sight, into a kind of chute that Desert Rat follows, I suddenly missed them—perhaps because we were finally all alone on the route.

Almost three hours later, I was on top of the Straights of Mallaca at the belay known as Singapore Slings, waiting beneath the great open maw of Jaws for Dade to clean the pitch below. I had just secured the haul bag alongside me, and the portaledges and caboose were hanging beneath it like great bats from a stalactite, waiting for dusk. It was already past seven, with direct sunlight only falling on the tops of the Cathedrals on the far side of the valley, the space between us cloaked in the dusky blue shadow that I'd only seen in Yosemite, which maybe comes from campfire smoke or dust or RV exhaust and which makes the sky seem almost tangible. I was psyched to be done for the day, but already dreading the Jaws pitch.

Jaws is an overhung chimney forty feet long, five feet wide at the bottom and two feet wide at the top. Originally done on aid with skyhooks on the inside of its three walls, it had been done as a free climb a few years before as a veritable solo with no protection until the very top of it. Dade was determined that we save time and pull it down free, and we'd decided that we'd flip for it in the morning.

We wrestled the portaledges into shape once Dade finished the pitch and set them up with Dade's red one resting just below my yellow one, tucked up tight in the Singapore harbor for the night—a harbor so high up that you can piss into thin air and know the stream will break apart and evaporate before it hits the ground.

It was still hot and humid, though cooler than it had been in the morning, and looking out across the Valley I noticed that, only a hundred feet away from me, there were swarms of puffy white seeds from cottonwood or poplar trees. They swelled and dipped in unison, their whiteness strangely phosphorescent in the dusk—as if the moon were shining on them, though there was no moon yet. I felt so happy for the white seeds that I found myself crying, and whether it was caused by the vacuum of retreating adrenaline or low blood sugar I didn't care. Soon my best friend Dade would take out the cans of stew and fruit we'd hauled for dinner and then we'd eat and pass out, two tiny specks hanging from a sheer wall with invisible zzz's floating above our heads. It was all so simple. This is why we were up there.

Hours later, though, long after Dade had begun to snore lightly, I was still awake, staring up into the void of Jaws—like I had been doing since before it had grown dark. Even though I was in complete darkness, I could still "see" it looming above me like an afterimage, its even angle burnt into my memory. My body was achy all over, especially my right index finger, which I'd bashed while pasting a copperhead. It felt like it were the size of a grapefruit, and I had to turn on my headlamp to convince myself it wasn't, the single bolt at the top of Jaws twinkling at me like a fat star—or maybe a glistening shark tooth. Just after I turned off my headlamp, I heard something out in the dark.

We were safe, I knew, protected by the overhang, but when I heard another whistle I unconsciously jerked in close to the wall: tiny stones were ripping through the air, and then something bigger fell past—the trilling buzz of a fist-sized block. Then all sound stopped. Was it just a little rockslide caused by a pigeon or a rat up on the ledge, or was Das Boot coming down? In spite of our Team Sandbag Sucker Punch coup, there was still the inescapable fact that Das Boot could fall anytime between now and twenty thousand years from now. So that meant it could fall the next day. It could even fall while we were climbing on it. Yikes.

In the deep silence, I wondered what Das Boot would sound

like if it broke free and fell past us right then, spinning slowly through the warm, dark air. Would it sound like a freight train with all engines pumping, or nothing but a bigger trilling than I'd just heard a moment ago? And would it hit like a meteorite, gouging the earth below and spreading trees out in a broad ring, or would it simply land with an enormous thud, standing upright for a moment like the Austrians' haul bag before slowly keeling over, just another domino in the chain?-

I wondered about the immense weight of it too. I remembered from some geology class that a cubic foot of granite weighs about 165 pounds—not much more than me—and tried to multiply the volume of Das Boot, maybe 20 feet by 30 feet by 80 feet times 165 pounds, but was immediately overwhelmed by the numbers, the zeroes drifting down upon me like sediment. The last thing I remembered before I fell asleep was a small pile of lead vests and shields that I saw inside the X-ray room in the Wyoming hospital, weight stacked upon weight stacked upon me, and then the weight compressed my waking world into a fossil that I wouldn't find again until morning.

THERE WERE MANY dreams, but the only dream I could really remember happened out on the immense, black field. I was holding Olive's face in my right hand in a very particular shape—as if I'd taken a climbing hold—with my right index on her left eyebrow, my thumb on her lip, and my middle and ring fingers on her left cheekbone. Her face seemed to be polished out of a thousand layers of amber, sealed inside the translucent petals of some honeyed flower. I knew that I could be with Olive and be happy, and she started out beaming at me, but then she grew angry with me and started yelling, though I couldn't hear her words. I realized that it was actually Ruby who was yelling at me, and then I felt a horrible, terrible pang of sadness—a great lightning bolt of a pang. Then I woke up in the pitch dark, my palms pressed to my eyes.

CHAPTER TWENTY-FOUR

S lack, goddammit—fuck!" bellowed Dade from deep inside Jaws the next morning. I'd called "Fish" to Dade's "Bowl"— one flip of my whirligig for all the marbles—and that left me belaying from my portaledge while Dade slapped and smeared his way up the forty feet of gear-less, glassy rock—trying not to fall into the valley air like the BASE jumpers who'd woken us up only a few hours earlier.

They ripped me from my sleep with a small explosion and I curled up tight with the fear that Das Boot was coming down, peering out of my sleeping bag only to see the blue and yellow canopy of a parachute to our west, followed by another dot far above him that resolved into the body of someone diving at the valley floor, arms thrust back and headfirst. After a few seconds, at our own height of about a thousand feet, that jumper released his canopy with another small boom, the sound lagging seconds after the sight, and tightly corkscrewed after the first to land somewhere in the meadows down below—where we'd been just two days before, looking up at the very stretch of rock we were now on.

"Easy hike up and then easy flight down . . ." Dade said when I looked over my ledge at him. "But I still think climbing's got to be the better sport."

He probably wasn't thinking that during the start of the Jaws pitch, when he had to stand on my shoulders like some East German *Kletterkoenig*. And he certainly wasn't thinking it when he reached the section of the chimney where it narrowed down to under three feet. That's where he had to shift from a spread-eagle to a position where his back was against one side and his feet the other, holding himself in place as if he were in the bottomless basket of a hot air balloon. Of course, the rope would stop him if he fell, but he was thirty feet out, which means over a sixty-foot fall. And that's still a long way to go, even if there's nothing to hit—as I had learned the hard way in my fall the day before.

"I got you, man, keep cranking," I yelled. I was sure he was going to fall and wished I'd anchored myself better for an upward pull, afraid I might smack my head where the inside slab of Jaws met the wall.

But somehow he slapped his back up into the rock and his right foot shot to the left wall and he was already moving in the new position, the veins in his arms and legs popping out as he tensioned himself in place. A minute later he was all crunched up at the apex of the pitch, where the slabs narrowed to under two feet, and I knew, though his body blocked it, that he was eyeing that bolt that had twinkled at me the night before, just above his head and inside the back of the shaft.

"You got it," I yelled, glad it wasn't me up there.

His voice came as if compressed by a great weight, as if he spoke any louder he'd wake up a sleeping ogre. "I can't reach the bolt . . . and I can't get any higher. I should have aided this mess . . ."

"Can you use the stiffy?" I asked. It's a long quickdraw with a couple of plastic chopsticks taped in place to help extend it. It was hanging on the outside of his harness, and I think I saw his lips move toward it, like a thirsty camel, as if they could unclip it for him.

"Oh, fuck me, I'm going to fall," he whispered, delicately

snaking his right hand between his chest and thighs to pull the stiffy off his harness. "I'm sorry."

And then Dade was a switchblade opening, falling and exploding and stopping the fall simultaneously, so that he hung from one arm which hung in turn off the stiffy, which had snapped raw into the bolt hanger.

"Slack!" he yelled, his whole body dangling from his right hand like a clapper in a bell until he smeared his feet on the wall. He jerked a bight of rope up into the bottom biner and then popped off, in the end hanging only a yard and a half below the clip—instead of thirty feet below me. Before I could say or do anything, he was winching himself up to the quickdraw, and then I was howling.

"You are a bad motherfucker!" I yelled, wishing my voice could echo through the whole valley. "The old man and the Seven Seas!"

But he could not share my elation, and his arms and legs hung limply from his torso: "I am the bad kitty that still had at least one life left, that's what I am. Again."

"You can have first crack at Gibraltar as your reward," I said before I realized I was saying it.

He nodded, his face somehow flushed and pale at the same time. "All right, I'll take you up on that."

That day we crossed the Pacific Proving Grounds, landing at the tiny belay ledges of Bikini Test Site and Eniwetok to reach the gorgeous, difficult pitches of Rhumb Line—three hundred feet of thin, arcing finger-tip cracks stacked on top of each other. Even though the Yosemite granite was smoother than Devil's Tower, offering less friction, the cracks were as good as any we'd climbed there, slightly overhung with positive feet and good gear placements, and I was incredibly focused while we were on them, my mind in my feet and my hands and everything in between—though not really in my head at all. For some reason, even immediately after my pitch, I wasn't able to replay it. In fact, I could barely remember a single thing about any of it—as if I had raced over the landscape in an airplane.

It wasn't until later in the afternoon, in the brutal heat, that things got bad. I was crossing the Tropic of Skin Cancer—an A5 full of tenuous, hollow flakes and even more tenuous placements—and eased in a small cam at the edge of the flake, completely focused. The flake turned out to be so flexible that the Lost Arrow I was hanging on shifted—but didn't blow—and my stomach screwed down to the size of a peach pit. There was a fine seam about three feet to my left, and I pawed through the rack to pull off the RPs, levering off my fifi hook to stretch and sneak a #1 into place. It would maybe hold body weight, but then there were all those other body-weight pieces behind me, simmering like popcorn kernels and getting ready to pop. I clipped my aider to it and started to weight the RP, all ginger and spice—then froze when it snapped its back like a baby rattlesnake.

Something was wrong. I imagined shattering my ankles on the ledge of Eniwetok below, of reeling backward and, even though I was wearing my helmet, cracking my skull with a dull "thuk" like Red had done. That's when I got "stuck" for the first time since Mudskipper in the Needles, stretched sideways off my fifi and unable to move, the RP trembling—still not completely weighted—but still in place.

"Fuck this freakin' aid climbing," I said, trying to stop the image of cracking my head open, "fuck it, fuck it, fuck it."

How did this happen so fast? My brain was a bowl of seething centipedes, my stomach compressed down to a black hole, the pulsing nowhere to be seen. I wanted to be curled up in a tight ball in my nest upstairs in *Makin' Bacon*. I wanted to sleep forever. Where was that "invincible" feeling?

"What's up?" Dade yelled after a minute. I was holding my breath then, my eyes closed.

"Shut the fuck up!" I hissed at the rock, and somehow this let off enough pressure for me to start breathing again—and to open my eyes in time to notice something flutter past me: just up and to my left in a tiny overhang there was a swallow nest, and a swallow there started peeping when a second one returned. I tried to peep back, to buck myself up, but my voice was too dry to sound right. The swallow stared at me, clinging to the edge of its home, its green feathers so dark they shone almost black, and then the bird seemed to swell like a drop of water and release to accelerate along the surface of El Cap, following the contours of the rock and disappearing in a heartbeat.

It's just like on Mudskipper, I thought. Dropping away . . . dropping ballast. Forget triggerism. *Make* this happen. Line the cherries up. I tried in that moment to drop ballast myself, faced again with the paradox that I was triggered to try to enact will, while believing that I was without true will. I wanted to get myopic and filter feed like I'd done at the Tower—like I'd done so many times in the last two days, when I had been calm and collected and climbing right.

I started talking to the other swallow looking down at me: "This guy's a chicken," I said about myself. "He's almost there and he can't be ruthless. He needs a trigger to make him lock on and do it."

The talking calmed me; I was able to slowly back my weight off the RP and look around. There was nothing I could reach, even beneath me, but then my eyes lit upon something: what seemed to be a hearty flake about fifteen above me, only four feet from the belay. I knew that bigger flakes and horns could be lassoed—or hooked—though I'd never done it. Then, really out of procrastination, out of needing to do anything else but weight the scary RP, I grabbed Dade's heavy, old Ring piton that he'd hammered into a hook, and tied the haul line into it. *What the hell*, I thought, *I can try it, and if it doesn't work, then I'll weight the RP.*

I looped about thirty feet of line in my left hand, then hefted the hook's weight a few times to judge the throw. Without warning, I wasn't anywhere else but there: the fifi hooking me to my top piece, my knees stable on the vertical rock. I remembered right then a game I used to play with my brother Gus: we'd toss Barrel of Monkeys plastic figures at the curled arms of the lamp above our kitchen table. The rounded hand of the monkey would catch the lamp maybe one time in twenty, but there was a way to toss it, to let it dead point just a little bit higher than the arm—like how our cat jumped onto the kitchen counter. I held this image in my mind and then swung my arm and gently let the hook fly, giving the rope in my left hand a little toss too. The hook seemed to twist on its way up, clattering into the rock a foot above the flake, but as it fell it caught the flake with its rounded curve, cupping it perfectly.

It was a desperate basketball toss the length of the court, just as the buzzer sounded; a lucky hole in one on a wind-blown Scottish golf course, though I didn't feel desperate—or lucky—at all. I tugged hard at it once, to test it, and then looked down at Dade, my stomach expanding with my smile. Then I had my ascenders out and was on my way up it—scary-careful with each pull on the thin line—until I had reached the flake and made a single hook move to top out on the two-foot square ledge known as Tasmania. The sense of dissolving fear, of leap-frogging a half-hour's work in seconds, of avoiding a terrifying fall 1,800 feet off the deck, got me incredibly psyched.

"I love this hooked piton!" I yelled, and I loved the ledge and I loved the RP that I hadn't used! I loved Dade too, and I yelled that down to him. Then I hooted out over the valley until I heard a whoop back. It was someone down in the meadows, standing on top of their car, waving their arms at us. I waved back, and so did Dade.

The world was good and right and not scary at all—until Dade, following the pitch, jugged up to that RP. He looked up at me, and then, just for the heck of it, weighted it with his aiders like I would have done if I hadn't landed the hook. The RP popped out like a rotten tooth—like it would have popped out with me.

And I would have fallen and zippered all the gear below it and hit the ledge and cracked my skull—a moment I re-imagined over and over as I lay in my portaledge that night—but I didn't have time to think about it sitting the ledge because a mini avalanche had started, a little to our right but bouncing in places to shoot over at us like shrapnel. I hunkered into the wall, hearing the whiz of what felt like bullets going by, while Dade hung in place, directly below the haul bag, about twenty feet below my ledge. One tiny piece of gravel pinged the center of my helmet, and then it was over.

When I looked up at Das Boot I swear I heard it groaning in the high air as pigeons flapped around it.

"That's no good," Dade said dryly, peeking out from beneath the bag.

I started hauling the bag as fast as I could while Dade skedaddled after it. Once we got up another fifty feet, we'd be in Mariana's Trench and would be protected until we went up and over the Roof of Good Hope, but I wouldn't be safe while belaying Dade from Tasmania.

"You'd better kick ass on this pitch," I said when he reached me.

"This is where the Schaefer Brothers bailed, isn't it? So . . . what exactly did the guy say?" Dade asked, not making eye contact with me.

I was able to gather enough of my little psyche from lassoing that flake to be a cheerleader: "Come on—we've been in worse stuff, even the choss on top of Spanish Prisoner was worse than this. And I just did another A5."

"You cheated yourself out of the A5 with that rodeo stunt, partner. And besides, the whole top of Devil's Tower wasn't about to come down when we did Spanish Prisoner—just look at that ominous bastard," he said, turning to point at Das Boot. "It's as big as Rhode Island and it's ready to come tumbling down."

It *was* ominous. The closer we got to it, the more we could see how its top hung out over its bottom—as if it had already started to fall, just in incredibly slow motion. It made my throat tighten up each time I looked at it. But I still wanted the wall.

"I'm an idiot. I should never have jinxed myself with this tattoo," Dade said, slapping his left arm, "or taken such risks. I'm going to end up like Red."

"There's no jinx—and you're the opposite of Red," I countered.

"All I know is that I wore out my luck clock again on Jaws and I don't want to make another mistake, and tomorrow we got, what, one pitch of A4+ and one of A5? And that's just to even get to Gibraltar—a crack almost as hard as the crux of Spanish Prisoner, except it will feel harder because we're exhausted and because Godzilla is up there threatening to launch bombs at us."

"All you can do is let yourself climb as well as you can, to not get in the way of yourself. Only you know if you're there or not," I said.

He laughed at me, bitterly: "Jesus, don't you see what you're doing? You're contradicting yourself, saying we don't have free will, but that I should use my free will."

"I'm just agreeing with what you said the other day. You know, about what if my words and ideas can trigger you to act that way— and I'm also triggered to say them? Like, I only know you through your actions, and you only know me through mine. Maybe you're terribly scared while aiding, nowhere near your rockhead, but you look cool and never let out a peep. And maybe I'm in my rockhead even while I'm cursing like a banshee—we'll never know. All you can see is that I threw the ring hook perfect the very first throw. All you can know of me is my outward actions. And all we can ever know about ourselves is from our outward actions too, because I sure as hell can't trust my memory. I mean, you hold some of my memories of Red's fall, and how can I know if you got it right? And if I can't trust my memory, then how can I ever know where my self is?"

"What are you talking about?"

"I'm just saying, 'Where's Atlas?' Nobody knows."

"You're right here," he said, rapping me on my helmet. "What the hell?"

"My actions, my words are right here. But do you know me?"

"I know when you'll suck it up or wimp out. I know that Ruby's got your heart so fucked up you can't even say her name. Or Olive's."

I ignored that last bit and kept going: "You think you know me, but really you have no way of knowing why I do anything— and I have no way of knowing why you do anything, either."

The conversation empowered me; I had put something

together again, something learned and lost, learned and lost, but I still couldn't express it right. It was the shell game again—only this time I was sure the self wasn't just hidden; it wasn't there at all. It was all just smoke and mirrors.

As we hung there in the wind, with Dade staring at me like I was crazy, I heard a voice come from right behind me: "Crap!" it said.

We both turned around to see a raven shoot upward, slowing down as it approached the apex of its flight about fifty feet above us, where it cracked its wings forcefully and flipped over backward into a sharp dive. As we watched it go, another raven, playing follow-the-leader, rose to the same spot in the sky the first had filled, cracking its wings too before peeling away, feathers chattering with the force of the turn, both of them racing for the tree line 1,800 feet below. When they shrank to just specks, I heard one of them make their call again—a honking "grack!"—and then the other one called back. It was beautiful and all at once I felt weepy, unbelievably happy. I loved the ravens and the rock and the lichen and Dade and even all our gear and the monkey rope between us. All of us were on the same team—we had come so far together— and here we were, poised to finish our biggest climb.

I'd been holding my hand out in the wind as I watched the ravens, my hand like a wing itself, fingering the air and feeling soft and loose and awash in this feeling of love for all things, when I realized in a freakish sense memory that my hand was in exactly the same shape as it had been when I touched the combined Olive-Ruby face in the dream the night before. All at once I felt my love for both of them rush up in me, almost breaking the surface before I snatched my hand away.

"If all I know about you is from your actions, my friend, then I'd have to say that you're nutty as a squirrel," said Dade.

There was nothing I could say about what had happened, so instead I looked up at the Roof of Good Hope just over three hundred feet above us. It would be hard to bail right after we did it, because if we tried to rappel the twenty-five–foot roof we'd be held away from the lower wall like kittens pinched by the scruff of their necks, unable to scratch the person who held them—unless we reversed the whole thing by back-aiding it.

"Are we going to finish this route or not?" I asked, looking upward to avoid looking into his eyes. I felt hard again, tough and tight. When he said nothing but started racking the gear, I took the rope and put him on belay.

CHAPTER TWENTY-FIVE

A few hours later, I was jugging in free air up to Dade right below the Roof of Good Hope, following the haul bag as it jerked upward in little beats. Before Dade's pitch I had freed Mariana's Trench, a sketchy layback pitch that took deep fingers, but which was slightly overhanging and so long that it seemed to leave the muscle cells in my calves and forearms fused together, melted by the hot myoelectricity leaping through them. Jugging after Dade, I was so tired I could only pull the ascenders once, then twice, before I had to rest, never able to get into my normal rhythm as I spun slowly on the rope, achieving alternating views of the valley and then the rock and then the valley again, where thick stratocumulus clouds had congealed as if to put a lid on the Valley's cubic miles of air. The clouds were fired up with the colors of the setting sun, but they also made the rock around me seem darker so that what had been golden was now gray, and what had been gray was now almost black—as if thin, colored layers of stone were being peeled away.

It made me think about the glaciers that formed the Valley. Before they pressed south the last time, this Valley had been a different one, with a different skin. If another ice age came and then went, ice again grinding down the rock walls, it would reveal another valley hidden inside this one—and a whole new world of routes would be left glistening in the sun. And behind that valley would lie another one, though smaller, and another, until there was nothing left but a bump on the surface of the earth. And I would be gone, and the Crackmeister's great, great-et-cetera inter-species granddaughter would be gone, and so would the entire human race.

"Atlas, a little help," yelled Dade then. The haul bag was stuck at a tiny overhang. I jugged up to it in ten exhausting pulls, then rocked it from side to side before it finally popped upward and over the lip it was caught on.

In that short amount of time the sun had almost set, spinning out a few great rays that cut sideways across the top of the Cathedrals. I stared out over the colors, relaxing with the knowledge that my day was almost over, that we'd come so far on the route, when something below caught my eye, something tumbling over itself while rising up through the dark toward me like some strange sea creature. It was maybe three feet long, an inch thick, and as it came closer to me I realized that it was gossamer—spider webs and silk strands that had found each other in the sky to form an independent mass. I'd seen gossamer before, but never a piece this large.

It floated up toward me, strangely alive as its surface caught sunlight reflected off the clouds, and it spun within a few feet of my outstretched hand before continuing up past Dade and the Roof of Good Hope, finally rising above Das Boot to the very lip of El Capitan. I lost it for a moment and then saw a glint of white as it blew back out over the valley—off to pick up some more spider silk—as the valley grew darker and the sky glowed with a gray that verged on green.

Forty feet above me, Dade was setting things up. Bright ovals cast by his headlamp landed on the rock, his portaledge, and his legs, then stretched into infinite parabolas, disappearing whenever he angled his head out toward the sky above us—or into the valley below. Down there, moving pins of light marked the road out of the Valley, where tourists, having had their fill of the Ansel Adams gallery and pizza stands, were driving home, unaware that millions of pounds of Das Boot were pulling at jillions of pounds of the earth, each of them trying to get closer to the other.

When I finally reached Dade, the rock seemed to flutter as if alive beneath my headlamp, and when I touched it I found it swimming with silverfish that leapt in all directions—including onto me. When I swept them off me they vanished into thin air, so light they probably never made it to the valley floor.

I exclaimed something about this, but Dade didn't seem to care. Then when I asked him if he'd seen the gossamer, he simply grunted. We had passed only climbing words between us— "Slack," "Rope," "Watch me!"—since our exchange four hundred feet below, those climbing words wedged between the sounds of metal on rock, of metal on metal, of nylon on nylon, and we set up my portaledge in the same conversational silence. It gave me a sudden pang.

What if his feeling of being jinxed, of his luck clock running out, was from some inexplicable awareness that came from seeing far enough into his own lines of triggerism to know something bad was on the way? Maybe his gut told him things like that, like my gut had told me to stay off that RP and try to hook the horn. I wondered this, but then again, I convinced myself that I was being triggered to worry about him—and triggered to think about this very thought.

Dade pretended to go to sleep right after we ate (I had a can of beef stew, a can of pears, and at least three bitter silverfish), and I lay down on my scoop of nylon to look out over the void, alone again. Usually you can see the stars well while on a wall, though the wall itself and the opposite side of the valley tend to narrow the sky as if looking through the ceiling slot of a telescope observatory. But this night, with the Roof of Good Hope decking me just as Jaws had the night before, I couldn't see anything above. I could *feel* Das Boot, though, clinging to the wall with the last of its strength only two hundred feet above us, a mere thirty feet to the right. We would reach it for sure the next day, even if Dade had to work out the moves on Gibraltar to redpoint it.

The thought of Das Boot coming down while I was sleeping rattled me, because if Das Boot could come down, why not the roof we were hanging under? Why not the whole damn wall of El Cap itself? What if there were an earthquake? It would be impossible for me to fall asleep with such worries, I remember thinking, and then suddenly I jerked awake, holding the whirligig in my right hand. The thing that had woken me was some kind of groaning nearby, though it also seemed like a great humming that came from far away, like the crash of ocean waves that are sometimes carried inland by sea winds. Or the clockwork of the triggered world, whirring away. Or maybe it was just Das Boot, still in its super–slow motion fall. I listened hard to the moonless dark, aware of some weather moving in, of the temperature dropping, the silverfish that had skittered all over the wall long gone.

Nothing. I must have dreamt the sound and then had the nightmare wake me up. The roof wouldn't come off—we were lucky to be hidden under it, and just a little bit unlucky that Das Boot hadn't fallen yet.

After my brief sleep, I realized how achy my body was, especially my hip crests from hanging at the belays, and wished I could take my harness off, though I knew it wasn't worth the risk; a portaledge buckle could break, pitching the ledge upside down, or I could have some sleepwalking dream, scooch right off the ledge and out into the darkness, and fall 2,200 feet. Of course, I could untie my rope in some sleepwalking madness too, I thought with a start.

And then I had to follow that thought: if I fell off the ledge while I dreamt of falling, and then woke up, how would I know which was which? As I thought about this, my thoughts chasing their own tails downward, I finally spun myself to sleep, forgetting all my nightmares except the last one, the one I woke up from: I was falling in that old falling dream, but this time I did not slow down. Instead, I just kept accelerating until I exploded into death, right into the earth.

CHAPTER TWENTY-SIX

C*a-rack!* I woke up to the sound of my body breaking, the day already light. But I was alive.

"Jumpers," I said to myself, trying not to think about the dream—and hoping the noise was just another parachute blowing open.

My whole body was thick from climbing, with nickel-sized scabs on the backs of both hands, a huge scab on my left forearm, and fingers so sore from handling all the metal that I could barely grasp the rain fly zipper. When I finally got it open I was hit by cool air, and peering out I was surprised to see that we were floating in fog—it was too cloudy for BASE jumping. Then I remembered waking up in the night, unable to hear the raindrops hit anything from our hide beneath the roof, but sure that drops were slipping past us in the cooling air. I must have lowered the fly then to keep out windblown rain, but I didn't even remember it.

"Just more rock fall," Dade said, his voice clear but delayed somehow, as if to reach me it had to travel over transatlantic phone lines. His red portaledge, put into soft focus by the fog, bumped around for a moment before Dade extended a Gatorade bottle out of his fly and poured pee out of it.

I could only follow it fifteen or twenty feet before it disappeared into the mist. Layers of cloud were moving in all directions below me—mesmerizing—then for one brief moment the spaces between them lined up to let me glimpse the dull grays and greens and tans of the valley floor.

"Seems like the rain is over," I said hopefully as I started to pack up my fly.

"I doubt the rock fall is. It was coming down all night."

"I guess I slept right through it."

"Passed out and talking the whole time," Dade said, finally flipping open the fly so I could see him. He looked like a madman. His hair was spiky and shot in all directions, his safety glasses barely clinging to his nose above a ragged, week-old beard. "I think you were mumbling 'Now. Now.' Then you said 'Catch me.'"

"Did you?" I asked.

He looked at me queerly, then disappeared again, his voice slightly muffled: "I dropped your rainfly for you, that's what I did. I can't believe you slept through it all. It sounded like some big blocks came off. Maybe washing machine–sized."

"Let's just hope we get over Good Hope," I said, "Then maybe it will be obvious."

It was. But first I had to aid through twenty-five skinny feet of the longest, wildest, most exposed horizontal crack I'd ever clung to the bottom of—with 2,300 feet of pure air between me and the floor of the valley. Roof cracks are a strenuous game because you're hanging free in the air, tensioning off your own aiders to reach the next ceiling placement, where you place, awkwardly and upside down, a pin or cam before tensioning over and onto the piece you've just placed. They're just as bad to second, since you have to take one step back for every two steps forward, weighting piece number two to free number one, then moving onto three before you can free two. When Dade followed it, he cursed steadily about the soggy, stretchy rope and the soggy air around us.

I just waited for him to finish, perched at the hanging belay at the edge of the roof, and got to watch as great, gray-white clouds broke apart and bounced off the Cathedrals in super slow motion, working their way up and out of the valley bowl as the sun cast their shadows sideways along the rock. This clearing also gave me a sightline to Das Boot, which seemed to arch out directly over us into the abyss, although it was maybe fifty feet to our right. That's when the rumbling started. When Das Boot started to fall.

There was a quaking and then a sharp boom that I felt more than heard, followed by another cracking boom as Das Boot began to pivot off its base. Clouds of dirt and granite dust burst outward while pigeons flapped in the opposite direction, and then the sky was falling.

I had never seen anything so large and full of potential acting in the world, and it was so far outside my understanding that it took seconds for the fear to hit, as if it lagged behind my comprehension like sound behind sight. This must have been the case for one of the pigeons too, because I saw its white body clinging to the top of the building-sized block for seconds before it finally flapped sideways away.

Once it was falling, a huge section of it—maybe a quarter of its length—broke free from the narrower bottom, while another truck-sized block burst forth from the top. In a trick of perspective it all seemed to be falling straight at us, and then appeared to be repelled as it ripped by, its great volume pushing gusts of air in two bursts as the biggest block rotated sideways, its corner slicing the air only twenty-five feet away from us—so close I could see individual splotches of pigeon guano that polished its top. It was all so big and so fast that it seemed for a moment that the whole of El Cap were coming down and that we'd come down with it. But then all three pieces were past, rotating sideways and also outwards in a half-revolution before they hit the base of Dog Daze. The biggest piece split lengthwise before crash-landing in the trees below, scattering them with great dusty explosions that we saw at first and then finally heard as muffled cracks and ba-booms as the trees snapped and the blocks rolled over. The crash sent up huge clouds of dust that rose for hundreds of feet, as if trying to meet halfway the smaller clouds of dust that were slowly filtering downward.

"Holy shit," said Dade, peering up at me from beneath the lip, crouching weirdly in his aiders. Then he started to giggle: "It's off, my man, the biggest trundle in the world—a good omen. And trundled by a night of light rain, no less."

Twigs and little clumps of dirt, light enough to be caught by the wind, were landing on us, and then another rockfall started with blocks the size of basketballs, some of them ripping the air only yards away from us. I ducked behind the haul bag but followed their path down to watch them bounce off the base and go careening into the trees.

What happened? There was air, and there was rock, and there was me. And there was a single moment, freezing Das Boot for a Planck's constant before letting it slip into another, its 10^{-43} seconds maybe tricking even the eye of the universe. It was the same kind of moment when I was inside of Ruby, our bodies held in a mold of space while her body held a cast of my own, the incredible distance between us just a surface where atom jostled atom. A line that was no line.

Right then, without looking over the haul bag at Dade, I knew, finally—though I'd learned it again and again and again—that his cells, my cells, the cells of silverfish and wall frogs and swallows, lie on this side of each moment, and there on the other side, through the tiniest of portals, lies the inanimate world of the dead: the world of Das Boot roaring and exploding and finally flattening its blind face to the earth.

With an excited burst, I knew that I hadn't really been in my rockhead yet on Seven Seas, but I had been near it. I knew too that the calm feeling that accompanied the pulsing as well as the awareness of density and dropping ballast had sunk into me completely. It was like when I'd learned how to ride a bike, where there was a jump to an "after" when it had become a part of me and I couldn't make myself fall over if I wanted to. All I had to do now was touch my whirligig and make the next climbing move, and then, if the world agreed, I'd get to make the next one after that. I peered over the haul bag at Dade and started to grin—and Dade grinned back.

The next two pitches went by as if in a dream. My most salient memory was of the repeated act of reaching up to touch my whirligig. It had become a button I could press to bypass my fear center, compressing all my senses together into a single, active state—my rockhead—that helped me know exactly where to go on the rock, exactly how to take a hold, exactly how to place a #3 nut, exactly how to breathe. I was so deep in this state, so focused on the arête on the first pitch over the roof, that it took Dade yelling for me to turn around and look down and behind me, where I saw one of the strangest phenomena (next to Das Boot falling) that I'd ever witnessed. An enormous specter had appeared on a cloud—a two-dimensional shadow of me but fifty feet tall, ringed in a brilliant halo that mimicked perfectly my every move. It was climbing its own giant arête, and waved a colossal, unfocused hand back at me when I waved at it.

It was another omen, I thought, and although I didn't know the word for this in English, I knew there was a word for it in German. I tried to remember the word my mother told me once—"something-*Gespenst*"—but couldn't find it, and by the time I neared the top of the pitch the cloud had grown so thin that the specter dissolved. Then there was only me again, climbing focused and passing auf as I reached the top of the arête.

Two hours later, the clouds all burned off, we were at the base of the famous Gibraltar pitch on the deep, two-part ledge called Tangiers. I was belaying from the protected, uppermost ledge that tucked right up under the start, and Dade was standing on the lower one about five feet beneath me, which jutted, unprotected from rock fall, further out into space. He was stretching out his forearms, then loosening up his shoulders and hips there. With the sheer scale of rock around us and Das Boot visible in relatively small pieces down on the valley floor, he may as well have been standing on the tip of a needle.

Then he was climbing up to me, his rack thinned down, his shoes cranked tight. Because we didn't know what he'd find up on top of this amazing pitch, which overhung ten feet in ninety and blocked our view of the pitches above it, I clipped the thin zip line to the back of his harness so I could send up a bolt kit and any other gear he might need to build a belay.

This was the pitch the rope guns could have climbed free and bagged if they'd been ballsier; that the Austrians might have had if they hadn't gotten injured. But we were there, a couple of house painters from east of Wyoming.

The route started out on super fine granite edges and led into a kind of channel that demanded smearing on the two overhung faces. Dade moved as if in shock at first, feeling tight, no doubt, from the hours of aid climbing he'd put in that morning. The shift from aid to hard free, I knew, was like the difference between laying a hardwood floor all day (with that gun to your head) and then loosening up enough to dance on top of it all night (still with that gun to your head).

Halfway up, where the smeary crux was supposed to be, he got stuck for a long time, trying to fiddle a nut into an opening in the seam. Just when I thought he was through with it he fell, shock-loading me and all the gear, jerking me hard against the wall and slapping himself against it too, though feet-first and okay.

"It's as hard as Spanish Prisoner," he yelled down, shaking out his hands, "but with great pro. The crux is probably placing that last piece—the crimp there is brutal."

He worked out the crux moves, and then, after a stretch of easier ground, hit some vicious gravity and took another short fall on a small stopper. Then another. At the very top of the pitch, looking onto the ledge that Das Boot used to rest on, he started yelling, but I couldn't understand him, and then he mantled over the edge, seeming to disappear right into sky.

I waited, staring up at the blue and down at the gray, and then Dade jerked the zipline three times—our old signal. I attached the bolt kit, a hammer, an assortment of pins and cams, and finally the rappel line, and then he pulled it up, the gear clanking and scuffing upward in short jerks. I heard him hammering in pins up there (none of them ringing with the pure, clean tones that signal safety), and then he hammered steadily for almost twenty minutes as he placed a bolt. The fact that he had to place a bolt where there must have been dozens of cracks made me a little nervous, and I grew even more nervous when he leaned out over the edge, 2,600 feet off the valley floor, and yelled that he was going to have to trundle some "gravel."

I tucked into the wall as tightly as possible, telling myself over and over that I was okay as a dozen large blocks and then a granite slab that would have made a mausoleum proud exploded on the lower of the two ledges—where Dade had stretched out only a couple hours before—spraying me with tiny shards as the larger pieces of rock fell and fell to ricochet off the wall and fall some more. The winds were so strong that I never heard the impact, while pieces of gravel light enough to be sucked in by its vortex pinged off my helmet and the haul bag and my shoulder. Then came another small avalanche, and, after a few minutes, another. If things were this bad on the ledge, what did it look like above it, where Das Boot had blown its moorings?

"It's a minefield up there," he said after he rappelled down to me, removing the gear on the way. "It took me the whole time to build a belay I could even half trust. If I don't send it this time, I'm just going to keep moving. We probably shouldn't be fucking around trying to get the redpoint."

I agreed. Dade rested and ate a protein bar, and an hour and half later he redpointed the beast like he'd already done it a dozen times. I'd been thinking of trying to free the route myself, but then thought again. I didn't care about it enough to not top out that day; I'd found what I was looking for—my rockhead—and we still had our mystery "first ascent" pitch after Gibraltar, and another pitch after that.

My thoughts about it were reinforced when I jugged up the rope after him, touching the seam where he had placed gear, amazed by how ridiculously crimpy and delicate the moves were and relieved that I wasn't going to try it myself.

When I reached the haul bag, hung up just beneath the ledge, I could suddenly smell the fall of Das Boot: the air seemed burnt somehow, as if it had been damaged by the grinding of the great block when it pivoted off its fulcrum, and when I finally snapped my ascender on the rope over the lip, I found Dade hanging from a bolt, shaking his head at me.

It looked like some giant had taken a twenty-foot wide chisel and hammered out a channel from the top all the way down to the ledge where the base of Das Boot had rested, leaving a pile of enormous white shards balanced together like a vicious game of pick-up sticks.

I worked my way over a dangerous block to Dade's belay—a nest of pins driven into cracks that scattered like spider webs up the main wall—and shook his hand. Then I smacked him on the helmet for good measure.

"You stud," I said.

He shrugged, clipping my rope into the belay with a clove hitch, so I could move around freely. "You've got some mess on your hands, Uhtlas, total choss. But once you're through it we're home free."

He was trying to sound solid—in control and confident—but I could tell that he was worried for me. This is how people die, we both knew: not climbing super hard on well-protected routes, but in rock fall, during a hasty rappel, in mixed terrain in bad light, when you're just too plain tired to think straight—and on chossy pitches like this. I'd have to pass auf for real.

Just as I was thinking this, I took a step backward and a hunk of granite, the size of a snowboard but six inches thick, started to slip from beneath my left leg, stretching me apart in a spread eagle to land me on my butt and almost pull me off the ledge in a backward roll. I was stopped by Dade, who grabbed my right ankle, but I yelled "Rock!" instinctively as the plank of stone scraped into thin air. I would have only fallen a few feet over the edge if I'd gone with it, since my rope was tied off, but I still would have been upside down and 2,700 feet off the deck and could've gotten hurt—or the slab could have cut the rope. The whole thing felt so hairy that I froze in place, waiting to find out if something else beneath me might shift too.

This time Dade didn't say anything, but his face turned pale. To do something that stupid after three days of being scared, of climbing so hard—I was an idiot. I got to my knees, awkwardly, and while Dade got ready to finish hauling the bag, I knocked and yanked hard on an oddly shaped horn near the edge, to make sure it was solid, before leaning on it to free the haul bag. The horn was shaped like an oversized mitten, complete with a thumb, and I turned my hand to grasp it, so that for a moment it felt as if I were shaking hands with the Capitan himself.

That calmed me a little, and I took a deep breath, then turned to face my options: The solid walls to either side of the Das Boot section were thin and hard to get to and would take many hours of aiding—even traversing over them to get to one of the other routes, like Dog Daze or Desert Fox, would take hours. And though we could also rappel down two pitches and cut over to Dog Daze and head up from there, with all our gear and the haul bag that would also take more than the rest of the day—and wouldn't let us finish Seven Seas. As I looked over at the top of Dog Daze I spotted a pair of climbers on the last pitch of the route, their journey, too, almost over. They must have been the ones who called to us our first day on the wall, thousands of climbing moves ago when I took that rattley fall off the pendulum traverse. I yelled to them and waved and they waved back, their "Whoo-Hoo!" carried to me on a sharp breeze, and this somehow buoyed me even more.

I knew what I had to do. The best option was to forge a new line right there—a line never done before because it had never before existed. It was the "Yosemite beneath Yosemite" that I'd imagined—the first of a thousand layers. The only real decision was which side of the channel to take. The right looked cleaner but ran directly above Dade, so there was less chance of pulling something off, but a greater chance of hitting him if I did. The left side was chossy and dicier, but would send rockfall mostly away from him. Either way I'd end up at old belay bolts at what used to be the top of the old Das Boot pitch.

"I'm going left," I said, pointing at it with my chin. "What should we call it?"

I wanted to call it whatever that word was for the specter we'd seen—the German word—but I still couldn't remember it.

"How about the Strait of Gibraltar—or, I know: the Pass Auf Pitch," said Dade.

"The Pass Auf Pitch—I like that," I said as I racked up the gear I might need.

The start was a horror show. The layers of rock that had been sheltered by Das Boot for millennia had suffered the effects of melting and freezing—without being able to exfoliate—and were friable and rotten with broken layers on top of layers. Every time I put my fingers in a crack I was ready for something above to shift and pinch them off—or for the rock to simply peel away—and felt as if I were climbing around vertical landmines. Dade seemed to think so too, and kept saying "You got it" and "Pass auf" and "Be ruthless," mentally pushing me up the route like I'd done for him not that many days before at Devil's Tower, when he almost took the way-whip but then didn't.

I couldn't place any solid gear for the first thirty feet in that overhung mess, and after a handhold pulled out on me and landed within a couple feet of Dade, I decided that the route was just too dangerous. I would down climb and aid my way over to Desert Fox and sacrifice the first ascent. I had just started to say as much to Dade, placing my foot on a hold I'd already used for my right hand, when the two-foot block popped out like an ice cube from its tray, my leg snapping at the air and almost knocking me off my handholds.

"Rock!" I yelled, though it had already hit the ledge. Instead of taking a load of precarious rocks off with it, it wedged itself perfectly between two shaky flakes. To reverse the move I'd just done had become a lot more difficult—plus I was worried that the rock behind where the cube had been might be sketchy too. The fear that I thought I'd moved beyond suddenly returned with a vengeance, and I couldn't even take my hand off the rock to touch my whirligig and get myself calm. But then Dade did it for me.

"I got you," he said, his voice truly calm. He was sitting on the haul bag, his legs akimbo, his arms resting on his knees, the rope secure in his hands, and he had his face turned up to me, trying to give me his strength. I don't know why, but I had a sort of waking dream of another Dade superimposed over this one, a Dade with a huge tree frog on one shoulder and a raven on the other. A Dade who was the God of Climbing and who had just told me to go for it and let this thing be the thing.

"What are you worried about?" I asked myself, my cracked lips brushing the rough granite before me. I was perched on a domino that was already falling, ready to trigger the dominos lined up after it. Just like with Olive and Ruby. Just like Dade's success on Spanish Prisoner. The moment had its momentum, and all I could do was ride out the Tilt-a-Whirl. There was no down-climb now; only doing the next move.

I minced my way through the next few moves to get to slightly better rock and my first truly solid piece of pro, then worked my way up the left corner of the gash with a few more crappy pieces of protection, and finally reached a solid, two-inch edge just beneath an overhang—eighty feet above Dade, maybe 120 feet from the top of El Cap. The edge and the overhang above it were new features, since this was where Das Boot once notched into the greater wall.

Just above that were the old bolts from the original belay station—a veritable island for shipwrecked souls like us—and I only had to make a few more moves to get to them. The safer, harder route would be to traverse further left to get to a vertical crack that circumvented the overhang. If I fell from there, assuming the gear was too worthless to change my descent, I'd probably go to the left of Dade's ledge and land in soft air. But that soft air was eighty feet times two, plus rope stretch, which would be over a 170-foot fall. And that's only if I didn't rip out Dade's sketchy belay completely and take us both down to crater into the remains of Das Boot. Yikes.

The second, quicker route would be to plug in a cam just over the lip of the overhang in a smooth, wedge-shaped crack and pull on it as aid to go more directly for the bolts. If something went wrong there, I'd probably rip all my gear and fall past Dade to go the length of the Gibraltar crack and finally hit the ledge of Tangiers, which jutted out from the Capitan like a torn hangnail. *Thuk.*

I let myself imagine that scenario for a microsecond, falling and ripping out my pro and dying on that outcrop, and then I shook all that fear out of my mind—and out of my hands. I wouldn't hit the ledge because I wasn't going to fall, and I wasn't going to fall because I would be so completely in my rockhead.

I had made thousands of decisions just like this one in the last three days, and this was just one more. I managed to touch my whirligig, and though my senses compressed into a single dense awareness that the rock was bad at the wedge-shaped crack above my head—that, really, I should go left—I had the immediate thought that it was no worse than what I'd been on for the last eighty feet. What the hell, I thought, I was riding that domino, right? Just keep moving. I threw a left heel hook over my head into the crack, to free a hand to pop in the cam, then clipped the rope into the cam.

The world had slowed down to three or four frames a second, and I swear I could feel every muscle fiber in my body, aware of every grain of rock that pressed into my fingers, the sling of the cam like a garrote on my palm, the rubber of my right shoe smearing and locking and smearing and locking in a slow-motion drift. I was passing auf as well as I ever had before, and I had conquered a fear that in the past might have frozen me. Everything I had learned over the last couple weeks—over my entire lifetime—was tied into this move. I was the God of Climbing I'd seen in Dade. I had the frog on one shoulder and the raven on the other, and the dominos were falling my way as I pulled hard on the cam and split the world, with great simplicity, into two. The *before* was lost in the first hundredth of a second. Here is what came in the *after*.

THE CAM AND the stone around it have exploded into his face and somehow knocked the Atlas right out of him, and while his body scrabbles in free air, clawing at rock that shreds like tissue paper, his self expands away from his body like waves of sound, pain rushing in to fill the void.

His body is surrounded by rocks the size of his torso, with stones the size of his fists, and though it is falling through sky with half a blue sky above, its eyes cannot see a thing except for a blur of black and gray streaks and the expanding blob of white that must be Dade's T-shirt.

This old rope smells just like lightning, the gear bursting in acceleration to unconnect his dots, and some part of his consciousness—swelling far beyond his body—flashes on the idea of counting down until he hears the thunder, just like his mother taught him—*eins-zwei*-what was that word? He knows this has to do with distance and with time but he can't remember the connection, just like he can't remember his own name.

He has no words for this next thought, though he does think it: He never knew that a moment can be so full it must divide into shells that nest inside each other, then beside each other. These shells right now are broken teeth, the smell of rock, a vacuum of fear—all of them falling at different rates, none of them keeping up with his accelerating body except for one, a shell so close to his body it remains a part of it, which contains a desperate love for what he approaches: the white blob of Dade that his eyes have almost focused on, the blob a part of him that is not his own self but still a self that he is part of.

And then another shell is spawned, a gossamer-ghost of un-told shells in the exact shape of his brain. It divides itself at the speed of light, bifurcating a trillion-fold in a blistering synaptic rush, nano-beetles rattling the cupboards of each neuron with a single-minded quest: to find the one memory or thought that could make this moment right. This is his life flashing before his eyes, but he won't ever know it—not unless he survives long enough for it to catch up with him.

As the only truly solid piece of gear rips out, just as his speed-ing body reaches the level of Dade, a head-sized rock falling alongside it appears on Dade's chest so suddenly it seems not to have landed there but to have been expelled from within, and in this infinitesimal moment their eyes tear a conduit through the air itself just long enough to register Dade's terror. Without words, because words have never moved this fast, Atlas thinks to Dade (all of it a single thought), *I've blown my chance to tell the*

truth. After Olive and Ruby and the shells of pain I gave them—of
my pushing all your buttons all at once. I know what I did wrong and
finally know what I should do.

But this fraction of the moment is gone almost before it starts,
and Atlas' body is reeling, curled in the shape of a question mark
as it accelerates past the belay with lengths of rope and tumbling
rocks falling along with it. Just as the wave of pain increases—and
once again too fast for words—he crunches this equation: too
much rope out + the Tangiers ledge hulking not far enough below
= pain on top of pain on top of pain.

Then a third thing comes—the image from an unremembered dream—of him passing through hard molecules of granite,
of splashing through the ledge as if through water, to sink inside
the mountain with a deep, bass groan.

There is a chattering, a scissoring of rope as his body jets down
through the great blue sky, and then a final something comes. It
is thinner and faster than all the others, it is his hard, tiny knot of
Olive and Ruby expanding—blooming—until he bursts with the
knowledge that there is something he can change, maybe something he can do, maybe one last time.

FROM EVERYWHERE AT once—but mostly from the edge of
space—his self senses the rift of Yosemite with El Capitan so
small it is just a bump casting shadows on a wide, convex field.
There are no clouds between his self and his body, and down past
the lip, inside the gray shadows of the valley, his body is falling
and this body is in pain and he wishes, like in the dream, that he
could crush the densities of all things into one to make the air
thick enough to stop its fall.

Above this falling body and the ledge that will kill it hangs
a great loop of rope, its other end anchored to Dade's belay plate.

The loop whips over the edge of Gibraltar only to be snatched up by the thumb-mitten horn, which pinches down on the rope, grinding the red sheath away with its stony thumb, until the sheath is gone and the core strands are snapping and the body slows until it is only inches from the Tangiers ledge, pinned to the air, one strand left . . .The body lands hard on all fours on a ledge the size of a butcher block, 2,600 pure feet off the ground, the rope chewed in two, as the Atlas-ness begins to rush in from everywhere. It carries with it that specter-word his mother had taught him—*eins-zwei-Brockengespenst*—which appears on his tongue as light as a mote of chalk, then falls away from his bloody lips riding a single, broken tooth.

ow. ow ow ow ow ow ow ow fuckfuckfuckfuckfuck fuck

"I was not in my rockhead, I am not in my rockhead, I have never been in my rockhead," I think as I come back into my body. The rockhead isn't "head" at all, and it isn't body, either. It's everything. Then I think something else, wincing on my hands and knees and looking at my tooth in a bloody slick of spit, and it's that *I am the one* who pushed Dade's buttons. I am the one who hurt Olive. I am the one who must find Ruby and listen to things I don't want to hear.

I can barely cobble the words to this coming thought, but I know that I am suspended by a million threads—by impossibly thin monkey ropes to Ruby and Olive and my family and my whirligig and everything I've ever held or smelled or beheld. They are repositories that hold parts of my self outside of me—just as Dade does. Especially Dade. Dade who is dying, maybe even dead. I am suspended by a great line of love to him, and when I look up to see the tattered rope above and finally the great, blue sky, I know that I can call this by its right name; that I fucking deserved this. And also: I am the one who can set things straight.

That cam and the crack—they were all wrong and I knew it—I knew that I should have gone left. I knew it and I rushed the moment. I was lazy and didn't let the thing be the thing at all. But now I will. If there are no other things, then the thing can only be itself.

Let the thing be the thing be the thing, I think, and let-the-thing-be-the-thing-be-the-thing falls in time with my breathing as the last of my greater pulsing self, finishing its descent from all of space, closes in on this body on the ledge like a smacked tether ball tightening quickly around its pole. Its speed paces my heart for a moment, then accelerates until it is vibrating along with the mitochondria in my cells, trilling along with the screaming pain in my mouth. I am back.

I reel the tattered lead rope in with my hands, up from the great void beneath me, and when I get to the ragged end, I have the feeling that I've been in this exact same place and touched these exact same fibers before, though I know I haven't. Déjà vu is not just a memory: it's when I incorporate the world; it's how I link neurons. It is where decisions are made.

In a hard, sharp break in time—a moment that is the opposite of deafening, the opposite of blinding—I think through every way to use the chewed-up rope, and then in total clarity I bundle it behind me to get it out of the way, and with this act I splice time back together.

I have found the logic made of ligaments and bones: I will climb without a rope, without a belayer, because to not need the rope is to not need to replace it, and to not need to replace it is to not waste time getting to Dade.

This is what the moment wants. I know this rock and the

air around me like I know the back of my bloody hands, like I know the pain pulsing out of my mouth where my eyetooth was smashed, my gum and lip still bleeding so much I must spit every few seconds down into the sky.

As I reach into the overhanging crack of Gibraltar, a pitch as hard as any I've ever climbed, my senses are compressed into a single intention: to the finding of things by searching with every fiber of my being. By searching with my will.

The sphere of this focused will runs 360 degrees around and above and below me, and takes in not just the rock and my body and my pain, but also completely for the first time the sweet air and the sun lighting up the dust at the Valley's lip and those millions of lines that suspend me. All of it. All at once.

No longer a domino but more like a top finally spinning so fast it can't be knocked over, my self has just approached its critical speed, though it is also a spinning coin that seems to spin fastest just before reaching its stillest state. In the wake of this stillness I am left humming with my own animation, throbbing with my own mass, and suddenly it's all so simple. My reason has come from outside of me, and it is to get to Dade. It is for the love of Dade.

My hands are dense but liquid, my mind of the same viscosity. I am filled with a single fluid substance, a single fluid intention. I am airy, molten rock, but at body temperature, and my mind, my hands, my eyes are all made of this sweet, gray granite.

Not from above anymore, but looking out from my granite eyes, reaching with my granite hands, I know that the edge I aim for and hit is a condensing of gravity. It is an inside-out bull's-eye where the stone will wrap around my fingers and where my fingers will sink into stone. I conform to become a perfect cast—a perfect cast of the entire planet—and I know, like I know my own name, that I have been frozen in these exact coordinates my entire life, with time and space moving through me so I could coalesce upon this shimmering act. I know that I'll never get another chance to get to Dade—to rise up to him and do this one thing right.

Right here, right now, I am finally climbing.

COOS BAY

ODOMETER: (2)01,683

LAT. 43.43° N LONG. 124.29° W

ALT. Ø FEET

JULY 26

EPILOGUE

B ev wanted to fly out, but she was in the middle of summer classes and Dade wouldn't let her—just like she wouldn't let him drive home in the Rig, leaving it for me to deal with. In fact, she said she'd be happy if she never saw the Rig again, and suggested that I should just push it off some high coastal road right into the Pacific. I'm not sure how serious she was, but I gave the idea some real thought. That's maybe how I ended up on the Oregon coast, standing on a black sand beach at dusk, watching the tide go out and throwing stones out into the waves.

When I got to the ledge on top of Gibraltar I found Dade propped up in his belay, unconscious, with that vicious, head-sized rock cradled gently in his lap. Although his heart was beating, I couldn't tell if he was breathing, and I grabbed that rock and hurled it off the ledge—into the abyss I'd just climbed out of. Then, afraid to even touch his chest, I gave him mouth-to-mouth with my bloody lips until he started to wheeze and cough up his own blood and I was sure he could breathe by himself.

Our second rope and haul line were both okay, and I planned to rappel to the base of Dog Daze and then, with Dade in the haul bag, solo-aid the final pitches of that route to bring him up out of the valley. But then I didn't need to do it alone; I got un-expected help from a Canadian couple—the two who had waved to us from the last pitch of Dog Daze had just topped out when I took my fall. They saw me land on the ledge and watched me solo

Gibraltar, and then hurried to rappel down to us, helping me ease Dade into the bag and haul him out on their fixed lines. This after four days of their own exhaustion.

It turned out Dade's left lung had been punctured and was full of fluid, and two ribs were so badly broken they had to be surgically reset. The doctors kept him in the hospital for six days and I was there with him the whole time, sleeping in the Rig the first night and then on a maternity recliner the nurse (breaking several rules) let me drag in.

When he came out of surgery and finally woke up, the first words out of his mouth—with a raspy croak—were that he couldn't fucking believe I'd soloed Gibraltar. He couldn't fucking believe it. He couldn't believe that I'd gotten to him in time. Then he wheezed out a laugh.

I was so relieved that I burst into tears right then and couldn't stop for minutes, then finally shook it off and told him he only made it because he was such a tough son of a she-goat, and how if I hadn't been so stupid and had just gone left instead of right we wouldn't be sitting there. But he just shook his head "No" and gave me that look that's the opposite of his boxing one. Then he made that V sign with his fingers and said "Myopic," but with a lisp, making fun of how I was talking with my missing tooth and my own swollen lip.

Since then I keep having these crying jags even though I'm happy. What's worse, they're usually triggered by the most mundane, ridiculous shit—like buying oatmeal in the cafeteria, or slamming the door of the Rig, or even just tying my shoes. I don't know when they'll stop. What I do know is that I will never be dizzy again.

Seven days after the accident, Dade was released, and I took him straight to the airport so he could get home to Bev. I tried to smile and held my hand out for our old carabiner handshake, but he waved me off, pulling me close instead so he could press the crook of his nose to my forehead. He didn't turn around or even say goodbye as the attendant wheeled him into security, though once through he yelled that he'd see me back in Minneapolis—and that the Rig better be in one piece.

Technically we didn't finish Seven Seas because I didn't complete the new Pass Auf pitch or the exit pitch above it, but I didn't care about that. I thought at first that my moment, my solo, was just the chemicals talking—a class six cataract from my adrenal glands, my well-being triggered by the flash flood of oxytocin. But in the week since the accident, I know that I have reached over into the other side and brought this thing back with me, as if I somehow smashed the monkey trap when I lost my tooth. It's a thing like happiness, but bigger, calmer, and I think it's become a part of me already, like riding a bike, like speaking another language. Except it's also more than that. It's more like I'm letting something out now. Or there's something that I'm no longer in the way of. Team Pulsing. Team Grown Up. Team Stayin' Alive.

It's ridiculous, I realize, whaling another fist-sized rock out into the water, that I don't feel like climbing at all. It's not about that right now. It's about other things.

Like Ruby and Olive and sorting us all out. I was on my way to find Ruby in San Francisco after leaving the airport yesterday, but just as I reached her exit I turned my blinker off and kept driving. I guess I just needed to not use words for a while. but I'll call her soon to let her know I'm okay—and that Dade's alive. With Olive, on the other hand, I'm not even sure where to start. Do I just show up at her doorstep in New York, ask for visitation with Meany and Mo, and try to explain it all from the beginning?

Somehow I ended up at this beach—one where Dade and I camped a few years ago on our way to the Valley, flush with a success on the Chief, in British Columbia. I was hell-bent to get here, but once I arrived I didn't know what to do with myself, and now I find myself still throwing stones into the water. Stones, and then, as if it were on fire, my whirligig—a kind of thank-you to the climbing gods for letting me have Dade back. I tear the laces out of its holes and sidearm the disc as hard as I can out into the ocean. It is caught by the gravity of the earth, the pull of the sea, and in that tension draws a long, clean arc before it cuts the black water. I imagine it tumbling slowly end over end, buffeted by currents beneath the waves before it reaches the dark sea floor, and I wonder what side it finally lands on, the *fish* or the *bowl*?

I drop the laces into the white of a broken wave, and as the wave retreats it beaches them in the exact shape of its foam, the shape of what it had been.

Suddenly I have an idea, if something that's been building for weeks can be called sudden. Or an idea. I walk back to *Makin' Bacon* and get in the passenger side, taking Olive's *Wyoming!* notebook out of my daypack. I open it up to the last page, where I'd written my questions about will and laziness and "Olive. Olive. Olive. Olive. Olive." at the start of my letter to her. The one I never managed to write. I think about the truth of what's happened and about calling things by their right name.

Climbing. Passing auf. My self. The triggers. Yosemite. The rockhead . . . love.

At the very least I need to explain all of this to Olive as well as I can—I owe her that much, I think, even if we never end up together. And so I draw a heavy line beneath the last words on the page and as I take a deep breath I write:

"'Yosemite,' he said to me in the dark. 'You and me and a big, bad wall.'"

The End

A CLIMBER'S TOAST

May your footwork be clean and easy,
Your rope always long enough,
May your sky be as wide as Wyoming,
And your partner smart and tough.

—Dade Eleutherios